Praise for the novels of Debbie Macomber

"Romantic, warm, and a breeze to read."
—*Kirkus Reviews* on *Cottage by the Sea*

"Exudes Macomber's classic warmth and gentle humor."
—*Library Journal* on *Three Brides, No Groom*

"Popular romance writer Debbie Macomber has a gift for evoking the emotions that are at the heart of the genre's popularity."
—*Publishers Weekly*

"Debbie Macomber is one of the most reliable, versatile romance writers around."
—*Milwaukee Journal Sentinel*

"Bestselling Macomber…sure has a way of pleasing readers."
—*Booklist*

"Macomber never disappoints."
—*Library Journal*

"Virtually guaranteed to please."
—*Publishers Weekly*

"It's impossible not to cheer for Macomber's characters…. When it comes to creating a special place and memorable, honorable characters, nobody does it better than Macomber."
—*BookPage*

DEBBIE MACOMBER

Summer Breezes

Previously published as
The Way to a Man's Heart and *Fallen Angel*

mira

mira™

ISBN-13: 978-0-7783-3184-1

Summer Breezes

Copyright © 2021 by Harlequin Books S.A.

The Way to a Man's Heart
First published in 1989. This edition published in 2021.
Copyright © 1989 by Debbie Macomber

Fallen Angel
First published in 1990. This edition published in 2021.
Copyright © 1990 by Debbie Macomber

This edition published by arrangement with Harlequin Books S.A.

For questions and comments about the quality of this book, please contact us at CustomerService@Harlequin.com.

Mira
22 Adelaide St. West, 40th Floor
Toronto, Ontario M5H 4E3, Canada
www.Harlequin.com

Printed in Lithuania

Recycling programs for this product may not exist in your area.

MIX
Paper from responsible sources
FSC® C021394

Midnight Sons

Alaska Skies
  (*Brides for Brothers* and
  The Marriage Risk)
Alaska Nights
  (*Daddy's Little Helper* and
  Because of the Baby)
Alaska Home
  (*Falling for Him,*
  Ending in Marriage and
  Midnight Sons and Daughters)

This Matter of Marriage
Montana
Thursdays at Eight
Between Friends
Changing Habits
Married in Seattle
  (*First Comes Marriage* and
  Wanted: Perfect Partner)
Right Next Door
  (*Father's Day* and
  The Courtship of Carol Sommars)
Wyoming Brides
  (*Denim and Diamonds* and
  The Wyoming Kid)
Fairy-Tale Forever
  (*Cindy and the Prince* and
  Some Kind of Wonderful)
The Man You'll Marry
  (*The First Man You Meet* and
  The Man You'll Marry)
Orchard Valley Grooms
  (*Valerie* and *Stephanie*)
Orchard Valley Brides
  (*Norah* and *Lone Star Lovin'*)
The Sooner the Better
An Engagement in Seattle
  (*Groom Wanted* and
  Bride Wanted)
Out of the Rain
  (*Marriage Wanted* and
  Laughter in the Rain)
Learning to Love
  (*Sugar and Spice* and
  Love by Degree)

You...Again
  (*Baby Blessed* and
  Yesterday Once More)
The Unexpected Husband
  (*Jury of His Peers* and
  Any Sunday)
Three Brides, No Groom
Love in Plain Sight
  (*Love 'n' Marriage* and
  Almost an Angel)
I Left My Heart
  (*A Friend or Two* and
  No Competition)
Marriage Between Friends
  (*White Lace and Promises* and
  Friends—And Then Some)
A Man's Heart
  (*The Way to a Man's Heart* and
  Hasty Wedding)
North to Alaska
  (*That Wintry Feeling* and
  Borrowed Dreams)
On a Clear Day
  (*Starlight* and
  Promise Me Forever)
To Love and Protect
  (*Shadow Chasing* and
  For All My Tomorrows)
Home in Seattle
  (*The Playboy and the Widow*
  and *Fallen Angel*)
Together Again
  (*The Trouble with Caasi* and
  Reflections of Yesterday)
The Reluctant Groom
  (*All Things Considered* and
  Almost Paradise)
A Real Prince
  (*The Bachelor Prince* and
  Yesterday's Hero)
Private Paradise
  (in *That Summer Place*)

*Debbie Macomber's
  Cedar Cove Cookbook*
*Debbie Macomber's
  Christmas Cookbook*

CONTENTS

THE WAY TO A MAN'S HEART

One

"Are you ready to order?" Meghan O'Day asked the man with the horn-rimmed glasses who was sitting in the booth beside the window. The gentleman was busily reading. Meghan withdrew the small tablet from inside her starched apron pocket and patiently waited for his response.

At her question, the reader's gaze reluctantly left the page of his book and bounced against her briefly. "The chicken potpie sounds good."

"Rose's potpies are excellent," Meghan said with a congenial smile. She noted that even before she'd finished writing down his order, the man had returned his attention to his reading. She grinned, not offended by his lack of notice. Some customers were chatty and openly friendly, while others preferred to keep to themselves. Meghan didn't mind. It was her job to make sure the clientele were served promptly and their needs seen to efficiently. Since Meghan was an avid reader herself, she didn't fault this gentleman for being more interested in his book than in ordering his meal.

Currently only a handful of customers dotted the diner, and the chicken-potpie order was up within a few short minutes. The reader, with his nose buried between the pages of his book, barely looked up when Meghan delivered his food.

"Is there anything more I can get for you?" she asked, automatically refilling his coffee cup.

"Nothing, thanks."

As she moved to turn away, Meghan noted that it was Geoffrey Chaucer's *Canterbury Tales*, that had captured his attention so completely. Excitement surged through her bloodstream.

Meghan herself was a devoted lover of classical literature. She set the glass coffeepot on the table and gave the reader a second look. Not bad. In fact he was downright handsome.

He glanced up at her expectantly. The only thing Meghan could do was explain. "I... Chaucer is one of my favorites."

"Mine, too." A slow, endearing smile eased across his face. He glanced down at the page and read in a clear, strong voice: "'Bifel that in that seson on a day, in southwerk at the Tabard as I lay—'"

"'—Redy to wenden on my pilgrimage to Canterbury with ful devout corage,'" Meghan finished reverently.

His face revealed his surprise. If she hadn't earned his attention before, she received it full force now. "You know Chaucer?"

Meghan felt a little silly and shook her head. "Not personally." Her fellow Chaucer fan didn't so much as crack a smile at her attempt at a joke. To her way of thinking, he was much too young to take life so seriously; but then she was only a waitress, not a psychologist.

"You're obviously familiar with his works." He frowned slightly and studied her as though he should be expected to recognize her and didn't.

"I've read it so many times that I've managed to memorize small portions of it. I guess you could say that Chaucer and I have a nodding acquaintance."

He chuckled at that, and planted his elbows on the table, grinning up her. "So you enjoy reading Middle English?"

"I'll confess it was difficult going at first," she said, feeling mildly guilty for interrupting his meal, "but I stuck it out and I'm glad I did. Frankly, when I read it aloud the first time, it sounded a whole lot like Swedish to me."

His face erupted into a full smile, as if he found her insights a bit irreverent, but nonetheless interesting.

A second volume rested on the seat beside him. He picked it up and ran his hand respectfully down its spine. "If you enjoy Chaucer, then you're probably a fan of Edmund Spenser, as well."

She noted that he was holding a well-read volume of *The Faerie Queene*. He continued to look at her expectantly, awaiting her reply. Feeling a bit chagrined, Meghan regretfully shook her head.

"You don't like Spenser?"

"Isn't he the one who wanted to write twelve books, each one celebrating a different knightly virtue?"

The reader nodded. "He only completed six."

"Actually, I don't think anyone minded." As far as Meghan was concerned, Spenser was a prime candidate for intensive counseling, but she couldn't very well tell her customer that. "I didn't mean to insult your tastes," she added quickly, not wanting to offend him.

The man reached for his fork, all the while studying her as if he were trying to place her. "Do I know you?"

Meghan shook her head. "Not unless you eat at Rose's Diner regularly and I don't remember seeing you before tonight."

"This is the first time I've been here, although I've heard

for years that Rose bakes the best pies in Wichita. Generally I'm not in this neighborhood." Still he continued to stare without the merest hint of apology.

"Rose will be pleased to hear that." Feeling a little foolish for lingering so long, Meghan picked up the coffeepot and took a step back. "Enjoy your meal."

"Thank you, I will." He continued to observe Meghan as she turned and headed toward the service counter. Even then, she felt his gaze.

Sherry Caldwell, the assistant manager, joined her there.

"Who's the hunk you were just talking to?"

"I don't know. He came in about twenty minutes ago, started reading Chaucer and ordered chicken potpie."

"He's cute, don't you think?" Sherry asked, eyeing him inquisitively. The assistant manager was a grandmother, but still young enough to appreciate a good-looking man when she saw one.

Meghan didn't think twice about nodding. There wasn't any doubt in her mind that this man was attractive. Everything about him appealed to her, especially his choice of reading material. Although he was sitting, Meghan could tell he was well over six feet. His dark hair was thick, cut short, and styled in a manner that gave him a distinguished air. He wasn't openly friendly, but he wasn't aloof, either. He was more of an introvert, she decided; distinguished and professional, too. Those traits wouldn't normally appeal to her, but they did in him—strongly.

From what she'd noticed, he seemed to be physically fit, but she couldn't picture him gliding down ski slopes or lifting weights. In fact, he didn't look like someone who cared much about muscle tone. He was dressed casually now, but something about him suggested he was more at home in three-piece suits and stiffly starched collars than the slacks and sweater he was wearing now.

"He's not the kind of guy one would expect to come in here, is he?" Sherry pressed.

Meghan shrugged. "I guess not, but we get all types."

Sherry chuckled. "Tell me about it, kiddo!"

The following evening, Meghan kept looking for the man who loved the literary classics, chiding herself for even expecting him to return. It wasn't like her to feel so strongly about a stranger, especially one whom she'd only talked to once and briefly at that. All day she thought about the handsome man who knew and loved Chaucer the same way she did. She would like to know him better, and wondered if he felt the same about her.

Just when the dinner rush had started to lull, Sherry strolled past her and muttered under her breath, "He's back."

Meghan's co-worker made it sound as if an FBI agent had just stepped into the diner and was preparing to consort with the KGB. Meghan was carrying three plates of chicken-fried steak, and daring not to hope, she paused to ask, "Who's back?"

Sherry rolled her eyes. "The good-looking guy from last night. Remember?"

"I can't say that I do." Meghan preferred to play dumb, being unwilling to let her friend know how much she'd thought about seeing "the reader" again.

"The chicken potpie from last night," Sherry returned, obviously frustrated. "The one you've been watching for all night, so don't try to fool me!"

"Chicken potpie?" Meghan repeated, continuing the pretense and doing a poor job of it. "Oh, you mean the guy who was reading Chaucer?"

"Right," Sherry teased. "Well, he obviously remembered *you*. He requested your section." Sherry wiggled her finely penciled brows up and down several times.

"He did?" By now Meghan's heart was doing cartwheels.

"That's what I just finished saying."

Meghan wasn't willing to put a lot of stock in this. "I don't suppose it occurred to that romantic heart of yours to assume he was pleased with the food and the service?"

"I'm sure he was," Sherry returned, trying to suppress a smile, and failing. "But I think he's far more interested in seeing you again. After all, he could order the same cooking from any one of us."

Meghan discounted Sherry's reasoning with a soft shrug, feeling disinclined to accept anything more than the fact the handsome man who read Chaucer was back.

"Go get him, tiger," Sherry teased. "He's ripe for the pickin'."

Meghan delivered the chicken-fried steaks and refilled coffee cups before approaching "the reader's" booth. Once again, his nose was deep in a well-worn leather volume.

"Good evening," she greeted, striving to sound friendly but not overly so—it wouldn't do to let him know how pleased she was to see him again. "You're back."

He closed the book and looked up at her. "I was in the neighborhood and decided to stop in."

"I'm glad you did." Her fingers tightened around the handle of the coffeepot. "I enjoyed our conversation last night."

"I did, too. Very much." His sober gaze continued to study her with undisguised admiration.

Meghan could tell that this man was earnest and serious. He wasn't the type to openly flirt or lead a woman on; in fact he seemed almost uncomfortable. This evening he was wearing a suit and tie and looked more dignified than ever. He was the only man in the entire diner wearing anything so formal.

He set the volume aside and looked up eagerly, reading her name tag. "It's good to see you again, Meghan."

"Thank you…and you too, of course." She set the coffeepot down, pulled her pad from the pink apron and held her pen poised, ready to write down his choice.

Instead of ordering, he held out his hand to her. "I'm Grey Carlyle."

She gave him her hand which he grasped in a firm handshake. Meghan had trouble pulling her gaze from his; his eyes were a mesmerizing shade of blue that reminded her of a midsummer Kansas sky.

"I'm pleased to meet you, Meghan—"

"O'Day," she filled in. "It's Irish," she mumbled, instantly wanting to kick herself for stating something so obvious. If her name wasn't enough of a giveaway, her bright auburn hair and deep blue eyes should have been.

Suddenly there didn't seem to be anything more to say. Grey glanced at the pad in her hand and announced, "I'll order the special—whatever it is."

"Chicken-fried steak," Meghan told him eagerly.

"That sounds fine."

Meghan took her time writing it down, wanting to linger and get to know him better. Instead she asked him, "Would you like soup or salad with your meal?"

"Salad."

She made a note of that. "What kind of dressing?"

He mulled this over as though it were important enough to involve national security. "Blue cheese, if you have it."

"We do." If they didn't she would stir up a batch herself.

"I don't suppose you've read Milton?" He turned over the book on the tabletop and showed her the cover.

Meghan held the order pad against her breast and smiled down on him. "I loved *Paradise Lost* and *Lycidas*, but the whole time I was reading his works I had the impression he was trying to get one up on Dante." The minute the words were out, Meghan wanted to jerk them back. She could feel the color sweep into her cheeks, and it was on the tip of her tongue to tell him she hadn't meant that.

The faint quiver of a smile started at the corners of his full mouth. "'Get one up on Dante'—I never thought of it quite like that before," he murmured. "But actually, you could be right."

A bell chimed softly in the background, reminding Meghan that one of her orders was ready and there were other customers who expected to be served. "I'd better get back to work," she said reluctantly. "I'll have your salad for you in just a minute."

"Before you go," he said abruptly, stopping her. "I'd like to know where you attended college?"

She cast her gaze down and shrugged, feeling slightly awkward. "I haven't."

"You haven't been to university?" Surprise elevated his voice.

Meghan looped a strand of shoulder-length hair over her ear and met his confused gaze.

"Do you mean to tell me you've done all this reading on your own?"

"Is that so unusual?"

He reached for his water glass. "Frankly, yes."

"If you'll excuse me now, I really have to get back to work."

"Of course. I'm sorry for detaining you this long."

"No, don't apologize. I enjoy talking to you. It's just that—"

"I understand, Meghan. Don't worry about it."

She stepped away from the booth, feeling uneasy with him for the first time. Literature was the one love of her life—her passion. She'd started reading early English literature when nursing her mother after she'd taken a bad fall. High school had given her enough of a taste for the classics that she'd sought out and begun to investigate major works on her own, later. While at home, she'd had ample opportunity to explore many of the literary greats, and in a short time had devoured volume after volume, making a whirlwind tour of six hundred years of English literature.

As Meghan headed toward the kitchen, she noticed Grey frowning. Now that he knew she didn't have a degree to back up her opinions, he probably wouldn't ask her what she thought of the classics again. It would have been better if she'd kept her thoughts to herself than to spout them as if she knew what she was talking about. The habit of blurting out exactly what she was feeling was one that continually plagued her. Grey Carlyle was a man of culture and refinement. Her guess was that he was a doctor or an attorney, or someone else equally distinguished. Obviously he knew a good deal more about literature than she ever would.

Greyson Carlyle watched Meghan move away from the table. In fact he couldn't stop looking at her. He'd embarrassed her when he'd started asking her about college, and he hadn't meant to do that.

When he'd first stepped into the diner the night before, he hadn't given her more than a second glance. It wasn't until she'd quoted Chaucer with such a deep-rooted love that he'd so much as looked at her. Once he *did* notice her, however, he found himself completely enthralled. It wasn't often a man could walk into a restaurant and meet a waitress as lovely and intelligent as Meghan. In fact, meeting Meghan had been downright unexpected. He loved the way her Irish blue eyes lit up and sparkled when she spoke of Chaucer and Milton. She knew these men and savored their works in much the same way he appreciated their craft and keen intelligence.

The things Meghan had said utterly intrigued him, for over the years, Grey had become far too accustomed to having his own opinions spouted back at him. Rare was the student who would have told him that Middle English sounded like Swedish. He couldn't keep from smiling at the thought.

The fact was Grey hadn't been able to stop thinking about the waitress all day. Hearing her outrageous statements was like sifting through sand and discovering pieces of gold.

He'd gone home the night before and found himself chuckling just thinking about Meghan O'Day. In the middle of a lecture the following morning, he'd paused remembering how the young woman had told him no one was sorry Spenser had only completed six of the twelve books he'd planned. He'd broken into a wide grin and had to restrain himself from bursting out laughing right there in front of his students. The freshman class had sat there staring at Grey as if they expected him to leap on top of his desk and dance.

Grey didn't know who'd been more shocked—his students or himself. But he'd quickly composed himself and resumed the lecture.

If Grey was going to be thinking about a woman, he chided himself later, he should concentrate on someone like Dr. Pamela Riverside. His colleague had been less than subtle in letting him know she was interested in getting to know him better. Unfortunately, Grey wasn't the least bit attracted to her.

Instead his thoughts centered on one Irish waitress with eyes warm enough to melt stone—a waitress with a heart for the classics.

He was getting old, Grey determined. It took someone like Meghan O'Day to remind him that life didn't revolve around academia and boring social functions. The world was filled with interesting people, and this waitress was one of them.

That evening, as he walked off the campus of Friends University, Grey impulsively decided to return to Rose's Diner. He would be discussing Milton with his students in the next day or two, and he longed to hear Meghan's thoughts on the seventeenth-century poet. He was certain she would have something novel to say.

"So?" Sherry asked, cornering Meghan the minute she approached the kitchen with Grey's order. "What did he want?"

Meghan stared at her friend and blinked, pretending not to understand. "'The reader'?"

"Who else could I possibly mean?" Sherry groaned.

"He wanted the special."

"I don't want to know what he ordered! Did he tell you why he was back again?"

Meghan chewed on the corner of her bottom lip. "Not actually. He asked what I thought of Milton, though."

"Milton? Who in heaven's name is Milton?"

Meghan smiled at her friend. "John Milton. He wrote *Paradise Lost* and *Paradise Regained* and plenty of other, lesser-known works."

"Oh, good grief," Sherry muttered. "It's those highfalutin Greeks you're always reading, isn't it? When are you going to give up reading that antiquated stuff? Wake up and smell the coffee, Meghan O'Day. If you're going to get anywhere in this life you've got to start reading real writers—like... Stephen King and... Erma Bombeck, God rest her soul." Sherry hesitated, then nodded once for emphasis. "Take Erma—now there's a woman after my own heart. She's got more to say in one newspaper column than those Greek friends of yours say in twenty or thirty pages."

"Milton was English," Meghan corrected, smiling inwardly at her friend's mild outburst.

"What's so intriguing about what these people wrote, anyway?"

"It's not the writer so much," Meghan said carefully, not wanting to insult her co-worker. "It's what they had to say about the things that affected their lives."

"Stephen King doesn't do that," Sherry countered. "And he's done all right for himself."

"He has, at that," Meghan agreed. It wouldn't do any good to argue with Sherry, but she wanted her to understand. "Listen to this," Meghan asked and inhaled deeply. When she spoke, her low voice was soft and well modulated. "'Know then thyself, presume not God to scan; The proper study of mankind is man.'"

Sherry was giving her an odd look. "That's Milton?"

"No. Alexander Pope. But don't the words stir your soul? Don't they reach out and take hold of your heart and make you hunger to read more?"

Sherry shook her head. "I can't say that they do."

"Oh, Sherry." Meghan sighed, defeated.

"I'm sorry, I can't help myself. That sounds like a bunch of mumbo-jumbo to me, but if that's what turns you on, I'll try not to complain."

When Meghan had finished adding salad dressing to the small bowl of lettuce and chopped tomatoes, she delivered it to Grey's table.

"Can I get you anything else before your dinner comes

up?" she asked, setting the salad in front of him along with a narrow tray of soda crackers.

"Everything's fine," he replied, and looked up at her. "Listen, I'd like to apologize if I embarrassed you earlier by asking you about your college education."

"You didn't embarrass me." It *had* somewhat, but she couldn't see that telling him that would help matters. Years before, she'd yearned to go to college, dreamed of it, but circumstances had kept her home. She didn't begrudge her lack of a formal education; it was part of her life and she'd accepted the fact long ago.

"I don't mean to pry," Grey said, frowning just a little, "but I'm curious why someone who loves the classics the way you do, wouldn't pursue your schooling?"

Meghan dropped her gaze. "The year I graduated from high school my mother fell down a flight of stairs and broke her hip. She needed surgery and was immobile for several months because of complications. With three younger brothers, I was needed at home. Later, after Mom had recovered, the family was strapped with huge medical bills."

"You're helping to pay those?" Grey pressed.

"They're mostly paid now, but I'm twenty-four."

"What's that got to do with anything?"

Meghan laughed lightly. "I'd be years older than the other freshmen. I wouldn't fit in."

Grey's brows drew together, forming a deep V over his eyes. Apparently he was considering something.

"I was wondering," he said, and hesitated. "I mean, you hardly know me, but there's a lecture on the poetry of Shelley and Keats at Friends University tomorrow evening that I was planning to attend. Would you care to go with me?"

Meghan stared back at him, hardly able to believe what

she was hearing. This distinguished man was actually asking her out on a date.

When she didn't immediately respond, he lowered his eyes to his salad. "I realize this is rather spur-of-the-moment."

"I'd love to go," she blurted out, scarcely able to disguise her enthusiasm.

"Shall we meet here in the parking lot…say, around seven-thirty?"

"That would be fine," Meghan responded eagerly. "I'm honored that you'd even think to invite me."

"The pleasure's all mine," Grey insisted with a boyishly charming smile.

"Until tomorrow, then," she said.

"Tomorrow," he repeated.

An hour later, Grey stood beside his car, his hand on the door handle, his thoughts excited and chaotic. He'd found a kindred spirit in Meghan O'Day. The minute she'd softly quoted Chaucer, his heart hadn't been the same. When he heard the reason she hadn't gone on to college, Grey knew he had to ask her to the lecture. Once she'd sampled the feast of rich works to be served the following night at the university, she would be hooked. He wanted this for her. Even if she was a few years older than the majority of the students, he knew she'd fit in. He could tell her this, but it wouldn't be nearly as effective as giving her a taste of what could be in store for her behind those walls of learning.

Grey wasn't an impulsive man by nature, but when he was with Meghan he found himself saying and doing the most incredible things. This invitation was just one example.

With an unexpected burst of energy, Grey tossed his car keys into the air and deftly caught them behind his back with his left hand. He was so stunned by the agile move that he laughed out loud.

A light snow had just begun falling when Meghan walked toward Grey in the well-lit parking lot in front of Rose's Diner the following evening. Snow had arrived early this year; Wichita had already been struck by two storms and it wasn't yet Thanksgiving.

"I hope I didn't keep you waiting long," Meghan said, strolling up to his side.

"Not at all."

He smiled down at her and the chill that had permeated Meghan's bones was suddenly gone, vanished under the warmth in his eyes.

Grey tucked her hand into the curve of his arm. "I think you'll enjoy this evening."

"I'm sure I will. Shelley and Keats are two of my favorites, although I tend to like Keats better."

Grey opened the car door for her. "I find their styles too similar to prefer one over the other."

"Oh, I agree. But I happened to read some of Shelley's letters," Meghan added conversationally, "and I've had trouble thinking objectively about him ever since."

"Oh?" Grey walked around the car and joined her in the front seat. "What makes you say that?"

Meghan shrugged. "His notes to his friends were full of far-out abstractions and so dreadfully philosophical. If you want my opinion, I think Shelley was stuck on himself. In fact, I've come to think of him as a big crybaby."

Grey's eyes widened. "I thought you said you liked Shelley?"

"Oh, dear," Meghan replied, expelling her breath. "I'm sorry. I've shocked you again, haven't I?"

"It's all right," he said, the frown slowly unfolding. "As it happens, Shelley is my all-time favorite and I'm having one heck of a time not defending him. You're right, though. He was big on himself. But who could blame him?"

"No one," Meghan agreed.

"You know what I like best about you, Meghan?"

She shook her head.

"You're honest, and that's a quality I admire. You aren't going to tell me something just because you think I want to hear it."

Meghan cocked her head to one side and expelled a sigh. "That—fortunately or unfortunately, as the case might be—is true. I have a bad habit of blurting out whatever I'm thinking."

"I find it refreshing," he said, reaching for her hand and squeezing her fingers. "We're going to enjoy tonight. And when the lecture is finished, we'll discuss Shelley again. I have the feeling your opinion's going to change."

Grey drove across town to Friends University. Although Meghan had passed the campus several times, she'd never actually been on the grounds. As she looked around at the ivy-covered structures, her gaze filled with longing. Some day, some way, she would find a way to further her education here.

"It really is lovely here, isn't it?" she said, once they'd parked. Grey walked around and opened her car door, his impeccable manners again impressing Meghan.

"Just standing here makes me want to curtsy to all these buildings," she commented, smiling.

"Meghan," he said kindly, tucking her hand once more into the crook of his arm. "I don't understand. You so obviously love literature, you aren't going to feel out of place once you sign up for a few classes. Yes, you would be older than the majority of first-year students, but not by much and really what would it matter?"

"It's a bit more than that," she said, looking away from him.

"If you can't afford the expense surely there are scholarships you could apply for."

"Yes, I suppose I could. But I haven't."

"Why not?"

She looked away, feeling uncomfortable. "The last thing I want to do is sit in some stuffy classroom and listen to some white-haired professor," she said defensively.

"Why not?"

Grey did a good job of disguising his shock, but Meghan could see that her words had rattled him. It seemed that his voice tensed a little, but Meghan couldn't be certain.

"If you really must know," she said nervously, "colleges and professors frighten me."

"Meghan, that's ridiculous. They're people like and you me."

"Yes, I suppose it *is* absurd, but it's the way I feel. I'm afraid a professor would look down his learned nose at me and think I'm full of myself."

"Listen," he said, placing his hands on her shoulders and turning on the pathway so that he faced her squarely. "There's something you should know."

In the distance, Meghan could hear footsteps approaching. Grey dropped his hands, apparently wanting to wait until the group had passed him.

"Evening, Professor Carlyle."

Grey twisted his head around and nodded. "Good evening, Paul."

"Professor Carlyle," Meghan muttered. "*You're* a professor?"

Two

Meghan felt the surprise splash over her, drenching her to the bone. Grey Carlyle was a university professor, specializing in English literature, no doubt! She couldn't believe how incredibly obtuse she'd been. Just looking at him, reading Chaucer and Milton in his crisp three-piece suit, precisely knotted tie and boot-camp polished shoes should have been a dead giveaway. Only Meghan hadn't figured it out. Oh, no. Instead she'd danced all around him in an effort to impress him with her dazzling insights and sharp wit— all the while making a complete nincompoop of herself.

Her gaze met his and quickly lowered. "I should have guessed," she muttered, forcing a smile.

"Is my hair that white?" he coaxed. "Do I really come off as so terribly stuffy?"

His words were a teasing reminder of the things she'd said about college and professors. "You could have gone all night without repeating that," she whispered, feeling the warm color rush into her face.

"I'm sorry, but I couldn't help myself."

"You're not the least bit sorry," she countered.

Grey chuckled and rubbed the side of his jaw. "You're right. I'm not."

"I should be furious with you, letting me go on that way!" Meghan continued, still not looking at him directly. If those students hadn't arrived when they did, there was no telling how much more she would have said.

"But you're not angry?"

"No," she said, releasing a pent-up sigh. "I probably should be, but I'm not." She'd done this to herself, and although she would have liked to blame Grey, she couldn't.

"I didn't know how to stop you," he admitted, frowning. "I wanted to say something—let you know before you'd embarrassed yourself. I suppose I just assumed you'd have figured it out. It was my own fault; I should have said something earlier."

"That's the problem," Meghan admitted with a rueful smile. "My tongue often outdistances my mind. I get carried away and say the most absurd things and then I wonder why everyone is giving me odd looks."

"Friends?" Grey prompted, holding out his hand.

His look was so endearing and so tender that Meghan couldn't have resisted had she tried. From the first moment she'd noticed Grey Carlyle reading Chaucer, she'd been attracted to him. Strongly attracted. Lots of good-looking men had passed through the doors of Rose's Diner, and plenty had shown more than a casual interest in her. But this was the first time Meghan had ever dated anyone she'd met at the restaurant after such a short acquaintance.

"Friends," Meghan agreed, slipping her hand into his. His touch was light and impersonal, and Meghan experienced a sensation of rightness about their being together. Perhaps it was best that she hadn't guessed his occupation earlier. If she had, she might not have been so candid.

They started walking toward the ivy-covered brick buildings. The pathway was lined by small green shrubs. "I wish now I'd worn my other shoes," Meghan commented casually. The one good thing about this date was that she'd cleaned out her closest while searching for the perfect outfit. After trying on anything and everything that was the least bit suitable, she'd chosen a red plaid skirt, white blouse and dark blazer, with knee-high leather boots.

Grey paused and glanced down at her feet. "Are those too tight?"

"No, especially since I've stuck my foot in my mouth a couple of times, but my other shoes are more subtle."

"Subtle?" he repeated.

"All right," she muttered. "More dignified. If I'd known I was attending this lecture with a full-fledged professor, I'd have dressed more appropriately for the occasion. But since I assumed you were just a regular, run-of-the-mill, classical literature lover, I thought the boots would do fine."

"You look wonderful just the way you are."

The open admiration in his gaze told her he was telling the truth. "It's nice of you to say so, but from here on out, it's my black patent-leather Mary Janes."

He burst out with a short laugh. The sound was robust and full but a little rusty, as though he didn't often reveal his amusement quite so readily.

Again he securely tucked her hand in the curve of his arm. "This is a prime example of what I was talking about earlier."

"What is?" Meghan wasn't sure she understood.

"Your honesty. There isn't any pretense in you, and I find that exceptionally rare these days."

Meghan was about to make a comment, when they strolled past a group of students.

"Hello, Professor Carlyle," a blond girl said eagerly and raised her hand. When Grey turned toward her, the teen smiled brightly. "I just wanted to be sure you knew I was here."

Grey nodded.

From all the smiles and raised hands directed toward Grey, Meghan guessed he was a popular professor. Heaven knew *she* liked him! Now that was an understatement if there ever was one. But at the same time she'd be a fool to hope that a man like Grey Carlyle would ever be romantically interested in her—and Meghan was rarely foolish. Obtuse, yes; foolish, no! She might amuse him now, but that wasn't likely to last.

Gavin Hall was only a short distance from the lot where Grey had parked his car. The auditorium was huge, and by the time they were seated near the back of the hall, it was more than a third filled.

Two men sat near the podium. The first Meghan recognized from the newspaper as Friends's president, Dr. Browning. The other man was obviously the speaker. To Meghan's way of thinking, he resembled a prune, though she chided herself for the uncharitable thought. The lecturer seemed to wear a perpetual frown, as though everything he saw displeased him. Either that or he'd recently been sucking lemons.

"There seems to be a nice turnout," Meghan commented, impressed by the number of students who appeared to have such a keen interest in Keats and Shelley.

Grey straightened the knot of his tie and cleared his throat. "Actually," he whispered out of the corner of his mouth, "I bribed my class."

"I beg your pardon?"

Grey didn't look particularly proud of himself. "Dr. Fulton Essary is a colleague of mine and a distinguished poet in his own right. We've had our differences over the years, but basically I value his opinions. I wanted a good showing tonight, so I told my classes that every one of my students who showed up would automatically receive an extra fifty credits toward his overall grade."

"Ah," Meghan said softly. "That was why the blond girl made a point of letting you know she was here."

"Exactly." Grey withdrew a piece of paper from the inside of his suit jacket and unfolded it as quietly as possible. As he scanned the auditorium, he started checking off names.

Within five minutes the lights dimmed and Dr. Browning approached the podium to make his introduction. Shortly afterward, Dr. Fulton Essary stepped up to the front of his audience and delivered his speech—in a dead monotone.

For one hour and five minutes Dr. Essary summarized the life and works of Percy Bysshe Shelley and John Keats. Although Meghan admired the talents of both nineteenth-century poets and was familiar with their styles and literary accomplishments, she was eager to learn something new.

Unfortunately, nothing she could do kept her thoughts from wandering. Dr. Essary was terribly boring.

After the first half hour, Meghan started shifting in her seat, crossing and uncrossing her long legs. At forty-five minutes, she was picking imaginary lint from the lap of her skirt.

The only thing she found riveting was the fact that someone who planned to talk for this amount of time could reveal such little emotion concerning his subjects. He might as well have been lecturing about the Walt Disney characters, Mickey and Minnie Mouse.

If anything in Keats's and Shelley's lives had personally touched him, Meghan would have never known it.

Once he finished there was a round of polite, restrained applause followed by what Meghan felt was a sigh of relief that rolled over the audience. The floor was opened for questions, and after an awkward beginning, one brave student stood and asked something that Meghan couldn't fully hear or understand.

Slowly Grey moved his head toward Meghan's and whispered, "What do you think?"

It was in her mind to lie to him, to tell him what he wanted to hear; but he'd claimed he admired her honesty, and she wouldn't give him anything less now. "The man's a bore."

Grey's eyes widened at the bluntness of her remark.

Meghan saw his reaction and immediately felt guilty. "I shouldn't have said that," she told him, "but I couldn't help it. I'm disappointed."

"I understand you may have found his delivery lacking, but what about content?"

Apparently the question-and-answer session was over with the one question, because just as Meghan was about to whisper her response, everyone started to stand. Happily leaping to their feet more adequately described what transpired, Meghan mused.

She supposed she wasn't the only one to notice, but it seemed to her that the hall emptied as quickly as if someone had screamed "Fire! Run for your lives!" Grey's students couldn't get out of there fast enough. Personally, she shared their enthusiasm.

Once they were outside, Grey helped her on with her coat, slipping it over her blazer, his hands lingering on her shoulders. "You were about to say something," he coaxed.

Meghan stared up at him blankly while putting on her gloves.

Burying his hands in the pockets of his thick overcoat, Grey matched his long strides to her shorter ones. "You didn't like the lecture?"

"I... I wouldn't exactly say that."

"You called the speaker a bore," he reminded her, frowning.

"Yes, well..."

"Is this another one of those times when your tongue got away with you?" he teased, but the amusement didn't quite reach his eyes.

Meghan slipped her hands inside her coat pockets, forming tight fists, uncertain how she should respond. She probably wouldn't be seeing Grey after tonight, so there wasn't any reason to pad her answer. She wasn't sure she could, anyway. After an hour and five minutes of such insipid drivel, she was having trouble holding her tongue.

"Perhaps referring to him as a bore was a bit of an exaggeration," she started, hoping to take the bite out of her blunt remark.

"So you've changed your mind." That seemed to please Grey.

"Not entirely."

His face fell. "You can't fault Dr. Essary. Honestly, Meghan, the man's a recognized genius. He's published his doctorate on Shelley and Keats. Mention the name Dr. Fulton Essary and the literary world automatically associates him with the two poets. His own published works have been compared to theirs. He's known all across America."

Meghan had never heard of him, but that wasn't saying much. Unfortunately, as far as she was concerned if someone were to mention the name Dr. Fulton Essary, her response would be a drawn-out yawn.

"I won't argue with you," she said, carefully choosing her words, "but there's no passion in the man."

"No passion? Are you saying he should have ranted and raved and pounded his fists against the podium? Is this how you think he should have delivered his lecture?"

"No—"

"Then just exactly what do you mean by passion?" Grey asked, clearly frustrated by her lack of appreciation for his colleague.

"Essary compared Keats to Shakespeare for the richness and confidence of his language, and I couldn't agree with him more, but—"

"Then what's the point?"

"The point is that for all the feeling your associate relayed, Keats could have written 'Mary Had a Little Lamb.' If what he was saying was so profound—and I think it could have been—then it should have come from his heart. I didn't feel anything from this friend of yours except disdain, as though he were lowering himself to share his insights to a group of students who are constitutionally incapable of understanding Keats's and Shelley's genius. Nothing he said gripped me, because it hadn't touched him."

Grey was silent for a minute. "Don't you think you're being unnecessarily harsh?"

"Perhaps, but I don't think so," she murmured. "Ask your students what they think. I'm sure one of them will have courage enough to be honest."

"It was a mistake to have brought you here," Grey said when they reached his car, his mouth a thin line of impatience.

He was angry and doing a remarkable job of restraining himself, Meghan noted. For that matter, she wasn't particularly pleased with him, either. He'd asked her what she thought and she'd told him. It was as if he expected her to say whatever it suited him to hear. Nor was she pleased with what he seemed to be implying. He made it sound as though she couldn't possibly know enough to make an intelligent evaluation of a man as brilliant as Dr. Essary. Good heavens! Even his name was pompous-sounding! All this evening did was reinforce the fact that she would never make it as a college student. If her supposed friend thought her stupid, what would strangers think?

Ever the gentleman, Grey helped Meghan into his car, firmly closing the passenger door and walking around to the driver's side.

The ride back to Rose's was an uncomfortable one. Grey didn't say a word and neither did Meghan. The silence was so loud she could barely hear anything else. It was in her mind to say something to ease the tension, but one look at Grey told her he wasn't in the mood to talk. Now that she thought about it, neither was she. She did feel badly, however. Grey had invited her to the lecture and she'd gone with an open mind, eager to learn; instead, she'd come away feeling depressed and sorry.

He eased his car into the restaurant parking lot and moved to turn off the engine.

"Don't," she said quickly, sadly. "There's no need for you to get out. I apologize for ruining your evening. Despite everything, I'm grateful you invited me to the lecture—I've learned some valuable lessons. But I feel badly that I've disappointed you. I wish you well, Professor Carlyle. Good evening." With that, she opened the car door and climbed out.

As she was walking away, Meghan thought she heard him call after her, but she didn't turn around—and he didn't follow her.

It was just as well.

Three

Grey couldn't remember a time when a woman had upset him more. Streetlights whizzed past him as he hurried back to Friends University, and he realized he was traveling well above the speed limit. With a sigh of impatience, he eased his foot off the gas pedal and reluctantly slowed his pace.

Grey had asked Meghan to Dr. Essary's lecture, believing she would be stimulated and challenged by the talk as well as the man. He'd liked Meghan, been attracted to her warmth and her wit; but now the taste of disillusionment filled him. In the space of only a few hours, he'd discovered that although she appeared intellectually curious, she wasn't willing to listen and learn from those who clearly had more literary knowledge than she. Being a professor himself, he felt it was like a slap in the face.

His invitation had been impulsive; and every time he acted spontaneously, Grey lived to regret it. This evening was an excellent example.

Meghan was a mere twenty-four-year-old with nothing more than a high-school education. She had no right to make such thoughtless statements about a man as eminent as Dr. Essary—a man who'd made a significant contribution to the world of literature. Just thinking about Meghan's comments infuriated Grey. The other man was brilliant, and she'd had the audacity to call him a bore. To worsen matters, she'd gone on to claim that Dr. Essary had revealed little emotion for his subject. Why, anyone looking at him would know differently. All right, Grey admitted, his esteemed colleague could use a few pointers on the proper method of delivering a speech of that length, but the audience wasn't a group of preschoolers with short attention spans. These were college students—adults.

What had upset Grey most, he decided, was Meghan's claim that Dr. Essary had displayed no passion. Of all the silly comments. Good grief, just exactly what did she expect—tears, dramatic gestures, or throwing himself down in front of the audience?

Grey had delivered plenty of lectures in his career, and his style wasn't all that different from that of his associate. No one had ever faulted Grey. No one had claimed he was a bore—no one would dare!

Back at Friends University, Grey sat inside his car for several minutes while the disillusionment worked its way through him. Rarely had he been more disappointed. Indignity burned through him like a fiery blade, hotter than what Meghan's comments warranted.

After a moment he slammed his hand against the steering wheel in a rare burst of emotion.

As he climbed out of the car, the lights from a coffeehouse called Second Life from across the street attracted his attention. A number of Friends students were known to hang out there. Grey started walking in the opposite direction to the faculty reception in honor of Dr. Essary, but stopped after only a few feet. Frowning, he abruptly turned around and headed toward the café.

* * *

Meghan secured the tie of her bright yellow housecoat around her waist and set the teakettle on top of the burner. Her apartment near Marina Lake was small and homey, but Meghan felt little of its welcome after this evening's disaster.

To prove exactly what kind of mood she was in, she'd walked in the door and gone directly to her bedroom to reach for her yellow robe. In fact, she hadn't even bothered to undress first.

Do not pass go. Do not collect two hundred dollars.

That was the way she felt—like a loser in a board game.

She'd blown her date with Grey. It was another one of those "open mouth and insert foot" incidents. He'd asked for her honesty, and she'd told him exactly what she thought of his friend. From there, the evening had quickly disintegrated. She should have known he wanted her to lie, and gone on and on about how wonderful the lecture had been.

Meghan didn't know if she was that good a liar. But it was clearly what he'd wanted to hear, and she should have given it to him and saved herself some grief.

So this was to be the end of her short-but-sweet relationship with Grey Carlyle. Unfortunately, it would take a while to work through the regret. Knowing the way she did things, it would take her a few days to pull herself together, to dissect the evening and put the incident into perspective so she could learn from what had happened. At the end of this blue funk she should walk away a little wiser.

The kettle let loose with a high-pitched whistle that broke the silence of the tiny kitchen. Meghan poured the boiling water into the teapot, added the herbal leaves and left them to steep for several minutes. She was just about to pour herself a cup when there was a knock at the door.

She glanced across the living room as though she expected there was some mistake. No one could possibly be coming to visit at this hour—unless, of course, it was one of her teenage brothers; but even that was unlikely this late in the evening.

"Who is it?" she asked.

"It's Grey. Could we talk a minute?"

Grey! Meghan's hands were trembling so badly she could hardly manage to twist the lock and pull open her front door. In that short time span, she didn't have a chance to school her reaction or her thoughts. The only thing she felt was an instant surge of jubilation. The smile that spread across her face came from deep within her heart. Meghan knew without even trying, there was no way to restrain the look of sheer joy that dominated her features.

"Grey," she said, stepping aside so he could enter her apartment.

He did so, standing awkwardly just inside the door. His gaze seemed to rest somewhere behind her and refused to meet her own. His expression was brooding and serious. The smile that had sprung so readily to her face quickly faded.

"I can see this is a bad time," Grey commented, once he looked directly at her and her yellow housecoat.

"No...this is fine," she replied hurriedly. "Would you like to sit down?" Embarrassed by the load of laundry that was piled on one corner of the sofa, she rushed over and scooped it up with both hands, smiled apologetically and deposited the clean clothes on the seat of the recliner.

"You look as if you were ready for bed," Grey observed, remaining standing. "Perhaps it would be better if I returned at a more convenient time."

"No, please stay." She removed the housecoat and draped

it over the back of the chair that contained her laundry. "I bought this robe several years ago when my family was on vacation in Texas," she felt obliged to explain. "Whenever I'm feeling depressed or unhappy about something, I put it on and pout for a while. My mother calls it the Yellow Robe of Texas."

Grey cracked a smile at that. "You're pouting now?"

"I was, but I'm not anymore." Meghan was delighted to see him, if only to let him know how much she regretted the way their evening had gone. She wanted to tell him how she'd felt when he'd lashed out at her, which had only driven home her own point that she wasn't cut out for college-level literature courses.

"I just put on a pot of tea. Would you like some?" she offered.

"Please."

Meghan moved into the kitchen and brought down her two best china cups, along with sugar and milk, and set them on a tray. When she turned around, she discovered Grey standing behind her, looking chagrined, his hands in his pockets.

"Aren't you the least bit curious why I'm here?"

With her heart in her throat, she nodded. The last person she had ever expected to see on the other side of her door was Grey Carlyle—*Professor* Grey Carlyle. "I'm equally curious to know how you knew where I live."

"When I went back to Rose's—I hoped you'd still be there—anyway, another waitress, I think her name was Sherry, gave me your address."

Meghan should have known the assistant manager would be willing to go against company policy for Grey. Normally the information would have had to be tortured out of her co-worker.

Grey freed one hand from inside his coat pocket and jerked his splayed fingers through his hair as though he weren't particularly pleased about something. "I told her you'd left something in my car that I thought you might need. I don't usually lie, but I felt it was important we talk."

Meghan's fingers tightened around the serving tray. "I understand."

Grey took the tray from her hand and set it on the round oak table that dominated what little space there was in her cramped kitchen. With him standing so close, the area seemed all the more limited. Despite herself, Meghan lifted her gaze to his.

Grey raised his hands to the rounded curves of her shoulders and his eyes caressed hers. "I owe you an apology."

"No," she said, and shook her head, more than willing to discount his words. "I should be the one to make amends to you. I don't know what came over me, or why I felt it was necessary to be so insensitive. I'm not often so opinionated—well, I am, but I'm usually more subtle about it. If it means anything, I want you to know I felt terrible afterward."

"What you said was true," he admitted bluntly, frowning. "Dr. Essary *is* an arrogant bore. The reason I took exception to your description of him is because Essary and I are actually quite a bit alike."

"I'm sure he's a fine man of sterling character—" Meghan stopped abruptly. "I beg your pardon?" She was sure she'd misunderstood Grey. He couldn't possibly mean to suggest that he was anything like his colleague. She didn't know Grey well, but everything about him told her Professor Carlyle was nothing like the other man.

"After dropping you off, I drove back to the university campus. I'll admit I was upset…more than I have been in a long time. I sat in my car fuming, feeling confused. I couldn't seem to put my finger on why I should be so insulted." He paused, pulled out a kitchen chair and gestured for Meghan to sit down. She did and he took the seat across from her.

"You were defending your friend, the same way he would have supported you," Meghan reassured him, silently chastising herself for her arrogant ways.

"Not true," Grey contradicted, his frown growing darker and more intense. "Fulton and I have never considered ourselves in those terms. You might even say there's friendly rivalry going on between us."

Since they were both sitting, Meghan poured the tea, handing Grey his cup. She didn't feel nearly as shaken now.

"Something you said, however, struck a note with me," he continued. "You suggested I ask my students what they thought. You seemed confident at least one of them would open up to me."

Meghan did vaguely remember suggesting that.

"A group of my pupils were having coffee after the lecture. I joined them and asked for their honest opinion." He hesitated, looking mildly distressed. "I asked. And by heaven, they gave it to me with both barrels."

Hearing that others shared her sentiments didn't cause Meghan to feel better about what had happened between her and Grey, but it helped.

While he was talking, Grey added both sugar and milk to his tea, stirring it in as though the sweetener were made of some indissoluble compound. "I took a long hard look at Fulton," Grey continued, "and what I saw was a sad reflection of myself."

"Grey, no." Her hand automatically reached for his.

"Meghan, you don't know me well enough to contradict me."

"But I do.... I realize we've only talked a few times, but you're not anything like Dr. Essary. I know it as surely as I'm convinced we're sitting here together."

He captured her fingers and squeezed lightly. "It's kind of you to say so, but unfortunately I know differently. My life has been filled with academia and its importance. In the process, I've allowed myself to become jaded toward life, forgetting the significance of what I thought were trivial matters. In the last few years, I've immersed myself in a disapproving, wet-blanket attitude."

"I'm sure you're mistaken."

His smile was sad, his features grim. "I've laughed more with you in the past few days than I have all year. I look at Fulton, so deadpan and serious, and I recognize myself. Frankly, I don't like what I'm seeing. If you feel there's no passion in him, you're right. But there's none in me, either. It's not something I'm proud to admit. Fun is often associated with frivolity. And as a learned man—an educator— I've looked upon fun as a flaw in the character of a man." He studied his cup as though he expected the tea leaves to spell out what he should say next. "I owe you much more than an apology, Meghan. In only a few short days you've revealed to me something I'd been too blind to recognize until now. I want you to know I'm truly grateful."

Meghan didn't know what to say. "I'm sure you're putting more stock than necessary in all this. The minute I met you I saw an intense, introverted man of undeniable intelligence who loved Chaucer and Milton the same way I did. I'm nothing more than a waitress at a popular diner, and you shared your love for the classics with me. If anything, that made you more appealing to me than a hundred other men." Meghan understood all too well the differences between them. Grey was accustomed to a refined, academic atmosphere while she was fun loving and slightly outrageous. From the moment she'd started talking to him Meghan had recognized Grey's type. He was analytical, weighing each fact, cataloging each bit of information before acting. Impulsive actions were as foreign to him as a large savings account was to her.

"What I saw was a bright, enthusiastic woman who—"

"Who doesn't know when to keep her mouth shut," Meghan finished for him.

They both laughed, and it felt good. Meghan took a sip of her tea, feeling almost light-headed. She realized it had taken a good deal of courage for Grey to seek her out and apologize.

He glanced at his watch, arched his brows as though he were surprised by the time, and stood abruptly. "I'm sorry for interrupting what remains of your evening, but I wanted to talk to you while I still had the nerve. The longer I put it off, the more difficult it would have been."

Meghan appreciated what it must have cost him to come to her, and her estimation of him, which was already high, increased a hundredfold. She didn't want him to leave, but she couldn't think of an excuse to delay him.

"I know how difficult it was for you to stop by. I'm glad you did."

"I am, too." He edged his way to the front door.

Meghan's mind was racing frantically in an effort to prolong his leaving. She thought to suggest a game of Monopoly, but was certain he'd find that childish. Cards weren't likely to interest him, either.

"Thanks for the tea."

"Sure," she said with a shrug. "Any time."

His gaze fell on the yellow robe that had been carelessly draped over the recliner and smiled. "Good night, Meghan."

She went to open the door for him, but his hand at her shoulder stopped her. She turned, and his narrowed gaze met hers in a lazy, caressing action. His eyes were filled with questions, but Meghan couldn't decipher what it was he wanted to know. A contest of wills seemed to be waging within him as his look continued to embrace her. Meghan returned his gaze, not understanding but wanting to help in any way she could.

"Every time I act on impulse I regret it."

She blinked, not knowing what to make of his comment. "Sometimes it's the only thing to do," she murmured. "My mother always claimed I should follow my heart. That's good advice—I suggest you do the same."

The frown left him, to be replaced by a determined grin. "You're right. Sometimes doing what seems natural is by far the best thing. I have the distinct feeling I won't regret this." With that, he lowered his head to hers and she felt the warm brush of his mouth across her own. He slipped his arm around her waist and gently pulled her against him, half lifting her from the floor. He touched the upper part of her lip with his tongue, lightly, and moistened the outline of her mouth.

A choppy rush of air escaped from her lips at this subtle attack on her senses. Meghan moaned softly and leaned into him, letting his weight absorb her own. Then, moving her head farther back, Grey rubbed his lips against hers, applying a gentle pressure until her mouth parted in welcome, eager for a more thorough exploration.

Meghan shouldn't have been so surprised that he would kiss her, but she was. She flattened her hands against his chest, her fingers clenching handfuls of his shirt as she gave herself over to the wealth of sensation that rocked through her.

It was a short kiss as kisses went; his mouth lingered over hers for only a heartbeat more and then quickly withdrew, leaving her hungering for more.

"I'd like to see you again," he said in a voice that sounded unlike his own, strained and reluctant. "Soon."

"Yes."

"Tomorrow night, at six? Dinner, a movie, anything you want."

Meghan made some kind of appropriate response, but the minute he was gone, she leaned against the door, needing its support. Several different emotions buzzed around her head. She felt disappointed that the kiss had been so short, and at the same time electrified and thrilled. With that brief kiss had come an immeasurable flash of excitement. She lifted her fingertips to her lips and examined them, half expecting there to be some lasting evidence of his touch. Her heart was pounding so hard, she felt as if her ribs were about to collapse. It wasn't that she'd never been kissed before; but no one had ever caused her pulse to react like this.

No one.

Four

The dishwasher was humming softly in the background when Meghan stepped into the shower late Saturday afternoon. She'd gone shopping and splurged on a new outfit, and had gotten home later than she would have liked. Normally she would have waited until the dishwasher was finished, but there wasn't time.

From the moment Grey had left her apartment the night before, her mind had been filled with romantic daydreams. She imagined him wining and dining her and then leading her onto a dance floor. Her fantasy showed him wrapping his arms around her and gazing into her eyes with undisguised admiration. Visions of him holding and kissing her filled her mind. Everything about this night was going to be perfect. They'd had such a rocky beginning, and she longed to make everything right.

Halfway through the shower, the water went freezing cold. Crying out in protest, Meghan turned off the knob and reached for a thick towel. A faint gurgling sound could be heard in the background. Thinking she should probably look into what was happening, Meghan wrapped the towel around her body and traipsed into the kitchen. Her wet hair fell over her face and she impatiently swatted it aside as she investigated the scene. An icy cold, wet sensation struck her toes the instant she moved onto the linoleum floor.

Meghan gasped and hurried back onto the carpet on her tiptoes.

Her dishwasher had overflowed.

"Oh, great," she moaned, running into the bathroom for some towels. As luck would have it, there was only one dry one and she was forced to search frantically through her laundry hamper for something to sop up the liquid. In her desperation she was tossing clothing left and right, hurling her panties and bras above her head.

Gathering up what she could, she hauled an armload of soiled clothes into the kitchen and quickly spread them over the floor. The first thing she had to do was to soak up as much water as she could as fast as possible. The whole time she was working, she was glancing at the clock.

What towels she could locate, plus a couple of shirts and two pairs of jeans, looked like mismatched puzzle pieces across her linoleum by the time she finished spreading them around. Still, water was puddled everywhere.

In an effort to help her clothes absorb as much as possible, Meghan danced over them, stomping her feet in a wild kind of jitterbug.

The doorbell chimed and Meghan froze. Please, she prayed, don't let that be Grey! Her gaze swung to the kitchen clock. It was still five minutes early. If there was an angel watching over her, then it wouldn't be Grey at her front door.

"Who is it?" she called out, holding the front of her housecoat together with one hand, bunching the material together so tightly her nails threatened to bend. Her hair was half dry by this time and stuck out in several different directions.

"It's Grey."

Meghan's faith in heavenly assistance quickly faded. She couldn't answer the door dressed in her robe and underwear with her hair resembling something out of a science-fiction movie. If that wasn't bad enough, her kitchen floor looked as if several bodies had recently been vaporized.

"Meghan?"

"Ah... I'm not quite ready," she responded, forcing a cheerful note into her voice. "Would it be possible for you to come back in a few minutes?"

Silence followed her request.

"That is if it wouldn't be too much of an inconvenience," she tried again, desperately hoping he would agree. When he returned she'd explain, but she couldn't let him see her like this.

"I did say six, didn't I?" he pressed.

"Yes," Meghan muttered.

"It's obvious that something else, or more likely *someone else*, has come by," Grey called back to her. "How long would you like me to disappear for? An hour? Two? Will that be long enough for you?"

Someone else! Grey thought she was trying to get rid of him because there was a man in the apartment with her? Her shoulders sagged in defeat. Without hesitating any longer, she yanked open the front door and stepped aside.

"You might as well come in and have a good laugh," she said, sweeping her hand in front of her. To her horror, her voice became a high-pitched screech, barely discernible. She tried several times to swallow, but all she could manage was to make more of the same wretched sounds.

She dared not look at him, because once she saw the

dismay in his eyes, she was bound to burst into tears, and that would only humiliate her further.

"Meghan, what happened?" He moved into her apartment and closed the door.

Her head hung so low that her chin was tucked against her collarbone. "I was in the shower when I heard funny gurgling noises.... My dishwasher died and there's water everywhere and I look like something from outer space." Desperate for oxygen, she sucked in a huge breath.

"Why didn't you say so in the first place?" Grey said.

He made it sound as though she'd purposely planned the whole disaster to evoke sympathy from him. "I wanted everything to be so special tonight—and then you seemed to think I'm keeping a man in here." She didn't dare admit that he was the only male she'd thought about from the minute he'd stepped into Rose's Diner. Her shoulders jerked up and down each time she tried to breathe.

"Meghan," he said, appealing to her with his hands. "I don't know what to say. I'm sorry, I thought—"

"I know exactly what you thought," she interrupted as the situation and his initial reaction started to get the better of her. "As you can see, something *has* come up and I won't be able to go out tonight." Pointedly she walked over to the door and opened it for him.

"The least I can do is help," he insisted.

Somehow the picture of Professor Grey Carlyle under a sink refused to take shape in her mind. This was a man familiar with George Bernard Shaw—not water pipes and broken-down dishwashers.

"I doubt that you know the least bit about plumbing," she remarked stiffly.

"I don't," he agreed, and then added under his breath, "and even less about women, it seems."

With her chin tilted at a defiant angle, Meghan stood with her back straight, her fingers tightening around the doorknob. "I appreciate the offer, but no thanks."

"You're sure you'll be all right?"

"Positive," she said, and flipped a damp strand of hair out of her eyes with as much dignity as she could muster, which wasn't much.

He proceeded to walk out but paused just outside the apartment door to exhale sharply and murmured, "I'm sorry, Meghan."

"So am I," she responded, feeling both miserable and defeated.

Ten minutes later, after Meghan had dressed and run a brush through her hair, she phoned the apartment manager, who was gone for the evening—naturally. Given no other choice, Meghan phoned her father.

Perhaps she'd been a bit hasty with Grey, she mused in the quiet minutes that followed her call home. He'd only been trying to help. Unfortunately his offer had followed on the heels of his implication that she was hiding a man in her apartment. For him to even suggest such a thing was enough to set her teeth on edge.

Both Meghan's parents arrived within the half hour.

"Hi, Mom. Hi, Dad," she greeted, hugging them both, grateful for their love and support.

Her father carried a toolbox with him. At fifty, Patrick O'Day was in his prime—healthy, fit, and handsome to boot. Meghan had always been close to both parents.

"What happened in your kitchen? A mass murder?" her father teased, then laughed at his own joke as he stepped over the sopping array of clothes.

"Thanks for coming over," Meghan told him sincerely. "I don't know what I would have done. The apartment manager wasn't in and more than likely he wouldn't be able to get anyone here until Monday morning, anyway."

Colleen O'Day removed her coat while studying Meghan. "Weren't you going out with that professor friend of yours this evening?"

In her excitement Meghan had phoned her mother and told her all about meeting Grey. "*Was* as in past tense! Obviously, something came up."

"Meghan, darlin', you must be so disappointed."

She nodded. There didn't seem to be anything more to say. This evening wasn't turning out the least bit the way she'd hoped.

When it came to Grey, she felt like someone eager to appear in a circus performing in the high-wire balancing act. Although she wanted badly to do it, she couldn't seem to find her footing. Each time she tried, she nearly slipped and fell.

"You look tired," her mother said next.

Meghan felt exhausted. For most of the day she'd been running on nervous energy, not taking time to eat lunch. Breakfast had been a glass of orange juice while on the run.

"It's not your dishwasher—you've got a broken pipe down here," her father shouted from beneath the kitchen sink.

"Surprise, surprise," Meghan answered with a soft chuckle. With her mother's help she removed the clothes and towels that littered the floor, placing them inside the empty laundry basket.

Her father had nearly completed the repair when her doorbell chimed. The teakettle whistled at almost the same second, and frustrated, Meghan paused, not knowing which to attend to first.

Debbie Macomber

"You get the door," her mother suggested, "and I'll take care of the tea."

It was Grey. He'd changed out of his pin-striped suit and into slacks and a sweater. He stood in front of her, holding a large book at his side.

"Before you get upset," he said, "I want you to know something."

Meghan's fingers curled around the doorknob. "You should know something, too," she returned.

"What?"

"I *have* got a man in my apartment—a handsome one who openly admits he loves me. This guy's crazy about me. Would you care to meet him?"

Anger flickered in Grey's eyes, and his mouth narrowed.

"Meghan?" her mother called out from behind her. "Who is that at the door?"

Reluctantly Meghan stepped aside. "Mom and Dad, I'd like you both to meet Professor Grey Carlyle. He teaches English literature at Friends University."

Grey stepped into the apartment, but his gaze centered on Meghan. "Your father?" he whispered.

She gave him a saucy grin.

"Professor Carlyle, how pleased we are to meet you," Colleen O'Day greeted, looking absolutely delighted to make his acquaintance.

Her father rose awkwardly to his feet and held out his hand to Grey, who shook it. "It seems my daughter was stuck in some hot water," Pat joked, "and had to call on her old man to rescue her."

"We were just about to have some tea, Professor. Please join us?"

Grey turned to Meghan, who didn't give him any indication she cared one way or the other. Actually, her heart was pounding so hard it was a wonder he couldn't see it beating against her sweatshirt.

"Thank you," he said, smiling up at Meghan's mother. "I'd enjoy a cup of tea."

"Pat?" Colleen asked, while Meghan brought cups down from the cupboard.

"Please." His reply was muffled as he was back under the sink.

"Can I do anything to help?" Grey asked, setting the book on the tabletop.

For the first time, Meghan could see the title, and when she did, she regretted her earlier display of anger. Grey had gone out and bought a book on plumbing repairs. Her insides went all soft at the thought that he should care so much.

"I'm almost finished here," her father told him. "I'll be with you in a couple of minutes. You sit down and I'll be there once I get this blasted fitting secure."

Her mother was busy pouring tea, which Meghan delivered to the small round table.

"I hope you're still hungry," Grey said when she approached him.

Her gaze shot to him and she blinked, not sure she understood.

"I've got two Chinese dinners in my car."

"I—"

"Why, that's thoughtful, isn't it, Meghan?" her mother interrupted. "Pat, don't you think we should be heading home? Danny needs to be picked up from the theater soon."

"I was going to have tea," he objected, and then hesitated, apparently reading his wife's expression. "Right," he said evenly. "I forgot Danny. Now that your pipe's fixed, Meghan, I guess I'll be leaving." Her father picked up the pliers and the other tools he'd been using and placed them inside his toolbox.

"Speaking of dinner," Colleen O'Day said, "why don't you come over to our house tomorrow for Sunday dinner, Professor? We've hardly had a chance to get to know you, and that way you could meet Meghan's three younger brothers."

Meghan's sip of tea moved halfway down her throat and refused to go any farther. It took several attempts to swallow it. Meghan didn't know what her mother could be thinking. Grey didn't want to meet her family. Why should he? He and Meghan barely knew each other, and every time they even tried to date, the evening ended in disaster.

"Thank you, Mrs. O'Day, I'd be honored."

Meghan realized his acceptance was only an excuse to be polite. After her parents left, she would let Grey know he shouldn't feel obligated.

"Okay, princess, everything seems to be working." To prove his point, Pat O'Day turned on the kitchen faucet, and after a few sputters the water gushed out normally.

"Thanks, Dad," she told him, kissing him on the cheek.

"It was a pleasure to have met you both," Grey said, in what Meghan was sure was his most courteous voice.

"You, too."

"We'll see you tomorrow at three, then," her mother prompted.

"I'll be there."

"Now, you two young folks try to enjoy the rest of your evening," Colleen O'Day suggested.

"We'll do that," Grey promised, his gaze reaching out and capturing Meghan's.

Five

Meghan braced her feet on the chair beside her, her knees raised as she held the small white box of spicy diced chicken directly below her chin. Grey might be accustomed to eating with chopsticks, but she wasn't.

"You're doing great."

She smiled lamely. "Right! I've got five different kinds of sauces smeared over the front of my sweatshirt and soy sauce dribbling down my chin." The piece of chicken that was balanced precariously on the end of her chopstick fell and landed in her lap, proving her point.

"Here." Grey handed her a paper napkin.

"Thanks."

Grey set aside the white container and reached for a small bag. "Are you ready for your fortune cookie?"

"Sure." She held out her hand, eager to discover her fate.

Grey gave her one and then promptly opened his first.

Meghan giggled at his shocked expression. "What does it say?"

"Ver-r-y inter-r-esting," he said in a feigned Chinese accent. "Cookie say professor must beware of waitress who read Shakespeare."

"Very funny," she returned, having a difficult time holding in her laughter. Setting aside the take-out container Meghan ceremonially split open her own fortune cookie.

"Well?" Grey prompted.

"It says I should beware of man who insists women eat with chopsticks."

Grey grinned. "I guess I asked for that."

"You most certainly did," she chided. "I don't suppose you want to hear my views on Shakespeare, do you?"

"Dear heavens, no. When it comes to literature, we can't seem to agree on anything."

"Literature," she echoed, "and just about everything else." That could very well be true, but when he was looking at her like this, his blue eyes warm and filled with humor, every argument she'd ever presented him with turned into melted ice cream. She was forced to pull her gaze away for fear of what he would read in her eyes.

"You'll be pleasantly surprised to know I'm crazy about Willie boy," she announced, popping half the fortune cookie into her mouth.

"Willie boy?"

"William Shakespeare."

"My faith in you has been restored," he said solemnly, dipping his head slightly.

"Oh, come now, Grey. Who couldn't like Shakespeare?"

"The same person who finds fault with Edmund Spenser is questioning my reserve toward another English great?" he asked, his eyes as round as paper plates. "I'd like to keep the peace as long as possible, if I can."

"Okay, okay. Forget I asked that." Still smiling, she stood and started to deposit the empty cartons into the garbage can.

Grey helped her. "Are you willing to discuss something else?" he asked.

He was so casual that Meghan assumed he was about to pitch another joke her way. "Now that all depends," she replied and tossed a wadded paper sack from behind her back. Her throw was a dead ringer, landing in the garbage can as though it were impossible for her to ever miss. Stunned, her mouth sagged open. "Did you see that?"

"Meghan, I'm serious."

She dropped her hands to her sides and turned to face him. "I know," she teased, laughter bubbling up inside her, "but I'm hoping once you get to know me, you'll lighten up a little."

His responding smile was feeble at best. "Meghan, would you please listen to me?"

The smile drained from her eyes when she realized that something was indeed bothering him. "Yes, of course."

He buried his hands in his pockets and walked over to the sink, staring at it for a couple of seconds before turning to face her. "Earlier, when I met your parents…"

"Yes?"

"I saw your face when your mother invited me to Sunday dinner. You weren't pleased. The fact is, you don't want me there, do you?"

Her first thought was to confirm his suspicion, but she realized it wasn't entirely true. She *did* long for him to meet her family, only she feared the outcome. "You're more than welcome," she said blithely, hoping to casually dismiss any reserve he'd sensed. "It's just that…"

"What?"

"I don't want you to feel obligated. Mom's one of those warm, wonderful people who insists on sweeping everyone she meets under her wing. I'm afraid you might feel pressured into joining my family just because my mother issued the invitation. If the plumber had been here, she probably would have invited him, too," Meghan said, making light of her parent's offer. "It's just Mom's way."

"I see."

From the stiff tone of his voice, it was clear Grey obviously didn't. "You have to understand," Meghan hurried to add. "My brothers would love nothing better than to get you involved in a hot little contest of touch football. And knowing Dad, he'd corner you the minute you walk in the door. He loves chess—anyone visiting is fair game. My dad's a wonderful man but he tends to be something of a poor loser." Meghan realized she was rambling, but she was frantically trying to make him believe that she had his best interests at heart.

She didn't even mention the ribbing her three brothers would likely give him. The annoyed look Grey had told her she was apparently doing a poor job of explaining the situation.

"But what it really boils down to is that I wouldn't fit in with your family," he announced starkly. "That's what you're really trying to say."

"Not entirely." It was; only she hadn't fully realized it. "You're welcome to come if that's what you want," she finished, feeling both frustrated and confused.

"You mean your mother's welcome is sincere, but yours isn't?"

"Oh, Grey, why do you have to complicate this? I told you the reasons I have my doubts, but whether you decide to come or not is entirely up to you."

"I see."

Meghan slapped her hands noisily against the sides of her legs. "I wish you would stop saying that."

"What?"

"*I see*, in that pitiful voice, as though I'd insulted you."

Earlier they'd sat and joked and teased each other like long-time friends, and now they were snapping at one another like cantankerous turtles. In the short time since they'd met, they'd muddled their way through several disputes. The last thing Meghan wanted was another one.

"I see," Gray said in exactly the tone she'd been talking about.

Meghan burst out laughing. She couldn't help herself, although it was clear that this reaction was the last thing Grey had expected of her.

"Professor Grey Carlyle, come here."

"Why?" His brows arched suspiciously, he studied her, clearly not trusting her.

"Never mind, I'll come to you." She did so, but the few short steps that separated them seemed more like miles. By the time she stood directly in front of him, Meghan had nearly lost her nerve. Boldly she slipped her arms around his neck, tilted back her head and looked squarely into his eyes.

Grey held himself stiff, with his hands hanging loosely at this sides, his brow puckered. "Kindly explain what you're doing!"

"You mean to tell me you don't know?" she asked softly. His mouth was scant inches from her own. Their soft, short breaths mingled and merged.

Very slowly, Meghan raised her lips to his and graced him with the briefest of kisses.

In response, Grey cleared his throat and moved his head farther away from hers, yet he didn't disentangle her arms from his neck or make any move to slip her out of his arms.

If he expected to thwart her with a scowl, it wouldn't work. Meghan stood on the tips of her toes and leisurely passed her mouth over his in a soft, almost chaste kiss.

This time neither moved, neither breathed. Kissing Grey the first time should have been warning enough. The second brief sampling only whetted Meghan's appetite for more.

His too, it seemed.

Grey lowered his head until his lips barely touched hers. He held himself completely immobile for a long moment, brushing his mouth back and forth over hers, savoring the velvet texture of her lips. The tip of his tongue outlined first her upper lip and then her bottom one until she felt her knees would buckle if he didn't give her a more complete taste. She moaned softly and he slipped his mouth over hers with a fierce kind of tenderness, molding her mouth to his own.

His fingers were planted on the curves of her shoulders when he gently pushed her away. His breathing was deep and ragged. Meghan's own wasn't any more controlled.

She'd meant to entice him, to take his mind off her mother's invitation to Sunday dinner and the problem that had created between them. Instead, Meghan's plan had backfired.

Everything went stock still. She swallowed uncomfortably and lowered her eyes. She couldn't have met his look, had the defense of Mother Earth depended upon it.

"Meghan?"

"I... I shouldn't have done that."

"Yes," he murmured, "you should have." He lifted his hand to her nape, urging her back into his arms. Without any argument, she went. This wasn't a game any longer. She was trembling, with both excitement and need.

Grey kissed her again, using his tongue to coax her lips farther apart, sending a wild jolt of elation through her.

By the time Grey's lips moved from hers and he buried

his face in the curve of her neck, Meghan had no strength left in her bones.

"All right," he whispered into her hair. "I'll conveniently forget the dinner tomorrow. You needn't worry I'll show up—I'll find some excuse to give your mother later."

Meghan tightened her arms around his neck. "I want you there. Only please remember what I said."

He laughed softly. "Meghan, it was obvious from the first that you didn't."

"I changed my mind," she said more forcefully this time. "Just be prepared for...my family."

"I suppose you're going to suggest I throw a game of chess, as well."

"That would be nice, but not necessary. It's time Dad owned up to the fact his strategy stinks."

A long moment passed in which Meghan felt they did nothing more than enjoy the feel of each other.

When her legs felt as if they could support her, she stepped away from him, but her heart was pounding like a charging locomotive. And yet she felt as weak as a new-born kitten.

"Please come," she said in as firm a voice as she could manage and wrote down her parents' address.

"You're sure about this?"

She pressed her forehead against his chest. "Yes."

"Then I'll be there."

Meghan was in the kitchen with her mother, peeling a huge pile of potatoes, when the doorbell chimed in the background. Ripping the apron from the front of her dress, she heaved in a calming breath to regain her composure and hurried into the living room.

Her parents' home was an older style built in the late

1920s, with a huge drawing room. An old brick fireplace with mantel was situated at one end, and bookcases along the other. A sofa, a recliner and two matching chairs with ottomans filled the rectangular area and were positioned around the television, where her father and brothers were watching a football game.

"That's probably Grey," she announced dramatically, standing in front of the TV set. It was the only way to completely gain their attention. "Now, please remember what I said," she cautioned, eyeing them severely.

"Oh, Meghan," thirteen-year-old Danny cried. "You make it sound like we're going to hurt him. He mustn't be much of a man if he can't hold his own in a little game of touch football."

"We've already been through this once, Daniel O'Day. You're not going to ask him to play football with you. Understand?"

"You sweet on this guy, Sis?" Brian asked, eyeing her with sparkling blue eyes and a mischievous grin.

"That's none of your business." As a high-school senior, Brian should know better than to ask. Meghan expected a little more understanding from her oldest brother. It was obvious, however, that she wasn't going to get it. Her mistake had been revealing to her younger siblings how much she *did* care about Grey.

"Dad… No chess, please."

"Princess, are you going to open the door or not? You're leaving the poor man to freeze to death on the front porch while you give everyone instructions on how to act around him."

"Grey's important to me."

"Oh, gee," fifteen-year-old Chad said, and hit his forehead with the palm of his hand. "We hadn't figured that one out, Sis."

Meghan stood in front of the door, sighed inwardly and smoothed her hands down the front of her dress. At the last moment, she twirled around and faced her father and brothers once more. "Please."

"Meghan, for heaven's sake would you kindly answer the door."

She did as her father requested, her smile forced. "Hello, Grey," she said greeting him with a wide smile and opening the screen door for him. "I'm pleased you could make it."

Grey stepped into the family home, carrying a bouquet of red rosebuds. He was dressed in a suit and tie, looking as dignified and professional as ever.

Meghan looped her arm around his elbow so they faced the O'Day men as a united force. "You remember my dad from last night?"

"Of course." Grey stepped forward and the two men shook hands.

Brian stood with his father and Meghan introduced him.

"I'm pleased to meet you, Brian."

"You too, Professor."

"Please call me Grey."

"Can I call you that, too?" Chad asked. He wasn't wearing his shoes, and his socks had huge holes in the toes.

"That's Chad," Meghan said, and prayed Grey didn't notice her brother's feet.

"I'm fifteen. How old are you?"

"Chad!" Meghan cried, closing her eyes.

"He looks too old for you, Meghan," Chad muttered under his breath. "Now I suppose you're going to get all mad at me because I said so."

She offered Grey a weak smile, which was the best she could do.

"I'm thirty-four," Grey answered without a pause. "And you're right, I *am* too old for Meghan."

"No, you're not," Danny piped up, walking over and holding out his hand, which Grey readily accepted. "I'm Danny."

Meghan could have kissed the freckles off her youngest brother's nose at that moment. Grey wasn't too old for her. In fact, their age difference had never come up before as she hadn't given the matter a second thought.

Danny, however, quickly destroyed all her goodwill by adding, "So, you don't play football? I always hoped that when Meghan got married her husband would like sports."

"Danny!" Meghan cried, feeling her face explode with color. "Professor Carlyle and I are just getting to know each other. We aren't going to be married."

"You're not?"

"Of course not. We only met a few days ago."

"Yeah, but from the way you've been acting all afternoon, I thought you were really hot for this guy."

Meghan cast him a look heated enough to boil water.

"All right, all right," Danny moaned. "I'll shut up."

"Meghan," her father advised discreetly, "if you let go of Grey's arm, he might be able to take off his coat and sit down."

"Oh, sorry," she said, smiling apologetically. She cast Grey a knowing glance and whispered, "I warned you."

"So you did," he mumbled back and removed his overcoat, keeping the bouquet of flowers with him.

"Would you like some tea or coffee or anything else before dinner?" Meghan asked him, just as her mother stepped into the room.

"Professor, how good of you to come," Colleen said graciously.

Grey handed her the roses. "Thank you for asking me, Mrs. O'Day."

"Colleen, please," she corrected. "Oh, my! Roses! Really, Professor, you shouldn't have, but I'm glad you did. It's been years since I've received anything so lovely."

"You brought the roses for my mom?" Danny asked incredulously. "What did you bring for Meghan? I thought you were sweet on *her*. You better watch it, 'cause she's got a temper."

"Danny," Meghan whispered, her eyes pleading with his. "Please don't say another word. Not one more word!"

"But..."

"Do me a favor and keep quiet for the rest of the afternoon."

The injustice of it all was nearly more than her youngest sibling could take and he tucked his arms over his chest and centered his concentration on the football game that blared from the television set.

"How are the Chiefs doing?" Grey asked, sitting down in the chair beside her father.

"Terrible," Pat O'Day muttered and sadly shook his head. "The Seahawks are running all over them. What they need is more power in the backfield."

"Dad's something of an armchair quarterback," Meghan explained.

"Do you like football, Professor?" Chad asked, leaning forward from his position on the ottoman, his hands clasped. His gaze was intent, as though the outcome of Grey's relationship with the O'Day family rested on his reply.

"I've been known to watch a game every now and again," Grey answered.

Meghan sighed her relief.

"That's great, because us men usually play a game or two ourselves after dinner," Chad informed him, as though expecting Grey to volunteer to join them.

It was all Meghan could do to keep from jumping up and down and waving her arms in an effort to remind her brothers of what she'd said. They'd promised not to involve Grey in any of this, but it looked as if Chad had conveniently forgotten.

"I'll take the flowers into the kitchen. Thank you again, Professor," Colleen said, gently sniffing them and smiling proudly. She turned toward her husband and sons. "Dinner will be ready in thirty minutes, so don't get so involved in this silly football game."

"Don't worry, Mom," Brian said. "The Chiefs are losing."

Meghan stood, her feet braced apart. She would have remained planted there, had her mother not dragged her back into the kitchen.

"Mom," she protested, looking back at Grey. "It's not safe in there for him. Grey isn't like other men."

"Oh?" Her mother's eyebrows arched speculatively and her eyes twinkled with amusement.

What Meghan really meant to say was that Grey wasn't anything like the other men she'd dated over the past few years. He was special, and she didn't want anything to happen that would destroy their budding relationship.

"I mean—" she hurried to add "—Grey's an only child. His whole life has revolved around academia. All Brian, Chad and Danny know is football. Grey was so smart he was sent to an advanced preschool class, for heaven's sake." Her mother looked impressed and Meghan continued, listing the details of his academic achievements. "From kindergarten he went straight into a gifted-students program. Grey's a lamb among wolves in there with Dad and the boys."

"He'll do just fine," her mother returned confidently.

"But—"

"Now come on, fretting isn't going to do any good, and neither is hurrying in there to rescue him from the fiendish plots of your younger brothers."

Meghan cast a longing glance over her shoulder, knowing her mother was right but longing to run interference. Grey meant more to her than any man she'd ever met. She and Grey were vastly different—almost complete opposites—and yet they shared several common interests.

Meghan's biggest fear, now that she'd had time to analyze it, was that his meeting her family would emphasize how different they were and discourage Grey from continuing their relationship.

"I'll set the table," Meghan offered when she'd finished dicing the tomato for the salad. The dining room was situated between the living room and the kitchen and offered Meghan the opportunity to check on Grey without being obvious. She opened the drawer to the china hutch and brought out the lace tablecloth. While she was there, she stuck her head around the corner and chanced a peek inside the living room. To her dismay, she discovered Grey and her father deeply involved in a game of chess. She groaned and pressed her forehead against the wall. As much as she loved her father, when it came to chess he was a fanatic and even worse, a terrible sport.

By the time Meghan finished setting the table and mashing the potatoes, dinner was ready. She stood with her hands braced against the back of a dining-room chair while the men gathered around the table.

"Professor, please sit next to Meghan," Colleen O'Day instructed, pointing toward the empty chair beside her daughter.

Grey moved to her side.

"I saw you and Dad," she muttered out of the side of her mouth. "How'd it go?"

"He won."

Meghan sighed, appeased. "Thank you," she whispered back.

"Fair and square, Meghan. I didn't throw the game."

"Dad won?" she asked, louder this time, her voice filled with surprise. She blinked a couple of times, hardly able to believe what she was hearing.

"I'm the world's worst chess player, only you never bothered to ask."

A smile quivered at the corners of her mouth and she shook her head. Once her father had claimed his place at the head of the table, the family bowed their heads as Pat O'Day offered the blessing.

Meals had always been a happy, sharing time for the O'Days, and Danny started in talking about what was lacking on the Kansas City Chiefs football team.

The buttermilk biscuits were passed around, followed by Yankee pot roast, mashed potatoes, thick gravy, small green peas and the fresh salad.

"Professor, Meghan was telling me you graduated from high school when you were fourteen," her mother stated conversationally, turning the subject away from football.

"Is that true?" Chad popped half a biscuit into his mouth and stared at Grey as if the older man had recently stepped off a spaceship.

Grey cleared his throat and looked self-conscious. "Yes."

Colleen O'Day looked on proudly. "Meghan was always the one who earned top marks in our family."

"That's because she's a girl," Danny objected. "Girls always do better in school—teachers like them better. Only sissies get good grades." As if he suddenly realized what he'd said, Danny's gaze shot to Grey and he quickly lowered his eyes. "Not *all* boys who get good grades are nerds, though."

Meghan wanted to kick Danny under the table, but she dared not. She was pleased that her mother didn't continue to drill Grey about his education. She could well imagine what her brothers would say if they knew he'd zipped through college and gone directly into a doctoral program. From there, he'd been accepted on the faculty of Friends University where he'd taught ever since.

"What about girls?" Brian asked, directing the question to Grey. "I mean, if you were so much younger than everyone else, who was there for you to date?"

"No one," Grey admitted frankly. "I didn't know many girls, as it was. There weren't any my age in the neighborhood and none at school, either. Until I was in my twenties, I rarely had anything to do with the opposite sex."

"Personally, I don't think they're worth the trouble," Danny said, completely serious. "Brian used to think that way, but then he met Allison and he's gone to the other side. Chad's not much better. There's a girl who calls him all the time and they talk all the time. I think he's turning traitor, too."

"It happens that way sometimes," Grey commented, sharing a knowing look with Meghan and doing an admirable job of disguising his amusement.

"You like my sister, don't you?" Danny continued, and

then added before Grey could answer, "I guess that's all right if she likes you. And she does. You wouldn't believe it. From the moment she arrived this morning, all she's done is give us instructions on what we could say to you and what we couldn't. I've forgotten half the stuff already."

"Obviously," Meghan said wryly.

"I think I can understand why Meghan likes you so much," Chad said with a thoughtful stare. "You teach literature, and Meghan really loves that stuff. She's always reading books dead people wrote."

Meghan stood abruptly and braced her hands against the edge of the table. "Anyone for dessert?"

An hour later, Meghan was helping her mother with the last of the dishes. Brian had cleared the table and the other boys had dealt with the leftovers and loading the dishwasher, leaving the few pots and pans that needed to be washed by hand. Grey and her father were in the living room playing a second game of chess.

"Meghan," her mother said with an expressive sigh, "I wish you'd relax. Grey is doing just fine."

"I know," she said, rubbing the palms of her hands together. "I suppose I'm overreacting, but I wanted him to feel at home with all of us, and I don't know if that's possible with the boys."

"He seems to be taking their teasing in his stride."

"What else can he do?" she exclaimed. "Challenge Danny to a duel?"

Her mother laughed at that. "I told you before there was nothing to worry about." She wiped her hands dry and reached for the hand lotion. "You like Grey, don't you, princess? More than anyone in a long while."

"Oh, Mom, I couldn't have made that any more obvious."

Colleen O'Day chuckled. "You're right about that."

"But we're different." She tucked an errant reddish curl around her ear and cast her gaze to the floor. She was Yankee pot roast and Grey was T-bone steak. "I like him so much, but he's intelligent and…"

"So are you," her mother countered.

"Educated."

"You're self-taught. You may not have an extensive education, but you've always had an inquiring mind and a hunger for the written word. Grey wouldn't be attracted to you if you weren't bright."

"But he's dignified and proud."

Her mother continued spreading the cream over her hands, composing her thoughts. "I don't see any real problem there. Just don't wear your purple tennis shoes around him."

Meghan laughed, and then chewed on the corner of her mouth. "I'm crazy about him, Mom, but I'm afraid I'm closing my eyes to reality. I can't understand why Grey is interested in me. It won't last, and I'm so afraid of falling in love with him. I expect him to open his eyes any minute and realize how irrational our being together is. It would devastate me. I'm excited and afraid at the same time."

Her mother was silent for a long moment. "When you were four years old, you were reading."

"What has that got to do with anything?"

Her mother smiled faintly. "From the time you could walk you were hauling books around with you everywhere you went. You were bound and determined to find out what all those letters meant and all their sounds. I don't suppose you remember the way you used to follow me through the house, pestering the life out of me until I'd give up and sit down with you. Once you were able to connect the letters with the sounds, you were on your own and there was no holding you back."

"It's not letters and sounds that I'm dealing with now. It's a man, and I feel so incredibly unsure of myself."

"Let your heart guide you, princess. You've always been sensible when it comes to relationships. You're not one to fall head over heels in love at the drop of a hat. If you feel so strongly about Grey, even if you've only known him a short time, then all I can advise you is to trust yourself."

"There isn't anything else I can do, is there?"

"He's a good man."

"I know."

Meghan's father drifted into the kitchen and reached for a leftover buttermilk biscuit. He paused and chuckled. "I've got to hand it to that young man of yours," he said to Meghan.

"What, Dad?" Meghan fully expected him to comment on the chess game.

"Chad and Danny talked him into playing football. They're in the front yard now."

Six

"But Grey's wearing a suit!" Meghan burst out as though that fact alone would prevent him from participating in any form of physical activity.

"Brian lent him an old sweatshirt of his."

"Oh, dear," Meghan cried, rushing toward the front of the house.

"He doesn't need you," her father called after her. "Your professor friend is perfectly capable of taking care of himself, don't you think?"

"Against Chad and Danny?" she challenged. "And Brian?"

Her father responded with a tight frown. "On second thought, maybe you'd better check on him."

Meghan grabbed her coat from the hall closet on her way out the door. Her first thought was to dash onto the lawn and insist all four of them stop their foolishness this minute. Instead, she stood on the porch with her hand over her mouth as she watched the unfolding scene.

Grey was bent forward, his hands braced against his knees. After shouting out a long series of meaningless numbers, Brian took several steps in reverse and lobbed the football to Grey. The ball soared through the air, the entire length of the yard, and no one looked more shocked than Chad and Danny when Grey caught it.

"Go for the touchdown!" Brian screamed at the top of his lungs.

"No!" Meghan called out. Unable to watch, she covered her face with both hands. A chill rippled down her spine that had nothing to do with the frosty November weather. Part of her longed to run into the middle of their scrimmage. She wanted to yank Grey off the grass before he got hurt, but she had no right to act as his guardian. As an adult, he must have known what he was getting himself into when he agreed to this craziness. He would be lucky, though, if he came out of this with nothing more than a broken bone.

From the hoots and cheers that followed, it became apparent that Grey had either scored or that Chad and Danny had stopped him cold. She couldn't decide which, and dared not look.

"Meghan?"

She whirled around to find Grey standing on the top step of the porch, looking worried. Her breath left her lungs in a sudden rush of relief. "Are you all right?"

"I'm more concerned about you. You're as pale as a ghost."

"I thought Chad was going to tackle you."

"He had to catch me first. I may not know much about football, but I'm one heck of a sprinter."

Meghan's relief was so great that she impulsively tossed her arms around his neck and squeezed for all she was worth. He felt warm and solid against her and she buried her face in his neck, laughing and fighting off the urge to cry at the same time.

Chuckling, Grey wrapped his arms around her waist and

swung her around. "I made a touchdown, and according to Brian, that makes me some kind of hero."

"Some kind of fool, you mean."

"You're not going to kiss her, are you?" Danny asked, making it sound the equivalent of picking up a slug.

Grey's gaze delved into Meghan's. He wanted to kiss her, she could tell, but he wouldn't. Not now. Later, his look promised. She answered him with a soft smile that claimed she was holding him to his word, even if it was unspoken.

"I think we better quit while we're ahead," Brian suggested, joining Meghan and Grey. "It's getting too dark, and personally, I don't think Meghan's heart can take much more of this. I thought she was going to faint when you caught that last pass."

"I was afraid Chad and Danny were going to murder him simply because he happened to catch it."

"We wouldn't have done that," Chad said with more than a hint of indignation. "This is touch football, remember?"

Danny scrunched up his face. "I might have tackled him, but I knew Meghan would kill me dead if I did."

Meghan looped her arm around Danny's neck in a headlock and rubbed her knuckles over the top of his head. "You're darn tootin', I would have."

With his arms squirming, her brother escaped and angrily glared at his older sister. "I hate it when you do that!"

Laughing, they all entered the house.

An hour later Grey followed Meghan back to her apartment and parked outside her building.

"Do you want to come up for coffee?" she asked. Looking at Grey now, she found it difficult to remember that he'd been playing football with her brothers only a short time earlier. His eyes were serious, his expression sober.

He seemed reserved and quiet after an afternoon filled with noise and fun.

"I'd love to come up for coffee," he answered automatically and smiled at her softly, "but regrettably, I can't. There's enough paperwork stacked on my desk to keep me up most of the night." He reached out and caressed the side of her face with his finger. "I enjoyed today more than I can tell you, Meghan. You have a wonderful family."

"I think so." She was close to her parents and all her brothers, although she'd wanted to throttle the boys when she saw that they'd managed to drag Grey into a football game. What had surprised her most was Grey's willingness to partake in her brothers' folly.

He continued to gently stroke the side of her face. Meghan knew he planned to kiss her, and she met him halfway, automatically slipping her arms around his neck. He lowered his lips to caress hers in a long, tender, undemanding kiss. Meghan felt certain that he meant to kiss her once and then leave, but instead, he tightened his arms around her waist, bringing her closer to him. The kiss deepened and she was treated to a series of slow, compelling kisses that made her weak with longing. Something special had sprung into existence between them from the first moment they'd met—something delicate and so tangible that Meghan could feel it all the way to the marrow of her bones.

She moaned at the erotic sensations that circled her heart and her head. Grey responded immediately to her small sigh of pleasure by prolonging the kiss. He parted her lips, then teased and tormented her with his tongue until Meghan was dazed almost senseless.

"Oh, Meghan," he whispered into her hair as though in a state of shock himself. "I can't believe the things you do to me."

"Me?" she asked, her laugh soft and mildly hysterical. Surely he must know that whatever physical electricity existed between them was mutual.

Grey moved away from her and rested his head against the wall, taking in several giant gulps of air. "One kiss. I told myself I was only going to kiss you once. You're quickly becoming addictive, Meghan O'Day."

Meghan's breathing was ragged, as well. "I'm sorry you can't come in for coffee, but I understand," she told him when it was possible to do so and sound as if she had her wits about her. "I enjoyed today, too. Very much."

His hand reached for hers. "There's a cocktail party I have to attend next Saturday night. It'll be dry and boring and filled with people who will remind you of Fulton Essary." He paused and grinned wryly, before adding, "They'll remind you a lot of me, too. Will you go with me?"

Meghan's heart leaped to her throat. Grey had boldly walked into her world and was issuing an invitation for her to explore his. Doubts buzzed around her head like pesky mosquitos at a Fourth of July picnic. "Are you sure you want me there?"

"I've never been more confident of anything in my life. You'll do just fine."

Meghan wished she shared his faith in her. "Before you go, I want to tell you about a decision I recently made," she said, smiling up at him. This small piece of news was something she'd been saving all day to tell him. "I've decided to visit Friends tomorrow."

His gaze widened briefly. "'Visit'?"

"You told me one of the reasons you invited me to hear Dr. Essary was to expose me to the richness of education that was available at the university. I've concluded that you're right. My being older than most first-year students shouldn't matter. There's no time like the present to go back to school. I'm so excited, Grey. I feel like a little kid again, and I have you to thank for giving me the courage to do something I should have done long ago."

The warmth of his smile caused her heart to leap.

"Classes don't start until after Christmas, and I'm only going to sign up for two the first time around and see how I do. That way, I can keep working for a while, as well." She felt a spontaneous smile light up her face as the enthusiasm surged through her. "I'm really trying to be sensible about all this."

"I think that's wise."

"When I first leafed through the catalog, I wanted to register for every literature class offered. But the more I thought about it, the more I realized that I've got to ease my way back into the habit of going to school. After all, it's been several years since I graduated."

"Meghan?"

He stopped her, and when she raised her gaze to his, she noted his brow had puckered into a frown. "Did you decide to take any of the classes I'll be teaching?"

She nodded eagerly. "The one on the American novel. But when I saw that we'd be reading *Moby Dick*, I had second and third thoughts."

"You don't like Melville?"

Meghan nearly laughed aloud at the look of dismay that briefly sparked in his clear blue eyes. "I read the book in high school and found it insufferable. All those allegories! And from what I see, they made such little sense."

Grey's frown darkened.

"He was a great writer, though," she said, hoping to appease Grey before she slipped into a black hole and couldn't find her way out. When it came to literature Meghan often found her views varied greatly from his. For the past two days, they'd been getting along so well that she'd forgotten how vehemently Grey defended the literary greats.

"Were you aware that *Moby Dick* is said to be the quintessential American novel?"

"I imagine Margaret Mitchell was upset when she heard that," Meghan returned jokingly. "Mark Twain, on the other hand, probably took the news in his stride."

"You can't compare those two to Melville."

What had started out in jest was quickly turning into something more serious. "Grey, honestly, Melville was tedious and boring to the extreme. Maybe he would have appeared less so if he'd made even a passing effort to be less obtuse."

He looked away from her and expelled his breath. "I can't believe you actually said that."

"I can't, either," she confessed. Her quicksilver tongue wasn't helping matters any. She didn't want to argue with Grey. She wanted him to be as excited as she was about attending Friends. "I didn't mean to start a fight with you, Grey. I just wanted to thank you for encouraging me."

He nodded. Although Meghan assumed their disagreement had been a minor one quickly forgotten, Grey was silent on the short walk upstairs to her apartment. Brooding and thoughtful, as well, she noted.

"Thank you for bringing me home," she said.

"Meghan, listen." He paused and raked his fingers through his hair, looking uneasy. "I'd prefer it if you didn't sign up for any of my classes. It would be the best thing all the way around, don't you think?"

Those words felt like a bucket of cold water unexpectedly dumped over her head. She couldn't really blame Grey. Already she'd proved how opinionated and headstrong she was. He was looking for a way to avoid problems, and she couldn't blame him. If she were his student, she would be nothing but a nuisance. Her pride felt more than a little dented, but she could do nothing but bow to his wishes.

"Of course. If that's what you want," she agreed stiffly.

"It is."

She cast her gaze downward, feeling wretched and sorry now that she'd even told him her plans.

"Good night," he said, leaning forward enough to brush his mouth over her cheek.

"Good night," she replied, doing her best to force some enthusiasm into her voice.

He waited until she was inside the apartment and the living area was lighted before he left her. "I'll call you later in the week," he promised.

She nodded, forcing a smile. The minute she closed the door after him, the smile vanished. Dropping her purse on the recliner, she walked directly into the kitchen and braced her hands against the countertop and stared sightlessly at her microwave. The lump in her throat felt huge.

Grey was well within his rights to ask her not to register for any of his classes, but she couldn't help taking it personally. She felt hurt and insulted.

An hour later, Meghan didn't feel much better. She sat in front of the television, wearing her yellow robe from Texas and watching a murder-mystery rerun. The phone rang, and heaving a sigh, she reached for it.

"Yo," she answered, certain it was her brother.

"Yo?" Grey returned, chuckling.

Meghan uncurled her bare feet from beneath her and straightened. "Grey?"

"Hello. I took a break a minute ago to make myself a cup of coffee and I got to thinking about something. When

I asked you not to register for any of my classes, there was a very good reason."

Meghan already knew what that was, but she didn't volunteer the information.

"The thing is, Meghan, I want tocontinue being with you as much as I can. If you're taking my American-novel class, it would be unethical for me to date you."

"Oh, Grey," she whispered, closing her eyes as a current of warm sensations washed over her. "I'm so glad you called. I was really feeling awful about it."

"Why didn't you say something?" he chided gently.

She brushed her bangs from her forehead and held her palm there. "I couldn't. I thought you objected because I can be so dogmatic and bullheaded when it comes to literature."

"I hadn't noticed," he teased.

"Oh, stop." But there was no censure in her voice. She felt as if a heavy weight had been lifted from her heart.

"You agree with me about not registering for my classes, don't you?"

"Of course. I should have realized why myself." She hadn't; and that only went to prove how insecure she felt about her relationship with him.

"Yes, you should have. I'm glad I phoned. I don't want any more discord between us. I guess for some people, politics is a touchy subject—for us it's literature."

Meghan chuckled. "You're right about that."

To enter the administration office at Friends University was like walking into a living nightmare. Bodies crammed each available space, and lines shot out in every direction imaginable. The noise was horrendous.

Once Meghan had managed to get inside the door, she

heaved in a deep breath and started asking questions of the first person she could.

"Pardon me, can I register for classes in this line?" she asked a gum-chewing brunette.

"Not here, honey, this one's for those of us needing financial assistance. Try over there," the girl told her, pointing across the room.

Meghan groaned inwardly and was forced to traipse through a human obstacle course, stepping over and around bodies that took up nearly every inch of floor space, until she reached the far side of the building.

She found a line and stood there, praying she was in the right place.

"Hi," a deep male voice greeted from behind her. "You work at Rose's Diner, don't you?"

Meghan turned to face a tall, rakishly good-looking man who looked vaguely familiar. "Yes. Do I know you?"

"There's no reason you should. I eat at Rose's every now and again. I don't know if you've waited on me or not, but I remember you from there. My name is Eric Vogel."

"Hello, Eric. I'm Meghan O'Day," she replied above the noise and they exchanged handshakes. "This place is a madhouse, isn't it?"

"It's like this every quarter."

"Don't tell me that, please."

"You're a senior?"

"I wish," she said. "I haven't been to school in years, and I'm beginning to feel like an alien—in with all these eighteen-and twenty-year-olds."

"How old are you?"

"Twenty-four."

"Hey, me too."

"I guess that qualifies us for a senior-citizen discount,"

Meghan teased. "I sincerely hope I'm in the right line for registration."

"You are," Eric said confidently, easing the pack off his back and setting it on the floor.

He apparently knew far more than Meghan did, and she was grateful he'd struck up a conversation with her.

"What classes are you planning to take?"

Awkwardly Meghan opened the catalog and showed him the two literature classes she'd chosen earlier, after much internal debate. Eric instantly started questioning her about her choices and it soon became apparent that they shared a love for the classics.

"You'll like Dr. Murphy's class," Eric assured her. "It's a whirlwind tour through six hundred years of British rhyme."

"A poetry-in-motion sort of class, then."

"Right," Eric said with a low chuckle.

The urge to ask her newfound friend if he'd ever taken anything from Grey was almost overwhelming, but Meghan resisted.

"Once we're done here, do you want to go over to The Hub and have a cup of coffee?" Eric suggested. "I'm meeting my fiancée there, and a couple of other friends. Why don't you join us?"

"I'll be glad to," Meghan said eagerly. The line was moving at a snail's pace and by the time they'd finished, it could well be close to noon. The student center seemed as good a place as any to have lunch.

Eric must have been thinking the same thing. "We might as well plan on having lunch together, from the way things are going here."

"It certainly looks that way," Meghan agreed.

Eric continued to leaf through the catalog. "By the way,

if you're interested in joining a reading group, there's one that meets Friday afternoons at two. We get together at The Hub, although I've got to confess we don't do as much reading as we'd like. Mostly we drink coffee and seek solutions to world problems. It's a literary group with bipartisan overtones, if you know what I mean. We seldom agree on anything, but love the challenge of a good argument."

The group sounded like something Meghan had been looking to find for years. "I'd love to come," she told him, having trouble keeping the excitement out of her voice.

Meghan had made her first college friend, and it felt good.

Grey's office lacked welcome when he let himself inside on Friday afternoon. He needed to phone Meghan and had put it off all week. He sat in his high-back leather chair and held a hand over his face as if the gesture would wipe out the image that kept popping into his mind.

He'd known Meghan was registering for classes Wednesday morning and had half expected her to stop off and see him afterward. When he'd talked to her the day before, he'd casually issued the invitation for her to come to his office, but he had a class at one and she had to be at Rose's before three, so the timing was iffy.

It had been pure chance that had taken Grey to The Hub early Wednesday afternoon. The faculty dining room was situated on the second floor and he was joining Dr. Riverside when he happened to catch sight of an auburn-haired woman who instantly reminded him of Meghan.

It *had* been Meghan, and a surge of adrenaline shot through him to have bumped into her so unexpectedly this way. It took a second longer for Grey to notice the two men and another woman who were sitting at the table with her.

The four were talking and laughing, obviously enjoying getting to know one another. One of the men, clearly attracted to her and doing his best to make himself noticed, had his arm draped along the back of her chair. He looked like a decent sort—clean-cut, preppy. Although it was difficult to tell from this distance, Grey thought he might have had the fellow in one of his classes a couple of years before.

The other man's arm was looped over Meghan's chair and was in no way territorial, but the emotions that shot through Grey certainly were. He felt downright jealous, and the fact stunned him. He had no right to feel so strongly about Meghan. Knowing he could experience such a powerful emotion toward her after so short an acquaintance shook him to the core. He'd left as soon as he could make his excuses to Dr. Riverside and returned to his office, badly shaken by the incident.

Two days had passed and Grey had yet to erase the image of Meghan from his mind. She hadn't stopped off at his office that afternoon, which had been just as well; she belonged with her friends. As soon as her classes started up, after the first of the year, she would come into contact with others like the ones she'd met Wednesday. With her vivacious, warm personality, she would soon have scores of new friends. These people would be her own age, and would share the same interests. They would open up a whole world to her—one in which Grey regretfully acknowledged that he wouldn't belong. There was only one thing left for him to do.

Only it wasn't easy.

Thursday, after giving the matter some heavy-duty thought, Grey had felt downright noble deciding to step aside for a man who would be far better suited to someone like Meghan O'Day. There would soon be several vying for her attention and Grey couldn't blame them. It would be all too easy for him to fall in love with her himself.

Meghan was sunshine and bright colors. Unfortunately, Grey's world was colored in black and white. He was staid; she was effervescent—the embodiment of warmth and femininity. And he was nothing more than an ivory-tower professor, secure in his own world and unwilling to venture far into another.

No. As difficult as it seemed now, it was better for them both if he stepped out of her life before either of them was badly hurt.

His feelings now, however, with the lonely weekend facing him were far less admirable. He might be doing the noble thing, but he didn't feel nearly as good about it.

It was hard to release a ray of sunshine. In fact, it was far more difficult than he ever imagined it would be. Meghan O'Day was someone very sweet and very special who drifted in and out of his life, leaving him forever marked by their all-too-brief encounter.

A cold sensation of regret lapped over him. First, he would phone Meghan and cancel their date for Saturday, and then he'd contact Pamela Riverside. Stiff and exceedingly formal, Pamela was far more compatible with him. If nothing more, they understood each other. And if he wasn't the least bit attracted to her, well, there were other things in life that made up for passion and excitement.

Feeling slightly guilty to be using Pamela to forget one sweet Irish miss with eyes as blue as turquoise jewels, Grey reached for the phone.

Meghan was busy folding clothes when her telephone pealed. Humming softly, she walked around the corner and lifted the receiver off the hook.

"Yo," she greeted cheerfully, easily falling into the greetings her brothers used so often. Meghan was in a marvelous mood. Life was going so well, lately. She'd missed seeing Grey on Wednesday and had felt badly about that, but by the time she'd left The Hub, she was shocked by how late it was. There hadn't even been time to run over and say hello.

"Meghan."

"Grey," she whispered on the end of happy sigh. "It's so good to hear from you. There's so much to tell you I don't know where to start," she said with a rush of excitement. "First of all, I'm sorry about the other day. I met someone while registering and we ended up having coffee with a couple of others, and the time slipped away without my even realizing it."

"I'm phoning about Saturday night," he announced brusquely.

"Oh, Grey, I'm really pleased you asked me to attend this cocktail party with you. Nervous, too, if you want the truth. You never did say how formal it was."

"Meghan," he said tightly. "Something's come up, and I'm afraid I'm going to have to cancel Saturday night."

"Oh." Meghan knew she'd been chattering, and immediately shut up.

"I apologize if this has caused you any inconvenience."

Grey sounded so formal that Meghan wasn't sure how to respond. "It's no problem. Don't worry about it."

"Good."

A short awkward silence followed, and Meghan decided the best thing to do was to ignore Grey's bad mood. "Oh, before I forget, Mom wanted me to ask you to dinner again next Sunday. Dad's eager to play chess again and the boys suggested you wear jeans so they won't have to worry about you ruining your suit pants."

"Meghan…"

"Grey, just wear what you're most comfortable in, and don't worry about my brothers."

"I won't be able to make it," he stated flatly. "Please extend my regrets to your family."

"All right," she replied wishing she knew what was wrong.

"I see that it's about time for you to leave for work," he said next, clearly wanting to end the conversation.

Meghan's gaze bounced to the face of her watch. "I've got a few minutes yet. Grey, is something the matter? You don't sound anything like yourself."

"I'm perfectly fine."

"It's not your health that concerns me, but your attitude."

"Yes, well," he said gruffly, "I've been doing a good deal of thinking over the last few days. It seems to me that since you're going to be attending Friends that it wouldn't do for us to continue to date each other."

An argument immediately came to her, but she quickly swallowed it. It was clear from the tone of his voice that his mind was made up and that nothing she could say would change it. The disappointment was enough to make her want to cry.

"I understand." She didn't, but that wasn't what Grey wanted to hear. He was giving her the brush-off and trying to do it in the most tactful way possible.

"We'll still see each other every now and again," he continued in the same unemotional tone as though it didn't matter to him one way or the other. "In fact it'll be unavoidable, since both your classes are in the same building as the ones I'm teaching."

Meghan wondered how he knew that. She hadn't even told him which classes she'd registered for. It was apparent he'd done a bit of detective work and had sought out the information himself.

"Yes, I suppose that it will be inevitable, won't it?"

"You're going to do very well at Friends, Meghan. If you have any problems, I want you to feel free to contact me. I'll be happy to do whatever I can to help."

"Thank you."

"Goodbye, Meghan."

The words had a final ring to them that echoed over the wire like shouts against a canyon wall.

"Goodbye, Grey," she whispered. By the time she replaced the telephone receiver, her stomach felt as if a concrete block had settled there.

Seven

Meghan's arms were loaded with books when she stepped into the ivy-covered brick faculty building. The directory in the entrance listed Grey's office as being on the third floor.

With doubts pounding against her breast like a demolition ball, she stepped into the elevator. The ride up seemed to stretch into eternity. It had been two weeks since Meghan had last talked to Grey and her mind stumbled and tripped over what she planned to say. She didn't know if she was doing the right thing in approaching him like this, but she found the persistent silence between them intolerable. Men had come briefly into her life in the past, but none had mattered more to her than Grey. She found accepting his rejection of her both painful and nerve-racking.

"May I help you?" a middle-aged woman who sat behind the computer asked when Meghan entered the series of offices. Apparently several professors shared the same assistant, who acted as both receptionist and assistant.

"Yes, please," Meghan answered, smiling broadly. "I'm here to see Professor Carlyle."

Frowning, the gray-haired women leaned forward and leafed through the appointment book. "Is he expecting you?"

"No. If he's busy I could come back when it's more convenient."

The woman gave Meghan a sharp look. "Professor Carlyle is always busy," she intoned. "Tell me your name and I'll ask if he'll see you."

By this time Meghan was convinced she was making a terrible mistake. She seemed to be shaking from the inside out. Dropping in on Grey like this, with such a flimsy excuse, would only complicate an already complex relationship.

"My dear girl, I don't have all day. Your name."

"Meghan O'Day," she answered crisply, then hurried to add, "Listen, I think perhaps it would be better if I came back another time—"

Before she could say anything more, the receptionist had pushed down the intercom switch and announced to Grey that Meghan was outside his office. Almost immediately afterward, a door opened and Grey stood not more than ten feet from her.

"Meghan."

His gaze revealed a wealth of emotion: surprise, delight, regret, doubt. Not knowing which one to respond to first, she forced a smile and said, "I hope I'm not interrupting anything important." She should be more concerned about making a fool of herself, she decided, but it was too late to do anything else now but proceed full steam ahead. She pasted a smile on her face and met his look, praying he wouldn't read the tumult boiling just beneath the surface.

"You're not interrupting anything. Come in, please." He stepped aside in order to admit her to his office. Meghan walked into the compact room and sat in a leather chair that was angled toward the huge mahogany desk. Grey's office was almost exactly the way she'd pictured it would be—meticulous in every detail. Certificates and honors lined one wall, and bookcases the other two. Behind his desk was a huge picture window that gave an unobstructed view of the campus below.

She noticed that shelf upon shelf of literary works were cramped together on the bookcases so that there wasn't a single inch of space available. In other circumstances, Meghan would have loved to examine his personal library.

"I should have called for an appointment first," she said, avoiding eye contact with him, "but I decided to stop by on the spur of the moment on my way back from the bookstore." She glanced down at the load of textbooks in her arms.

By this time, Grey was seated in the swivel chair behind his desk.

"I'll admit this is a surprise. It's been what, now—two weeks since we last talked?"

Two weeks, three days and four hours, Meghan tallied mentally. "It's been a little longer than two weeks, I guess," she responded, hoping she didn't look half as nervous as she felt. Her stomach was in complete turmoil. She tightened her arms around the load of books, holding them against her breast as though she expected Grey to hurl something at her, which was completely ridiculous.

Now that she was here, she was convinced she'd made a drastic mistake.

Grey looked at her, waiting.

"It's been really cold lately, hasn't it? I feel we're going to be in for a harsh winter."

"Yes, it has been."

His look told her he had better things to do than discuss the weather. "I was on the campus to pick up my textbooks," she tried again.

He nodded reminding her that she'd already told him that.

"How have you been, Meghan?"

"Good. Really good." Her response was eager and she scooted to the edge of her seat. "And you?"

"Fine, just fine."

Not knowing how else to proceed, she said, "I thought I'd take two classes this first time, since it's been so many years since I was in school.... I guess I already told you that didn't I?"

"Yes, I believe you mentioned that before." A heavy silence followed until Grey asked, "How's your family?"

"They're fine. Mom's busy preparing for Thanksgiving." Her grip tightened all the more around the books until the inside of her arms ached from the unnecessary pressure.

A pulsating stillness followed. They'd exhausted the small talk and there was nothing left for Meghan to do but state the reason for her visit, which at best would sound terribly feeble.

"I've been coming to a reading group the last couple of Fridays here on campus," she began, forcing some enthusiasm into her voice. "I was thinking that you might like to join us sometime."

"I appreciate the fact you thought of me, but no," he said crisply.

She hadn't really expected him to accept her invitation, but she hadn't anticipated that his answer would be quite so abrupt. He hadn't even taken time to give the suggestion any thought. "I know you'd like the others," she felt obliged to add. "They share your views on a lot of subjects; they're thoughtful and intelligent and not nearly as opinionated as me." That was only a half-truth, but she was getting desperate.

"I don't have the time for it," he added starkly.

"I know you don't.... I should have realized that." She

stood suddenly, with her heart pounding so fast and furiously, she was certain her ribs would soon crack.

"Meghan?"

"It was wrong to have come here. I'm sorry, Grey." As quickly as she could propel her legs, she hurried out of his office. If this were happening in a movie instead of real life, the elevator would have been open and ready to usher her away from the embarrassing scene. Naturally it wasn't, and she didn't have the time or patience to stand still for it.

"Meghan, wait!"

She couldn't. She should never have come to him like this. If making a fool of herself wasn't enough, she felt like crying—which added to her humiliation. If he saw them it would be that much worse.

Somehow she made it to the stairway, yanking open the door as hard as she could and vaulting down the stairs, taking two at a time until she feared she would stumble if she didn't slow down. Grey called her one last time, but she was forever grateful that he didn't try to follow her.

"The party at table twenty-two is waiting for his check," Sherry said as she brushed past Meghan that night at Rose's Diner.

"I've got it right here," Meghan replied, thanking her friend with a grin. She didn't know where her mind was tonight, but she'd felt sluggish and out of sorts all evening. On second thought, she did know where her mind was, but thinking about Grey was nonproductive and painful. She paused and checked through the slips in her apron pocket and took the coffeepot with her as she delivered the tab to table twenty-two.

"Are you sure I can't talk you into a piece of pie?" she

asked the elderly gentleman who was waiting there. "Rose's pecan is the special of the month."

"No, thanks," he said, patting his extended belly. "Rose's cooking has already filled me to the gills." He chuckled at his own joke and reached for his check.

Meghan went around the room refilling coffee cups when Sherry strolled past her a second time. "Don't look now, but trouble with a capital T just strolled in."

"Who?"

"Your professor friend," Sherry whispered, giving her a look that suggested Meghan had been working too many hours lately.

"Oh, great," Meghan groaned. She didn't want to face Grey—not after their disastrous confrontation earlier in the day.

"He requested your section, too."

"Sherry," Meghan pleaded, gripping her co-worker's forearm, "wait on him for me. Please, I can't. I just can't."

"Yes, you can!"

"I thought you were my friend."

"I am," she said, looking Meghan straight in the eye. "That's why I'm going to insist as assistant manager that you wait on your own customer. Someday you'll thank me for this."

"There'll be air-conditioning in hell before I do," she told her friend, her teeth clenched.

Sherry giggled and Meghan reached for a water glass and a menu to deliver to Grey's table. Once more, she noted, he sat in the booth by the window. A book lay open on the tabletop and he was intently reading, which meant he wasn't paying any attention to her. That was just as well.

As unobtrusively as possible, Meghan set down the water glass and menu and walked away. From out of the corner of her eye, she watched as Grey briefly picked up the plastic-coated menu and scanned its offerings. Either he made up his mind quickly or he wasn't particularly hungry, because he set it aside no more than a second or two after reading it over.

His novel didn't seem to be holding his attention, either, because he closed that and pushed it away. His brow was pleated, his look brooding.

Meghan gave him an additional three minutes before she approached his table, her tablet in her hand. "Are you ready to order?"

"Why did you run out of my office today?"

"The special is excellent this evening," she announced, ignoring his question. "Liver and onions—which I'm sure is one of your personal favorites."

"Meghan, please." He removed his horn-rimmed glasses, tucked them inside his jacket pocket and stared up at her.

Her eyelids drifted closed as embarrassment burned through her. "Pecan pie is the special of the month."

"I don't care about the pie," he said forcefully, causing several patrons to glance in his direction. Grey smiled apologetically and added softly, "But I care about you."

Her eyes shot open. In his office, she'd felt inane and foolish, but now she was furious. "You care about me?" she echoed with disbelief.

"It's true."

She rolled her eyes. "Oh, please, spare me. You broke our date two weeks ago and I haven't heard from you since. Believe me, Professor Carlyle, I got your message—loud and clear."

"I—"

"You gave me a polite, educated brush-off in what I'm sure you felt was the kindest way possible. I can't say that

I blame you. After all, you're a college professor and I'm nothing more than a waitress with a love for the classics. You're educated and brilliant. I'm simply not good enough for the likes of you."

Anger flared into his eyes, sparking them a bright blue. "You couldn't be more wrong."

Meghan doubted that, and sucked in a steadying breath before continuing in a sarcastic tone. "Hey, don't worry about it. I'm a big girl," she returned flippantly. "I can accept the fact you don't want to see me again."

"Then why were you at my office this afternoon?"

Meghan's mouth made trout-like movements as her mind staggered to come up with a plausible explanation. "Yes... well...that was a tactical error on my part." Then she remembered she'd had an excuse for being there—all right, not a very good one, but a reason. "I honestly thought you might enjoy joining the reading group," she claimed righteously, holding her head high.

Grey's gaze scanned the diner. "I can see that an explanation is going to be far more complicated than I thought. How much longer before you're off work?"

It was on the tip of her tongue to inform him he could wait all night and it wouldn't do any good because she had no intention of talking to him—ever. But that would have been a lie. As much as she longed to salvage her pride by suggesting he take a flying leap into the Arkansas River, Meghan wanted desperately to talk to him. She'd been utterly miserable for the past two weeks, missing Grey more than she'd thought it was possible to yearn for anyone she'd known so briefly. It was as if all the expectation had gone out of her life; and with it, all the fun and excitement.

"Another half hour. Would you like a piece of pecan pie while you wait?"

"Do you have custard pie?"

She smiled—the first genuine one in weeks. She should have known Grey would prefer custard over pecan. "Yes. I'll bring you a piece of pie and tea," she said, knowing he favored tea over coffee.

"Thank you."

While Meghan was slicing the custard pie, Sherry strolled past her and remarked, "Well, my friend, from the looks of things, the temperature in hell is several degrees cooler." She moved on past, chortling as she went.

The last fifteen minutes of Meghan's shift seemed to drag by. Sherry let her go a few minutes early, and Meghan changed out of her uniform in record time.

Grey was waiting for her in the parking lot. "Do you want to talk at your apartment, or would you prefer coming to my place?"

"Yours," Meghan replied automatically

For some reason, Meghan had assumed Grey lived in an apartment near the university, but she was wrong. She followed him to a house, a very nice two-story brick one with a sharply inclined roof and two gables.

She walked in the front door, doing her best not to ogle. The interior was decorated in a combination of leather and polished wood. As his office had been, the walls of his living room were lined with shelf upon shelf of obviously well-read books.

"Go ahead and make yourself comfortable," he said, taking her coat from her and hanging it in the entryway closet. "Would you like some coffee?"

"Please." She followed him into the kitchen where all the appliances were black and the sink was made of stainless steel. Everything was in perfect order, reminding Meghan that her own kitchen looked like something out of the Star

Wars movie. Her stomach rumbled and she placed a hand over her abdomen, silently commanding it to be quiet.

"You're hungry. Didn't you have dinner?"

She shrugged. "Actually, I wasn't in the mood for anything tonight." She'd been too depressed and miserable to think about anything as mundane as eating.

"Can I fix you a sandwich?"

"No, thanks," she returned, although the mere mention of food was enough to make her mouth salivate. Now that she had time to think about it, she was famished.

Grey pulled out a white cushioned stool with a wicker back for her to sit on while he busied himself with the coffee. He seemed to be composing his thoughts as he filled the coffee machine with water.

"I saw you in The Hub," he said as he opened the cupboard and took out two coffee cups. The dark liquid had just started to leak into the glass pot.

"When?" She'd only been there a handful of times.

His back was to her. "The day you registered for classes."

He seemed to place some importance on that fact that Meghan didn't seem to understand. "Yes, I was there."

"Making new friends?" he coaxed.

"Yes. That was the day I met Eric Vogel and the others in the reading group."

"I see."

"*What* do you see?" Meghan pressed. He was using those same words again and in that identical tone of voice that she'd come to dread.

He turned around, his face as tight and constrained as his voice. "You and those other students looked right together."

She frowned. "I don't understand."

He gripped the edge of the counter behind him. "No, I don't suppose you do." His gaze studied the polished black-

and-white checkered linoleum floor. "A whole new world is about to open up for you, Meghan," he said, smiling wryly. "You've devoted yourself to your family and your job since the time you finished high school. As soon as you start at the university, you're going to meet lots of new friends."

"Yes, I suppose I will." She still had no idea what he was getting at.

"What I'm trying to tell you, and apparently doing a poor job of it, is that you could have any man you wanted."

Meghan was so shocked that for a minute she didn't speak. "Grey, honestly, you seemed to have overestimated my charms." She couldn't very well announce that the only man who interested her was him! "And even if what you're saying is true, and it isn't, what has it got to do with you and me?"

"Everything." He looked surprised that she would even raise the question.

Meghan couldn't believe what she was hearing. Her stomach gurgled again and she pressed her hand harder against her midriff. "Let me see if I understand your reasoning—"

"There's nothing to understand. I don't want to stand in your way."

"Stand in my way?" she echoed, and jumped off the stool. Her stomach was churning and growling again, making her all the more unreasonable. "Oh…just be quiet," she cried.

Grey looked positively shocked.

"I wasn't talking to you."

"Is there someone else here I don't see?"

"My stomach won't stop making noise."

"Good grief, Meghan, why didn't you accept the sandwich I offered?"

"Because I'm too furious with you!" She was pacing now, lost in a free-fall of thoughts and emotions.

"I'll make you something to eat and you'll feel better," he suggested calmly.

"Stand in my way of what?" she pressed, ignoring his offer of food.

"Of finding someone special like Eric or any one of the others. I noticed how interested in you they all seemed to be. Frankly I couldn't blame them. You're warm and witty, and—"

"Miserable."

"I know you're hungry," he persisted, opening his refrigerator. "I'll have a sandwich ready for you any minute." Already he was gathering the fixings on the kitchen counter.

"I don't want a sandwich," she told him, clenching and unclenching her hands at her side.

"Soup, then?"

"You might have asked me how I felt before making that kind of decision. What gives you the right to decide who I should and shouldn't see? Don't you think it would have been better to discuss this with me first? I've been miserable, Grey, and all because you thought Eric and I looked good together. By the way, Eric's fiancée may think differently about that."

He stopped and turned to face her, a frown creasing his brow. "I have the distinct feeling we're discussing two entirely different subjects here. I thought we were discussing making a sandwich."

"A sandwich? We're talking about my life!"

"Oh." He looked both flustered and uneasy.

"Are you really so insensitive?"

"Actually," he said, boldly meeting her gaze, "*insecure* would be a more appropriate word. I didn't realize you'd been hurt by this until today when you came to my office. Frankly, I was more than a little surprised. I assumed you'd start dating any one of the others and quickly forget me."

"Both insensitive *and* insecure, then," she whispered.

A hush followed her statement. Meghan watched, standing as stiff as a new recruit in front of a drill sergeant, waiting. Her chin was elevated to a haughty angle.

Grey had revealed no faith in her or the attraction she felt for him—none. He'd seen her as a flighty teenager easily swayed by the charms and attention of another.

"Will an apology suffice?" he asked after an elongated moment, meeting her look.

"An apology and a sandwich would be an excellent start. Anything beyond that will need to be negotiated separately."

"Meghan, there's no need for you to be so nervous," Grey said as he pulled his car into a parking space outside Dr. Browning's home.

Grey had insisted she attend this party with him at the elegant home of the president of Friends University. Meghan had hoped that Grey would introduce her to his friends gradually, but he claimed this would be much easier. Easier for him, perhaps, but exceptionally hard on her nerves.

"What, me worried?" she joked, doing her best to disguise her nervousness. Grey may have insisted she attend this party with him, but she doubted he would include her in another. Her heart was in her throat, and she hadn't said more than a dozen words to him from the minute he'd picked her up at the apartment. During the half-hour drive to Dr. Browning's home, it was all Meghan could do to keep from wringing her hands.

"You're as pale as a sheet." He reached for her hand,

squeezing it reassuringly. "Everyone's going to love you, so stop worrying."

"Right," she said, forcing some eagerness into her voice. She'd never dreaded a party more. In the beginning, she'd been pleased and excited that Grey had asked her to accompany him; it had meant so much at the time. But now Meghan would have done just about anything to come up with a plausible excuse to get out of this formal gathering. Her mind kept repeating the line about fools rush in where angels fear to tread.

Grey came around to her side of the car and opened the passenger door.

Meghan tightened her fingers around her small evening bag and sucked in her breath. "Grey, I know this is going to sound crazy, but I feel a terrible headache coming on.... Maybe it would be best if you drove me home."

"Nonsense. I'll ask Joan to get you an aspirin."

An over-the-counter drug wasn't going to help her, but arguing with him wouldn't do any good, either.

"You're sure about this?" She felt she had to ask him that and give him the opportunity to back out gracefully before she said or did anything that would embarrass them both.

"Positive," he returned confidently.

Meghan's fingers felt like blocks of ice. The chill extended up her arms and seemed to center someplace between her belly and her heart.

"Before we go inside would you do something for me?" she asked hurriedly.

"You mean other than take you home?" he chided gently, smiling at her.

"Yes."

"Anything, Meghan. What do you need?"

She was sitting sideways in the car, half in and half out, wondering if she'd lost her mind.

"Meghan?"

"I… I don't know what I want," she whispered.

"You're cold?"

She nodded so hard, she feared she would ruin her hair, and she'd spent hours carefully weaving every strand into place to make an elaborate French braid. It seemed exactly the way she should style it for this evening, although she rarely wore her shoulder-length curls any way except loose.

"I think I know what you need," he said, and looked over his shoulder before leaning forward slightly and planting his hands on her shoulders.

Meghan blinked her eyes a couple of times, wondering at this game, when Grey lowered his mouth to hers in a soft, gentle kiss that spoke of solace more than passion. He pressed his lips to hers in the briefest of contacts.

Meghan sighed and braced her hands against his fore-arms, needing something to root herself in reality. Was this Grey holding her? The same man who would nor-mally frown upon kissing where there was a chance of their being seen?

He kissed her a third time and then a fourth as though a sample weren't nearly enough to satisfy him and he needed much, much more.

When he lifted his head, she could feel the color return-ing to her face and she was beginning to experience the faint stirrings of warmth seep back into her blood.

"There. How do you feel now?"

"Almost kissed."

He frowned slightly. "I suppose that was unfair, but I couldn't think of any other way to get some rosiness back into your cheeks. You looked as if you were about to faint. Are you ready now?"

"As ready as I'll ever be."

He discharged his breath and linked his fingers with hers. "Just be yourself, Meghan. There's nothing to worry about. Try to enjoy tonight."

"I know I will," she murmured, although she knew that would be impossible.

Together, hand in hand, they strolled up to the large Colonial-style home of the university president.

Nearly immediately, Meghan realized her fears were mostly unfounded. The first people she met were President Browning and his wife, Joan. From the moment she was introduced to her, Meghan liked Joan Browning, who was warm and personable—gracious to the marrow of her bones.

"Greyson's mentioned you several times," Joan stated while the two men engaged in brief conversation. "Both John and I have been looking forward to meeting you for weeks."

Meghan did a good job of disguising her surprise. "Thank you for including me."

"Nonsense. Thank you for coming."

They moved into the house and Grey slipped his arm around Meghan's waist. "There, that wasn't so bad, was it?"

"No," she had to agree. Surprisingly, it had been rather painless. She'd liked Joan Browning, who had gone out of her way to make sure that Meghan felt comfortable and welcome.

"Are you ready to meet a few of the others?" Grey asked.

"Not until I've had some champagne," she said lightly, knowing the alcohol would help her relax. One glass was her limit, but she knew some of her nervousness would disappear with that.

Obligingly Grey fetched them each a glassful of champagne, leaving Meghan for a few short moments. He returned and smiled down at her with both warmth and humor.

"Have I told you how lovely you look tonight?"

"About four times, and I appreciated hearing it every time."

He chuckled. "I feel fortunate to have you with me this evening."

"I'm the one who should be saying that," Meghan whispered, knowing all too well that *she* was the fortunate one. "Grey, who's that woman sitting across the room from us?" she asked, when she couldn't ignore the other woman any longer. "She's been sending daggers my way from the moment we walked in. Do you know her?"

Meghan felt Grey tense. "Yes, well…" He paused and cleared his throat. "I'm sure you're imagining things."

"I'm not. Who is she?" Meghan prodded.

"That's Dr. Pamela Riverside." He was clearly uneasy. He finished the last of his champagne in one swallow and set the tall thin glass aside.

"I think it's time you introduced us, don't you?" Meghan asked, realizing that the champagne had given her the courage necessary to suggest such a thing.

"Frankly, no."

Eight

"Hello, I'm Meghan O'Day," Meghan said, greeting the woman with steel-blue eyes who'd been glaring at her for the past half hour. If Grey wasn't going to make the introductions, then she would see to it herself. The minute Meghan had been free to do so, she'd slipped away from Grey, who'd been engaged in conversation.

"I'm Dr. Pamela Riverside," the other woman said stiffly, holding on to her champagne glass as though she expected it to protect her against alien forces. "I… I'm a colleague of Dr. Carlyle's."

"I assumed that you were."

"Greyson's never mentioned me?" the other woman asked softly, lowering her gaze, looking vulnerable and desperately trying to hide it.

"Grey may have, but I don't recall that he did," Meghan said, after searching through her memory and drawing a blank as far as Dr. Riverside went. From his reaction earlier, Meghan was almost certain that Grey hadn't said a word about his colleague. In fact, it seemed obvious that he was doing everything he could to keep the two of them apart.

"I didn't think he had," Pamela responded in a hurt voice that trembled just a little.

Meghan's pulse started to accelerate at an alarming rate. The thoughts that flashed through her mind seared her conscience. If Dr. Riverside was shooting daggers in Meghan's direction, then there was probably a very good reason. Perhaps Grey had jilted the other woman, and had left her with a battered and bleeding heart. The more Meghan studied the female professor, the more she realized she wore the look of a woman done wrong by her man. She was taller than Meghan by several inches, and thin to the point of being gaunt. Her dark hair was styled in a severe chignon that did little to soften the sharp contours of her cheeks and eyes. Without much effort, she could have been appealing and attractive, but her style of clothing was outdated and she didn't even bother with lipstick or eye shadow.

"Actually, there isn't any reason why Grey should have said anything about me," Pamela continued, looking more miserable by the minute. "He's never been anything but the perfect gentleman with me. If I were to tell you anything different, it would be a lie."

"I don't suppose he mentioned me, then, either," Meghan muttered. Grey had always been "the perfect gentleman" with her, as well. Meghan doubted that he would ever be anything else.

"No, I can't say that he did," Dr. Riverside confirmed brusquely, looking pleased to be telling Meghan as much.

That didn't help Meghan to feel any better. In fact she felt downright discouraged. She wasn't so naive to believe there hadn't been women in Grey's past. He might even be involved with someone now, although she doubted it.

"Actually, there isn't any reason he should tell you about me, either," Meghan admitted with some reluctance.

The beginnings of a smile came over Pamela. "That's where you're wrong."

"Wrong?" Meghan didn't like the sound of this.

"He didn't have to tell me anything about you. I knew almost from the first."

Meghan wondered briefly exactly *what* it was the other woman knew. "I'm not sure I understand," she said, wishing now that she hadn't refused a second glass of champagne. This convoluted conversation wasn't making much sense.

"By my calculations, I'd guess that you and Grey started going out the last part of October."

Meghan nodded, confirming the other woman's conjecture. She wasn't sure how Pamela Riverside had known that, and wasn't convinced she even wanted to know. Meghan was about to ask another question, when Grey casually strolled up and joined them.

"Pamela," he said as a means of greeting her, dipping his head slightly. He held himself as stiff as a freshly starched shirt collar, his hands buried deep in his pockets. "I can see you've met Meghan O'Day."

"We introduced ourselves," Meghan explained.

Grey's deep blue eyes revealed his disapproval, which surprised Meghan all the more. From everything he'd been saying and doing, it was obvious he didn't want Meghan to have anything to do with his colleague. But his efforts to keep them apart only served to pique Meghan's interest.

"There are some people I'd like you to meet," Grey stated, possessively slipping his arm around Meghan's waist. "If you'll excuse us, Pamela."

"Of course," Pamela murmured, but some of the stiffness returned to her voice. "It was nice meeting you, Meghan."

"You, too," she answered, genuinely meaning it. "We'll talk again soon."

"I'd like that."

Grey tensed and then led Meghan away. Although it could have been her imagination, it seemed that he was unnecessarily eager to remove her from the other woman's presence.

An hors d'oeuvre table had been set up, and several of the guests were milling around there, talking. Meghan recognized a couple of professors from her few visits to the Friends campus, but the others were all strangers.

It soon became apparent that there wasn't anyone in particular Grey meant to introduce her to and that he'd used the ploy as an excuse to get Meghan away from Dr. Riverside. He eased them into line and handed Meghan a small plate and napkin.

Once they'd served themselves, Grey escorted her into the family room. Only one other couple had opted to sit there and they were on the other side of the room, deeply involved in their own conversation. Grey directed Meghan to the sofa, sitting next to her but twisting around so that his back was braced against the armrest and he could look at her.

"I suppose you're full of questions now," he muttered disparagingly.

"No," Meghan fibbed. Her head was buzzing, wanting answers, but she'd intended to ask them in her own good time.

"There never has been anything between me and Pamela, no matter what she told you," he volunteered, his voice elevated and sharp. "Never."

"She didn't suggest that there was."

Grey sagged with relief as the tension slackened between his shoulder blades. "Pamela's ripe for marriage and she's going to make some man an excellent wife—but not me!"

He said this with such vehemence that Meghan nearly swallowed her cracker whole. "I see," she said, not meeting his look.

Grey paused and studied her through eyes that had narrowed suspiciously. "I understand now why you dislike it so much when I say that," he mumbled, clearly all the more troubled. "Exactly what did she tell you?"

"Nothing much." There hadn't been time.

He paused and briefly rubbed the back of his neck. "Pamela and I have been part of the university's literature department for several years. We've worked closely together, and I suppose it's only natural for her to assume certain things. Our backgrounds are similar, and through no fault of our own we've often been coupled together." He rearranged the appetizers on his plate, shifting them around as if doing so was vital to their discussion.

"She's in love with you."

Grey's head shot up so fast, Meghan wondered if he'd strained his neck. "She told you that?"

"She didn't need to. I realized it almost from the moment we walked in here tonight."

"I've never done anything to encourage her, Meghan. I swear to you that's true. We've been thrown together socially for years, and I suspect that several of the university staff have assumed that the two of us were romantically involved. But that isn't true, I promise you it isn't."

"Okay," she said, taking a bite of a cheese-stuffed cherry tomato. "Hmm, this is delicious. Are you going to eat yours?"

Grey's gaze was disbelieving, as though he couldn't quite believe that she could comment on an hors d'oeuvre when the fate of their budding relationship hung in the balance. "You mean you aren't angry?"

"Should I be?"

"No," he claimed fervently, pushing his hand through his hair until his fingers made deep grooves in the dark mane. "There's absolutely no reason for you to be!"

"Like I said before I'm not angry."

"You're sure?"

"Positive." She reached for the cheese-stuffed cherry tomato on his plate. If he didn't want it, she did. "As far as I can see, there isn't any reason to be jealous, either. So I won't be."

His jaw sagged open as though he expected an argument and was almost disappointed when Meghan didn't give him one.

"Grey, you don't have to do this," Meghan urged, her gaze holding his. She still had trouble believing that he'd allowed her two youngest brothers to talk him into this craziness. It was the Wednesday before Thanksgiving and Meghan had a free evening in the middle of the week, which was rare indeed. Sherry had given her the night off to compensate for having her work on the holiday.

"To be honest, I'm not quite sure how they talked me into this, either," Grey replied, chuckling lightly, "but it's something I'd like to do—especially since you're able to come with us."

He parked his car in front of her family home and the minute he did, Chad and Danny burst out the door as if they couldn't get away fast enough.

"It isn't like the boys never get to go to the movies," Meghan reminded him. "They should never have phoned you and asked you to take them."

"From what Chad said, they needed someone over seventeen to accompany them because this movie has a high degree of violence."

"Brian's over seventeen."

"He's busy."

"And you're not?"

"Meghan—" he reached for her hand "—I want to do this. I haven't been to a movie in years, and this was the perfect excuse to see *Chainsaw Murder, Part Twenty-Three.*"

"But you didn't see the others, and if you had, I'm fairly certain you wouldn't be interested in the sequel. In fact, I'm absolutely positive you're going to hate this movie."

"Let me be the judge of that."

"Don't say that I didn't warn you." If what Grey said was true and he hadn't been to a movie in years, then he was about to receive the shock of his life. Horror films weren't what they once were. There were blood and guts and gore enough to affect even the most hard-hearted.

"Hi, Professor," Danny greeted as he leaped into the backseat of Grey's car with the enthusiasm of a herd of charging elephants. "We're really glad you're taking Chad and me to the movies, aren't we, Chad?"

"Yeah." Chad's enthusiasm wasn't nearly as keen as his brother's. "But I didn't know Meghan was coming along," he added, eyeing his sister skeptically.

"I felt I should, since you two blackmailed Grey into this evening's outing. Whose bright idea was it to call him, anyway?"

"Danny's," Chad shouted.

"Chad's," Danny retorted in the same loud voice as his brother's.

"I don't mind," Grey insisted, reminding Meghan a second time that he'd been a willing victim of her brothers' schemes.

"But I saw the previews to this movie," Meghan told him. "It's really bloody and violent."

"I can stand a little blood."

"Yeah, so can I," Chad said with the eagerness only a teenager could understand.

"Me, too," Danny chimed in.

"Well, as long as it isn't my own blood, I guess I'm out-voted," Meghan murmured, accepting her fate.

Chad released a huge sigh of relief. "I was afraid when I saw Meghan that she was going to force us to go see something else, like a love story. Yuck!"

"It could be worse," Danny muttered under his breath. "Meghan could have insisted we see a musical."

"Come on, you guys, it's not that bad." Grey was good to her brothers. This wasn't the first time he'd gone out of his way to take them somewhere. Her own mother was half in love with him herself, and it was little wonder. Grey had been to the house twice, and each time he'd brought her roses and faithfully mailed her thank-you cards for having him over for dinner. If Grey had set out to win her family, he couldn't have done a better job. They were all as crazy about him as she was. In some ways it troubled Meghan, the way he catered to them all. But it was only natural that, as an only child, he would be attracted to her fun-loving family. He worked so hard to be a part of them—playing chess with her father, subjecting himself to football with her younger brothers. Deep inside her heart, Meghan was thrilled that he cared enough to strive to be one of them. Yet a small, doubting part of herself worried that it was her family that Grey was attracted to, and that being with her was just a bonus. As much as possible, however, Meghan tried to ignore the negative thought.

Grey found a suitable parking place at the Wichita Mall and escorted them into the cinema.

"We don't have to stay with you two, do we?" Danny asked, once he was loaded down with popcorn and a drink. "We'd look like a bunch of wimps if we had to sit with you guys."

"We *can* sit on our own, can't we?" Chad repeated his brother's concern.

"Sit where we can see you, that's all I ask," Meghan answered for Grey.

"Why?" Chad and Danny demanded together. "We aren't little kids, you know."

"In case something happens and we have to leave early, I want to know where you are so I don't have to rove the aisles to find you," she insisted.

The boys rolled their eyes and then glared at each other as though they suspected Meghan had been talking to their mother too frequently. If they had any further protests, they chose to forget them and hurried off on their own.

Carrying the popcorn and drinks, Grey paused at the back of the theater. "Is there any place special you want to sit?" he asked Meghan.

"Near the back, so when the blood and guts start flowing, I can make a quick escape." Grey chose seats in the second to the last row. In contrast, Chad and Danny were in the third row from the front so that the huge white screen loomed in front of them. If they were any closer, their noses would have touched it. Neither one, it seemed, wanted to miss any of the gory details. Once seated, Meghan's two brothers twisted around and when they saw their sister, gave a short, perfunctory wave.

When Grey seemed sure Meghan was comfortable, he handed her a box of popcorn. She shoved a handful of kernels into her mouth, chewing as fast as possible. She figured she should eat what she could now because once the movie started she wouldn't have the stomach for it.

The lights dimmed and Meghan held her breath while the credits started to roll across the screen. The minute the violence started, Meghan covered her eyes and scooted so far down in her seat that her forehead was level with the backs of the chairs in front of her.

"Meghan," Grey whispered. "Are you all right?"

"No."

He scrunched down, too, so his that face was even with her own. "Do you want to leave?"

"Chad and Danny would never forgive me." She kept her eyes closed. "Is the girl dead yet?"

"The girl?"

"The one in the movie," Meghan whispered heatedly. Who else could she possible mean, for heaven's sake?

"Yeah, and her friend, too."

"Oh, thank goodness." Meghan uncovered her eyes and sat upright. "I'm going to have nightmares all week because of this stupid movie."

Grey straightened, and then looped his arm around her back, cupping her shoulder. "Does this help?"

She smiled into the darkness and nodded.

"And this?" Gently he pressed her head close to his shoulder.

"That's even better." Meghan leaned her head against the cushion of his chest as he shared his warmth and his strength with her. Only when she was so close to Grey could Meghan ignore the grisly details of the graphically played-out murder story.

Content, Meghan looked up at Grey and their gazes met

in the dark. Grey gently smiled down at her, and the movie, at least for Meghan, faded into oblivion.

What surprised Meghan most was how much a smile from Grey could affect her. Her heart, which had been beating hard anyway, accelerated, stopped cold and then started up again. She longed for him to kiss her, and her eyes must have told him as much, yet she could feel Grey's resistance. Meghan couldn't blame him—she was asking for the absurd. They were in a crowded theater; anyone could see them.

"Meghan," he whispered.

"I know," she murmured, her eyes downcast. "Later."

"No," he growled softly. "Now." He bent his face toward hers, and his breath fanned her upturned face. Their lips met in the gentlest of kisses—velvet against satin, petal-soft, sweet, gentle, addictive.

Grey breathed in harshly and leaned his forehead against her own. "Sweet Meghan O'Day, the things you do to me."

A tornado could have descended on her at that moment, and Meghan wouldn't even have noticed. The mighty wind that would destroy everything in its path wouldn't have fazed her. Nothing could have compared to the rush of emotion that rocked through her. She was falling in love with Professor Greyson Carlyle—head over heels in love with him. Up to this point she'd been attracted to him, infatuated with him and challenged by the differences between them; but her feelings went beyond all that now.

Some time after the cocktail party at President Browning's house and before tonight, she'd willingly surrendered her heart to this man. The precise time and place remained a mystery.

Grey kissed her one last time, and the kiss was long and

thorough. Their lips clung to each other and when they broke apart, it was with heavy reluctance.

Meghan hardly noticed the remainder of the film. At several places in the movie the audience gasped at some gruesome sight, but all Meghan did was sigh and lean against Grey, soaking up his warmth.

When the film was finally over, light filled the theater. Meghan straightened and Grey disentangled his arms from around her.

"We might as well wait for the boys in the lobby," Grey suggested. He helped Meghan on with her coat after she stood.

Behind them, she heard two girls whispering.

"That *is* Professor Carlyle," came the first voice, clearly female.

"It can't be," returned the second, also feminine. "Old Stone Face? Think about it. Professor Carlyle never cracks a joke or hardly ever smiles. He just isn't the type to pay money to see this kind of movie. It couldn't possibly be the same man."

"I know you're right, Carrie, but I swear it looks just like him."

"He's got a woman with him, too. Someone young."

A short silence followed. Meghan was sure that Grey couldn't help overhearing the conversation any more than she could. Catching his gaze, she tried to reassure him with a timid smile, but if he saw it, he didn't respond.

"I read somewhere that everyone has a twin in this world," the whispering continued. "I bet that man's Professor Carlyle's twin."

"She's too young for him, don't you think?"

On the way out of the aisle, Grey kept his arm tucked around Meghan's waist. He stopped at the last row, paused and looked down at the two teenage girls, who remained sitting. They glared up at him, their mouths gaping open.

"Good evening, Carrie… Carol," he said evenly.

Both teens straightened in their seats as though they'd been caught doing something illegal. "Hello, Professor Carlyle."

"It's good to see you again, sir."

With his hand guiding Meghan at the base of her spine, he directed her into the lobby.

Meghan waited until they were near the exit doors before she spoke. "Greyson Carlyle, that was cruel and unusual punishment."

"Perhaps," he agreed, his smile noticeably forced.

Chad and Danny walked out of the main part of the theater looking as though they could hardly wait to see yet another episode of *Chainsaw Murder*. Meghan cringed at the mere thought of having to sit through another sequel to the dreadful horror film. If Grey had any intention of saying anything more to her about what they'd overheard earlier, the chance was gone.

"Wasn't that super rad?" Chad asked, looking to Grey for his approval. "Danny and I want to thank you for taking us—we probably wouldn't have been able to go if it hadn't been for you."

The comment was designed to cause Meghan to feel guilty for not being more willing to accompany her brothers to such important events, but she refused to be so much as tempted by the emotion. If it had been up to her, they would have gone to see a musical—and both Chad and Danny knew it.

"The movie was rad?" Grey repeated, arching his brows and glancing in Meghan's direction.

"Rad means cool, groovy—you know," Chad explained conversationally.

Grey nodded, his blue eyes serious. What humor shone there seemed forced. "Now that you mention it, I *do* know what that means. Banana splits are rad, aren't they? I wonder if you two boys would be game for one?"

"Are you nuts? We'd love it," Danny answered for them both.

"Grey, you're spoiling them," Meghan protested, but not too strenuously. She enjoyed watching Grey interact with the boys, and it was obvious they were equally fascinated with him.

"Oh, Meghan, don't ruin it for us. Grey's not spoiling us. He offered all on his own, without any coaxing."

"Yeah. We didn't even have to ask—" Danny tagged on his own feelings "—Grey's just being a pal."

"That's right," Grey said, and wrapped his arm around Meghan's shoulders.

He led the way outside, keeping Meghan close, but she felt him withdrawing even as he offered to take the boys out for dessert.

"From what I hear about your uncle Harry," Grey said to Meghan, "I'm going to need all the friends I can find for tomorrow."

Meghan had nearly forgotten that her infamous uncle would be joining the O'Day family for the Thanksgiving festivities the following day. Uncle Harry was a known teaser, who delighted in saying and doing things that were sure to embarrass the younger generation. Usually he had a trick or two up his sleeve, and he delighted in fooling all the family members.

"I don't think you have much to worry about, Grey,"

Meghan assured him. "Uncle Harry's mellowed out the last several years."

"Does he play chess?"

"Not with my father," Meghan explained, chuckling. The only one brave enough to tackle Pat O'Day was the man whose arm was draped over her shoulder.

"What about football?"

"Loves it, as long it's on a screen and doesn't involve anything more than a few choice words of advice for the referees and coaches. You're in luck. He hasn't personally touched a football in years."

Grey nodded. "Then he sounds like my kind of man."

Following banana splits at the ice-cream parlor, Grey dropped Chad and Danny off at the house, stopping in briefly to say hello to Meghan's parents. Then he drove Meghan back to her apartment. He was unusually quiet the whole way there, and she longed to bring up the incident in the theater, but wasn't sure how. A couple of times she was tempted to make a joke of it, then decided it would be better if Grey mentioned the episode himself. She didn't know why Grey should be so troubled by it, but he obviously was. Their evening had been perfect until two of his students had recognized him and commented.

"You'll come up for coffee, won't you?" she invited, hoping that he would. Then at least there was the chance they would talk this matter out.

"You're not too tired?" he asked, then promptly yawned. He looked almost embarrassed as he placed his hand over his mouth.

"I'm fine. But from the look of it, you're exhausted."

"It's been a hectic week." He yawned a second time, looking chagrined. "Maybe I'd better just walk you to your door and say good-night there."

He escorted her to her apartment door and brushed his lips over hers in the briefest of kisses, leaving Meghan feeling frustrated and cheated.

"Good night."

"Good night, Grey. I'll see you tomorrow."

His answering smile was lame at best. Meghan bit into her bottom lip to keep from calling out for him to come back. Instead, she moved inside her apartment and plopped herself down on the sofa, letting her disappointment work its way through her.

The following morning when Meghan walked into her family home, she was immediately greeted with the pungent smells of sage and pumpkin-pie spices.

"Meghan, I'm glad you're here," her mother greeted and kissed her on the cheek. "Grey just phoned. He told me he tried to catch you, but apparently you'd just left the apartment."

Meghan dipped her finger into the whipped topping and promptly licked it, savoring the sweet taste. Her mother insisted upon using real cream in her recipes and not the imitation products that had become so popular over the years.

"Is Grey going to be late?" Meghan asked, examining the variety of dishes that lined the kitchen counter.

"No," her mother said sadly. "He called to give us his regrets. He won't be able to spend the day with us, after all. Apparently something's come up."

Nine

"Something's come up?" Meghan echoed her mother's words, hardly able to believe what she'd heard. "What did Grey mean by that?"

"I don't know, princess, but he hardly sounded like his usual self." Her mother was busy whittling away on a huge pile of potatoes. Once they were peeled, she let them fall into a large pot of salted water.

Normally Meghan would have reached for a paring knife and lent a helping hand, but she was too upset. She started pacing the kitchen, her arms wrapped around her waist, her gaze centered on the ceiling while her thoughts collided in a wild tailspin. She should have guessed something like this would happen following the incident with two of Grey's students in the theater.

"I was afraid this would happen," she muttered, discouraged and disappointed—in both Grey and herself. She should have insisted they talk about what happened before he left her apartment.

"Did you and Grey have a falling-out, dear?" her mother asked, reaching for another potato.

"Not really." Meghan leaned her hip against the sink and

appealed to her mother with her hands. "Do you think I'm too young for Grey?"

"Sweetheart, what I think is of little importance," she said matter-of-factly. "That's something that should be settled between you and Grey, not you and me."

"I know you're right." Meghan hesitated then exhaled sharply, thinking it might help to discuss the matter with her mother. "Last night a couple of Grey's students were in the theater. They were whispering and we couldn't help overhearing what they said. Those girls seemed to think Grey was too old for me. Honestly, Mom, it doesn't bother me. Dad's eight years older than you and it's never been an issue."

"Seven and a half years," her father corrected as he sauntered into the kitchen. He reached inside the cupboard above the refrigerator and brought out a huge bag of salted peanuts.

"Don't be ruining your dinner, Patrick O'Day," Colleen warned, shaking her index finger at him.

"I won't, but a man's got to have some nourishment." He wrapped his arms around his wife's waist and nuzzled her neck. "You can't expect me to live on turkey and stuffing alone, you know."

"Oh, get away with you." Colleen chuckled and squirmed out of his embrace. "Dinner will be ready by one."

"We're eating early this year, aren't we?"

"I've got to be to work by three, Dad," Meghan reminded her father. She hesitated and glanced at the kitchen clock. If she hurried, there would be enough time for her to drive over to Grey's house and talk some reason into him. With any luck, she would be able to convince him to join her and the rest of her family at least for dinner, if not all day. To allow those two thoughtless students to ruin the holiday would be wrong, but the fact that Grey had allowed the matter to upset him to this extent troubled her even more.

"Mom," she said hurriedly. "Do you need my help in the kitchen, or can I leave you for a few minutes?"

"No, everything's under control—your aunt Theresa's due any time. Are you going over to Grey's? Good—you convince him to come to dinner. Remember the way to a man's heart often leads through his stomach."

Smiling, Meghan nodded, not surprised that her mother had read her thoughts. "That sounds like a good idea," Colleen agreed, surprising Meghan. "Don't come back without him, you hear?"

"I won't." Meghan kissed her mother's cheek, appreciating her understanding. "I shouldn't be any more than an hour. But it might be longer if he proves to be stubborn."

Colleen O'Day laughed softly. "Then I won't look for you for at least two hours."

All the way over to Grey's house, Meghan prepared her arguments. Her mother was right—more than right! Neither one of them could afford to allow what others thought to dictate their relationship. The instant she arrived, she planned on kissing Grey long and hard. *Then* he could tell her she was too young for him. The strategy had merit, and Meghan grinned, knowing full well that Grey wouldn't have a leg to stand on!

Smiling at this novel plan of attack, she parked her car on the street in front of his house. Excited now, she hurried up the steps, rang the doorbell and waited impatiently.

"Meghan." Her name was issued on a rush of surprised pleasure when Grey opened the door.

"Now listen here, Greyson Carlyle, what's this about you not coming over for Thanksgiving dinner," she accused, her eyes flashing with mischief. "Mom gave me some flimsy excuse not even worth mentioning. I want to know exactly what you think you're doing, and I want to know right now." She punctuated each word by playfully poking a finger in his stomach. With each thrust, Grey took a step in reverse, his eyes wide and disbelieving.

"Meghan…"

He tried to get her to listen, but she wouldn't let him. "I can't believe you'd let what two students said disturb you this way. If you're worried about our age difference, then I dare you to take me in your arms. I challenge you to kiss me and then argue the point."

"Greyson, who is this woman?"

The sober, dry voice came from behind Grey, in the direction of the kitchen.

Stunned, Meghan looked beyond him to face an austere middle-aged woman with silver-white hair that was severely tucked away from her face. She wore a dark blue suit and black shoes—and no smile. Meghan blinked, certain she'd inadvertently run into Pamela Riverside's mother.

"Meghan O'Day, I'd like to introduce my mother, Dr. Frances Carlyle."

"How do you do, Dr. Carlyle?" Meghan said, the teasing laughter in her eyes wilting away under the solemn stare of the older woman. Meghan stepped forward and the two exchanged a brisk handshake. Her legs felt as if they'd turned to water and the size of the knot in her throat would have rivaled a golf ball.

"Are you a student of Greyson's?" his mother asked, her gaze boring holes into Meghan. Her tone wasn't openly unfriendly, but it lacked any real interest or warmth.

"No—we're friends," Meghan quickly explained.

"I see."

There was that phrase again. Meghan longed to share a knowing look with Grey, but she dared not.

"Mother was here waiting for me when I returned last night," Grey explained. He motioned toward the recliner, indicating that Meghan should take a seat. Apparently he noticed she was having trouble remaining in an upright position.

"Would you like some tea?" Frances Carlyle asked.

"Please." Meghan accepted, hoping that once Grey's mother had vacated the room, she could talk to him. She wished with everything in her that she hadn't charged into his home, stabbing him with her finger and chiding him at the top of her voice, demanding that he kiss her.

"I'll be just a minute."

Meghan was convinced his mother had told her that as a means of warning her, but as far as Meghan was concerned, a minute was exactly long enough. She waited until the older woman had left the living room and then covered her face with both hands.

"Good heavens, Grey!" she wailed in a thick whisper. "How could you have let me go on that way?" She wanted to crawl inside a hole, curl up and die. Within a matter of two minutes, she'd given his mother the worst possible impression of herself.

"Meghan, listen..."

She lowered her hands. "I feel like such a fool, barging in here like King Kong. And you let me do it."

"Could I have stopped you?"

She shrugged, then admitted the truth. "Probably not."

"I tried phoning you this morning."

Meghan bit into the corner of her bottom lip. "I know. Mom told me." She could have saved herself a lot of grief had she hadn't let her cell phone battery wear down.

"My not coming to dinner had nothing to do with what happened last night," Grey said, reaching for her hand. He reluctantly released it when he heard movement from inside the kitchen. Meghan gave him a reassuring smile; she didn't need his touch when his gaze was so warm and gentle.

"I can just imagine what your mother thinks," she whispered, feeling all the more miserable.

Grey was about to say something more when Frances Carlyle walked into the room, carrying a tray. Grey stood and took it from his mother and set it on the coffee table.

"Cream or sugar, Meghan?"

"Just plain, thank you," she responded, scooting to the edge of the cushion. There were four cups on the tray, but she didn't give the matter more than a passing thought until Pamela Riverside casually strolled into the room with all the dignity of one who knows she has "arrived." The size of the lump in Meghan's throat doubled in size. She turned her gaze to Grey, and her breath jammed in her lungs.

"When I wasn't home last evening, Mother phoned Dr. Riverside," he said, his gaze holding Meghan's and seeming to plead for understanding.

"Dear Pamela was kind enough to come to the airport on such short notice and drive me to Greyson's house," his mother added in a light, accusing tone.

Meghan noted that Grey's jaw tightened slightly. "I would have been more than happy to come for you myself, Mother, had I known you were arriving."

"It was a surprise, and I hated to ruin it. I suppose it was wrong of me to assume you'd be home, but I couldn't imagine what you'd be doing out the evening before Thanksgiving."

"You were with Ms. O'Day?" Pamela asked, stirring sugar into her tea with a dainty flip of her wrist.

"We were at the movies."

"How quaint." Grey's mother smiled for the first time, but once more Meghan read little amusement or welcome in the other woman's gaze.

"That must have been...fun," Pamela commented, seeming to search for the right word, although she did appear genuinely interested.

If Dr. Riverside was the least bit uncomfortable, it would have been impossible to tell. Actually, there was no reason for her to feel any annoyance, Meghan mused. She was the chosen one, basking under the glow of Frances Carlyle's approval. And who could blame her? Not Meghan.

"What movie did you see?" Pamela pressed.

Meghan should have known that one was coming. She lowered her gaze and mumbled the title, hoping the others wouldn't understand and would let it pass. *"Chainsaw Murder, Part Twenty-Three."*

Frances Carlyle gasped softly, doing her best to disguise her shock. "I'm sure I misunderstood you."

"It's not as bad as it sounds, Mother," Grey said, and his voice carried a thread of amusement.

"I never dreamed my own son would lower himself to view such rubbish," Frances said, fanning her face a couple of times as though the room had suddenly become too warm. "Naturally, I've heard Hollywood is making those disgusting films, but I certainly didn't think that sort of rubbish would appeal to you, Greyson."

"I'm sure it doesn't," Meghan inserted, automatically defending him. "My brothers were the ones who wanted to see that particular film and they conned Grey into taking them."

"Your brothers 'conned' my son?" Grey's mother echoed, her look all the more aghast. She held on to her cup with both hands and it looked for a split second as though she were going to drop it. The cup wobbled precariously, then steadied.

"I didn't mean it quite like that," Meghan hurried to explain. Every time she opened her mouth, she dug herself deeper into a pit of despair. She cast a pleading look in Grey's direction, wanting to let him know how sorry she was for muddling this entire conversation. "The boys mentioned how much they wanted to go, and Grey, out of the goodness of his heart, volunteered to take them."

"I hardly think that is the type of movie for young boys."

"They're fifteen and thirteen." On this matter, Meghan actually found herself agreeing with Grey's mother. But she couldn't force her tastes on Chad and Danny, who seemed to thrive on horror films of late.

"Meghan's family had invited me over for Thanksgiving dinner," Grey said, directing the comment to his mother. "I phoned earlier and made my excuses."

Frances Carlyle nodded approvingly. "Pamela and I will be preparing our own Thanksgiving dinner," she explained, and smiled fondly at the other woman. "However, it was kind of your parents to invite him, but Greyson's with his family now."

From the look Grey's mother cast at Pamela, it was all too apparent that she'd personally handpicked her son's future wife. She'd done everything but verbally announce the fact.

Meghan's heart was so heavy it was a wonder she was able to remain sitting in an upright position. The differences between her and Grey's social position hadn't actually bothered her until that moment. Whenever they were together, Meghan had been swept up in the magic that sparked so spontaneously between them. But it was all too clear that

Grey's mother wasn't interested in hearing about magic; she would be far more concerned with passing on the proper genes and balancing out intelligence quotients.

Meghan leaned forward and set her cup back on the tray. She'd barely tasted the tea, but she couldn't endure another minute of this awkward conversation.

"I have to be getting back," she said as calmly as she could. "We're eating earlier this year, because I have to be at work before three."

"What kind of employment involves working on a holiday?" Frances Carlyle asked.

Once more, Meghan had exposed herself without realizing what she was doing. She would have given anything to quietly inform Grey's mother that she was a brain surgeon and was needed for an emergency procedure within the hour. Instead, she calmly announced, "I'm a waitress at Rose's Diner." She didn't bother to look at Grey's mother, knowing the woman's expression would only reveal her disapproval.

"I see," Frances Carlyle said in a tone so like Grey's that it would have been comical if it hadn't hurt so much.

"I'll walk you to your car," Grey insisted.

"That won't be necessary," she said, keeping her voice as even as possible and having trouble doing so.

"Nonsense, Meghan. I'll see you to your car."

Frances Carlyle stood with Meghan and Grey. "There's no need to expose yourself to the cold, son. You can say goodbye to your...friend here."

Certain everyone could see how badly she was trembling, Meghan reached for her purse, buttoned her coat and headed toward the front door.

Ignoring his mother's advice, Grey followed her outside.

"Meghan, I'm sorry," he said, taking her by the shoulders when they reached her car. His eyes were troubled, his expression grim. "I had no idea my mother was planning to fly in at the last minute like this." He frowned and his face darkened momentarily.

"There's no need to apologize. I understand." By some miracle, Meghan was able to force a smile.

"I didn't know anything about this. Apparently Pamela and my mother have been planning this little surprise for the last several weeks."

Meghan would take bets that they'd arranged this about the time Grey had started dating her. She had to give Pamela Riverside credit. Grey's colleague had used the most effective means possible to show Meghan how ill-suited she was to Grey. All the arguments in the universe couldn't have said it more eloquently than those few stilted moments with his mother. Meghan knew that no matter what Grey felt for her, she would never fit into his world. His family had already rejected her with little more than a passing thought.

Meghan had faced this argument before, but always from her own perspective. She'd stood on the other side of the fence, knowing that her family and friends would accept Grey without a moment's hesitation. The one sample of her meeting Grey's colleagues had been slanted in her favor; for the majority of the evening, she'd stayed glued to his side. It was impossible to calculate how the evening had actually gone.

"I'll phone you tomorrow," Grey promised.

"I'm working." She wasn't due in until three, but twenty-four hours wasn't long enough for her to analyze her feelings. If she could delay dealing with this until her head was clear and her mind wasn't clouded with emotions, Meghan knew she would cope better. "When's your mother leaving?"

"Not until Sunday afternoon."

"It probably would be better if you waited until then to contact me, don't you think?" This was Meghan's subtle method of keeping the peace for Grey's sake. She didn't doubt he would get an earful later. His mother was bound to tell him how improper a relationship with Meghan was the minute she drove out of sight. On second thought, Frances Carlyle was intelligent enough to relay the message without ever having to utter a word. She would probably do it in the same manner Pamela Riverside had delivered her own missive to Meghan.

"What my mother thinks or says isn't going to change the way I feel about you," he said tightly.

Meghan loved him so much at that moment that it took every ounce of self-control she possessed not to break down and weep. She raised her fingers and lovingly ran her hand down the side of his face.

"Thank you for that," she said, her voice little more than a broken whisper. She lowered her eyes, fearing that if she looked at him much longer, she wouldn't be able to hold back the emotion straining for release. Her eyes burned and her chest ached.

She started to turn away from him, but his grip on her shoulders tightened and he brought her back against him. Surprised, Meghan raised her gaze to his, only to discover that Grey meant to kiss her. A weak protest rose in her, but she wasn't allowed to voice any objection. With infinite tenderness, he settled his mouth firmly over hers. His hands on her shoulders were strong enough to lift her onto the tips of her toes.

Meghan opened her mouth to him, kissing him back with all the longing stored in her heart. She gripped the front of his shirt, bunching the material with her fists, holding on to him as though she never intended to let go. She moaned softly as his mouth moved with tender ferocity over her own until they were leaning against each other.

"Meghan," he whispered, planting a series of soft kisses over her eyes and cheeks. He threaded his fingers through her hair, keeping her close. "I'd rather spend the day with you and your family. I'm sorry it has to be like this."

"Don't apologize. I understand, Grey." She clung to him, her eyes closed. But when she looked up, she happened to notice his mother standing in the picture window, looking out at them. The older woman's face was creased into a look of disapproval so sharp that Meghan could feel its pointedness all the way across the yard. With some effort, she eased herself out of Grey's arms.

He opened her car door for her. "I'll call as soon as I can, but it probably won't be until Sunday afternoon."

She nodded, and looked away.

"Have a nice Thanksgiving."

"You, too," she said, and slipped inside the car and inserted the key into the ignition.

"Meghan," her mother said softly, taking the chair beside her in the kitchen after the Thanksgiving meal was over. "We haven't had to a free moment to talk since you got back from Grey's. Did you two argue?"

"No. He's got company from out of town."

"You hardly touched your dinner."

"I guess I wasn't hungry." The excuse was weak, but it was the best she could come up. She made a show of looking at her watch. "I suppose I should think about heading off to work."

"Isn't it a little early yet?"

"I'm sure Sherry's swamped," Meghan explained, hoping her mother would accept that rationalization without voicing an objection. "She'll appreciate an extra pair of hands."

"Hey, Meghan," Danny interrupted, strolling into the kitchen, gnawing on a turkey drumstick. "Can you call Grey and tell him we need him for touch football. We're one man shy."

"I already told you he won't be coming today," she replied sharply. She hadn't meant to snap at her brother, but the words had slipped out uncensored before she could put a stop to them.

Danny's eyes rounded and he shrugged expressively, giving her a wounded look. "Well, I'm sorry for livin'. I thought he'd want to come over, that's all."

"I'm sure he did want to join us," Colleen O'Day assured her son, arching a thoughtful brow in Meghan's direction.

Meghan stood, pushing in her chair. Her fingers bit into the cushion on the back of the seat. "I'm sorry, Danny, I didn't mean to jump all over you."

"Will you tell Grey the next time you see him that we missed him?" her brother pressed. "Hey, you're not breaking up with him, are you? Grey's neat. I like him."

"Don't worry about it, all right? What I do is my own business."

"You *are* going to keep dating him, aren't you?" Danny demanded, not satisfied with her answer.

"Who's breaking up with whom?" Brian asked, strolling into the kitchen. Allison Flynn was with him and the two had been holding hands from the minute she arrived. Meghan had watched them during dinner and marveled at how they'd ever managed to eat.

"Meghan and Grey are on the outs," Danny informed

his oldest brother. "He's the best thing that ever happened to her and she's dumping him."

"What?" Brian cried.

"Listen, you two, this isn't any of your business," their mother reminded them. "Whatever happens between Meghan and the professor is their own affair."

"I suppose this means you want us to stay out of it. Right?" Danny asked.

"Exactly," Meghan told him sternly.

"But, Meghan," Danny whined, "where would you ever find anyone as nice as Grey? None of your other boyfriends ever took Chad and me to the movies. I like him. Think about that before you go throwing away the greatest guy in the world."

Unfortunately, it wasn't up to Meghan. Grey's mother would be flying out Sunday. Frances Carlyle had four long days to convince Grey how wrong Meghan would be for him, and how perfectly Pamela Riverside would fit into his life.

If Meghan didn't hear from him Sunday afternoon, she would know exactly how successful his mother had been. It was almost comical when she stopped to think about it. Meghan could have saved Dr. Frances Carlyle a good deal of trouble. She'd already made up her mind about where her relationship with Grey was going.

Nowhere.

Grey lay on his bed, his hands linked behind his head, staring at the ceiling. If he lived to be a hundred and ten he would never forget the look on Meghan's face when she met his mother. She'd marched into his house, insisting he kiss her and heaven knew he'd been tempted. Then she'd looked around Grey and discovered his mother standing just inside the kitchen, looking at Meghan as though she were the devil incarnate come to corrupt her only child.

Regrettably, Frances Carlyle was no Colleen O'Day. Grey's mother meant well, but he'd long ago given up letting her dictate his life. One of the reasons he'd accepted his position with Friends University in Wichita was in order to escape his mother's constant interference.

For the past three days, Grey had been forced to hear her list Pamela Riverside's fine qualities over and over again until he'd wanted to shout for her to cease and desist. When that ploy didn't seem to be working, his mother had gone on to tell how she prayed she would live long enough to enjoy her grandchildren. This was followed by a short sigh, as if to suggest that her stay on earth was only a matter of time and Grey shouldn't expect her to hang on much longer.

Actually, his mother had missed her calling; she should have been in the theater. And as for grandchildren, Grey sincerely doubted that Frances would want anything to do with his children until they were old enough to conjugate verbs.

Over the course of the same few days, Grey had tried to talk to his mother about Meghan, but every time he mentioned her name, the subject had been subtly changed. Yes, Meghan was "a dear girl"; it was unfortunate she was so… "common."

Grey chuckled in the dark. Meghan common! His mother had a good deal to learn about the Irish miss. Meghan O'Day was about as common as green eggs and ham. She was sunshine and laughter, unfathomable, unnerving and incomprehensible. And he was in love with her.

Meghan had been concerned that he would be upset by what Carol and Carrie had whispered in the theater the other night. To be frank, he *had* been troubled at first, but

he'd tried not to let it bother him. The age difference between him and Meghan was almost ten years, but it hadn't
seemed to affect her. If that was the case, he shouldn't allow
it to worry him.

The one thing that had shaken him more than anything
was knowing that his students referred to him as "Stone
Face." He smiled. He had a reasonable sense of humor.
Now that he'd met Meghan, it was becoming a little more
fine-tuned. His students would notice the changes in him
soon enough.

The following afternoon, Grey drove his mother to the
airport. He did his best not to show his enthusiasm. This
visit had been more strained than usual. Frances tried,
but she really wasn't much of a mother—the instincts just
hadn't been there. Her idea of mothering had to do with
manipulation and control. She loved him as much as it was
possible for her to care about anyone, and he loved her. She
was, after all, responsible for giving him life and for nur-
turing him to the best of her capabilities.

Frances hugged him close. "Keep in touch, Greyson."

"Yes, Mother," he said, and dutifully kissed her on the
cheek.

"And please consider what I said. It's time you thought
about settling down."

If he settled down any more, his chest would start sprout-
ing corn, but he kept his thoughts to himself.

"Pamela is a dear, dear girl. I do hope you'll try to arrange some time to get to know her better."

He answered that with a weak smile.

"She's crazy about you, Greyson, and just the type of
woman who will help you in your career. Your father, God
rest his soul, would be pleased. Marriage can't be taken
any too lightly, especially by someone in your position.

You need a woman who will give you more than attractive children. You must marry someone your equal." She paused and looked directly into his eyes. "You *do* understand what I'm saying, don't you?"

"Yes, Mother." Grey clenched his hands into fists, battling down the anger that flared to life so readily. He only needed to hold on a little while longer. She would be gone in a matter of minutes.

"Good." Frances Carlyle nodded once, looking pleased that her message had been received. She gave her son a smug look and headed into the airport.

Grey hurried home. In fact, he could hardly get there fast enough. The minute he could, he reached for his cell, punching out Meghan's number with an eagerness that had his fingers shaking. He let it ring ten times before he cut off the call. Meghan wasn't answering.

Ten

"Hello, Eric, it's good to see you again," Meghan said, draining whatever energy she had by coming up with a smile. For three nights straight, she hadn't gotten more than four hours' sleep. She was exhausted mentally, physically and emotionally. Filling his coffee cup, she handed him a menu, then automatically recited Monday's special—all-you-can-eat spaghetti and meatballs.

"You look terrible," her college friend commented, studying her through narrowed eyes. "What happened? Did you just lose your best friend?"

In a manner of speaking, that was exactly what had happened. Meghan brushed off his concern with a light laugh. "Don't be silly."

"Meghan, sweetie, I recognize men problems when I see them. If you need a shoulder to cry on, you come to Uncle Eric, okay? Or better yet," he said enthusiastically, "let me arrange for you to talk to Don Harrison."

"Who?"

"Don Harrison. You met him two weeks ago at the reading group. Actually, Don's interest doesn't lie so much in the classics as it does in you. He's been pumping me with questions about you every day for the last two weeks, but I've discouraged him because I knew you were seeing someone steadily."

Meghan didn't even remember meeting Don, but that wasn't unusual. The reading group had ten faithful members who showed up every week and nearly as many others who came and went as the spirit moved them.

"Listen," Eric continued, undaunted by her apathy. "I'll call Don and let him know you could use some cheering up. He'll be thrilled to hear it."

"I'd rather you didn't," Meghan told him. She just wasn't in the mood to see anyone new. Maybe in a few weeks, when her heart was on the mend; but not now. It was too soon. And she felt too raw and vulnerable.

"Why wouldn't you want to see Don? He'll provide the right kind of therapy to help you get over this guy who's making you so miserable."

It was apparent that Eric wasn't going to listen to her objections, but she was equally persistent and shook her head. She took the pad out of her pocket, hoping Eric would take the hint and order.

"Give it some thought and let me know, all right?"

"Okay," she murmured. But she had no intention of dating this guy.

"Everything will look better in the morning," Eric said confidently. "Just wait and see. Now don't argue with your uncle Eric, because he's all-wise and he knows all about these things because he's suffered a few broken hearts in his time. By the way, I'll take the spaghetti and meatballs and a piece of the cherry sour-cream pie."

Rarely had she been more woeful, she realized. It took effort just to get through the day. No one had ever told her that loving someone could be so painful. All her life, she'd grown up believing that when she fell in love there would be birds chirping some sweet song, apple trees blossoming in the distance and enchantment swirling about her like champagne bubbles.

What a farce love had turned out to be.

Meghan didn't even know what she was going to say to Grey. Avoiding him, which she'd succeeded in doing for the last couple of days, wasn't going to work forever. Sooner or later she would have to answer her phone. If she didn't, he would simply arrive unannounced at Rose's, and then she wouldn't be able to escape him.

With that thought in mind, Meghan went on her break. She sat in the employees' lounge and after a few heart-pounding moments of indecision, she picked up her phone and slowly, deliberately, dialed Grey's number.

"Meghan, where have you been?" he cried, then promptly sneezed. That outburst was followed by a loud, nasty-sounding cough. "I've been trying to reach you for two solid days."

"I... I've been busy. How did your visit with your mother go?"

Grey emitted a short laugh. "About as well as they ever do. I know she went out of her way to intimidate you Thanksgiving morning, but I'm hoping you didn't let anything she said bother you."

"No, not in the least," Meghan lied. Dr. Frances Carlyle had looks that would make a Mafia hit man tremble. In those few minutes she'd spent with the other woman, Meghan had sat with her back straight and her hands neatly folded in her lap. Words she rarely used kept slipping out of her mouth—words and phrases like *indeed*, *quite so* and *most certainly*.

"My mother often means well," Grey continued, "but

I refuse to allow her to rule my life. And before you say another word, I didn't have anything to do with Pamela's joining us for dinner that day. I'm not interested in her and never will be. I'm hoping you realize that by now."

"You don't need to worry, Grey. Having Dr. Riverside join you didn't bother me in the least." However, Meghan was willing to wager a month's worth of tip money that his mother would convince him Pamela was the woman of his dreams before the year was out. Meghan was all too aware that this ploy to marry Grey off to Pamela hadn't been all his mother's doing. Grey's esteemed associate had done her share—subtly of course, but effectively.

"Good, I—" He stopped abruptly and let loose a series of turbulent sneezes. "Sorry. I can't seem to stop once I get started."

"You sound terrible, Grey." Now that she wasn't so concerned with her own emotional pain, she realized how miserable he seemed to be.

"It's nothing but a nasty cold. I'll be over it in a couple of days, but I'm sure I'll feel better by Saturday. This is probably just a twenty-four hour virus."

Meghan tightened her grip on the telephone receiver. "Saturday night?"

"We've been invited to a dinner party. I mentioned it the other night while we were eating ice cream, remember?"

No, she didn't. Not at first. Then vaguely her memory was stirred. Knowing how nervous she was about attending these formal affairs with him, Grey had offered to let her scoop up the last of his hot fudge topping if she would agree to let him escort her to a holiday dinner party at the home of Dr. Essary. High on her love for Grey and his generosity to her brothers, Meghan had willingly agreed to the exchange. Now she felt like a dimwit. All things considered, the last thing she wanted to do was attend a social function with him.

"Remember?" he coaxed a second time.

"Yes, I guess I do."

Grey coughed and excused himself, returning a moment later. "I'm sure I'll improve before Saturday."

Meghan squeezed her eyes shut as the pain washed over her in swelling waves. "Seeing that you're a little under the weather, and Saturday is up in the air, would you mind terribly if I canceled our date?"

"Meghan, Meghan, Meghan," he chided in a singsong voice that sounded amazingly like his rendition of *I see*. "You're not going to get out of this dinner party that easily. Honey, the more often you accompany me to these functions, the more relaxed you'll become. I want you with me."

"From the sounds of this virus, you're going to get worse before you get better." Meghan had no idea if that was true or not, but she was grasping at straws.

"If I am still under the weather, we'll cancel."

"But I'd like to make other plans. I don't want to be left on hold like this," she said, digging to the bottom of the barrel for excuses.

"I don't understand. What do you mean by 'other plans'?"

"I've been asked out by…one of the men from the reading group, and frankly, I'd forgotten all about the dinner party." This was elasticizing the truth to the very limit. But according to Eric, she could have a date with Don Harrison if she wanted one. She didn't. But Grey didn't need to know that. At this point, her only intention was to convince him she didn't want to see him any longer before either of them suffered any more from a dead-end relationship.

"One of the men from the reading group," Grey repeated.

He sounded as though he were reeling from this news; his voice was barely audible.

"Since you're not feeling well, anyway, I can't see where it would hurt any to cancel our plans."

"Is it Eric Vogel?"

"No. I already told you, he's engaged."

"I see." He paused then asked, "And you'd prefer to go out with this other guy?"

"Yes," she whispered, then regrouped her thoughts and stated calmly, "That is, if it isn't too much of a problem for you, since I had committed myself to you first."

This was so much more difficult than she'd thought it would be.

The silence that followed was loud enough to break the sound barrier. What felt like sonic booms slammed against her eardrums until her head was shaking and her whole body was trembling in their aftermath.

"I hadn't realized your social calendar was so crowded."

Meghan recognized the anger in his voice and it was like inflicting a wound upon herself. "I'll call you later in the week and see how you're feeling."

"Don't worry about Saturday night. Go ahead and date your friend or any other men you might meet between now and Saturday." His words felt like a cold slap in the face.

"Thank you for understanding. Goodbye, Grey."

He may have bid her farewell, but if he had, Meghan didn't hear him. All she'd heard was another series of sneezes and coughs.

For a full minute after the line had been disconnected, Meghan kept her hand on the receiver. Taking in deep breaths seemed to help, but it didn't help control her desire to bury her face in her hands. She didn't do that, of course—not when she had customers waiting.

* * *

A violent sneeze ripped the flimsy tissue in half, and Grey automatically reached for another. His head felt as if someone had turned him upside down and all his blood had pooled in his sinuses. His chest hurt even worse; it felt as though a two-ton truck had decided to park there and had no intention of moving. He was utterly miserable! And he had three classes to get through before he could head home.

Meghan wasn't helping matters any. She'd come up with this cock-and-bull story about wanting to go out with another man Saturday night, and he'd fallen for it hook, line and sinker.

At first.

He'd been so infuriated with her that he was sure the elevation in his temperature had been due to his short conversation with Meghan the day before.

Once he'd settled down, sat back and reflected on their discussion, he realized she'd been lying, and doing a poor job of it. If he hadn't been so irritated with her, he would have easily seen through her deception.

In the light of a fresh day, Grey downright refused to believe she was interested in someone else. He couldn't very well claim that at age thirty-four he hadn't been in love before now, but the powerful emotion he felt for Meghan O'Day went far beyond anything in his limited experience. He'd been infatuated, captivated and charmed by any number of women over the years. But it was this one sweet Irish miss who laid claim to his heart. He couldn't love Meghan the way he did and not know when she was making something up.

Grey guessed all this nonsense about her dating someone else related directly to his mother's visit. That aristocratic old lady had buffaloed Meghan into believing she wasn't good enough for him. Grey would bet cold cash on that fact. He couldn't blame Meghan for letting Frances browbeat her into such thinking. Grey's mother had done a good job on Meghan, who'd had no experience in dealing with his manipulating parent. Grey, on the other hand, had had a lifetime of practice; and he wasn't about to let his own mother cheat him out of the best thing that had ever happened to him: Meghan O'Day.

Noticing the time, Grey reached for his tweed jacket, his overcoat and his briefcase. He hesitated long enough to line his jacket pocket with tissues. He was through the worst of this stupid cold—at least that was what he continued to tell himself, but then immediately broke into a series of loud coughs that racked his throat and chest.

"Professor Carlyle, are you all right? Perhaps I should make a doctor's appointment for you."

"Don't worry, I'm fine," he said, waving off his assistant's concern.

"If you're not better in the morning, I really think you should see someone."

The first person who flashed into his mind that he should see was Meghan. A slow smile eased its way across his face. The Milton-quoting waitress would make an excellent nurse—unlike Pamela Riverside, who would probably insist he take cod-liver oil and stay away from her in case he was contagious. Naturally, if Meghan were around, he would have to exaggerate the extent of his sickness. But the mere thought of Meghan sitting at his side, running her cool hands over his fevered brow and whispering sweet nothings in his ear, was far more appealing than a heavy dose of antibiotics or Pamela Riverside.

Before he left the building, Grey turned up the collar of his overcoat. Dear grief, it had been cold lately. A fresh batch of snow had thickly carpeted the campus grounds. Several students had taken to building snowmen, and their merriment filled the crisp afternoon air.

Grey heard the sound of Meghan's musical laughter long before he found her in the crowd. A smile teased the corners of his mouth as he paused in the shoveled walkway, holding his briefcase close to his side while his gaze scanned the large group of fun-making young people.

A flash of auburn-colored hair captured his attention and his gaze settled there. It was Meghan, all right. *His* Meghan. Only she was standing with her arms wrapped around another man and her eyes were smiling up at him.

The amusement left Grey's expression to be replaced by a weary kind of pain that struck sharp and deep. It took a moment for him to find his breath. When he did, he held his head high and continued down the pathway as though nothing had happened. He sincerely doubted that Meghan would ever know that he'd seen her.

"Mom!" Meghan cried, flying into the house, her voice filled with alarm. "I need you."

The kitchen door swung open. "Honey, what is it?"

"Grey. He's ill!" She gripped her mother's forearms and swallowed several times before she could continue. Her own heartbeat sounded like a cannon in her ear. "I was on campus earlier and overheard a student comment that Grey hasn't been to school in three days and all his classes have been canceled."

"Aren't you jumping to conclusions?"

"No. When I talked to him Monday night, he sounded like he had a dreadful cold then. Apparently he's much worse now."

Colleen O'Day tucked in a few strands of gray hair behind her ear and casually strolled back into the kitchen where she'd been folding clothes on the round oak table. "I thought you told me you'd decided not to see your professor friend anymore."

"Yes, but he's sick now and—"

Her mother raised her hand as if she were stopping traffic. "Although it was difficult at the time, I bit my tongue, figuring this is your life. You're twenty-four and old enough to be making your own decisions. Whether I happen to agree with you or not, is something else entirely."

"I'm worried about Grey. Surely you can understand that."

Colleen O'Day fluffed out a thick towel and neatly folded it in thirds. "From what you were telling me the other day, you'd decided you didn't much care for the professor anymore."

"Mom," Meghan said with an impatient sigh, "I didn't come here for a lecture."

"Then why are you here?"

"I want you to make your special soup for Grey. I know once he's had some of your broth, he'll feel better. I always did. Remember when I was a little girl how you used to tell me the soup had magical healing powers?"

"Meghan—" Colleen issued her daughter's name on an exasperated sigh and reached for another towel "—how do you expect to get the soup to him? According to what you said, you have no intentions of seeing him again. Do you expect leprechauns to deliver it?"

"Don't be silly."

"From what you said, you're not worthy enough to lace that distinguished man's shoes, let alone be seen with him. To hear you tell it, the good name of O'Day is sure to tarnish the professor's reputation and possibly ruin his career.

You didn't seem to mind, though, because you'd made up your mind that he was too pompous and dignified for the likes of you anyway."

"You're exaggerating, Mother, and that's not like you. I care enough about Grey to want the best for him. Isn't that what loving someone means?"

Her mother held the laundry basket against her stomach and sadly shook her head. "Perhaps I am stretching the facts a bit, but that's because I disagree with you so strongly. Loving a man often does call for sacrifice, but not the kind you're making. But as I said earlier, it's your life. If you want to break your own heart, far be it for me to stand in your way and gift you with forty-odd years of wisdom."

Meghan knotted her fists at her side. "Will you make the soup or not?"

"And who's going to take it to him?"

"You?" Meghan proposed hopefully.

"Me?" Her mother laughed at the mere suggestion. "I'm not traipsing halfway across town to deliver my special healing soup to your old boyfriend, Meghan Katherine O'Day. If you don't care to go out with him any longer, then why should I care if he's ill? He's your friend, not mine."

"How can you say that?" Grey had brought her mother flowers, complimented her cooking and gone out of his way to let her know how much he appreciated sharing Sunday meals with them. She couldn't understand her mother's attitude.

Colleen O'Day shrugged as though what happened to Professor Carlyle was of little concern to her. "All I know is that my daughter wants nothing more to do with the man."

"He's ill."

"Why should that bother you?" Colleen pressed. "You don't plan to see him again."

Frustrated, Meghan closed her eyes. "Will you make the soup, or not?"

"Not."

Meghan was so shocked, her mouth fell open.

"But I might be persuaded to share the family recipe with my only daughter. It's time she learned of its miraculous healing powers herself. My one wish is that it will loosen a few of her own brain cells so she can see what a terrible mistake she's making."

The two mason jars were securely tucked inside the shopping bag when Meghan entered the faculty building. Grey's office was on the third floor of the same structure, but that wasn't where she was headed.

When her mother had copied the recipe, Colleen O'Day had done so with the express hope that Meghan would deliver the soup to Grey herself and in the process settle her differences with Grey. Unfortunately Meghan couldn't do that, but she hadn't wanted to disillusion her mother with the truth. She planned to deliver the soup in a roundabout manner and pray that her mother never found out.

Dr. Pamela Riverside would take the soup to him.

After some heavy-duty soul-searching, Meghan had devised a plan of action. She was going to show Pamela Riverside the way to this particular man's heart. It was obvious the poor woman needed help. She might balk now, but someday she would appreciate Meghan's efforts.

As Dr. Riverside's office was on Grey's floor, the same receptionist announced Meghan. Meghan didn't wait, however, but saw herself into Dr. Riverside's room.

Grey's colleague was seated behind a meticulously clean desk in a spotless office that wasn't marked by a single personal item other than her books.

"Ms. O'Day," Pamela greeted, rising to her feet. "This is a pleasant surprise."

But she didn't look pleased, which was just as well. Meghan closed the door and stepped forward, not stopping until she stood directly in front of the other woman's desk.

"Do you love him?"

The other woman sucked in her breath. "I beg your pardon."

"Dr. Carlyle! Do you love him?"

"I hardly think my feelings for Greyson Carlyle are any of your business."

"No, I don't suppose you would." Setting the shopping bag on top of the desk, Meghan crossed her arms and battled down an overwhelming sense of sadness. "You're exactly the right kind of woman for him. His mother knows it. You know it. And I know it."

Pamela Riverside cast her gaze downward. "Unfortunately Greyson hasn't seemed to have figured it out yet."

"And he won't with you looking like that."

Pamela slapped her hand against her breast in shock and outrage. "Exactly what are you saying?"

"Your clothes," Meghan cried, waving her hand at the fastidious dark blue suit as though she were a fairy godmother and held the powers of transformation in the tips of her fingers. "I haven't seen you in anything but that same dark suit and jacket in all the times we've met. That thing looks twenty years old."

"I'll have you know I bought this only last month."

"And have five exactly like it hanging in your closet."

Pamela sucked in a tiny breath that told Meghan she'd hit the peg square on the head. "And those horrible shoes have got to go."

With her hands braced against her hips, Grey's associate

glared down at her feet. "These are the most comfortable shoes I've ever worn. I refuse to let you—"

"Of course, they're comfortable. That's because your grandmother broke them in for you. Go shopping, Dr. Riverside, throw caution to the wind and try a new department store. Start with a silk teddy and go from there."

The woman's mouth opened and closed several times, as though she couldn't say everything she wanted to fast enough. "If you insist upon insulting me, Ms. O'Day, then perhaps you should leave."

"Take the pins out of your hair."

"I can't believe I'm hearing you correctly."

"Your hair," Meghan repeated, pointing her finger at the professor, unwilling to brook any argument. "And do it now."

With her face growing more pale by the minute, Pamela reached behind her head and released the tightly coiled chignon. The dark length unrolled down her back and she loosened it so that it fell about her face.

The transformation was remarkable. Pleased, Meghan nodded quietly as she studied Pamela's facial features in a fresh light. "Much better. While you're at the department store make an appointment with a beautician. Have her cut about an inch all the way around, and don't ever wear it up again."

"Well, I never!" she barked.

"Well, it's time you did."

Grey's colleague looked so shocked that she snapped her mouth shut.

"He's sick, you know, and in his weakened condition he'll be more receptive to gestures of concern from you. Go shopping and make sure everything you have on is new. Have your hair done the way I said and then go and visit him. And last but not least, take him this soup and tell him you made it yourself."

"I rarely cook. Greyson knows that."

"Lie."

"Ms. O'Day, I'll have you know I'm as honest as the day is long."

"These are the shortest days of the year, Dr. Riverside. Take advantage of it." Meghan paused and drew in a quivering breath. "Make him happy, or by heaven, you'll wish you had." With that, she marched out of the office.

Tears brimmed in Meghan's eyes, making it almost impossible for her to navigate her way to the elevator.

Grey was on the mend. For the last four days he'd been living on orange juice, canned chicken soup and peanut butter—tasting nothing. The chill that had permeated his bones was gone, but the cough that seemed to convulse his intestines lingered on. He hadn't talked to Meghan in those four days, and it felt like four years. His heart was heavy, his head stuffy and his thoughts more twisted than an old pine tree's limbs. The combination left him in no mood for company, and Pamela Riverside had just phoned claiming she had to talk to him; she possessed urgent information that he must act upon immediately.

Given no choice, he'd changed clothes and put on water for tea, awaiting her arrival with as much enthusiasm as the settlers greeted Indians on the warpath in the 1800s. He would have refused to see Pamela if it weren't for the fact that she sounded highly agitated, which in itself was rare. Whatever was troubling her probably was linked to some problem within the department, and he would prefer to deal with it now instead of on Monday morning.

A car door closing echoed in the distance and Grey braced himself for the inevitable confrontation.

"Hello, Pamela," he said, when he opened the door for her, wondering if she even suspected he wasn't particularly welcoming.

She marched into his living room, her eyes flashing with indignation and her hands knotted into tight fists at her sides. "That woman belongs in jail."

"Calm down," he said, leading her to a chair. Once she was seated, he handed her a cup of freshly brewed tea, adding the cream and sugar he knew she favored.

Waving her hand as though directing a world-class orchestra, Pamela announced, "She pranced right into my office as brazen as can be. I demand that you do something, Greyson."

Grey took the seat across from her, braced his hands on the arms of the chair and dug his fingers into the material, praying for patience. Pamela hadn't so much as asked how he was feeling. It was amazing the things that went through his mind at a time like this.

"Don't you even care?"

Frankly, he didn't. "*Who* pranced into your office as insolent as could be?"

"That...girl you've been dating. Meghan O'Something."

Grey couldn't believe his ears. He uncrossed his legs and straightened, digging his fingers deeper into the pads of the leather chair. "Meghan did? Exactly what did she say?"

Pamela's hand went into action a second time. "You're going to love this! She insulted me and threatened me and insisted I lie to you." She said all this in a rush, as though the memory of it were more than she should be asked to bear. When she'd finished, she let a soft cry part from her mouth, then bit down on her lower lip as outrage filled her once again.

"She insulted you?" That didn't sound anything like Meghan, and Grey honestly refused to believe it.

"Yes," Pamela cried. "She made several derogatory statements about my clothes and demanded that I never wear my hair up again. Right in my own office, Greyson. I mean to tell you, I've never been so insulted in my life."

"I see." Grey frowned. He didn't know what was going on in Meghan's loveable, confused mind, but he fully intended to find out.

"I'm sure you *don't* see," Pamela insisted vehemently. Her gaze sharpened all the more. "Something has to be done about this woman.... She belongs in a...mental ward. I'm still shaking. Just look!" To prove her point, she held out her hand for his inspection, and in fact it was trembling.

"You said Meghan also threatened you."

"Indeed, she did." Tilting her head at a lofty angle, Pamela drew in a short breath as if to suggest she needed something more to calm her before she continued with this tale of horror.

Grey was growing impatient. The more he was with Pamela, the more he realized that she'd attended the same school of dramatics as his mother.

"She claimed that if I didn't make you happy, she'd make sure I wished I had. Now I'm not exactly sure what she meant by that, but the whole torrid conversation started out by her demanding answers to what I consider highly personal and confidential questions." She paused long enough to draw in a second quivering breath. "The thing that concerns me most—because it's obvious now more than ever before—is that this...friend of yours is suffering from some kind of mental flaw, which is probably genetic. Did I tell you that she insisted I lie to you?"

Grey gritted his teeth to keep from defending Meghan, but it was necessary that he hear everything before voicing his thoughts. "Yes," he coaxed, hoping to encourage her to speak freely. "About the lying."

"She delivered some disgusting-looking broth and demanded that I take it to you. What I found most amazing was she wanted me to tell you I'd cooked it up myself. Now you and I both know that while I'm an incredibly talented woman in many areas, my expertise doesn't extend to the kitchen. From everything else this loony woman did, I strongly suspect she could be trying to poison you and then blame me for it. Naturally, the more I thought about the situation, the more plain it became that I had to come straight to you."

"What did you do with the broth?"

"I threw it in the garbage right away. Greyson, it was the only thing to do."

Grey nodded. The soup was a loss, but he was grateful beyond words that Pamela had come to him, although he questioned her purpose. "I'm most appreciative, Pamela."

A smug smile replaced the look of fabricated horror. "Just what do you intend to do about this?"

He tapped his index finger over his lips while mulling over the information. When he'd finished, he straightened and eagerly met Dr. Riverside's gaze.

"I believe I'll marry her."

Eleven

"You want to know what I think?" Meghan asked a group of friends who were sitting in a circle on her living-room carpet. She held up a full glass of cheap wine as if to propose a toast.

"What does Meghan think?" three others chimed in, then held up their glasses, eager to salute her insights.

Tears of mirth rolled down her face and she wiped them aside. This get-together with Eric, his fiancée, Trina Montgomery, and Don Harrison was exactly what she needed to see her through these first difficult days without Grey.

"I think," she said, starting again, trying her best to look somber, "Henry David Thoreau wrote *Walden* when he should have been going for a killing on the stock market." She said this with a straight face, as serious as she'd been the entire evening. Then she ruined everything by loudly hiccuping in a movement so jolting that it nearly dislodged her head. Shocked and embarrassed by the involuntary action, she covered her mouth. Until that moment, she hadn't realized how precariously close she was to being tipsy.

"I bet he made all his students use recycled paper," Trina added, then laughed until the tears streamed down her face.

"Right," Don agreed, nodding. "He missed his calling in life, he should have been a—"

"Boy Scout leader," Meghan supplied.

The others doubled over with laughter as though she'd said the funniest thing in the world.

"I love it," Eric said, slapping the floor several times.

"What I said?" Meghan asked, thinking he might be referring to the continued hiccuping.

Eric and the others were laughing too hard to answer her.

The doorbell chimed and the merriment stopped abruptly. Don glanced toward the door, looking mildly guilty. "Shh," he said, putting his finger over his mouth. "We must be making too much of a racket."

"I don't think we were," Meghan said, doing her best to sober up before going to the door.

Trina covered her mouth with her palm, then lowered it to whisper, "Someone might have called the police."

"What for?" Eric chided. "The worst thing we've done all night is make a few derogatory remarks about Thoreau."

The doorbell chimed a second time.

"I think you'd better answer it," Trina whispered to Meghan. "It's your apartment, and it could be one of the neighbors. Tell them we promise to be quiet."

"Tell whoever it is to lighten up," Don muttered. "It's barely eight o'clock."

Getting to her feet was far more difficult than it should have been. Meghan teetered for a second as the room started to tilt and sway. She walked across the floor and stood in front of her door. Taking in a deep, steadying breath, she smoothed her hair away from her face and squared her shoulders.

"Who is it?" she called out in a friendly voice.

Whoever was on the other side obviously didn't hear because her question was followed by repeated loud knocking.

Startled by the unexpected noise, Meghan's hand flew to her breast. She gasped and jumped back a step.

Immediately Don Harrison leaped to his feet. He was short and a little stocky, but exactly the type of friend Meghan needed right now. She doubted that she would ever feel anything romantic toward him, but he was friendly, patient and kind, and Meghan genuinely liked him.

"I'll answer it for you," Don announced, and readjusted the waistband of his pants as if to suggest he was about to walk into the middle of the street with a six-shooter in his hand and gun down anyone who was crazy enough to upset Meghan.

"No...it's all right." Hurriedly she waved off his concern, twisted open the dead bolt and threw open the door. Her gaze collided with a solid male chest. She squinted, greatly relieved that it wasn't the uniform of a policeman that confronted her. Slowly she raised her head, but when she did, her eyes clashed with a pair of deep China-blue ones that were all too familiar.

"What are you doing here?" she demanded.

"Dr. Carlyle," Don exclaimed from behind her. His shock echoed across the room like a cannon firing into the wind.

"He's going to arrest us for what we said about Thoreau," Trina wailed. "I knew something like this was going to happen. I just knew it." She released a small cry and covered her face with a decorative pillow.

"Dr. Carlyle, sir," Eric cried, struggling to come to his feet. "We didn't mean anything by what we said. Honest."

"May I come inside?" Grey asked, ignoring the others and centering his gaze on Meghan.

Had the fate of the free world rested on her response, Meghan couldn't have answered.

The professor's narrowed eyes then surveyed the room,

slowly taking in the scene. He focused on each face, finally drawing his gaze back to Meghan. "May I?" he repeated.

"Oh, sure—I guess." Meghan squared her shoulders, then hiccuped despite her frenzied effort to look and act sober.

"Don't let him intimidate you," Don encouraged, placing his arm around Meghan's shoulders.

"I won't," she whispered.

Grey's look swung accusingly back to Don, and the other man immediately dropped his hold on Meghan, retreating several steps under the force of Grey's eyes.

"You're drunk—you all are," Grey announced.

"I'm not," Meghan insisted righteously, then laughed and pointed her index finger toward the ceiling. "Yet."

"I want to know how he heard what we were saying," Eric mumbled, looking confused. "Does he have Superman hearing, or what?"

"I don't want to know how he found out," Trina mumbled from behind the pillow. "Oh no, there goes my quarter grade. I'll never make it out of his class alive."

Don just sat looking dumbstruck and disoriented.

"You need coffee," Grey announced, and moved past all four and into the kitchen.

Meghan lowered herself onto the arm of the chair. Her knees had started to shake and she wasn't sure she could remain upright much longer.

"He walked into your kitchen as if he had every right in the world to do so," Eric interjected, pointing in that direction. "He can't do that, can he?"

"He said we needed coffee," Don reminded the others.

"But how can he walk into a stranger's home and know where everything is and—" Eric stopped abruptly as if a new thought had flashed into his mind. He exchanged knowing looks with Don.

Don was apparently thinking the same way as Eric. His gaze widened considerably. "You wouldn't by chance happen to have met Dr. Carlyle before tonight?" Don asked Meghan then swallowed convulsively.

"I…" Meghan found herself too flustered to talk. "Yes," she admitted in a small, feeble voice.

"He isn't—" Eric glanced toward the kitchen and paled. His Adam's apple worked up and down his throat a couple of times. "No." He shook his head, answering his own question. "It couldn't be."

"What couldn't be?" Trina demanded.

Eric's eyes rounded considerably. "The reason we came over here tonight," he muttered under his breath.

"We came to cheer up Meghan," Trina replied, looking bewildered.

"Because…" Eric prompted.

"Because she was on the outs with her—" Trina stopped hastily then slowly shook her head. "It couldn't be."

"Did you see the look he gave *me*," Don whispered. "I'm lucky to be alive."

Eric turned to face Meghan. "Do you know Dr. Carlyle…personally?"

Without meeting his gaze, she nodded.

"Professor Carlyle wouldn't happen to be the guy you've been so upset over, would he?"

Once more Meghan nodded.

"That's it," Trina lamented, wrapping her arms around her middle. "I'm flunking out of college. My dad's going to disinherit me."

"Don't be ridiculous," said Don, looking disgruntled.

Trina ignored him. "My mother will never forgive me for doing this to her. My life is over—and all because I wanted to help the friend of the man who in two months is vowing to love and protect me for the rest of my life."

"Grey isn't going to do anything to you three," Meghan insisted, feeling close to tears. The wine, which had gone to her head earlier, had settled in the pit of her stomach now and she felt wretched. The walls refused to stop moving and she dared not look at the floor for fear it would start pitching and heaving. She was grateful to be sitting down.

"You obviously don't know Professor Carlyle the way we do," Trina whispered, shooting a worried glance over her shoulder as if she expected Grey to return any minute.

"You're taking a class with him?" Meghan asked Trina. She nodded wildly. "Eric, too."

"I did last year," Don admitted. "All of a sudden I have this sneaky suspicion that he's going to find a way to go back and flunk me."

"You're all being ridiculous," Meghan told them. She hesitated. "Do you want me to get rid of him?"

"No," all three chorused.

"No way," Don said, moving his hands like an umpire declaring a runner home safe.

"That'll only make matters worse," Eric explained.

It looked as if he planned to say more, but he stopped abruptly when Grey entered the room, carrying a tray laden with four mugs of steaming coffee.

Silently Grey passed the cups around, leaving Meghan to the last.

"I haven't been drinking," Eric proclaimed as he lifted the cup from the tray.

Grey paused in front of Eric and glared down at him suspiciously.

"It's true. I was planning to drive home," Eric persisted,

his voice high and a little defensive. "I'm just in a fun-loving mood," he offered as a means of explanation.

"It's true," Meghan confirmed softly.

"Is anyone here capable of telling me what was going on when I arrived? I'm particularly interested in your comments about being arrested for what you said about Thoreau."

Meghan noted that the other three were all staring at their coffee as if they expected something to pop up and start floating on the surface.

"Meghan?" Grey coaxed. "Perhaps you could explain."

She swallowed uncomfortably and shrugged. "We were just having some fun."

"Apparently at Thoreau's expense."

"I don't think he'd mind," she said weakly. "He had more of a sense of humor that most educators give him credit for."

"Is that a fact?"

"I mean it, Grey."

"Grey?" Don echoed. He looked at the others and his shoulders moved up and down with a sigh of defeat. "She calls him Grey." This was spoken with such seriousness that Meghan wondered at his meaning.

"Maybe we should just leave," Trina suggested, her voice elevated and hopeful. "It's obvious the professor wants to talk to Meghan alone."

"Yeah," Don seconded. "We should all just leave before—" He let the rest of what he was going to say fade.

"You don't need to worry, I can drive without a problem," Eric promised. Before anyone could say anything more, Eric hurried over to Meghan's closet and jerked his coat off the hanger. While he was there, he retrieved both Trina's and Don's jackets.

He was opening the front door before Meghan even had a chance to protest. Now that her head had started to clear, she wasn't sure that being alone with Grey was such a brilliant idea. At least with the others around, there was a protective barrier for her to hide behind.

"I'll see you to the door," Meghan offered.

"There's no need," Grey countered. "I will."

A part of Meghan wanted to cry out and protest that this was her home and these friends were her guests and she would be the one to see them off. But she wasn't feeling particularly strong at the moment, and arguing with Grey now would demand more energy than she could afford to waste.

Grey seemed to take his time with the task, Meghan mused a couple of minutes later. The four were engaged in a whispered conversation for what seemed an eternity; and although Meghan strained to hear what they were saying, she couldn't make anything out of it but bits and pieces.

All too soon, Grey closed the door and turned around to face her.

Meghan lowered her head so much that the steam from her coffee cup was about to bead against her face.

"Hello, Meghan."

"Hi." Still she didn't look up. "I see that you recovered from your cold."

"Yes, it's mostly gone now."

"That's good news. You sounded miserable the last time we spoke."

"I was, but the cold wasn't responsible for that."

"It wasn't?"

"No."

From the sound of his voice, Meghan knew he was moving closer to her. If there had been any place for her to run and hide, she would gladly have done so. Unfortunately her apartment was tiny, and knowing Grey, he would only follow her.

"The cold was a bear, don't misunderstand me," Grey

continued. "But the real reason I was feeling so crummy had to do with you."

"Me?" This came out sounding much like a squeaky door badly in need of oiling. "I'm sure you're mistaken."

"Yes. You, Meghan Katherine O'Day. Plotting so I'd see you making a snowman with your arms wrapped around another man. I'll have you know you nearly had me convinced."

He was so close that all she had to do was look up from her perch on the arm of the chair and meet his gaze, but she was afraid he would read the truth in her eyes if she did. She *had* carefully planned that scene and was shocked that he'd figured it out.

He advanced a step.

Meghan swallowed and, losing her balance, slid backward. A soft gasp escaped her lips as her posterior slithered over the material. She was abruptly halted when her back slammed against the opposite arm of the chair. It was a minor miracle that the coffee didn't end up spilling down her front.

"Are you all right?" Grey asked, clearly alarmed.

It took Meghan a couple of seconds to gather her scattered wits. "I'm fine." Although she made a valiant effort, she couldn't right herself in the chair. Grey pried the coffee cup out of her fingers, and once her hands were freed, she used those for leverage, twisting around so she could sit upright. She did so with all the pomp and ceremony her inebriated condition would allow.

"There," she announced, as if she'd accomplished a feat of Olympic proportions. She brushed her palms together several times, feeling utterly pleased with herself. "Now, what was it you were saying?"

Grey was quiet for so long that she dared to chance a look in his direction. She found him pacing the small area in front of her chair much like a caged animal. He stopped and turned to look at her, then threaded his fingers through his hair in what she thought looked like an outburst of indecision.

"I don't know if this is the best time for this conversation or not," he admitted dryly.

"It's probably not." Meghan was more than willing to delay a confrontation. Her head was spinning, and she was sure it wasn't the wine this time, but the fact that Grey was so close to her. He'd always had this dizzying effect upon her. "You shouldn't even try to talk to me now. You probably haven't noticed, but I happen to be...a little tipsy."

"A little!" he shouted. "You're plastered out of your mind."

"That's not entirely true," she protested, just as vehemently. "And if I am, it's all your fault."

"Mine? Where do you come up with that crazy notion?"

That was the last thing Meghan planned to reveal to him. She tilted her head at a regal angle, then pinched her lips together. With a dignified air, she pantomimed locking her mouth closed and stuffing the imaginary key into the front of her bra. Once she'd finished, she realized how silly this must have looked, and decided that if she was ever going to gather her moonstruck wits about her, the time was now.

Her actions seemed to frustrate Grey all the more, and Meghan began to experience a sense of power. She, a lowly waitress, had managed to flap the unflappable Professor Greyson Carlyle.

"All I want to know," he asked with stark impatience, "is why? And then I'll be out of here."

"Why what?"

"Why did you go to Pamela Riverside's office?"

Meghan's head shot up. "She told you?" That much was obvious. Good grief, the woman was said to have a genius IQ, yet she was displaying all the intelligence of a piece of mold. "That's the last thing in the world she should have done."

"Pamela claims you insulted her and threatened her and demanded that she lie to me. Is that right?"

Meghan crossed her legs then cupped her hands over her knees, praying her look was sophisticated and suave, but knowing it wasn't. "In a manner of speaking, I suppose she's right." If it were in her power now, Meghan would like to have another serious discussion with Grey's associate. It was all too obvious that what the woman lacked in clothes sense she also lacked in common sense. The last thing she should have done was confront Grey and tell him about their tête-à-tête.

"Threatening someone else doesn't sound anything like the warm, generous woman I know."

"Maybe you don't know me so well, after all," Meghan muttered.

"After tonight, I'm beginning to believe that myself."

"Then maybe you should just leave…because as you so kindly pointed out, I'm plastered."

"Maybe I should, but I'm not going to—not until I find out why you'd even approach Pamela…especially when I've gone out of my way to let you know I feel nothing for her."

"She's in love with you."

"She doesn't know the meaning of the word."

"That's not true," Meghan cried, defending the other woman and ignoring the woozy rushes of dizziness that enveloped her. Grey had misjudged Pamela Riverside, and Meghan could understand the other woman's frustration. She remembered all too well how vulnerable his colleague had looked the night Meghan had met her at the cocktail party. Pamela had seen Meghan with Grey and had been devastated. His colleague might have her faults, but she was still a woman and as hungry for love and acceptance as any other female. Strangely, for all her brilliance, Dr.

Riverside was shockingly naive when it came to men and the male-female relationship.

"Pamela Riverside possesses all the warmth of a deep freeze," Grey continued, his patience clearly tested. "You can argue with me all you want, but I'm not leaving here until you tell me the reason you found it so necessary to go to her office."

"Because." Her voice was so soft and small. She was certain Grey hadn't been able to hear her, so she repeated herself. "Because." It came out more firmly, but unfortunately it made absolutely no sense.

Grey knelt down in front of her and braced his hands on the overstuffed arms of the chair. "Because? That doesn't tell me much."

"She's perfect for you," Meghan pronounced, not daring to look at him. Although she'd tried several times to push the pain-inducing thought from her mind, Meghan kept imagining what Grey and Pamela's children would look like. All she could envision were dark-haired boys with horn-rimmed glasses, and blue-eyed little girls in two-piece business suits and black tie-up shoes.

"Pamela's perfect for me," Grey repeated and shook his head as if the mere thought brought with it a discordant note. "Honestly, Meghan, if I didn't love you so much, that could be considered an insult."

"An insult!" She'd made the biggest sacrifice of her life for him, and now Grey was calmly telling her that she'd affronted him by gallantly relinquishing him to the woman who was far better suited to his lifestyle. The unfairness of it all came crashing down on her like a ton of concrete. "I can't believe you'd say that to me. I was so unselfish, so noble and—" She stopped and jerked her head up. "What was it you just said? The first part, about...loving me?"

Grey's face was so close to her own that his features had blurred. Then Meghan realized that it was the tears in her eyes that had misshaped his visage. Sniffling, she rubbed a hand down her face. His words sobered her faster than ten cups of strong, black coffee.

"I love you, Meghan O'Day."

"But how can you…? Oh, Grey!" She leaned forward and pressed her forehead against his while struggling not to cry. "You can't love me, you just can't."

"But I do. And I have no intention of ever loving anyone else as long as I live."

From somewhere deep inside, Meghan found the strength to break away from him. She stiffened her shoulders and rubbed her cheeks dry of any moisture. Her heart felt like a thundering herd of horses galloping inside her chest. "I'm really sorry to hear that."

"You love me, too," he stated evenly. "So banish the thoughts of coming up with a bunch of lies to convince me otherwise. I'll refuse to believe you, anyway."

Meghan blinked several times, her lashes dampening the high arches of her cheeks. She reached out and lovingly traced her fingers down the side of his face. "I don't think I could lie, even if I tried," she whispered. "Oh, Grey, how could we have let this happen?"

He brushed the wisps of hair away from her cheekbones and his thumbs lingered there as though he couldn't keep from touching her. "You make it sound as if our falling in love were some great tragedy. From the moment I met you, my life has been better. You're laughter and love and warmth and excitement. I'll always be grateful to have found you."

"But your mother…"

"You won't be spending the rest of your life with her. I'm the one you're going to be marrying."

"What?" Meghan was convinced she'd misunderstood him. "Who said anything about getting married?" The thought was so baffling to her that she jumped up in the cushion of the chair and pointed an accusing finger at him, waving it several times. "You've lost your mind, Greyson Carlyle."

"Okay, we'll live in sin. But to be honest, that may put my career in jeopardy. Dr. Browning lives by a high moral standard, and frankly, he's not going to approve."

"I can't marry you." She wouldn't have thought it possible, but her heart was pounding faster and faster until it felt like a timed device ready to explode within her breast.

"Meghan," Grey murmured, rising to his feet. "Would you kindly climb down off that chair?"

"I...don't think I should. What would be better is if you left, and then maybe I could think clearly and we could forget you ever suggested...what you just did." She couldn't even say the word.

"Don't be silly. Now, come down from there before you fall." He held out his hand to assist her, but she pretended not to see it.

"Meghan," he cried, clearly exasperated.

"If I step down, you're going to kiss me."

"I'll admit the thought has crossed my mind," he said with a devilish smile.

"And if you do, it'll weaken my defenses."

"As it should."

It took both her hands to brush the hair off her forehead. "I can't let that happen. In fact I think you should leave— you've got me at a distinct disadvantage here. I'm dizzy and weak, and everything you're saying is making me dizzier and weaker."

"I love you."

"See what I mean," she persisted. She slumped back

down in the chair, bracing her heel against the edge of the cushion and resting her chin on her bent knees. To her way of thinking—which she had to admit was unclear at the moment—she could hurt Grey's career if they were to marry. "I'm a waitress," she whispered. "Have you forgotten?"

"No, love, I haven't. Are you ashamed of it?"

"No!"

He knelt down in front of her and grinned. His smile carried with it all the warmth of a July sun. "My feelings wouldn't change if you mopped floors for a living. You're honest and proud, and I'm crazy in love with you. I'd consider myself the most fortunate man in the world if you'd honor me by being my wife."

All the resistance seeped out of her like air whooshing out of a balloon. She was crazy in love with him herself, and had been for weeks. He studied her for a long moment, and her reluctant gaze met his. It didn't take long for her to recognize that everything he said was true. He did love and want her, and she would be a fool to even consider turning him away. A smile courted the corners of her mouth even as a tear ran down the side of her face.

Grey reached out and brushed her cheekbone with his cool fingertips. The moment was so tender, so sweet, that Meghan squeezed her eyes shut in an effort to savor these marvelous feelings.

Grey was right; she wouldn't be marrying his mother. It would take time and patience, but eventually Frances Carlyle would come to accept her. Meghan couldn't allow their lives to be dictated by someone else. Her mind clouded with fresh objections, but her heart quickly overrode those, guiding her to where she belonged and where she wanted to be—in Grey's arms.

She reached out to him, looping her arms around his

neck. He heaved a sigh of relief and crushed her against him, holding her as though he'd snapped her out of the jaws of death.

"Meghan, my love, you've led me on a merry chase."

She wanted to tell him so many things, but she was kept speechless as he rained countless kisses upon her face— moist darts of pleasure upon her flushed features, some burning against her eyelids and others scorching the pulse points in her neck.

"You *are* going to marry me, aren't you?" he asked after a long moment, still kissing her.

"Yes. Oh, Grey, I love you so much."

Grey moaned and returned his mouth to hers, tantalizing her with a series of soft kisses that quickly turned to intense ones that sent her pulse soaring and left her temples thundering. She tangled her fingers in his hair, and arched her body against his.

He kissed her so many times, Meghan felt spineless in his arms. When he buried his face in the soft slope of her neck, they were both trembling.

"I'm not going to let you change your mind," he said on a husky note.

"I have no intention of doing so," she assured him.

Grey paused and reached inside the pocket of his tweed jacket and brought out a jeweler's box. When he lifted the lid, Meghan gasped at the size of the diamond resting between the folds of black velvet.

He removed the ring, reached for her hand, and gazing into her tear-rimmed eyes, he slipped it onto her finger.

With that simple action, the waitress became forever linked with the professor.

Epilogue

"Meghan," Grey called up the stairs from the living room, "hurry or we're going to be late. We should have left five minutes ago."

Squirting on some cologne, Meghan rushed into the bedroom and searched frantically for her dress heels. Grey's side of the room was meticulously organized, while hers was a disaster area. She could hear him moving up the steps to find out what was taking her so long. Angry with herself for not knowing where her shoes had disappeared, she got down on her knees and tossed whatever was on the floor onto the top of the bed.

"Meghan, we're going to be late," Grey said a second time, standing in the doorway. Their nine-month-old son, Kramer, squirmed in his arms, wanting down so he could crawl to Mommy and play her silly game.

"I can't find my white heels," Meghan cried, lifting up the bedspread and peeking underneath.

"Honey, you shouldn't be crawling around down there in your condition," Grey muttered, lowering Kramer to the carpet. Soon all three were on the floor looking for Meghan's shoes.

"I'll have you know you're responsible for my condition," Meghan teased, her gaze locking with his.

"I know." Grey's look caressed her and his hand moved around her waist to pat the gentle swelling of her abdomen. "I worry about you having the two so close."

"It's the way I wanted it," she reminded him. Still kneeling, she turned and looped her arms around his neck and playfully kissed him, darting her tongue in and out of his mouth in a familiar game of cat and mouse, letting her kisses tell him how much she loved and desired him.

"I think we should have waited. Irish twins—I still can't believe it. Kramer born in January and this baby due in December." His hand rested against the sides of her stomach, caressing her there.

Making gurgling noises, Kramer agilely crept between his parents, his headful of bright red curls leading the way. Once he'd maneuvered himself into position, he stood upright, looking around. He hurled his small body against Meghan, laughing as though to tell her he'd won their game. From the moment he was born, he'd been a sweet, happy baby.

"Oh, Kramer," Meghan exclaimed, swinging him into her arms. "You're going to be walking soon, you little rascal."

Kramer squealed with delight as she raised him above her head.

"That's just what we need," Grey said, frowning just a little.

"What?" she asked, busily keeping her son's eager hands out of her hair.

"Kramer walking at ten months. My mother already believes he's a genius, and if he starts walking that early, it will only prove as much in her eyes."

"She surprised me," Meghan admitted thoughtfully. Her

mother-in-law had delivered several surprises over the past year, all of them pleasant ones.

"Surprised *you*?" he returned with a short laugh. "You could have bowled me over with a dirty diaper when I realized she was going to be the doting-grandmother type. When Kramer was born, I thought she was going to buy out the toy store."

"Dirty diapers *do* bowl you over," she reminded him, smiling.

He shrugged. "That was just a manner of speech."

"Your mother loves Kramer."

"And you," he said. "She told me not so long ago how you've become much more than a daughter-in-law to her." He paused and rubbed the side of his face. "To hear her tell it, she was the one responsible for getting us together."

"I suppose she's right. Only she used reverse psychology."

"She absolutely insists you get your degree."

"I will, in time—so she needn't worry. But for now, I'm more concerned with raising my family. I've got a year in already and will take more classes when I can."

Grey's eyes brightened and he quickly crawled across the floor, holding up one pair of white high-heeled shoes that were partially hidden behind the dresser. "Here they are."

Kramer crawled after his father, his little knees moving at top speed.

Meghan quickly rose to her feet, slipped on the white shoes and reached down for her son. "This'll be your first wedding, son, so behave," Meghan told him, nuzzling his neck playfully.

"I think it was nice of Pamela to request that we bring Kramer along this afternoon," Grey said.

"He stole her heart, right along with your mother's,"

Meghan pointed out. "She wouldn't think of excluding him on this important day."

Grey stood, brushing any traces of lint from his pant legs. "Do you think Pamela and Fulton are going to be happy?"

"Yes, I do," Meghan replied, setting her son down and reaching inside her closet for a light coat. "I was the one who was shocked when Pamela came over to tell us she was marrying Dr. Essary. I hope I was able to hide my surprise."

"What I can't figure out is why we didn't realize it sooner. The two of them make the perfect couple, when you stop to think about it."

"What amazes me is how falling in love has changed the two of them. They're completely different people than when I first met them."

"I'm completely different, too," Grey reminded her. "Thanks to one sweet Irish miss who stole my heart and changed the way I view everything from Milton to French toast."

Clinging to the skirt of his mother's dress, Kramer Carlyle struggled into a standing position. Gurgling happily, he looked at his father and took two distinct steps, then promptly fell onto his padded bottom.

"I knew it all along," Meghan said with a happy laugh. She leaned over and picked up her son. "We've got ourselves a little genius."

* * * * *

FALLEN ANGEL

One

The least it could do was rain! What was the use of living in Seattle if it wasn't going to so much as drizzle? And Amy was in the mood for a cloudburst.

She bought herself an order of crispy fried fish and chips simply because she felt guilty occupying a picnic table in the tourist-crowded pier along the Seattle waterfront. The mild June weather had refused to respond to her mood and the sun was playing peekaboo behind a band of thin clouds. No doubt it would ruin everything and shine full force any minute.

"Excuse me—is this seat taken?"

Amy glanced up to discover a man who looked as though he'd just stepped out of a Western novel and was searching for Fort Apache standing opposite her. The impression came from a leather band that was wrapped around his wide forehead and the cropped-waisted doeskin jacket.

"Feel free," she said, motioning toward the empty space opposite her. "I'll be finished here within a couple of minutes."

"It doesn't look like you've even touched your meal."

"I couldn't possibly eat at a time like this," she said, frowning at him.

His thick brows shot upward as he lifted his leg over the wooden table and sat opposite her. "I see."

Amy picked up a fat French fry and poised it in front of her mouth. "I've been home exactly two weeks and it hasn't so much as rained once. This is Seattle, mind you, and there hasn't even been a heavy dew."

"The weather *has* been great."

"I'd feel better if it rained," she returned absently. "It's much too difficult to be depressed when the sun is shining and the birds are chirping and everyone around me is in this jovial, carefree mood."

The stranger took a sip of his coffee, and Amy suspected he did so to cover a smile. It would be just her luck to have a handsome stranger sit down and try to brighten her mood.

He set the cup on the picnic table and leveled his gaze at her. "You look to me like a woman who's been done wrong by her man."

"That's another thing," Amy cried. "Everything would be so much simpler if I'd been born a male."

Her companion's brown eyes rounded. "Is that a fact?"

"Well, of course, then I wouldn't be in this mess...well, I would, but I'd probably be happy about it."

"I see."

Feeling slightly better about the situation, Amy tore off a piece of fish and studied it before popping it into her mouth. It tasted good, much better than she'd anticipated. "It wouldn't be nearly this difficult if I didn't have the most wonderful father in the world."

His dark eyes softened. "Then you shouldn't need to worry."

"But it just kills me to disappoint him." Amy took another bite of the battered fish. "After all, I am twenty-three—it's not as though I don't know what I want."

"And what *do* you want?"

"How would I know?" she muttered. "No one even asked me before."

Her newfound friend laughed outright.

Amy smiled, too, for the first time in what seemed like years. "If I'm going to be spilling my guts to you, I might as well introduce myself. I'm Amy Johnson."

"Josh Powell." He held out his hand and they exchanged quick handshakes.

"Hello, Josh."

"Hello yourself," he returned, grinning broadly. "Are you going to be all right, Amy Johnson?"

She expelled a harsh sigh, then shrugged. "I suppose." Another French fry made its way into her mouth. When she reached for the fish, she noted that Josh had stopped eating and was studying her.

"Is there a reason you're wearing that rain coat?" he asked.

She nodded. "I was hoping for a downpour—something to coordinate with my mood."

"I thought you might have heard a more recent forecast. An unexpected tropical storm or something."

"No," she admitted wryly.

"Frankly, I'm surprised by the weather myself," Josh stated conversationally. "I've been in Seattle several days now, and the sun has greeted me every morning."

"So you're a tourist?"

"Not exactly. I work for one of the major oil companies, and I'm waiting for government clearance before I head for the Middle East. I should fly out of here within the week."

Her father owned a couple of oil wells, but from what

Amy could remember they were in Texas and had been losing money for the past few years. If her father was experiencing minor financial problems with his vast undertakings, then it was nothing compared to what was bound to happen when *she* stepped into the picture. He had such high hopes for her, such lofty expectations. And she was destined to fail. It would be impossible not to. She had about as much business sense as Homer Simpson. Her college advisers had repeatedly suggested she change her major. Personally, Amy was all for that. She worked hard and even then she was considered borderline as to whether she would be accepted into the five-year joint BA and MBA program. She'd been number three on a waiting list. Then her father had donated funds toward a new library, and lo and behold, Amy and everyone else on the list had been welcomed into the prestigious school of business with open arms.

"I'm impressed with what I've seen of Seattle," Josh went on.

"It's a nice city, isn't it?" Amy answered with a soft smile. She leaned forward and plopped her elbows on top of the picnic table. "Do you think it would work if I feigned a fatal illness?"

"I beg your pardon?"

"No," she said, answering her own question. "It wouldn't." Knowing her father, he would call in medical experts from around the world, and she'd be forced into making a miraculous recovery.

Josh's amused gaze met hers.

"I'm not making the least bit of sense, am I?"

"No," he admitted dryly. "Do you want to talk about it?"

Supporting her cheek with the palm of one hand, she stared into the distance, wondering if discussing the matter with a stranger would help. At least he would be unbiased.

"My father is probably one of the most dynamic men you'll ever meet. Being around him is like receiving a charge of energy. He's exciting, vibrant, electric."

"I know the type you mean."

"I'm his only child," Amy muttered. "You may have noticed that Dad and I don't share a whole lot of the same characteristics."

Josh hedged. "That's difficult to say—we only met a few minutes ago, but from what I've seen, you don't seem to lack any energy."

"Take my word on this, Dad and I aren't anything alike."

"Okay," he said, then gestured toward her. "Go on."

"I recently acquired my MBA—"

"Congratulations."

"No, please. If it had been up to me I would have hung around the campus for as many more years as I could, applied for a doctorate—anything. But unfortunately that option wasn't left open to me. According to my father, the big moment has finally arrived."

"And?"

"He wants to take me into the family business."

"That isn't what you want?"

"Heavens, no! I know Dad would listen to me if I had some burning desire to be a teacher or a dental assistant or anything else. Then I could talk to him and explain everything. But I don't know what I want to do, and even if I did, I'm not so certain it would matter anyway."

"But you just said—"

"I know, but I also know my father, bless his dear heart. He'd look at me with those big blue eyes of his, and I'd start drowning in this sea of guilt." She paused long enough to draw in a giant breath. "I'm the apple of his eye. According to him, the sun rises and sets on my whims. I can't disappoint him—Dad's got his heart set on me taking over for him."

"You've never told him this isn't what you want?"

She dropped her gaze, ashamed to admit she'd been such a coward. "Not in so many words—I just couldn't."

"Perhaps you could talk to your mother, let her prepare the way. Then it won't come as any big shock when you approach your father."

Once more Amy shook her head. "I'm afraid that won't work. My mother died when I was barely ten."

"I see—well, that does complicate matters, doesn't it?"

"I did this to myself," Amy moaned. "I knew the day was coming when I'd be forced to tell him the truth. It wasn't like I didn't figure out what he intended early enough. About the time I entered high school, I got the drift that he had big plans for me. I tried to turn the tide then, but it didn't do any good."

"Turn the tide?" Josh repeated. "I don't understand."

"I tried to marry him off. The way I figured it, he could fall in love again, and his new wife would promptly give birth to three or four male heirs, and then I'd be off the hook. Unfortunately, he was too busy with the business to get involved with a woman."

"What if *you* married?"

"That wouldn't..." Amy paused and straightened as the suggestion ricocheted around the corners of her brain. "Josh...oh, Josh, that's a brilliant idea. Why didn't I think of that?" She nibbled on her lower lip as she considered his scheme, which sounded like exactly the escape clause she'd been wanting. "If my father would be willing to accept any excuse, it'd be something like that. He's a big-hearted romantic, and if there's one thing he wants more than to see me in the business—it's grandchildren." Her blue eyes flashed with excitement as she smiled at Josh. Then it struck her, and she moaned. "There's one flaw to this brilliant plan, though." She raised her fingers to her mouth and stroked her lips while she gave the one weakness some thought.

"What do you mean there's a flaw?" Josh repeated, sounding impatient.

"I'm not in love."

"That's not such a difficult hang-up. Think. Surely there's one man you've met in your life that you like well enough to marry?"

She considered the list of men she'd dated and her shoulders sagged with defeat. "Actually, there isn't," she admitted reluctantly. "I dated in college, but only a little, and there was never anyone I'd seriously consider spending the rest of my life with."

"What about the boys who attended high school with you? Five years have passed, and things have changed— perhaps it's time you renewed those old friendships."

Once more Amy frowned, then regretfully shook her head. "That won't work, either. I attended a Catholic girls' school." She closed her eyes, prepared to mentally scan through a list of potential men she might consider marrying. Unfortunately, she couldn't think of a single one.

"Amy," Josh whispered, "are you all right?"

She nodded. "I'm just thinking. No," she said emphatically, as the defeat settled on her shoulders like a blanket of steel, "there's no one. I'm doomed."

"You could always have a heart-to-heart talk with your father. If he's as wonderful as you claim, then he'll be grateful for the honesty."

"Sure, and what exactly do I say?"

"The truth. You might suggest he train someone else to take his place."

Despite the fact that Josh was serious, Amy laughed a little. "You make it sound so easy...you couldn't possibly realize how difficult telling him is going to be."

"But necessary, Amy."

The second to the last thing Amy needed was the cool voice of reason. The first had been a handsome stranger introducing himself to her. When a person is depressed and miserable, she decided, everything seems to fall apart!

"Talk to him," Josh advised again.

As much as Amy wanted to argue with him, he was right. Her eyes held on to his as if she could soak up his determination.

"The sooner you get it over with the better," he added softly.

"I know you're right," she murmured. "I should do it soon...before I find myself behind a desk, wondering how I ended up there."

"What's wrong with *now?*"

"Now?" Her startled gaze flew to Josh.

"Yes, now."

Her mouth opened to argue with him, but she realized there really wasn't any better time than the present. The corporate headquarters was within walking distance, and it would be best to face her father when she was charged with righteous enthusiasm. If she delayed the confrontation until dinnertime, she might chicken out.

"You're absolutely right. If I'm going to talk to my father, I've got to do it immediately." In a burst of zeal, she charged to her feet and offered Josh her hand. "Thank you for your advice."

"You're most welcome." He smiled and finished his coffee. "Good luck."

"Thanks, I'm going to need it." Securing the strap of her purse over her shoulder, she deposited what remained of her lunch in the trash and marched toward the sidewalk in smooth strides of military precision. When she reached the street, she turned to find Josh watching her. She raised her hand in a gesture of farewell, and he did the same.

An hour later, Amy sat in the back row of the Omnitheater at the Seattle Aquarium, slouched down as far as she could in her seat without slipping all the way out of it and into the aisle. Her hand covered her eyes. A documentary about the Mount St. Helen's disaster was about to start.

Disasters seemed to be the theme of Amy's day. Following her trip to the Rainier Building on Fifth Avenue, she'd walked to the waterfront area where her car was parked. The thought of returning home, however, only added to her misery, so she'd opted for the documentary.

Her bravado had been strong when she reached the fifty-story structure that housed Johnson Industries. She'd paused on the sidewalk outside and glanced up at the vertical ribs of polished glass and concrete. About half of all the people inside were a part of the conglomerate that made up her father's enterprise.

Her mistake had been when she'd started working with the figures. Calculating two hundred people per floor, that came to twenty thousand workers inside the Rainier Building—when full—of which a possible ten thousand were Johnson employees.

Of all those thousands, very few would stand equal to or above Amy in the capacity her father had chosen for her.

She wasn't exactly stepping into an entry-level position.

Oh, no, she'd been groomed for a much loftier point on the corporate scale. Her father's idea had been to place her as a director, working her way through each of the major sections of the company until the most important aspects of each department had been drilled into her. Naturally, Harold Johnson planned to stay on as president and chief executive officer until Amy had learned the ropes, but "the ropes" felt too much like a hangman's noose to suit her.

The lights lowered in the Omni-theater, and Amy heard someone enter the row and sit next to her.

"I take it the confrontation with your father didn't go well."

Amy's hand flew away from her face. It was Josh. "No," she whispered.

"What happened?"

She flopped her hands over a couple of times, searching for a way to start to explain. "It's a long story."

The man in front of them twisted around and glared, clearly more interested in hearing the details of the natural disaster than Amy's troubles.

"I've already seen the movie once," Josh said. "Do you want to go outside and talk?"

She nodded.

As she suspected, the sun was shining and the sky was an intense shade of blue. Even the seagulls were in a jovial mood.

"Do you want some ice cream?" Josh asked when they reached the busy sidewalk. He didn't wait for her reply, but bought them each an enormous double scoop waffle cone, then joined her in front of the large, cheerful water fountain.

Amy sat on the edge of the structure, feeling even more pathetic than she had earlier that afternoon.

"I take it you talked to your father?"

"No," she muttered. "I didn't get past Ms. Wetherell, his executive assistant." She lapped at the side of the cone, despite everything enjoying the rich, smooth taste of the vanilla ice cream. "I don't think I've ever really looked at that woman before. She reminds me of a prune."

"A prune?" Josh repeated.

"She might have been a pleasant plum at one time, but she's been ripened and dried by the years. I think it might be the fluorescent lighting." Amy knew she would look just like Ms. Wetherell within six months. She was going to hate being trapped indoors with no possibility of escape.

"The prune wouldn't allow you to talk to your own father?"

"He was in an important meeting." She turned to Josh and shrugged. "I was slain at the gate."

"Amy…"

"I know exactly what you're going to say, and you're absolutely right. I'll talk to my dad tonight. I promise you I will."

"Good."

He looked proud of her, and that helped. "How'd you happen to be in the Omni-theater?" she asked. It had to be more than coincidence.

"I saw you go inside and was curious to find out what happened."

He'd removed the leather jacket and draped it over his shoulder, securing it with one finger. His eyes were deeply set, his nose prominent without distracting from his strong male features. His ash-blond hair was longer than fashionable, but well kept. It seemed to Amy that calendar and poster manufacturers were constantly searching for men with such blatant male appeal. Men like Josh.

"Is something wrong?" he asked her unexpectedly.

"No," she said, recovering quickly. She hadn't realized she'd been staring quite so conspicuously.

"Your ice cream is melting," he told her.

Hurriedly, she took several bites to correct the problem. The green-and-white ferry sounded its horn as it approached the pier. It captured Josh's attention.

"Did you know that Washington has the largest ferry system in the United States and the third largest in the world?" Amy asked, in what she hoped was a conversational tone.

"No, I didn't."

"When you consider someplace like the Philippines with all those islands, that fact is impressive." Amy realized she was jabbering, but she wanted to pull attention away from herself and her problems. "Our aquarium is the one of only a few in the world built on a pier," she said, adding another tour-guide fact. "Have you been up to the Pike Place Market yet?"

"Several times, and I've enjoyed it more each visit."

"It's the largest continuously operated farmers' market in the nation."

"You seem to be full of little tidbits of information."

She smiled and nodded. Then she closed her eyes and expelled her breath in a leisurely exercise. "I really do love this city."

"It's home," Josh said quietly, and Amy sensed such a longing in his voice that she opened her eyes to study him.

"Would you like to walk with me?" he asked her unexpectedly. Standing, he offered her his elbow.

"Sure." She tucked her arm around his, enjoying the feeling of being connected with him. Josh had been a friend when she'd needed one. They barely knew each other—they'd exchanged little more than their names—and yet she'd told him more about her problems than she had any-one. Ever. Even her closest college friends didn't know how much she dreaded going to work for her father. But Josh Powell did. A stranger. An unexpected friend.

It took them forty minutes to walk from the waterfront area to the Seattle Center on Queen Ann Hill. They stood at the base of the Space Needle, which had been built for the 1962 World's Fair and remained a prominent city land-mark. Feeling it was her duty to relay the more important details, Amy told him everything she could remember about the Space Needle, which wasn't much. She finished off by asking, "Where's home?"

"I beg your pardon?"

"Where are you from?"

He paused and looked at her for a tense moment. "What makes you ask that?"

"I… I don't know. When I told you how much I love Se-attle, you claimed that was because it was home. Now I'm curious where home is for you."

His eyes took on a distant look. "The world—I've taken jobs just about everywhere now. The Middle East, South America, Australia, Europe."

"But where do you kick off your boots and put up your feet?"

"Wherever I happen to be," he explained.

"But—"

"I left what most others would consider home several years ago. I didn't ever intend to go back."

"Oh, Josh, that's so sad." Her voice sounded as if she'd whispered into a microphone, low and vibrating.

"Amy…" He paused, then chuckled softly. "It wasn't any big tragedy." Burying his hands in his pockets, he strolled away, effectively ending the conversation. He paused and waited on the pathway for her to join him.

Glancing at the time, Amy sighed. "I've got to get back to the house," she said with reluctance.

"Tell me what you're going to do tonight."

"Nothing much," she hedged. "Watch a little television probably, read some—"

"I don't mean that, and you know it."

"All right, all right, I'm going to talk to my father."

"And then tomorrow you're going to meet me at noon at the seafood stand and tell me what happened."

"I am?"

"That's exactly what you're going to do."

Her heart started to pound like an overworked piston in her chest, but that could have been because she would soon be confronting her father, and her success rate with making dragons purr was rather low at the moment. But the reaction could well have been due to the fact that she would be meeting Josh again.

"Any questions?" he asked.

"One." She paused and looked up at him, her eyes wide and appealing. "Will you marry me?"

"No."

"I was afraid of that."

Two

Manuela had served the last of the evening meal before Amy had the courage to broach the subject with her father. She looked at him, watching him closely, wanting to gauge his mood before she unloaded her mind. His disposition seemed congenial enough, but it was difficult to tell exactly how he would respond to her news.

"Did you have a pleasant afternoon?" Harold asked his daughter, glancing at her.

His unexpected question thumped her out of her musings. "Yes… I took a stroll along the waterfront."

"Good," he said forcefully, and nodded once. Harold Johnson took a bite of his shrimp-stuffed sole. He was nearly sixty-five and in his prime. His hair had gone completely white in the past few years, but his features were ageless, as sharp and penetrating as Amy could ever remember. He watched what he ate, was physically and mentally fit and lived life to the fullest. Nothing had ever been done by half measure. Harold Johnson was an all-or-nothing man. There were few compromises in attitude, health or personality.

He was the type of man who, when he saw something

he wanted, went after it with everything he had. He would never accept defeat, only setbacks. He claimed his greatest achievements had been the result of patience. If ever he would need to call upon that virtue, it was now, Amy mused. She loved him just the way he was and prayed he could accept her for who she was, as well.

"Ms. Wetherell said you stopped in to see me," he added, when he'd finished his bite of fish.

"You were in a meeting," she answered lamely.

Her father's responding nod was eager. "An excellent one as it turned out, too. I told a group of executives in five minutes how they can outsell, outmanage and outmotivate the competition."

"You said all that in five minutes?"

"Less," he claimed, warming to his subject. "Mark my words, Amy, because you're going to be needing them soon enough yourself."

"Dad—"

"The first thing you've got to do is set your goals—you won't get any place in this world if you don't know where you're headed. Then visualize yourself in that role."

"Dad—"

He held up his hand to stop her. "And lastly, and this is probably the most important aspect of success, you must learn to deny the power of the adverse. Now you notice, I didn't say you should deny the negative, because there's plenty of that in our world. But we can't allow ourselves the luxury of thinking adversity can get control over us. Because the plain and simple truth is this—misfortune has power only when we allow it to. Do you understand what I'm saying?"

Amy nodded, wondering if she would ever get a word in edgewise and, if she did, how she could possibly say what she needed to tell him.

"You come to the office tomorrow," her father went on to say, smiling smugly. "I've got something of a surprise for you. I was saving it for later, but I want you to see it now."

"What's that?"

"Your own office. I've hired one of those fancy interior decorators and I'm having the space redesigned. Nothing but the best for my little girl. New carpet, the finest furniture, the latest technology, the whole nine yards. Once that's completed, I want you working with me and the others. Together, you and I are going to make a difference in this country—a big one." He paused and set aside his fork. When he looked up, his gaze was warm and proud. "I've been waiting for this day for nearly twenty years. I don't mind telling you how proud I am of you, Amy Adele. You're as pretty as your mother, and you've got her brains, too. Having you at my side will almost be like having Mary back again."

"Oh, Dad…" He was making this so much more difficult.

"These years that you've been away at school have been hard ones. You're the sunshine of my life, Amy, just the way your mother always was."

"I'd like to be more like her," she whispered, knowing her father would never understand what she meant. Her mother had always been behind the scenes, acting as a sounding board and offering moral support. That was where Amy longed to be, as well.

Her father reached for his wineglass. "You're more and more like Mary every day."

"Mom didn't work at the office though, did she?"

"No, of course not, but don't you discount her worth to me. It was your mother's support, love and encouragement that gave me the courage to accomplish everything I have done over the years. Never in all that time did Mary and I dream we'd come so far or achieve so much."

"I meant what I said about being more like her," Amy tried once again. "Mom…was more of a background figure in your life and I…think that's the role I should play, too."

"Nonsense! You belong at my side."

"Dad, oh, please…" Her voice trembled like loose change in an oversize pocket. "You just finished telling me how important it was to visualize yourself in a certain role, and I'm sorry, but I can't see myself cooped up in an office day in and day out. It just isn't me. I—"

"You can't what?"

"See myself as an important part of Johnson Industries," she blurted out in one giant breath.

Her announcement was followed by a short silence.

"I can understand that," Harold said.

"You can?"

"Of course. It's little wonder when all you've done, so far is book learning," her father continued confidently. "Business isn't sitting in some stuffy classroom listening to a know-it-all professor spouting off his views. It's digging in with both hands and pulling out something viable and profitable that's going to affect people's lives for the better."

"But I'm not sure that's what I want."

"Of course you do!" he countered sharply. "You wouldn't be a Johnson if you didn't."

"What about Mom, and the support she gave you? Couldn't I start off like that… I mean…be a sounding board for you and a helpmate in other ways?"

"Years ago that was all you could have done, but times have changed," her father argued. "Women have fought for their rightful place in the corporate world. For the first time in history women are getting the recognition they deserve.

You're my daughter, my only child—everything I've managed to accumulate will some day belong to you."

"But—"

"Now, I think I understand what you're saying. I should have thought of this myself. You're tired. Exhausted from your studies. You've worked hard, and you deserve a break. I wasn't thinking when I suggested you start working with me so soon after graduation."

"Dad, I'm not *that* tired."

"Yes, you are, only you don't realize it. Now I want you to take a vacation. Fly to Europe and soak up the sun on those fancy beaches. Then in September we'll talk again."

"Vacationing in Europe isn't going to change how I feel," she murmured sadly, her gaze lowered. The lump in her throat felt as large as a grapefruit. She loved her father , and it was killing her to disappoint him like this.

"We aren't going to talk about your working until September. I apologize, Amy, I should have realized you needed a holiday. It's just that I'm a bit anxious to have you with me—it's been my dream all these years and I've been selfish not to consider the fact you're in need of a little time to yourself."

"Dad, please listen."

"No need to listen," he said, effectively cutting her off. "I just said we'd talk about it in the fall."

It took everything within Amy just to respond to him with a simple nod.

"You don't understand," Amy told Josh the following afternoon. "Before I could say a word, Dad started telling me how I was the sunshine of his life and how he'd waited twenty years for this day. What was I supposed to do?"

"I take it you didn't tell him?"

"I did—in a way."

"Only he didn't listen?"

Her nod was slow and reluctant. "It's obvious you've met my father, or at least someone like him. I don't blame Dad—this isn't exactly what he wanted to hear. The best I could do was to admit I couldn't see myself working with him in the office. Naturally, he didn't want to accept that, so he suggested I take the rest of the summer off to unwind after my studies."

"That's not such a bad idea. You probably shouldn't have expected anything more. Frankly, I think you did very well."

"You do?" she asked excitedly, but her mood quickly deflated. "Then why do I feel so rotten?"

"It's not going to get any easier. Last night was difficult, but at least you've gotten yourself a two-month reprieve. Perhaps, in the coming weeks, you'll come up with some way of making him understand."

Amy lowered her gaze and nodded. "Maybe." She raised the cup to her mouth and took a sip of coffee. "What about you, Josh? Did you hear about the government clearance?"

"No—nothing." His voice was filled with resignation.

"I know it's selfish of me," she admitted with a soft smile, "but I'm glad."

"It's easy enough for you to feel that way, you're not the one sitting on your butt waiting."

They exchanged smiles, and Josh brushed a stray strand of hair from her cheek. His fingers lingered as his eyes held hers.

"I'm grateful you came up and asked to share that table with me," Amy admitted. "I was feeling so low and miserable and talking to you has helped."

A reluctant silence followed, before he said, "Actually, I'd been watching you for some time."

"You had?"

Josh nodded. "I waited around for ten minutes to see if someone was going to join you before I approached the table. I was pleased you were alone."

"I wish there was more time for us to get to know each other," she whispered, surprised by how low and sultry her voice sounded.

"No," he countered bluntly, "in some ways it's for the best."

They stood at the end of the pier behind a long row of tourist shops, and Amy walked away, confused and uncertain. She didn't understand Josh. There wasn't anyone else nearby, and when she turned around and looked up, prepared to argue with him, she was taken aback to realize how close they were to one another—only a scant inch or two separated them.

Josh took the coffee from her hand and set it aside. Then he settled his hands on top of her shoulders, and his spellbinding gaze was stronger than the force of her will. His eyes searched hers for a long moment. She knew then that he intended to kiss her, and her immediate response was pleasure and anticipation. All morning, she'd been thinking about meeting Josh again and her heart had leaped with an eagerness she couldn't explain.

With unhurried ease, he lowered his head to settle his mouth over hers. He was surprisingly gentle. The kiss was slow and thorough, as if rushing something this sweet would spoil it. Amy sighed, and her lips parted softly, inviting him to kiss her again. Josh complied, and when he'd finished, a low moan escaped from deep within his throat.

"I was afraid of that," he said, on the ragged end of a sigh.

"Of what?"

"You taste like cotton candy...much too sweet."

Amy felt a little breathless, a little shaken and a whole lot confused. In one breath Josh had stated that it was better if they didn't get to know each other any better, and in the next he'd kissed her. Apparently, his mind was just as muddled as hers was.

"Amy, listen—"

"You don't like the taste of cotton candy?" she interrupted, her eyes still closed.

"I like it too much."

"Then maybe we should try kissing one more time...you know...as an experiment."

"That might be a bad idea," Josh countered.

"Why?"

"Trust me, it just could."

"Okay," she murmured, disappointed. He placed his fingertips to the vein that pounded in her throat and his thumb stroked it several times as if he couldn't help touching her.

"On second thought," he whispered, a little breathlessly, "maybe that wouldn't be such a big mistake after all." Once more his mouth settled over hers. His kiss was a leisurely exercise as his lips worked from one side of her lips to the other. The heat he generated within her was enough to melt concrete.

He was so tender, so patient, as if he understood and accepted her lack of experience and had made allowances for it. Timidly, Amy slid her hands up his chest and clasped them behind his neck, and when she leaned into him, her breasts brushed against him. He must have felt them through her thin shirt because he moaned and reluctantly put some space between them.

Amy struggled to breathe normally as she dropped her hands.

"You taste good, too," she admitted. That had to be the understatement of the year. Her knees felt weak, and her heart—well, her heart was another story entirely. It seemed as though it was about to burst out of her chest, it was pounding so hard and fast.

Josh draped his wrists over her shoulders and supported his forehead against hers. For a long time he didn't say a word.

"I've got to get back to the hotel. I have a meeting in half an hour."

Amy nodded; she was disappointed, but she understood.

"Can I see you tomorrow?"

"Yes. What time?" How breathless she sounded. How eager.

"Dinner?"

"Okay."

He suggested a time and place and then left her. Amy stood at the end of the pier, her gaze following Josh for as long as he was within sight, then she turned to face the water, letting the breeze off the churning green waters cool her senses.

With his hands buried deep in his pants pockets, Josh stood at the window of his hotel room and gazed out at the animated city below. His thoughts were heavy, confused.

He didn't know why he was so strongly attracted to Amy Johnson, and then again he did.

All right, he admitted gruffly to himself, she was different. Her openness had caught him off guard. From the first moment he'd seen her, something had stopped him. She had looked so miserable, so troubled. He wasn't in the business of counseling fair maidens, especially blond-haired, blue-eyed ones. Even now he was shocked at the way he'd stood and waited for someone to join her and then did so himself when he was certain she was alone. Somehow, the thought of her being friendless and troubled bothered him more than he could explain, even to himself.

It wasn't his style to play the part of a rescuer. Life was complicated enough without him taking on someone else's problems. He'd convinced himself the best course of action was to turn and walk away.

Then she had looked straight at him, and her slate-blue eyes had been wide with appeal. He had realized almost immediately that although she had been staring in his direction, she wasn't seeing him. Perhaps it was then that he recognized the look she wore. Resignation and defeat flickered from her gaze. It was like looking in a mirror and viewing his reflection from years past.

In Amy he saw a part of himself that he had struggled to put behind him, to bury forever. And there it was, a look in a lovely woman's eyes, and he couldn't refuse her. He waited for a moment, not knowing what to do, if anything, then he had ordered the fish and chips and approached her table.

Now the travel clearance he had been waiting for had arrived. For the past fourteen days, he had been looking for government approval before he headed for the oil-rich fields of Saudi Arabia. By all rights, he should be taking the first available flight out of Seattle. He should forget he had even met Amy Johnson, with the blue angel eyes and the soft, sweet mouth. She wasn't the first woman to attract him, but she was the first to touch a deep part of himself that he'd assumed was beyond reach.

In many ways Josh saw Amy as a complete opposite to himself. She was young and vulnerable. The world hadn't hardened her yet, life hadn't knocked her off her feet and walked over her. Her freshness had been retained, and her honesty was evident in every word she spoke.

Yet, in as many ways as they were different there was an equal number that made them similar. Several years back, Josh had faced an almost identical problem to Amy's. He'd loved his father, too, longed to please him, had been willing to do anything to gain Chance Powell's approval.

It was his father's betrayal that had crippled him.

For Amy's sake, Josh prayed matters would resolve themselves differently for her and her father than they had for him and his own. He couldn't bear the thought of Amy forced to face the world alone.

Moving away from the view of downtown Seattle, Josh sat at the end of his mattress, where his suitcase rested. The problem was, he didn't want to leave Amy. His mistake had been kissing her. It was one thing to wonder what she would feel like in his arms, and something else entirely to have actually experienced her softness.

When he had suggested she tell him what had happened once she talked to her father, he had promised himself it would be the last time. Then he had kissed her, and even before he realized what he had been saying, he had suggested dinner. She had smiled at the invitation, and when she spoke, she had sounded eager to see him again.

Only he wouldn't be there. Josh had decided not to show up for their dinner date. It wouldn't take Amy long to figure out that his visa had been approved and he'd had to leave. He was being cruel in an effort to be kind. Funny, the thought of disappointing her troubled him more than anything he had done in a good long while.

"Amy," her father called, as she rushed down the curved stairway. "Why are you running like a wild anilmal through this house?"

"Sorry, Dad, I'm late," she said with a laugh, because he

tended to exaggerate. She hadn't been running, only hurrying. She didn't want to keep Josh waiting.

"Late for what?"

"My date."

"You didn't mention anything about a dinner date earlier."

"I did, at breakfast."

Her father snorted softly. "I don't remember you saying a word. Who is this man you're seeing? Is he anyone I know?"

"No." She quickly surveyed herself in the hall mirror and, pleased with the result, reached for her jacket.

"Who is this young man?" her father repeated.

"Josh Powell."

"Powell... Powell," Harold echoed. "I can't recall knowing any Powells."

"I met him, Dad, you didn't."

"Tell me about him."

"Dad, I'm already five minutes behind schedule." She grabbed her purse and dutifully kissed him on the cheek.

"You don't want me to know about him? This doesn't sound the least bit like you, Amy. You've dated several young men before, but you've always told me something about them. Now you don't have the time to talk about him to your own father?"

"Dad." She groaned, then realized what he said was partially true. She was afraid he wouldn't approve of her seeing someone like Josh and hoped to avoid the confrontation—a recurring problem with her of late.

Dragging in a deep breath, she turned to face Harold Johnson. "I met Josh on the waterfront the other day. He's visiting Seattle."

"A tourist?"

She nodded, hoping that would satisfy him.

"How long will he be here?"

"I...don't know."

Her father reached for a Havana cigar and stared at the end of it as if that would supply the answers for him. "What aren't you telling me?"

It was all she could do not to groan. She was as readable as a first-grade primer when it came to her father in certain areas, while in others he had a blind eye. "Josh works for one of the oil companies—he didn't mention which one so don't think I'm hiding that. He's waiting for his visa to be approved before he leaves."

"And when will that be?"

"Anytime."

Her father nodded, still gazing at his fat cigar.

"Well?" She threw the question at him. "Aren't you going to tell me not to see him, that he's little more than a drifter and that I'm probably making a big mistake? Josh certainly doesn't sound like the kind of man you'd want me to become involved with."

"No. I'm not going to say a word."

Amy paused to study him. "You're not?"

"I raised you right. If you can't judge a man's character by now, you'll never be able to."

Amy was too shocked to say anything.

"So you like this oil worker?"

"Very much," she whispered.

A smile came over Harold as he reached for a gold lighter. The flames licked at the end of the cigar and he took two deep puffs before he added, "Frankly, I'm not surprised to discover you met someone. Your eyes are as bright as sparklers on the Fourth of July, and you can't get out of this house fast enough."

"I'd leave now if one nosy old man wasn't holding me up by asking me a bunch of silly questions."

"Go on now, and have a good time," he said with a chuckle. "I won't wait up for you."

"Good."

Her father was still chuckling when Amy hurried down the front steps to her car. She felt wonderful. Just when she was convinced her life was at its lowest ebb, she'd met Josh. He was a cool voice of reason that had guided her through the thick fog of her doubts and worries. She had opened up to him in ways she hadn't with others, and in doing so, she had unexpectedly discovered a rare kind of friend. His kiss had stirred up sensations long dormant, and she held those emotions to her chest, savoring them until she was able to see him again.

Fifteen minutes after she left home, Amy walked into the French restaurant near the Pike Place Market. A quick survey of the dim interior confirmed that Josh hadn't arrived yet.

Her heart raced with excitement. She longed for him to kiss her once more, just so she'd know the first time had been real and that she hadn't built it up in her mind.

"May I help you?" the maître d' asked when she stepped into the room.

"I'm meeting someone," Amy explained, taking a seat in the tiny foyer. "I'm sure he'll be along any minute."

The man nodded politely and returned to his station. He paused, glanced in her direction and picked up a white sheet of paper. "Would your name happen to be Amy Johnson?"

"Yes," she said and straightened.

"Mr. Powell phoned earlier with his regrets. It seems he's been called out of town."

Three

"Do you mean he's left?" Amy's voice rose half an octave with the question. A numb feeling worked its way from her heart to the ends of her fingertips.

The maître d' casually shrugged his thin shoulders. "All I know is what the message says."

He handed it to her, and Amy gripped the white slip and glared at the few words that seemed so inadequate. "I see," she murmured. They hadn't exchanged phone numbers so there'd been no way for him to contact her one last time and let her know his clearance had arrived.

"Would you like a table for one?" the maître d' pressed.

Amy glanced at the angular man and slowly shook her head. "No. Thanks." Her appetite vanished the moment she realized Josh wouldn't be joining her.

The man offered her a weak smile as she headed for the door. "Better luck next time."

"Thank you." The evening had turned exceptionally dark, and when Amy glanced toward the sky, she noted that thick gray thunderclouds had moved in. "Just in time," she mumbled toward the heavens. "I didn't think it was ever going to rain again, and if I was ever in the mood for it, it's now."

With her hands buried in the pockets of her long jacket, she started toward her car, which was parked in the lot across the street.

So Josh was gone. He had zoomed in and out of her life with a speed that had left her spinning in its aftermath, and in the process he had touched her in ways that even now she didn't completely understand.

She recalled the first time she had seen him standing above her, holding an order of fish and chips, wanting to know if he could share the picnic table with her. The look in his expressive dark eyes continued to warm her two days later.

Alone now, she stood at the curb, waiting for the light to change, when she heard her name carried in the wind. Whirling around, she noticed someone running toward her with his hand raised. Her heart galloped to her throat when she realized it was Josh. Briefly, she closed her eyes and murmured a silent prayer of thanksgiving. Turning abruptly, she started walking toward him, too happy to care that it had started to rain.

Josh was breathless by the time they met. He stopped jogging three steps away from her, and when he reached her, he wrapped his powerful arms all the way around her waist, half-lifting her from the sidewalk.

His hold was so tight that for a second Amy couldn't breathe, but it didn't matter. Happiness erupted from her, and it was all she could do not to cover his face with kisses.

"What happened?" she cried when her feet were back on the ground.

The rain was coming down in sheets by this time, and

securing his arm around her shoulders, Josh led her into the foyer of the restaurant.

"Ah," the maître d' said, looking pleased. "So your friend managed to meet you after all." He lifted two oblong menus from the holder on the side of the desk and motioned toward the dining room. "This way." His voice took on a formal tone and relayed a heavy French accent that had been noticeably absent earlier.

Once they were seated and presented with the opened menus as if there was insider information from Wall Street to be mindfully studied, Amy looked over to Josh. "What happened?" she asked again. "I thought you'd left town."

His smiling eyes met hers above the menu. "I'm still here."

"Obviously!" She was far more interested in talking to him than scanning the menu. Their waiter arrived and introduced himself as Darrel. Holding his hands prayerfully, he recited the specials of the day, poured their water and generally made a nuisance of himself. By the time he left their table, Amy was growing restless. "Your clearance came through?"

"Yesterday afternoon."

"Then you *are* leaving. When?"

He glanced at his watch as the waiter approached their table once more. "In a few hours."

"Hours," she cried, and was embarrassed when the conversations around them abruptly halted and several heads turned in her direction. Feeling the heat creep into her cheeks, she felt obligated to explain. "I... I wasn't talking about our dinner."

A couple of heads nodded and the talk resumed.

"Would you care to place your order?" Darrel inquired, his eyes darting from Amy to Josh and back again.

"No," she said forcefully. "Could you give us ten more minutes?"

"Of course." He dipped his head slightly and excused himself, looking mildly irritated.

Amy smoothed the white linen napkin onto her lap as the realization hit her that if Josh was scheduled to depart in several hours, then he must have decided earlier not to meet her. But for some unknown reason, he'd changed his mind. "What made you decide to see me?" she asked starkly.

Josh's eyes clashed with hers, and a breathless moment passed before he answered her. "I couldn't stay away."

His answer was honest enough, but it did little to explain his feelings. "But why? I mean why did you want to leave Seattle without saying goodbye?"

"Oh, Amy." He said her name on the end of a troubled sigh, as if he didn't know the answer himself. "It would have been best, I still believe that, but heaven help us both, here I am."

The look in his eyes caused her to grow hot inside, and she reached for her glass, tasting the cool lemon-flavored water.

"I knew the minute I kissed you I was in trouble." He was frowning as he said it, as though he couldn't help regretting that moment.

"Despite what you think, our kissing wasn't a mistake," she said softly, smiling, "It was fate."

"In any case, I'm flying out of Sea-Tac in a little less than seven hours."

Amy's eyes sparked with eagerness as she leaned toward him. "You mean, we have seven whole hours?"

"Yes." Josh didn't seem to share her excitement.

She set her menu aside. "Are you really hungry?"

Josh's gaze narrowed. "I'm...not sure. Why are you looking at me like that?"

"Because if we've got seven hours, I don't think we should waste them sitting in some elegant French restaurant with a waiter named Darrel breathing down our necks."

"What do you suggest?"

"Walking, talking...kissing."

Josh's Adam's apple moved up his throat as his eyes bored straight into hers. "I don't think so... Besides, it's raining." He dismissed her idea with an abrupt look of impatience.

Darrel returned with a linen cloth draped over his forearm, looking more like an English butler than ever.

"I'll have the lamp chops," Josh announced gruffly, handing him the menu. "Rare."

"Escalope de veau florentine," Amy said when their waiter looked expectantly in her direction. She would rather have spent these last remaining hours alone with Josh, but he was apparently going out of his way to avoid that.

Twice now, he'd claimed that kissing her had been problematic, and yet she knew he'd enjoyed the exchange as much as she. In fact he looked downright irritated with himself for having changed his mind about coming this evening. But he'd professed that he couldn't stay away. He was strongly attracted to her, and he didn't like it one bit.

"Amy, would you kindly stop looking at me like that?"

"Like what?" she asked, genuinely confused.

"You're staring at me with my grandmother would call 'bedroom eyes.'"

He was frowning so hard that she laughed out loud. "I am?"

He nodded, looking serious. "Do you realize I'm little

more than a drifter? I could be a mass murderer for all you know."

"But you're not." Their salads arrived and she dipped her fork into the crisp greens.

"The fact that I wander from job to job *should* concern you."

"Why?" She didn't understand his reasoning.

"Because just like that—" he snapped his fingers to emphasize his point "—I'm going to be in and out of your life—I won't see you again after tonight. I don't intend on returning to Seattle. It's a nice place to visit, but I've seen everything I care to, and there isn't any reason for me to stop this way again."

"All right, then let's enjoy the time we have."

He stabbed his salad with a vengeance. "I don't know about you, but I'm having a fantastic time right here and now."

"Josh," she whispered. "Why are you so furious?"

"Because." He stopped and inhaled sharply. "The problem is, I'm experiencing a lot of emotions for you that I have no right feeling. I should never have come here tonight, just the way I should never have kissed you. You're young and sweet, and most likely a virgin."

Despite herself, Amy blushed.

"I knew it," he muttered, setting his salad fork aside and sadly shaking his head. "I just knew it."

"That's bad?"

"Yes," he grumbled, looking more put out than ever. "Don't you understand?"

"Apparently not. I think we should appreciate what we feel for each other and not worry about anything else."

"You make it sound so simple."

"And you're complicating everything. You were there

for me when I needed a friend. I think you're marvelous, and I'm happy to have met you. If we've only got seven hours—" she paused and, after glancing at her watch, amending the time "—six and a half hours left together, then so be it. I can accept that. When you're gone, I'll think fondly of you and our brief interlude. I don't expect anything more from you, Josh, so quit worrying."

He didn't look any less disturbed, but he returned to his salad, centering his concentration there as if this was his last meal and he was determined to enjoy it.

They barely spoke after their entrées arrived. Amy's veal was excellent, and she assumed that Josh's lamb was equally good.

When Darrel carried their plates away, Josh ordered coffee for them both. When the bill arrived, he paid it, but they didn't linger over their coffee.

"The dinner was very good," Amy said, striving to guide them naturally into conversation. "I'm glad you came back, Josh. Thank you."

He looked as if he was tempted to smile. "I've been rotten company. I apologize."

"Saying goodbye is never easy."

"It has been until now," he said, his eyes locking with hers. "You're a special lady, Amy Johnson, don't sell yourself short. Understand?"

Amy wasn't sure that she did. "I won't," she answered.

"You're far more capable than you give yourself credit for. I don't think your father is as blind as you believe. Once you're in the family business and get your feet wet, you may be surprised by how well you do."

"Et tu, Brute?"

Josh chuckled. "Do you want any more coffee?"

She shook her head.

Josh helped her out of her chair and they left the restaurant.

The rain had stopped for the moment, and a few brave stars poked out from behind a thick cluster of threatening clouds.

With her hands in her pockets, Amy stood in front of the restaurant. "Do you want to say goodbye now?" He didn't answer her right away and, disheartened, Amy read that as answer enough. Slowly, she raised her hand to his face and held it against his clean-shaven cheek. "God speed, Joshua Powell." She was about to turn away when he took hold of her wrist and closed his eyes.

"No," he admitted tightly. "I don't want to say goodbye just yet."

"What would you like to do?"

He chuckled. "The answer would make you blush. Let's walk."

He looped her hand in the crook of his elbow and pressed his fingers over her own. Then he led the way down the sidewalk, their destination unknown, at least to her. His natural stride was lengthy, but Amy managed to keep pace with him without difficulty. He didn't seem inclined to talk, which was fine, since there wasn't anything special she wanted to say. It was such a joy just to spend this time with him, to be close to him, knowing that within a matter of hours, he would be gone forever from her life.

After the first couple of blocks, he paused and turned to her. His eyes were wide and restless as they roamed her features, as though setting them to memory.

"Do you want to talk?" she asked, looking around for a place for them to sit down and chat. The area was shadowy, and most of the small businesses had closed for the day. The only illumination available was a dim streetlight situated at the end of the block.

He shook his head. "No," he said evenly, his gaze effectively holding hers. "I want to kiss you."

Amy grinned. "I was hoping you'd say that."

"We shouldn't."

"Oh, I agree one hundred percent. If it was cotton candy the first time, there's no telling what we'll discover the second. Caramel apples? Hot buttered popcorn? Or worst of all—"

He chuckled and silenced her by expertly fitting his mouth over hers. His kiss was so unbelievably tender that it caused her to shiver. His grip tightened, bringing her more fully into the circle of his arms. Amy linked her hands to the base of his neck, leaning into him and letting him absorb the bulk of her weight. She strained upward, standing on the tips of her toes, naturally blossoming open to him the way a flower does to the summer sun.

When they broke apart, they were both trembling.

It had started to rain again, but neither of them seemed to notice. Josh threaded his fingers through her hair as he kissed her once more, rocking his lips slowly back and forth, creating a whole new range of delicious sensations with each small movement.

He shuddered when he finished. "You're much too sweet," he whispered, taking a long series of biting kisses, teasing her with his lips and his tongue.

"So you've said...just don't stop."

"I won't," he promised, and proceeded to show her exactly how much he enjoyed kissing her.

A low moan escaped, and Amy was surprised when she realized the sound had come from her.

"You shouldn't be so warm and giving," Josh continued. He held her close as if loosening his grip would endanger her life.

Amy felt her knees about ready to give. She was a rag doll in his arms. "Josh," she pleaded, caressing the sides of his face and the sharp contours of his jawline.

He continued to mold her softness to him and braced his forehead against hers while he drew in several deep breaths. Amy couldn't stop touching him; it helped root her in reality. Her hands cherished his face. She ran her fingertips up and down his jaw, trying to put the feel of him into her memory, hoping these few short moments would last her for all the time that would follow.

"It's raining," Josh told her.

"I know."

"Cats and dogs."

She smiled.

"You're drenched."

"The only thing I feel is your heart." She flattened her hand over his chest and dropped her lashes at the sturdy accelerated pulse she felt beneath her fingertips.

"If you don't get dry, you could catch cold," he warned as if he were searching for an excuse to send her away.

"I'll chance it."

"Amy, I can't let you do that." He slipped his arm around her shoulders and guided her east, toward the business-packed section of the downtown area. "I'm taking you to my hotel room. You're going to dry yourself off, and then I'm going to give you a sweater of mine."

"Josh…"

"From there, I'll walk you to your car. We'll be in and out of that hotel room in three minutes flat. Understand?"

Her eyes felt huge. He didn't trust himself to be alone with her in his room, and the thought warmed her from the inside out. Amy didn't need his sweater or a towel or anything else, but she wasn't about to tell him that.

By the time they reached the lobby of his hotel, her hair was so wet that it was dripping on the carpet. She was certain she resembled a drowned muskrat.

Josh's room was on the eighteenth floor. He opened the door for her and switched on the light. The suite was furnished with a king-size bed, chair, television and long dresser. His airline ticket rested on the dresser top, and her gaze was automatically drawn to that. The ticket forcefully reminded her that Josh would soon be out of her life. The drapes were open, and the view of the Seattle skyline was sweeping and panoramic.

"This is nice," she said, smiling at him.

"Here." He handed her a thick towel, which she used to wipe the moisture from her face and hair.

"What about you?" she asked, when she'd finished.

He stood as far away from her as he possibly could and still remain in the same room. His eyes seemed to be everywhere but on her.

"I'm fine." He scooted past her, keeping well out of her way. His efforts to avoid brushing against her were just short of comical. He seemed to breathe again once he was safely out of harm's way. From the way he was acting, one would suspect she carried bubonic plague. He opened the closet and took out a long-sleeved sweater. "There's a mirror in the bathroom if you need it."

She actually did want to run a comb through her hair and moved into the other room.

"Do you remember the other day when you asked me if I didn't go in to my father's business what I wanted to do instead?"

"I remember." His voice sounded a long way off, as though he was on the other side of the room.

"I've given the question some thought in the last few days."

"What have you come up with?"

She stuck her head around the door. She was right; Josh stood with his back to her in front of the windows, although she doubted that he was appreciating the view. "If I tell you, do you promise not to laugh?"

"I'll try."

She eased his sweater over her head and smoothed it around her hips, then gingerly stepped into the room, hands dangling awkwardly at her sides. "In light of all the advancements in the feminist movement, this is going to sound ridiculous."

"Try me." He folded his arms over his broad chest and waited.

"More than anything, I'd like to be a wife and a stay-at-home mother." She watched him carefully, half expecting him to find something humorous in her confession. Instead, his gaze gentled and he smiled.

"I treasure the memories of my mother," she continued. "She was so wonderful to me and Dad, so loving and supportive of everything we did. I've already explained my father's personality, so you know what he's like. Mom was the glue that held our family together. Her love was the foundation that guided him in those early years. I don't know if she ever visited his office, in fact, I rather doubt that she did, and yet he discussed every decision with her. She was his support system, his rock. She was never in the limelight, but she was a vital part of Dad's life, and his business."

"You want to be like her?"

Amy nodded. "Only I'm more greedy. I want a house full of children, too."

Josh's gaze moved deliberately to his watch. "I think we'd better go," he said, sounding oddly breathless.

"Josh?"

He stiffened. "I promised you we'd be in and out of here in a matter of minutes. Remember?"

"I'd like to stay."

"No," he said forcefully, shaking his head. "Amy, please, try to understand. Being alone with you is temptation enough—don't make it any more difficult."

"What about the sweater?" She ran her fingers down the length of the sleeves. "Won't you want it back?"

"Keep it. Where I'm headed it's going to be a hundred degrees in the shade. Trust me, I'm not going to miss it."

"But—"

"Amy!" Her name was a husky rumble low in his chest. "Unless you'd like to start that family you're talking about right now, I suggest we get out of here."

"Soon," she told him firmly, refusing to give in to the shock value of his statement.

Twin brows arched. "Soon?" he repeated incredulously.

"Come here." Her back was pressed against the door, and her heart was pounding so hard that it had long since drowned out what reason remained to her. She had never been so bold with a man in her life, but she knew if she was ever going to act, the time was now. Otherwise, Josh was going to politely walk her to her car, kiss her on the cheek and wish her a good life and then casually stroll away from her and out of her world.

"Amy." His mouth thinned with impatience.

"Say goodbye to me here," she said, smiling, then she motioned with her index finger for him to come to her.

He shoved his hands into his jeans pockets as if he didn't trust them to keep still at his sides. He paused and cleared his throat. "It really is time we left."

"Fine. All I'm asking is for you to say our farewells here. It will be much better than in a parking lot outside the restaurant, don't you think?"

"No." The lone word was harsh and low.

She shrugged and hoped she looked regretful. "All right," she murmured and sighed. "If you won't come to me, then I guess I'll have to go to you."

Josh looked shocked by this and held out his hand as if he were stopping traffic.

The action did more to amuse her than keep her at bay. "I'm going to say goodbye to you, Joshua Powell. And I'm warning you right now, it's going to be a kiss you'll remember for a good long while."

Everything about Josh told her how much he wanted her. From the moment they had stepped into his room the tension between them had been electric. She didn't understand why he was putting up such a fight. For her part, she was astonished by her own actions. Until she had met Josh, she had always been the timid, reserved one in a relationship. Two minutes alone with him and she had turned into a hellcat. She wasn't sure what had caused the transformation.

"Amy, please, you aren't making this easy," Josh muttered. "We're playing with a lighted fuse here, don't you understand that? If I kiss you, sweetheart, I promise you it won't stop there. Before either of us will know how it happened, you're going to be out of that dress and my hands are going to be places where no one else has ever touched you. Understand?"

She felt the blood drain out of her face as quickly as if

someone had pulled a drain from a sink. Blindly, she nodded. Still, it didn't stop her from easing her way toward him.

Josh groaned. "I knew it was a mistake to bring you up here." His face was tight, his eyes dark and brilliant. "We're going to end up making love, and you're going to give me something I don't want. Save it for your husband, sweetheart, he'll appreciate it more than I will."

Her heart went crazy. It felt like a herd of charging elephants was stampeding inside her chest. She moistened her lips, and whatever audacity had propelled her into this uncharacteristic role abruptly left her at the threat in his words. Pausing, she drew in a deep, calming breath and forced a smile.

"Goodbye, Josh," she whispered. With that, she turned and bolted for the door.

He caught her shoulder and catapulted her around and into his chest before she made it another step. He cursed under his breath and locked her in his arms, rubbing his chin back and forth over the crown of her head in a caressing action, silently apologizing for shocking her.

"Oh, Amy," he groaned, "perhaps you're right. Maybe it *is* fate." She felt his warm breath against the hollow beneath her right ear.

Her head fell back in a silent plea, and he began spreading warm kisses over the delicate curve of her neck. With his hands holding each side of her face, he ran his lips along the line of her jaw, his open mouth moist and passionate. When she was sure he meant to torment her for hours before giving her what she craved, he lowered his mouth to hers, softly, tenderly in a kiss that was as gentle as the flutter of a hummingbird's wings. A welcoming rasping sound tumbled from her lips.

He made a low, protesting noise of his own as his lips

caressed hers, tasted her, savored her, his mouth so hot and compelling that she felt singed all the way to the soles of her feet. When they broke apart, they were both breathless.

"Amy... I tried to tell you."

"Shh." She kissed him to silence his objections. She had no regrets and longed to erase his. "I want you to touch me...it feels so good when you do."

"Oh, angel, you shouldn't say things like that to a man."

"Not any man," she whispered, "only you."

Josh inhaled a sharp breath. "That doesn't make it any better."

"Why don't you just shut up and kiss me again?"

"Because," he growled, "I want so much more." He ground his mouth over hers as if to punish her for making him desire her so much.

Amy bit into her lower lip at the powerful surge of sensations that assaulted her like a tidal wave. Before she knew what was happening, he had removed the sweater he had given her to wear. His fingers were poised at the zipper at the back of her dress when he paused, his breathing labored. Then, with a supreme effort, he brought his strong loving hands to either side of her face, stroking her satiny cheeks with the pads of his thumbs.

"It's time to stop, Amy. I meant what I said about saving yourself for your husband. I won't be coming back to Seattle."

She dipped her head and nodded, accepting his words. "Yes, I know." Gently she raised her lips to his and kissed him goodbye. But she kept her promise. She made sure it was a kiss Joshua Powell would well remember.

Josh secured the strap of his flight bag to his shoulder and glanced a second time at his watch. He still had thirty minutes before he could board the plane that would carry him to his destination in Kadiri. He had been filled with excitement, eager for the challenge that awaited him in this Middle Eastern country, and now he would have gladly forfeited his life savings for an excuse to remain in Seattle.

His mind was filled with doubts. He had said goodbye to Amy several hours earlier and already he was being eaten alive, caught between the longing to see her again and the equally strong desire to forget they had ever met.

His biggest mistake had been trusting himself alone with her in his hotel room. The temptation had been too much for him, and she certainly hadn't helped matters any. The woman was a natural-born temptress, and she didn't even know it. She couldn't so much as walk across the room without making him want her. All his life, he would remember her leaning against his door and motioning for him to come to her with her index finger. She was so obviously new to the game that her efforts should have been more humorous than exciting. Unfortunately, everything about her excited him.

To complicate matters, she was innocent. When she started talking about building a secure home life for her husband and wanting children, he knew that she was completely out of his league. They were as different as fresh milk and aged Scotch. She was hot dogs and baseball and freshly diapered babies. And he was rented rooms, a dog-eared passport and axle grease.

He had to bite his tongue to keep from asking for her number. He didn't often think of himself as noble, but he did now. The sooner he left Amy, the sooner he could return to his disorderly vagabond lifestyle.

However, Josh was confident of one thing—it would be a long time before he forgot her.

As Josh stood in the security line at SeaTac Airport he checked the flight time and gate number on his ticket.

"Josh."

He jerked around to discover Amy hurrying down the concourse toward him. For one wild second, Josh didn't know if he should be pleased or not.

It didn't take him long to decide.

Four

"Amy." Josh rushed out of the line at security and gripped her shoulders as his eyes scanned hers. "What are you doing here?" She was still breathless and it took her several moments to speak. "I know I shouldn't...have come, but I couldn't stay home and...and let it all end so abruptly."

"Amy, listen to me—"

"I know." She pressed the tips of her fingers over his lips, not wanting him to speak. He couldn't say anything that she hadn't already told herself a dozen times or more. "I'm doing everything wrong, but I couldn't bear to just let you walk out of my life without—"

"We already said goodbye."

"I know that, too," she protested.

"How'd you know where to find me?"

"I saw your airline ticket on the dresser, and once I knew which airline, it wasn't difficult to figure out which secrurity checkpoint you'd be going through. Oh, Josh, I'm sorry if this embarrasses you." She was so confused, hot and cold at the same time. Hot from his kisses and cold with apprehension. She was making a complete idiot of herself, but after weighing her options, she'd done the only thing she could.

"Here," she said, thrusting an envelope toward him.

"What's this?"

"In case you change your mind."

"About what?" His brow condensed with the question.

"About ever wanting to see me again. It's my contact information, and for good measure I threw in a flattering photo of myself, but it was taken several years ago when my hair was shorter and…well, it's not much, but it's the best I have."

He chuckled and hauled her into his arms, squeezing her close.

"You don't have to email me," she told him, her voice steady with conviction.

"I probably won't."

"That's fine…well, it isn't, but I can accept that."

"Good."

He didn't seem inclined to release her, but buried his face in her neck and drew in a short breath. "Your scent is going to haunt me," he grumbled. "I'm going halfway around the world and all I'll think about is you."

"Good." Her smile was weak at best. She'd done everything she could by pitching the ball to him. If and when he decided to swing at it, she would be ready.

The security guard tapped him on the shoulder. "Are you going or not, cause you're blocking the line." Moving over slightly, Josh wrapped her in a warm embrace, he brushed his hand across her cheek, his touch was tender, as though he was caressing a newborn baby. "I have to go," he said, his voice low and gravelly.

"Yes, I know." Gently she smoothed his sweater at his shoulders and offered him a feeble smile. "Enjoy the Middle East," she said, "but stay away from those belly dancers."

Amy dropped her arms and stuffed her hands inside her

pockets for fear she would do something more to embarrass them both. Something silly like reaching out and asking him not to leave, or pleading with him to at least contact her.

She did her utmost to beam him a polished smile. If he was going to hold on to the memory of her, she wanted to stand tall and dignified and give him a smile that would make Miss America proud. "Have a safe trip."

He nodded, turned and took two steps away from her.

Panic filled Amy—there was one last thing she had to say. "Josh." At the sound of her voice, he abruptly turned back. "Thank you...for everything."

He offered her a weak smile.

She nodded, because saying anything more would have been impossible. She kept her head tilted at a proud angle, determined to send him off with a smile.

"Amy." Her name was a low growl as Josh dropped his flight bag and stepped toward her.

"Go on," she cried. "You'll miss your plane."

He was at her side so fast she didn't have time to think or act. He hauled her into his arms and kissed her with a hunger and need that were enough to convince her she would never find another man who made her feel the things this one did. His wild kiss was ardent, but all too brief to suit either of them.

Josh pulled himself away from her with some effort, picked up his bag and headed into the security checkpoint. Amy stood frozen to the spot he'd left her, following him with her eyes, until he was out of sight, her head demanding that she forget Joshua Powell and her heart claiming it was impossibile.

Harold Johnson was sitting in the library smoking a cigar when Amy quietly let herself into the house. The lights from the crack beneath the door alerted her to the fact her father was up and waiting for her return.

"Hi," she said, letting herself into the room. She sat in the wingback leather chair beside him and peeled off her coat. Slipping off her shoes, she tucked her feet beneath her and rested her eyes.

"You're back."

She nodded. "I saw Josh off at the airport. I gave him all my contact information and for good measure a photo of myself."

"Smart idea."

"According to Josh it was a mistake. I can't understand why he thinks that way, but he does. He made it clear he has no intention of keeping in touch."

"Can you accept that?"

To Amy's way of thinking, she didn't have a choice. "I'll have to."

Her father's low chuckle was something of a surprise. "I don't mind telling you that your interest in this young man is poetic justice."

"Why's that?"

"All these years, there've been boys buzzing around this house like bees in early summer, but you didn't pay a one of them a moment's heed. For all the interest you showed, they could have been made of marble."

"None of them was anything like Josh."

"What makes this one so different?" her father asked, chewing on the end of his cigar.

Amy swore he ate more of it than he smoked. "I don't know what to tell you. Josh is forthright and honest—to a fault sometimes. He's the type of man I'd want by my side if anything was ever to go wrong. He wouldn't back away from a fight, but he'd do everything within his power to see that matters didn't get that far."

"I'd like him, then."

"I know you would, Dad, you wouldn't be able to stop yourself. He's direct and sincere."

"Pleasant to look at, I suspect."

She smiled and nodded. "He wears his hair a little longer than what you'd like, though."

"Hair doesn't make the man." Harold Johnson puffed at the cigar and reached for his glass of milk.

"What are you doing up this late?" she asked after a moment of comfortable silence.

"After we talked when you came home from dinner, I heard you roaming around your bedroom for an hour or two, pacing back and forth loud enough to wake the birds. About the time I decided to find out what was troubling you, I heard you leave. Since I was awake, I decided to read a bit, and by the time I noticed the hour, it wasn't worth going back to bed."

"I'm sorry I kept you awake."

"No problem." He paused and yawned loudly, covering his mouth with the back of his hand. "Maybe I *will* try to get in an hour or two of rest before heading for the office."

"Good idea." Amy hadn't realized how exhausted she was until her father mentioned it.

They walked up the stairs together and she kissed his cheek when she reached her bedroom door. "Sally and I are playing tennis tomorrow morning, and then I'm doing some volunteer work at the homeless center later in the afternoon. You didn't need me for anything, did you?"

"No. But I thought you were going to take the summer off?"

"I am," she said, and yawned. "Trust me, Dad, tennis is hard work."

Josh had never been fond of camels. They smelled worse than rotting sewage, were ill-tempered and more stubborn than mules. The beasts were the first thing Josh saw as he stepped off his small plane that had delivered him to the oil fields. He had the distinct impression this country was filled with them. And soldiers. Each and every one of them seemed to be carting a machine gun. A cantankerous camel strolled across the runway followed by two shouting men waving sticks and cursing in Arabic.

Joel Perkins, Josh's direct superior and best friend, was supposed to meet him in the crowded Kadiri airport. Kadiri was a small town rich in oil. The company that employed Josh had recently signed a contract for oil exploration and drilling with the Saudi government.

It was like stepping back in time when Josh stepped off the plane. The terminal, if the building could be termed that, was filled with animals and produce and so crowded that Josh could barely move.

Ten minutes in this part of the country and already his clothes were plastered to his skin; the temperature must have been over a hundred degrees inside, and no telling what it was in the direct sunlight.

At six foot four, Joel Perkins was head and shoulders above most everyone, so it was easy enough for Josh to spot his friend. Making his way over to him, however, was another matter entirely.

"Excuse me," Josh said twenty times as he scooted around caged chickens, crying children and several robed men.

"Good to see you," Joel greeted him, and slapped his hand across Josh's back. "How was the flight?"

"From Seattle to Paris was a piece of cake. From Paris to Kadiri...you don't want to hear about it, trust me."

Joel laughed. "But you're here now and safe."

"No thanks to that World War II wreck of a plane that just landed."

"As you can see, the taxis are out of service," Joel explained. "We're going to have to ride into the city on these."

Josh took one look at the ugliest-looking camel he had ever encountered and let out an expletive that would have curled Amy's hair. He stopped abruptly. Every thought that drifted through his mind was in some way connected to her. He hadn't stopped thinking of her for a single minute. Every time he closed his eyes, it was her lips that smiled at him, her blue eyes that flashed with eagerness, her arms that reached toward him.

What he had said to her about her scent haunting him had been prophetic. In fact, he had strolled along the streets of Paris until he had found a small fragrance shop. It took him an hour to discover the perfume that reminded him of her. Feeling like a fool for having wasted the proprietor's time, he ended up buying a bottle. He didn't know what he was going to do with it. Mail it to his seventy-year-old Aunt Hazel?

"What's the matter?" Joel asked. "Has the heat gotten to you already?"

"No," Josh said. "A woman has."

Joel's eyes revealed his surprise. "A woman? Where?"

"Seattle."

Joel laughed.

"What's so funny?" Josh demanded.

"You. It does me good to see you aren't as immune as you'd like others to believe."

Josh muttered under his breath, regretting saying anything about Amy to his friend.

Joel slapped him across the back as his eyes grew dark and serious. "Are you going to do anything about it?"

Josh didn't need to think before he answered. "Not a damn thing."

Joel expelled his breath in a slow exercise. "Good. You had me worried there for a minute."

A week later, Josh had changed Joel Perkins's mind.

Exhausted, Amy let herself in the back door of her home. Her face was red, and she wiped it dry with the small white towel draped around her neck. Her tennis racket was in one hand, and after securing it under her arm, she poured herself a tall glass of iced tea.

"Manuela, is the mail here?"

"Nothing for you, Miss Amy," the Spanish-American housekeeper informed her.

Amy tried to swallow the disappointment, but it was growing increasingly difficult. Josh had been gone nearly two weeks, and she'd hoped to hear from him before now. No emails, no messages. She'd hoped he at least might write. Nothing yet and she was beginning to believe she wouldn't hear from him. The thought deeply depressed her.

Her phone rang, as she went to answer it she noted that the display read private. "Hello," she said, walking out of the kitchen. Her words were followed by an eerie hum. Amy blinked and was about to disconnect when someone spoke.

"Amy, is that you?"

Her heart raced into her throat. "Josh?"

"What time is it there? I wasn't sure of the time difference and I hope it isn't the middle of the night."

"It's not. It's three in the afternoon."

He sounded so different. So far away, but that didn't detract from the exhilaration she was experiencing from hearing the sound of his voice.

"I'm so glad you called," she said softly, slumping into her father's desk chair. "I've been miserable, wondering if you ever would. I'd just about given up hope."

"It was Joel's idea."

"Joel?"

"He's a friend of mine. He claimed that if I didn't call you, he would. Said I had my mind on you when I should be thinking about business. I guess he's right."

"If he were close by, I'd kiss him."

"If you're going to kiss anyone, Amy Johnson, it's me, understand?"

"Yes, sir."

"What's the weather like?"

"Seventy-five and balmy. I just finished playing two sets of tennis. I've been doing a lot of that lately… If I'm exhausted, then I don't think of you so much. What's the weather like in Kadiri?"

"You don't want to know. A hundred and five about ten this morning."

"Oh, Josh. Are you going to be all right?"

"Probably not, but I'll live." There was some commotion and then Josh came back on the line. "Joel's here, and he said I should email you."

Her heartbeat slowed before she asked, "Is that what you want?"

An eternity passed before he responded. "I don't know what I want anymore. At one time everything was clear to me, but after two weeks, I'm willing to admit I was a fool to think I could forget you. Yes, Amy, I'll be in touch. I'll try and get a message off to you now and again, but I'm not making any promises."

"I understand."

"Listen, I put something in the mail for you the other day, but it'll take a week or more before it arrives—if it ever does. The way everything else goes around here, I doubt that it'll make it through customs intact."

"Something from Kadiri?"

"No, actually, I picked this up in Paris."

"Oh, Josh, you were thinking of me in Paris?"

"That's the problem, I never stopped thinking about you." Once more there was a quick exchange of muffled words before Josh came back on the line. "Joel seemed to think it's important for you to know that I haven't been the best company the last couple of weeks."

Amy closed her eyes, savoring these moments. "Thank Joel for letting me know."

"Be sure and tell me if that package arrives. If it does, there's something else I'd like to send you, something from Kadiri." His words were followed by heavy static.

"Josh. Josh," she cried, certain she'd lost him.

"I'm here, but I can't say for how much longer."

"This is probably costing you a fortune."

"Don't worry about it. Joel's springing for the call."

A faint laugh could be heard in the distance, and Amy smiled, knowing already that she was going to like Josh's friend.

"As soon as you contact me I'll email you back, I promise." It was on the tip of her tongue to tell him how much she had thought about him and missed him since he'd left. Twice now, she had gone down to the waterfront and stood at the end of the pier where he had first kissed her, hoping to recapture those precious moments.

"I swear living in Kadiri is like stepping into the eighteenth century. This phone is the only one within a hundred miles, so there isn't any way to reach me."

"I understand."

"Amy, listen." Josh's voice was filled with regret. "I've got to go. Joel's apparently bribed a government official to use this phone, and we're about to get kicked out of here."

"Oh, Josh, do be careful."

"Honey," he said, and laughed. "I was born careful."

At that precise moment, the line was severed.

Amy sat down at the dinner table across from her father and smoothed the napkin across her lap, feeling warm and happy.

"So you got another email from Josh today?"

"Yes," she said, glancing up. "How'd you know?"

"You mean other than that silly grin you've been wearing all afternoon? Besides, you haven't played tennis all week, and before his phone call, you spent more time on the tennis courts than you did at home."

Amy reached for the lean pork roast and speared herself an end cut. "I don't know what tennis has to do with Joshua Powell."

Her father snickered softly. He knew her too well for her to disguise her feelings.

"Little things say a lot, remember that when you start working at the end of the summer. That small piece of advice will serve you well."

"I will," she murmured, handing him the meat platter, avoiding his gaze.

"Now," her father said forcefully, "when am I going to meet this young man of yours?"

"I... I don't know, Dad. Josh hasn't written a word about when he's leaving Kadiri. He could be there for several months—perhaps longer. I have no way of knowing."

Her father set the meat platter aside, then paused and rested his elbows on the table, clasping his hands together. "How do you feel about that?"

"I don't understand."

"I notice you're not dating anyone. Fact is, you've been

living like a nun. Don't you think it's time to start social-
izing a little?"

"No." Her mind was too full of Josh to consider going
out with another man, although she was routinely asked.
Not once in all the weeks since Josh had left Seattle had the
thought of dating anyone else entered her mind.

Harold Johnson brooded during the remainder of their
meal. Amy knew that look well. It preceded a father-to-
daughter chat in which he would tell her something "for
her own good." This time she was certain the heart-to-heart
talk would have to do with Josh.

Amy didn't have a single argument prepared. Harold was
absolutely right, she barely knew Joshua Powell. She'd seen
him a grand total of three times—four if she counted the fact
they'd met twice that first day and five if she included her har-
ried trip to the airport. It wouldn't have mattered if she'd seen
him every day for six months, though. But her father wouldn't
understand that. As far as Amy was concerned, she knew
everything important that she needed to know about him.

When their talk was over, Amy went to her room, took
out her computer and read the email she'd received and
sat on the bed.

Dear Amy,

I opened your email this morning. There are no words to tell
you how pleased I was to see it. It seems weeks since we
talked on the phone, and with Joel standing over me, it was
difficult to tell you the things that have been going through
my head. Now, as I sit down to type, I realize it isn't any
easier to find the words. I never was much good with this
sort of thing. I work well with numbers and with my hands,
but when it comes to expressing my feelings, I'm at a loss.

I suppose I should admit how glad I was to see you at the

airport. As I headed to the airport to catch my flight I told myself it was best to make a clean break. Then, all of a sudden, you were there and despite everything, I was thrilled you came. I still can't believe you came and how you knew when and where to find me. Anyways like I said before, I'm not much good at this. Email be back when you can.

Love, Josh

Needing to think about her response, Amy waited a day to reply.

Dearest Josh,

The perfume arrived in today's mail. The fragrance is perfect for me. Where did you ever find it? The minute I opened the package, I dabbed some behind my ear and closed my eyes, imagining you were here with me. I know it sounds silly, but I felt so close to you at that moment, as if it was your fingers spreading the fragrance at my pulse points, holding me close. Thank you.

Today was a traumatic one for me. Dad brought me in to work with him to show me how he'd had an office completely remodeled for me. It was so plush, so... I don't know, elaborate. Everything was done in a dark wood, mahogany I think. I swear the desk had to be six feet long. I don't suppose this means that much unless you've ever seen my dad's office. He's used the same furniture for twenty years... same office assistant, too. At any rate, everything about my dad's office shouts humble beginnings, hard work and frugality. He should be the one with the fancy furniture—not me. I swear the guilt was more than I could bear.

It made me realize that the clock is ticking and I won't be able to delay telling him my feelings much longer. I've got to tell him...only I don't know how. I wish you were here. You made me feel so confident that I'm doing the right thing. I don't feel that anymore. Now all I am is confused and alone.

Love, Amy

P.S. You haven't been seeing any belly dancers, have you?

Dearest Angel Eyes,

I swear this country is the closest thing to hell on earth. The heat is like nothing I've ever known. Last night, for the first time since I arrived, Joel and I went swimming. We were splashing around like a couple of five-year-olds. The whole time I was wishing it was you with me instead of Joel.

Later I lay on the sand and stared at the sky. The stars were so bright, they seemed to droop right out of the heavens. I had the feeling if I reached up I could snatch one right out of the sky. First chance I get I rush to my computer at the end of the day and I'm happy as a kid in a candy store when an email arrives from you. Then the next thing I know I'm gazing at the stars, wondering if you're staring at them, too. What have you done to me, Amy Johnson?

Joel keeps feeding me warnings. He tells me a woman can be too much of a distraction, and that I've got to keep my head screwed on straight. He's right. We're not exactly here on a picnic. Don't worry about me, if I'm anything it's cautious.

I put a surprise in the mail for you today. This is straight from the streets of Kadiri. Let me know when it arrives.

Love, Josh

P.S. No, I haven't seen any belly dancers. What about you? Any guys from the country club wanting you for doubles on the tennis courts?

My dearest Josh,

I love seeing the picture of you and Joel. You look so tan and so handsome. It made me miss you all the more. I sat down and studied the photo for so long the image started to blur. I miss you so much, it seems that we barely had a chance to know each other and then you were gone. Don't mind me for complaining. I'm in a blue funk today. Dad took me to lunch so I could meet the others from the office and when I jumped on the computer I saw your email.

It made me wish I could sit down and talk to you.

By the way, Joel's so tall. I'm pleased he's there with you. Thanks, too, for your vote of confidence in handling this situation with Dad. He seems oblivious to my feelings. Come September, I probably will move into my fancy new office because I can't honestly see myself confronting him. My fate is sealed.

Your Angel Eyes

It was one of those glorious summer afternoons that blesses the Pacific Northwest every August. Unable to resist the sun, Amy was venting her energy by doing laps in the pool.

"Miss Amy, Miss Amy!"

Manuela came running toward the pool, her hands flying. She stopped, breathless, and a flurry of Spanish erupted from her so fast and furiously that even after two years of studying the language, Amy couldn't make out a single word.

"Manuela," she protested, stepping out of the pool. She reached for her towel. "What are you saying?"

"You left your phone on the counter…long distance… man say hurry."

Amy's heart did a tiny flip-flop. "Is it Josh?"

The housekeeper's hands gestured to the sky as she broke into her native tongue again.

"Never mind," Amy cried, running toward the phone in her hand. "Josh... Josh, are you still there?"

"Amy? Who answered the phone? I couldn't understand a word she said."

"That's Manuela. I'm sorry it took me so long. How are you? Oh, Josh, I miss you so much."

"I miss you, too, angel. I read your email from yesterday, and I haven't been able to stop thinking about you since."

"I was in such a depressed state when I wrote that... I should never have pressed the Send button."

"I'm glad you did. Now, tell me what's happening between you and your father."

"Josh, I can't—not over the phone."

"You're going to work for him?"

"I can't see any way out of it. Are you going to think me a coward?"

"My Angel Eyes? Never."

"I figured the least I could do was give it a try. I don't hold out much hope, but who knows, I might shock everyone and actually be successful."

"You sound in better spirits."

"I am...now. Oh, before I forget, the traditional dress from Kadiri arrived, and I love it. It's so colorful and cool. What did you say the women call it again?"

"Btu-btu."

"I wore it all last night, and the whole time I had this incredible urge to walk around the house pounding drums and singing 'Kumbah Ya.'"

Josh laughed, and the sound did more to elevate Amy's mood than anything in two long months.

"Amy, listen, I've only got a few more minutes. We were

able to get use of the phone again, but I don't know how long it's good for so if we're cut off again, don't worry."

She nodded before she realized he couldn't see her gesture of understanding. She closed her eyes to keep the ready emotion cornered. "I can't tell you how good it is to hear your voice."

"Yours, too, Angel Eyes."

She laughed. "I loved the picture of you and Joel. Thank you so much for sending it. You look even better than I remember."

"I'm coming back to Seattle."

Amy's head snapped up. "When? Oh, Josh, you don't know how many times I prayed you would."

"Don't get so excited, it won't be until December."

"December," she repeated. "I can wait another five months...easy. How about you?"

"I swear to you, Amy, I don't know anymore. I've never felt about a woman the way I do about you. Half the time I'm so confused by what's happening between us that I can't understand how this company can pay me the money it does. Joel keeps threatening to fire me; he claims he doesn't need anyone as lovesick as me on his crew."

Lovesick. It was the closest Josh had ever come to admitting what he felt for her.

"Hold on a minute," Josh shouted. He came back on the line almost immediately. "Honey, I've got to go. I'm thinking about you, angel—"

"Josh... Josh," she cried, "listen to me. I love you."

But the line had already gone dead.

A man could only take so much, Josh reasoned as he walked among the huge drilling structures that had been brought into Kadiri by SunTech Oil. Joel, acting as general foreman, had left his instructions with Josh, but Josh had been running into one confounding problem after another all morning. There wasn't any help for it. Josh was going to have to find Joel and discuss the situation.

It was as he was walking across the compound that he heard the first explosion. The force of it was powerful enough to hurl him helplessly to the ground.

By the time he gathered his wits, men had panicked and were running, knocking each other down, fighting their way toward the gates.

"Joel," Josh cried when he didn't see his friend. Josh searched the frantic, running crowd, but battling through the workers was as difficult as swimming up a waterfall.

"Joel," Josh shouted a second time, then grabbed a man he recognized by the collar. "Where's Joel Perkins?"

The trembling man pointed toward the building that was belching smoke and spitting out flames from two sides. Something drove Josh forward. Whatever it was had nothing to do with sanity or reason or anything else. The only conscious thought Josh had was the brutal determination to go inside and bring out his friend.

Two men tried to stop him, screaming a word that Josh found unintelligible. Covering his mouth with a wet cloth, Josh shoved them both aside with a superhuman strength, then, without thought, stormed into the building.

He recognized two things almost immediately. The first was that Joel Perkins was dead. The second was more devastating than the first. The building was going to explode, and there was nothing he could do to get himself out alive.

Five

"Amy."

Her father's gentle voice stirred her from a light sleep. She rolled over onto her back to discover him sitting on the edge of her bed, dressed in his plaid robe, his brow puckered in a dark frown. He'd turned on her bedside lamp to its lowest setting.

"Dad?" she asked, softly. "What is it?"

His eyes pooled with regret, and instantly she knew.

"It's Josh, isn't it?"

Her father nodded. "The call came an hour ago."

He'd waited an hour. A full hour? Struggling into a sitting position, she brushed the hair from her temples, her hands trembling. She hadn't heard from him in almost two weeks and had already started to worry. Her heart had told her something was wrong.

"Tell me," she whispered. Her tongue felt thick and uncooperative, but she had to know even if it meant she'd lost him forever. "What's happened?"

Harold Johnson placed his hands on her shoulders. "He's been seriously injured. There was an accident, an explosion. Five men were killed. Josh wasn't hurt in the initial explosion, but he went back for his friend. Apparently, he was too late; his friend was already dead."

Amy covered her mouth with her palm and took in deep, even breaths in an effort to curtail the growing alarm that churned in her like the huge blades of a windmill, stirring up dread and fear. "But he's alive."

"Yes, baby, he's alive, but just barely. I can't even tell you the extent of his injuries, only that they're life threatening."

Fear coated her throat. "How did SunTech Oil know to contact me?" Whatever the reason, she thanked God they had. Otherwise, she might never have known.

Her father gently brushed the hair from her brow, his eyes tender and concerned. "Josh listed you as his beneficiary in case of his death. Since he hadn't written down anyone as next of kin, yours was the only name they had. I can't tell you any more than that. The line was terrible, and it was difficult to understand anything of what the official was saying."

Without waiting for anything more, Amy tossed back the covers. "I'm going to him."

Her father shook his head meaningfully. "Somehow I knew you'd say that."

"Then I suppose you also knew I'd want the next flight out of here for Kadiri?" She paused and thought for a moment. "What about a visa?"

"As a matter of fact, I thought of both those things," he admitted, chuckling softly. "There's a connecting plane in Paris, but the only flight into Kadiri flies on Wednesdays."

"But that means I'll have to wait an entire week." She used her thumb and index finger to cup her chin and frowned. "Then I'll get to Paris and hire a private plane to fly me into Saudi Arabia. If I have to, I'll walk from there."

"That won't be necessary," Harold told her.

"Why not?" She whirled around, not understanding.

"You can take the company jet. I'm not sending you off to that part of the world without a means of getting you out of there."

Despite the severity of the situation she smiled, tears glistening in her eyes. "Thank you, Dad."

"And while I was at it, I talked to a friend of mine in the State Department. You've been granted a six-week visa, but you won't be able to stay any longer—our relations with the Middle East are strained at best. Get in and out of there as fast as you can. Understand?"

Her mind was buzzing. "Is there anything else I need to know?"

"Yes," Harold said firmly. "When you come home, I want Josh with you."

When Josh awoke, the first thing that met him was pain so ruthless and severe that for a moment he couldn't breathe. He groaned and dragged in a deep breath, trying to come to terms with the fact that he was alive and not knowing how much longer he wanted to live if being alive meant this excruciating pain. Blissfully, he returned to unconsciousness.

The second time, he was greeted with the same agony, only this time there was a scent of jasmine in the air. Josh struggled to hold on to consciousness. The flower brought Amy to the forefront of his mind. His last thoughts before the building exploded had been of his Angel Eyes, and regret had filled him at the thought of never seeing her again. Perhaps it had been that thought that had persuaded death to give him a second chance. Whatever it was, Josh was grateful. At least, he thought he was, until the pain thrust him into a dark world where he felt nothing.

Time lost meaning. Days, weeks, months could have silently slipped past without him ever realizing it. All he experienced were brief glimpses of consciousness, followed by blackouts for which he was always grateful, because they released him from the pain.

The scent of jasmine was in the wind whenever he awoke. He struggled to breathe it into his lungs because it helped him remember Amy. He held on to her image as long as he could, picturing her as she stood at the airport, determined to send him off with a smile. So proud. So lovely— with soulful eyes an angel would envy. It was then that he had started thinking of her as Angel Eyes.

The sound of someone entering his room disturbed his deep sleep. He heard voices—he had several times. They disturbed him when all he wanted to do was sleep. Only this time, one soft, feminine voice sounded so much like Amy. He must have died. But if this was heaven, then why the pain?

"No," he cried, but his shout of protest was little more than a whisper. It wasn't fair that he should fall in love for the first time and then die. Life wasn't fair, he'd known that from the moment he walked out of his father's office, but somehow he'd always thought death would be...

"Josh," Amy whispered, certain she'd heard him speak. It had been little more than a groan, but it had given her hope. "I'm here," she told him, clasping his hand in her own and pressing it to her cheek. "I love you. Do you understand?"

"Miss Johnson," Dr. Kilroy, Josh's English doctor, said with heavy reluctance. "I don't think he can hear you; the injuries to his body have been catastrophic. I don't think your friend is going to make it. We've only given him a fifty percent chance to live."

"Yes, I know."

"He's been unconscious for nearly three weeks."

"I know that, too."

"Please, you aren't helping him by staying at the hospital day and night. Perhaps if you returned to your hotel room and got a decent night's sleep."

"You'll have to get used to my presence, Doctor, because I'm not budging." She turned toward the bed and swallowed back the alarm, as she had every time her gaze rested on Josh. His injuries were multiple, including second-degree burns on his arms, a broken leg, cracked ribs, a bruised kidney and other internal damage, not to mention a severe concussion. Mercifully, he'd been unconscious from the moment she arrived, which had been five days earlier. Not once had she left his side for more than a few minutes. She talked to him, read to him and wiped the perspiration from his brow, touching him often, hoping her presence would relay her love.

The weak sound he'd made just a moment before was the first indication she'd had that he was awake.

"Miss Johnson, please," Dr. Kilroy continued.

"Doctor, I'm not leaving this hospital," she returned sternly.

"Very well," he acquiesced and left the room.

"Josh." She whispered his name and lightly ran her hand across his forehead. "I'm here." His eyes were bandaged, but Dr. Kilroy had assured her Josh hadn't been blinded in the accident.

Another soft cry parted his lips, one so unbelievably weak that she had to strain to hear it. Cautiously, she leaned over the hospital bed and placed her ear as close to his mouth as she could.

"Angel Eyes? Jasmine?"

"At your service," she said, choking back the tears. She didn't know who Jasmine was, but she wasn't going to let a little thing like another woman disturb her now. "You're awake?" It was a stupid question. Of course he was.

"Dead?"

It took her a moment to understand his question. "No, you're very much alive."

"Where?"

"We're here in Kadiri."

Gently, he shook his head and then grimaced. The action must have caused him severe pain. She could tell that talking was an effort for him, but there wasn't anything more she could do to help.

"Where?" he repeated. "Hell? Heaven?"

"Earth," she told him, but if he heard her, he didn't give any indication.

She ran for the nurse but by the time they arrived at the room Josh was unconscious again.

Another twenty-four hours passed before she was able to communicate with him a second time. She had been sitting at his bedside, reading. Since his eyes were wrapped it was impossible to tell if he was asleep or awake, but something alerted her to the fact that he had regained consciousness.

"It's Amy," she said softly, taking his hand and rubbing his knuckles gently. "Here, touch my face."

Very slowly he slid his thumb across the high arch of her cheek. Amy was so excited that it was impossible to sit still. She kissed the inside of his palm. "I love you, Joshua Powell, and I swear I'll never forgive you if you up and die on me now."

A hint of a smile cracked his dry lips. "Earth," he said and his head rolled to the side as he slipped into unconsciousness.

"Dad," Amy shouted into the heavy black telephone receiver. It made her appreciate the effort Josh had made to contact her by phone, not once but twice.

"Amy, is that you?"

She could almost see her father throwing back his covers and sitting on the edge of his mattress. By now, he would have reached for his glasses and turned on the bedside lamp.

"It's me," she cried. "Can you hear me all right?"

"Just barely. How's Josh doing?"

"Better, I think. The English doctor SunTech Oil flew in says he's showing some signs of improvement. He knows he's alive, at any rate. He's said 'earth' twice now."

"What?"

Amy laughed. "It's too difficult to explain."

"Are you taking care of yourself?"

"Yes...don't worry about me."

"Amy." Her father paused and continued in his most parental voice. "What's wrong?"

"Wrong?" she repeated. "What could possibly be wrong? Oh, you mean other than the fact I've flown halfway around the world to be at the deathbed of the man I love?"

"You just told me Josh is improving."

"He is. It's just that...oh, nothing, Dad, everything is fine. Just fine."

"Don't try to feed me that. There's something troubling you. Whatever it is—I can hear it in your voice even if you *are* eight thousand miles away. You can't fool me, sweetheart. Tell me what's up."

Amy bit her lower lip and brushed the tears from her

eyes. "Josh keeps asking for another woman. Someone named Jasmine. He's said her name three or four times now, and he seems to think I'm her."

"You're jealous?"

"Yes. I don't even know who she is, but I swear I could rip her eyes out." No doubt she'd shocked her dear father, but she couldn't help it. After spending all this time with Josh, praying he would live, nursing his injuries, loving him, it was a grievous blow to her ego to have him confuse her with another woman.

"Do you want to come home now?"

"Josh can't travel."

"Leave him."

Amy realized the suggestion was given for shock value, but it had the desired effect. "I love him, Dad. I'm here for the long haul. Whoever this Jasmine woman is, she's got a fight on her hands if she thinks I'm giving Josh up quite so easily."

Her father chuckled, and Amy felt rejuvenated by the sound. It had taken her the better part of three hours to place the call to Seattle, but the time and effort had been well-spent.

"Take care of yourself, Amy Adele."

"Yes, Dad, I will. You, too."

When she returned to Josh's room, she found a nurse and Dr. Kilroy with him. He was apparently in a good deal of pain and was restlessly rolling his head back and forth. Amy walked over to his bedside and clasped his hand between her own.

"Josh," she said. "Can you tell me what's wrong? How can we help you?"

His fingers curled around hers and he heaved a sigh, then apparently drifted into unconsciousness.

"What happened?" Amy asked.

The doctor lifted the patient's chart and made several notations. "I can't be sure. He apparently awoke soon after you left the room and was distressed. He mumbled something, but neither the nurse nor I could understand what he was trying to say. It's apparent, however, that you have a calming effect upon him."

It wasn't until later that night that Josh awoke again. Amy was sitting at his bedside reading. She heard him stir and set her novel aside, standing at his bedside.

"I'm here, Josh."

His hand moved and she laced her fingers with his, raising his hand to touch her face to prove she was there and real and not a disembodied voice in the distance.

"Joel's dead," he said in a husky murmur.

"Yes, I know," she whispered, and her voice caught. Instinctively, she understood that his uneasiness earlier in the afternoon had been the moment he realized his friend had been killed in the explosion.

"I'm so sorry." A tear crept from the corner of her eye and ran down the side of her face. He must have felt the dampness because he lifted his free hand and blindly groped for her nape, forcing her head down to his level. Then he buried his face in the curve of her neck and held her with what she was certain was all the strength he possessed. Soon his shoulders started shaking, and sobs overtook him.

Amy wept, too. For the life that was gone, for the man she never knew, for the dear friend Josh had tried to save and had lost.

She fell asleep that night with her head resting on her arms, which she'd folded over the edge of the mattress. She awoke to feel Josh caressing her hair.

"Good morning," she whispered, straightening.

"Thank you," he returned, his voice still incredibly weak.

No explanation was needed. Josh was telling her how grateful he was that she'd been with him while he worked out his grief for his friend.

She yawned, arching her back and lifting her arms high above her head. "Are you in a lot of pain?"

"Would you kiss me and make it better if I said I was?"

"Yes," she answered, smiling.

"Amy," he said, his voice growing serious. "You shouldn't be here. I don't know how it's possible, you being here. It took me weeks to get my visa remember?"

"I remember." She bent over and kissed his brow.

"Leave while you can."

"Sorry, I can't do that." She pressed a warm kiss along the side of his mouth. "Feel better yet?"

"Amy, please." He gripped her wrist with what little strength he had. "I'm going to be fine…you've got to get out of here. Understand?"

"Of course."

"I thought your father had better sense than this. You should never have come."

"Josh, you don't need to worry about me."

"I do… Amy, please."

She could tell the argument was draining his strength. "All right," she lied. "I'll make arrangements to leave tomorrow."

"Promise me."

"I…promise."

Amy could see the tension ease out of him. "Thank you, Angel Eyes."

He seemed to rest after that. Amy felt mildly guilty for the lie, but she couldn't see any way around it.

The following day when Josh awoke, he seemed to know instinctively that she was there. "Amy?"

"I'm here."

"No! You promised. What happened?"

"Kadiri Airlines only flies on Wednesday."

"What day is it?"

"I don't know, I lost track." Another white lie. But the minute he learned it was Tuesday, he would get upset and she didn't want to risk that.

"Find out."

"Dr. Kilroy said he was going to remove the bandages from your eyes today. You don't expect me to leave without giving you at least one opportunity to see me, do you?"

"I'm dying for a glimpse of you," he confessed reluctantly.

"Then I'd better make it worth your while. I have an appointment to get my hair done at eleven." There wasn't a beauty salon within five hundred miles of Kadiri. Josh had to know that.

"Any chance of getting me a toothbrush and cranking up the head of this bed?"

"I'll see what I can do."

It took Amy fifteen minutes to locate a new toothbrush and some toothpaste. Josh was asleep when she returned, but he awoke an hour later. She helped him brush his teeth while he complained about the taste of Kadiri water. She didn't have the heart to tell him he was brushing with flat soda water.

By the time they'd completed the task, Dr. Kilroy entered the room. The man reminded her of a British Buddy Holly. He turned off the lights and removed the bandages while Amy stood breathlessly waiting.

The minute the white gauze was unraveled from Josh's

head, he squinted and rotated his head to where Amy was standing. He held out his hand to her. "I swear, you've never looked more beautiful."

Knowing that after weeks of having his eyes covered, she couldn't be anything more than a wide blur against the wall, she walked to his side and wrapped her arms around his neck. "Joshua Powell, you don't lie worth beans."

He curved his hand around her neck and he directed her mouth down to his. "I've waited three long months to kiss you, don't argue with me."

Amy had no intention of doing anything of the sort.

Josh moved his mouth over hers with a fierce kind of tenderness, a deep, hungering kiss that developed when one had come so terribly close to losing all that was important, including life itself. He shaped and fitted her soft lips to his own, drinking in her love and her strength.

Dr. Kilroy nervously cleared his throat, mumbled something about seeing his other patients and quickly vacated the room. Amy was grateful.

"Josh," she whispered while he continued nibbling at her lips, catching her lower lip between his teeth and tugging at it sensuously before he lay back and rested his head on the pillow. Still he didn't fully release her. He closed his eyes and his smile was slanted, full and possessive.

"Angel Eyes," he whispered. "I can't tell you how good it feels to kiss you again."

"Yes," she agreed, her own voice pathetically weak.

He brought his hand back to her nape, stroking and caressing, directing her mouth back to his own. Amy held back, fearing too much contact would cause him pain.

"I'm afraid I'll hurt you," she whispered.

"I'll let you know if you do."

"But, Josh—"

"Are you going to fight with me?"

Their mouths were so close that their breaths merged. Amy could deny him nothing. "No..."

"Good."

He touched his tongue to her lips, gently coaxing them open, and then she complied to his unspoken request.

Shudders of excitement braided their way along her backbone, and her heart was hammering like a machine gun inside her chest. When she flattened her palms against Josh's chest, she noted that his heart was beating equally strongly. The movement was reassuring.

Taking in a deep breath, Josh ended the kiss and rested his forehead against hers. Their mouths were moist and ready, their breaths mingling.

"Go back to Seattle, Amy," he pleaded, running his hands through her hair.

"One kiss and you're dismissing me already?"

"I want you home and safe."

"I'm safe with you."

He chuckled lightly. "Honey, you're in more danger than you ever dreamed. Is that door open or closed?"

"Open."

He muttered a curse.

She dipped her mouth to his and kissed him long and slow, taking delight in sensuously rubbing her mouth back and forth over his, creating a slick friction that was enough to take the starch from her knees. By the time they broke apart, she was so weak, she'd slumped against the side of the bed.

"Maybe... I should close it," she said, once she'd found her voice.

"No...leave it open," he said with a sigh as he ran his palms in wide circles across her back as though he had to keep touching her to make sure she was real. "Amy, please, you've got to listen to me."

"I can't," she told him, "because all you want to do is send me away." She leaned forward and pressed her open mouth over his, showing him all that he had taught her in the ways of subtle seduction. "Here," she whispered. "Feel my heart." She pulled one of his hands from her back and pressed it to her chest.

"Amy!" He sucked in a wobbly breath.

"Josh, I love you," she said, kissing him once more, teasing him with the tip of her tongue.

"No...you shouldn't...you can't."

"But I do."

He closed his eyes to deny her words, but he couldn't keep his body from responding. He moved his hand and lovingly cupped her chin, then brushed the edges of her mouth. "I can't get over how good it feels to hold you again."

She leaned into his embrace, experiencing a grateful surge of thanksgiving that he was alive and on the mend.

"You promised me you were going to leave," he reminded her quietly.

"Yes, I know."

"Are you going back on your word?"

"No." Eventually she would fly out of Kadiri, but when she did, Josh would be with her. Only he didn't know that yet.

"Good. Now kiss me once more for good measure and then get out of here. I don't want to see you again until I'm in Seattle."

"Josh," she argued. "That could be weeks—"

"Honey, will you stop worrying?" He was exhausted. Resting his head against the pillow, he closed his eyes.

It took him all of two seconds to fall asleep. Carefully,

Amy lowered the head of his bed, then tenderly kissed his forehead before silently slipping out of the room.

Amy felt better after she'd showered and eaten. From the moment her father had come to her bedside that fateful night all those weeks ago, she hadn't done anything more than nibble at a meal.

She slept better than she had in a month. Waking bright and early the following morning, she dressed in the traditional Kadiri dress Josh had mailed her and walked down to the public market. With her blond hair and blue eyes, she stuck out like a bandaged thumb. Small children gathered around her, and, laughing, she handed out pieces of candy. The eyes of the soldiers, with rifles looped over their shoulders, anxiously followed her, but she wasn't frightened. There wasn't any reason to be.

Amy bought some fresh fruit and a colorful necklace and a few other items, then lazily returned to the hospital.

"How's Josh this morning?" she asked Dr. Kilroy when they met in the hallway.

The doctor looked surprised to see her. "He's recovering, but unfortunately his disposition doesn't seem to be making the same improvement."

"Why not?"

The thin British man studied her closely. "I thought you'd left the country."

Amy smiled. "Obviously, I haven't."

"But Mr. Powell seems to be under the impression that you're back in America."

"I let him think that. When I leave Kadiri, he'll be with me."

Dr. Kilroy lifted his thick, black-framed glasses and

pinched the bridge of his nose. "Personally, I don't want to be the one who tells him."

"You won't have to be."

"Oh." He paused.

"I'm going that way myself. Is there anything else you'd like me to tell him?"

Dr. Kilroy chuckled, and Amy had the impression that he was a man who rarely laughed.

"No, but I wish you the best of luck with your friend, Miss Johnson. I fear you're going to need it."

With a smile on her lips, Amy marched down the hall and tapped lightly against Josh's door. She didn't wait for a response, but pushed it open and let herself inside.

"I told you, I don't want any breakfast," Josh grumbled, his face turned toward the wall. The drapes were drawn and the room was dark.

"That's unfortunate, since I personally went out and bought you some fresh fruit."

"Amy." He jerked his head around, wincing in pain. "What are you still doing here?"

Six

"What does it look like I'm doing here?" Amy answered, gingerly stepping all the way into the room. "I brought you some fresh fruit."

Josh closed his eyes against what appeared to be mounting frustration. "Please, don't tell me you bought that in the public market."

"All right," she answered matter of factly. She brought out a small plastic knife and scored the large orange-shaped fruit. It looked like a cross between an orange and a grapefruit, but when she'd asked about it, the native woman she'd bought it from apparently hadn't understood the question.

"You *did* go the market, didn't you?" Josh pressed.

"You claimed I wasn't supposed to tell you." She peeled away the thick, grainy skin from the succulent fruit then licked the juice from the tips of her fingers.

"You went anyway."

"Honestly, Josh, I was perfectly safe. There were people all around me. Nothing happened, so kindly quit harping about it. Here." She handed him a slice, hoping that would buy peace. "I don't know what it's called. I asked several people, but no one seemed to understand." She smiled at the memory of her antics, her attempts to communicate with her hands, which were no doubt humorous to anyone watching.

Josh accepted the slice. "It's an orange."

"An *orange?* You mean I flew halfway around the world and thought I was buying some exotic fruit only to discover it's an orange? But it's so big."

"They grow that way here."

She found that amusing even if Josh didn't. She continued to peel away the skin and divided the sections between them. After savoring three or four of the sweet-tasting slices, she noted that Josh hadn't sampled a single one of his.

"You promised me you were leaving Kadiri," he said, his words sharp with impatience. His eyes were dark and filled with frustrated concern.

"I am."

"When?"

She sighed and crossed her long legs. "When you're ready to travel, which according to Dr. Kilroy won't be for another two weeks, perhaps longer. Josh, please try to understand, you've received several serious injuries. It's going to take time, so you might as well be tolerant."

"Amy—"

"Nothing you can say or do is going to change my mind, Joshua Powell. Nothing. So you might as well be gracious enough to accept that I'm not leaving Kadiri unless you're with me."

Joshua shut his eyes so tightly that barbed crow's feet marked the edges of his eyes. "How in the name of heaven did you get to be so stubborn?"

"I don't know." She wiped the juice from her chin with the back of her hand. "I'm usually not, at least I don't think I am, it's just that this is something I feel strongly about."

"So do I," he returned vehemently.

"Yes, I know. I guess there's only one solution."

"You're leaving!"

"Right," she agreed amicably enough. "But you're coming with me."

Amy could see that she was trying his patience to the limit. His tan jaw was pale with barely suppressed exasperation. If there had been anything she could do to comply with his demands, she would have done it, but Josh was as obstinate as she, only this time she was fortunate enough to have the upper hand. He couldn't very well force her out of the country.

In a burst of annoyance, Josh threw aside the sheet.

"Josh," she cried in alarm, leaping to her feet, "what are you doing?"

"Getting out of bed."

"But you can't...your leg's broken and you're hooked up to all these bottles. Josh, please, you're going to hurt yourself."

"You're not giving me any choice." The abrupt movements were obviously causing him a good deal of pain. His face went gray with it.

"Josh, please," she cried, his agony causing her own. Gently she pressed her hands against his shoulders, forcing him down. Josh's breathing was labored, and certain that he'd done something to harm himself, she hurried down the hall to find Dr. Kilroy.

The doctor returned with her to Josh's room. Almost immediately he gave Josh a shot to ease the pain and warned them both against such foolishness. Within minutes, Josh was asleep and resting relatively comfortably.

Amy felt terrible. When Dr. Kilroy invited her to have tea with him, she accepted, wiping the tearstains from her face.

"Josh seems to think my life is in imminent danger," she confessed. "He wants me out of the country." She stared into the steaming cup of tea, her gaze avoiding his. Even if the doctor agreed with Josh, she was bound and determined not to leave Kadiri unless Josh was at her side.

The good doctor, fortyish and graying, pushed his glasses up the bridge of his nose as if the action would guide his words. "Personally, I understand his concern. This is no place for an American woman on her own."

"But I just can't leave Josh here," she protested. "Are you sure it's going to be two more weeks before he can travel comfortably?"

"Three." He added a small amount of milk to his tea and stirred it in as if he were dissolving concrete. "It'll be at least that long, perhaps longer before he can sit for any length of time."

"What about laying down?"

"Oh, there wouldn't be any problem with that, but there aren't any airlines that provide hospital beds as a part of their flying options," he said dryly.

"But we could put a bed in my father's jet. I flew into Kadiri in a private plane," she rushed to explain. "It's at my disposal for the return trip as well."

Propping his elbows against the tabletop, Dr. Kilroy nodded slowly, thoughtfully. "That changes matters considerably. I think you might have stumbled upon a solution."

"But what about when we land in Seattle? Will Josh require further medical care?"

"Oh, yes. Your friend has been severely injured. Although the immediate danger has passed, it'll be several weeks—possibly months—before he'll be fully recovered. For the next two or three weeks it is critical he gets medical care only available at a hospital."

Amy knew the minute Josh was released from the Kadiri Hospital he wouldn't allow anyone to admit him to another one stateside.

"Josh isn't one to rest complacently in a hospital," she explained.

"I understand your concern. I fear Mr. Powell may try to rush his recovery, pushing himself. I only hope he realizes that he could do himself a good deal of harm that way."

"I could make arrangements for him to stay at my family home," she offered hopefully. "Would a full-time nurse be adequate to see to his needs? Naturally he'd be under a physician's care."

It didn't take the doctor long to decide. "Why, yes, I believe that could work quite well."

"Then consider it done. The plane's on standby and can be ready within twenty-four hours. Once we're airborne and we can contact Seattle, I'll have my father make all the necessary arrangements. A qualified nurse can meet us at the airport when we arrive."

"I can sedate Mr. Powell so the journey won't be too much of a strain on him...or anyone else," Dr. Kilroy added. It was agreed that a nurse would travel with them, although Amy would have preferred it if Dr. Kilroy could make the trip with them himself.

"I believe this will all work quite well." The British man looked pleased. "Now, both you and Mr. Powell can have what you want."

"Yes," Amy said, pleased by the unexpected turn of events.

When Josh awoke early in the afternoon, Amy was at his bedside. He opened his eyes, but when he saw her sitting next to him, he lowered his lids once more.

"Amy, please…"

"I'm flying out this evening, Josh, so don't be angry again."

His dark eyes shot open. "I thought you said Kadiri Airlines only flew on Wednesdays."

"They do. I'm going by private jet."

His lashes flew up to his hairline. "Private jet?"

"Before you find something else to complain about, I think you should know you're coming with me."

If he was shocked before it was nothing compared with the look of astonishment on his face now. " Amy…how… when…why?"

"One question at a time," she said, smiling softly and leaning over him to press her lips to his. "The how part is easy. Dr. Kilroy and I had a long talk. We're flying you to Seattle, hospital bed and all."

"Whose plane is this?"

"Dad's. Well, actually," she went on to explain, "it technically belongs to the company. He's just letting us use it because—"

"Hold on a minute," Josh said, raising his hand. "This jet belongs to your father's company?"

"Right."

His eyes slammed shut, and for one breathless moment he didn't say a word. When he opened them once more, his gaze held hers while several emotions flickered in and out of his eyes. Amy recognized shock, disbelief and a few other ones she wasn't sure she could identify.

"Josh, what is it?"

"Your father's name wouldn't happen to be Harold, would it?"

"Why, yes. How'd you know?" To the best of her knowledge she'd never mentioned her father's first name. But she hadn't been hiding it, either.

The harsh sound that followed could only be described as something between a laugh and a snicker. Slowly, Josh shook his head from side to side. "I don't believe it. And here I thought your father was just some poor devil who wanted to make you a part of a wholesale plumbing business."

Josh wasn't making the least bit of sense. Perhaps it was the medication, Amy reasoned. All she knew was that she didn't have time to argue with him, nor would there be ample opportunity for a lot of explanations. He looked so infuriated, and yet she was doing exactly what he wanted. She couldn't understand what was suddenly so terribly wrong.

The red flashing lights from the waiting ambulance were the first things Amy noted when they landed at Boeing field near Seattle some fifty hours later.

Amy was exhausted, emotionally and physically. The flight had been uncomfortable from the moment they'd taken off from the Kadiri Airport. Josh, although sedated, was restless and in a good deal of pain. Amy was the only one who seemed capable of calming him, so she'd stayed with him through the whole flight.

Harold Johnson was standing alongside the ambulance, looking dapper in his three-piece-suit. He hugged Amy close and assured her everything was ready and waiting for Josh at the house.

"Now what was this about me finding a nurse with the name of Brunhilde?" he asked, slipping his arm around her thin shoulders. "You were joking, weren't you? I'll have you know, Ms. Wetherell contacted five agencies, and the best we could come up with was a Bertha."

Amy chuckled, delighted that her father had taken her message so literally. "I just wanted to make sure you didn't hire someone young and pretty."

"Once you meet Mrs. White, I think you'll approve." Her father laughed with her. The worry lines around his mouth and eyes eased, and Amy realized her journey had caused him a good deal of concern, although he'd never let on. She loved him all the more for it.

"It's good to have you back, sweetheart."

"It's good to be back."

The ambulance crew were carrying Josh out of the plane on a gurney. "Just exactly where are you taking me?" he demanded.

"Josh." Amy smiled and hurried to his side. "Stop being such a poor patient."

"I'm not going back in any stuffy hospital. Understand?"

"Perfectly."

He seemed all the more flustered by her easy acquiescence. "Then where are they taking me?" His words faded as he was lifted into the interior of the ambulance.

"Home," she called after him.

"Whose home?"

The attendant closed one door at the rear of the ambulance and was reaching toward the second before Amy could respond to Josh's question.

"My home," she called after him.

"No you're not. I want a hotel room, understand? Amy, did you hear me?"

"Yes, I heard you."

The second door slammed shut. Before he could argue with her, the vehicle sped off into the night.

* * *

"It's good to be home," Amy said with an exhausted sigh. She slipped her arm around her father's trim waist and leaned her head against his strong shoulders. "By the way, that was Josh. In case you hadn't noticed, he isn't in the best of tempers. He doesn't seem to be a very good patient, but who can blame him after everything he's been through?" She lifted her gaze to her father's and sucked in a deep breath. "I almost lost him, Dad. It was so close."

"So he's being a poor patient," her father repeated, obviously trying to lighten her mood.

"Terrible. Mrs. White's going to have her hands full."

Harold Johnson took a puff of his cigar and chuckled softly. "I always hated being ordered to bed myself. I can't blame him. Fact is, I may have a good deal in common with this young man of yours."

Amy smiled, realizing how true this was. "I'm sure you do. It isn't any wonder I love him so much."

Josh awoke when the golden fingers of dawn slithered through the bedroom window, creeping like a fast-growing vine over the thick oyster-gray carpet and onto the edges of his bed. Every bone in his body ached. He'd assumed that by now he would have become accustomed to pain. He'd lived with it all these weeks, to the point that it had almost become his friend. At least when he was suffering, he knew he was alive. And if he was alive, then he would be able to see Amy again.

Amy.

He shut his eyes to thoughts of her. He'd been in love with her for months. She was warmth and sunshine, purity and generosity, and everything that was good. She was the kind of woman a man dreams of finding—sweet and innocent on the outside, but when he held her in his arms, she flowered with fire and ready passion, promising him untold delights.

Yet somehow Josh was going to have to dredge up the courage to turn his back and walk away from her.

If he was going to fall in love, he cried silently, then why did it have to be with Harold Johnson's daughter? The man was one of the wealthiest men in the entire country. His holdings stretched from New York to Los Angeles and several major cities in between; his name was synonymous with achievement and high-powered success.

Josh couldn't offer Amy this kind of life, and even if he could, he wouldn't. He had firsthand experience of what wealth did to a man. By age twenty-five, he had witnessed how selfishness and greed could corrupt a man's soul.

The love for money had driven a stake between Josh and his own father, one so deep and so crippling that it would never be healed. Eight years had passed, and not once in all that time had Josh regretted leaving home. Chance Powell had stared Josh in the eye and claimed he had no son. Frankly, that information suited Josh well. He had no father, either. He shared nothing with the man who had sired him—nor did he wish to.

Josh's mother had died when he was in college, and his only other living relative was her sister, an elderly aunt in Boston whom he visited on rare occasions. His Aunt Hazel was getting on in years, and she seemed to make it her mission in life to try to bridge the gap between father and son, but to no avail. They were both too proud. Both too stubborn.

"I see you're awake," Bertha White, his nurse, stated as she stepped into the room. She certainly dressed for the

part, donning white scrubs with the dedication of a con-
quering army.

Josh made some appropriate sound in reply. As far as he
was concerned, Bertha White should be wearing a helmet
with horns and singing in an opera. She marched across
his room with all the grace of a herd of buffalo and pulled
open the blinds, flooding the room with sunlight. Josh noted
that she hadn't bothered to ask him how he felt about letting the sun blind him. Somehow he doubted that she cared.

She fussed around his bedside, apparently so he would
know she was earning her salary. She checked his vital
signs, dutifully entering the statistics in his chart. Then she
proceeded to poke and prod him in places he didn't even
want to think about. To his surprise, she graciously gave
him the opportunity to wash himself.

Josh appreciated that, even if he didn't much care for
the woman, who was about as warm and comforting as a
mud wrestler.

"You have a visitor," she informed him once he had
finished.

"Who?" Josh feared it was Amy. It would be too difficult
to deal with her now, when he felt weak and vulnerable.
He didn't want to hurt her, but he wasn't sure he could do
what he must without causing her pain.

"Mr. Johnson is here to see you," Bertha replied stiffly,
and walked out of the room.

No sooner had she departed than Amy's father let himself in, looking very much the legend Josh knew him to
be. The man's presence was commanding, Josh admitted
willingly. He doubted that Harold Johnson ever walked
anywhere without generating a good deal of attention. Everything about him spelled prosperity and accomplishment.

This one man had achieved in twenty years what three normal men couldn't do in a lifetime.

"So you're Josh Powell," Amy's father stated, his eyes as blue as his daughter's and just as kind. "I would have introduced myself when you arrived last night, but you seemed to be in a bit of discomfort."

They shook hands, and Harold casually claimed the chair at Josh's bedside, as if he often spent part of his morning visiting a sickroom.

"I'll have you know I had nothing to do with this," Josh said somewhat defiantly, wishing there was some way he could climb out of his bed and meet Johnson man-to-man.

"Nothing to do with what?"

"Being here—I had no idea Amy planned to dump me off in your backyard. Listen, I don't mean to sound like I'm ungrateful for everything you've done, but I'd like to make arrangements as soon as I can to recover elsewhere."

"Son, you're my guest."

"I would feel more comfortable someplace else," Josh insisted, gritting his teeth to a growing awareness of pain and an overabundance of pride.

"Is there a reason?" Harold didn't look unsettled by Josh's demands, only curious.

The effort to sit up was draining Josh of strength and conviction, which he struggled to disguise behind a gruff exterior. "You obviously don't know anything about me."

Harold withdrew a cigar from his inside jacket pocket and examined the end with a good deal of consideration. "My daughter certainly appears to think highly of you."

"Which doesn't say much, does it?"

"On the contrary," Harold argued. "It tells me everything I need to know."

"Then you'd better..." A sharp cramp thrust through

his abdomen and he lay back and closed his eyes until it passed. "Suffice it to say, it would be best if I arranged for other accommodations. Amy should never have brought me here in the first place."

"My daughter didn't mean to offend you. In fact, I don't know if you've noticed, but she seems to have fallen head over heels in love with you."

"I noticed," Josh admitted dryly. Amy. Her name went through his mind like a hot blade. He had to leave her, couldn't her father understand that much? They were as different as the sun and the moon. As far apart as the two poles, and their dissimilarities were in ways that were impossible to bridge. Harold Johnson should be intelligent enough to recognize that with one look. Josh would have thought the man would be eager to be rid of him.

"You don't care for her?" Harold asked, chewing on the end of the cigar.

"Sir, you don't know anything about me," Josh said, taking in a calming breath. "I'm a drifter. I'm hardly suitable for your daughter. I don't want to hurt her, but I don't intend to lead her on, either."

"I see." He rubbed the side of his jaw in a thought-filled action.

It was apparent to Josh that Amy's father did nothing of the sort. "And another thing," Josh said, feeling it was important to say what was on his mind. "I can't understand how you could have let her fly to the Middle East because of me. Kadiri was no place for her."

"I agree one hundred percent. It took me an hour to come to terms with the fact she was going no matter what I said or did, so I made sure the road was paved for her."

"But how could you let her go and do a thing like that?" Josh demanded, still not understanding. Someone like Harold Johnson had connections, but even *his* protective arm could only stretch so far.

"I was afraid of being penalized for defensive holding," Harold said firmly.

Josh was certain he'd misunderstood. His confusion must have shown in his face, because the older man went on to explain.

"Amy's recently turned twenty-four years old and beyond the point where I can tell her what she can and can't do. If she wants to take off for the far corners of the world, there's little I can do to stop her. She knows it, and so do I. For that matter, if she's going to fall in love with you, it's not my place to tell her she's making a mistake. Either the girl's got sound judgment or she doesn't."

"I'm not good enough for her," Josh insisted.

The edges of the man's mouth lifted slightly at that. "Personally, I doubt that any man is. But I'll admit to being partial. Amy is, after all, my only child."

Josh closed his eyes, wanting to block out both the current pain and the one that was coming. If he stayed it would be inevitable. "I'm going to hurt her."

"Yes, son, I suspect you will."

"Then surely you realize why I need to get out of here, and the sooner the better."

"That's the only part I can't quite accept," Harold said slowly, his tone considerate. "As I understand it, you don't have any family close at hand?"

"None," Josh admitted reluctantly.

"Then perhaps you'd prefer several more weeks in a hospital?"

"No," Josh answered.

"Then you've made other arrangements that include a full-time nurse and—"

"No," Josh ground out harshly.

Harold Johnson's eyes filled with ill-concealed amusement.

"Your point is well taken," Josh admitted unwillingly. He didn't have a single argument that would hold up against the force of the other man's logic.

"Listen to me, son, you're welcome to remain here as long as you wish, and likewise, you're free to leave anytime you want. Neither Amy nor I would have it any other way."

"The expenses...?"

"We can discuss that later," Harold told him.

"No, we'll clear the air right now. I insist upon paying for all this... I want that understood."

"As you wish. Now, if you'll excuse me I'd better get into the office before my assistant comes looking for me."

"Of course." Josh wanted to dislike Amy's father. It would have made life a whole lot easier. If Harold Johnson had been anything like his own father, Josh would have moved the Panama Canal to get as far away from the Johnson family as humanly possible. Instead, he'd reluctantly discovered Amy's father was the kind of man he would have gladly counted as a friend.

"Sir, I don't want you to think I don't appreciate everything you've done." Josh felt obliged to explain. "It's just that this whole setup makes me uncomfortable."

"I can't say that I blame you. But you need to concentrate on getting well. You can worry about everything else later."

It commanded a good deal of effort for Josh to nod. Swirling pain wrapped its way around his body, tightening its grip on his ribs and his leg. Amy's father seemed to understand that Josh needed to rest.

"I'll be leaving you now."

"Sir." Josh half lifted his head in an effort to stop him.

"If you could do one small favor for me, I'd greatly appreciate it."

"What's that?"

"Keep Amy away from me."

Harold Johnson's answering bellow of laughter was loud enough to rattle the windows. "It's obvious you don't know my daughter very well, young man. If I couldn't prevent her from flying to Timbuktu and risking her fool neck to be at your side, what makes you think I can keep her out of this sickroom?"

Josh felt an involuntary smile twitch at the corners of his mouth. Harold was right. There was nothing Josh could do to keep away Amy. But that wasn't the worst of it. He wanted her with him, and he wasn't fooling either of them by declaring otherwise.

He must have fallen asleep, because the next thing Josh knew Bertha White was in his room, fussing around the way she had earlier in the morning. Slowly, he opened his eyes to discover the elderly woman dragging a table across the room with a luncheon tray on it.

A polite knock sounded on the door. "Ms. White."

"Yes?"

"Would it be all right if I came in now? I brought my lunch so I could eat with Josh."

"No," Josh yelled, not waiting for the other woman to answer. His nurse shot him a look that reminded him of his sixth grade teacher, who Josh swore could cuff his ears with a dirty look. "I don't feel like company," he explained.

"Come in, Miss Johnson," Mrs. White answered, daring Josh to contradict her. "I've brought the table over next to the bed so you can sit down here and enjoy your visit."

"Thank you," Amy said softly.

Josh closed his eyes. Even her voice sounded musical.

Almost like an angel's… He might as well accept that he wasn't going to be able to resist her. Not now, when he was too weak to think, much less argue.

Seven

"Hi," Amy said, sitting down at the table. She carried her lunch with her—a shrimp salad and a tall glass of iced tea. Try as he might, Josh couldn't tear his eyes away from her. If her voice sounded like an angel's, it didn't even begin to compare with the way she looked. Sweet heaven, she was lovely.

"Are you feeling any better?" she asked, her eyes filled with gentle concern.

Josh thought to answer her gruffly. If he was irritable and unpleasant, then she wouldn't want to spend time with him, but one flutter of soft blue eyes and the battle was lost.

"I'm doing just fine," he muttered, reluctantly accepting defeat. He couldn't seem to look away. She might as well have nailed him to a wall, that was how powerless he felt around her. Why did she have to be so sweet, so wonderful? Before she came to visit him, he'd tried to fortify his heart, build up his defenses. Some defenses! One glance and those defenses crumbled at his feet like clay.

"You're not fine," Amy countered swiftly, with a hint of indignation. "At least, that's not what I heard. Mrs. White claimed you had a restless night and have been in a good deal of pain."

"I wouldn't believe everything Robo-nurse says if I were you."

Amy chuckled, then whispered, "She is a bit intimidating, isn't she?"

"Attila the Hun incarnate."

Josh momentarily closed his eyes to enjoy the sound of her merriment as it lapped over him like a gentle wave caressing the shoreline. How he loved it when Amy laughed.

She hesitated before spreading a napkin across the lap of her jeans. "I thought it was best if we cleared the air," she said, stabbing a fat pink shrimp with her fork. She carefully avoided his gaze. "You seemed so upset with me when Dad met us at the airport the other night. I didn't mean to take charge of your life, Josh, I honestly didn't. But I suppose that's how you felt, and I certainly can't blame you." She paused long enough to chew, but while she was eating, she waved her fork around like a conductor, as if her movements would explain what she was feeling.

"Amy, I understand."

"I don't think you do," she said, once she'd swallowed. "You wanted me out of Kadiri, and I saw the perfect chance to get us *both* out, and I grabbed it. There wasn't time to consult with you about arrangements. I'm sorry if bringing you here went against your wishes. I... I did the best I could under the circumstances." She stopped long enough to suck in a giant breath. "But you're right, I should have consulted with you. I want you to know I would have, except Dr. Kilroy had heavily sedated you, and he thought it best to keep you that way for the journey. Then when we arrived everything happened so fast, and you—"

"Amy, I understand," he said quickly, interrupting her when he had the chance.

"You do?"

"Yes."

The stiffness came out of her shoulders, like air rushing from a balloon as she relaxed and reached for another shrimp. His gaze followed her action, and when she lifted the fork, she paused and smiled at him. Her happiness was contagious and free-flowing. It assailed him in a whirlwind of sensations he'd desperately struggled to repress from the moment he learned she'd flown to Kadiri to be with him.

"Want one?" she asked, her voice low and a little shaky. Her lips were moist and slightly parted as she leaned forward and held the fork in front of his mouth.

Their eyes met, and obediently he opened his mouth for her to feed him the succulent shrimp. It shouldn't have been a sensuous deed, but his heart started beating hard and strong, and the achy, restless feeling of needing to hold and kiss her fueled his mind like dry timber on a raging fire.

He longed to touch her translucent skin and plow his fingers through the silky length of her hair. But most of all, he realized, he wanted her warm and naked beneath him, making soft sounds of pleasure in his ear, and with her long, smooth legs wrapped around his.

His stomach knotted painfully. He leaned back and closed his eyes to the image that saturated and governed his thoughts.

She was at his side immediately, her voice filled with distress. "Should I get Mrs. White? Do you need something for the pain?"

The idea of a shot taking away the discomfort in his groin was humorous enough to curve up the edges of his mouth.

"Josh!" she blurted out. "You're smiling."

"I've got a pain, all right," he admitted, opening his eyes. He raised his hand, and trailed his fingertips across the arch of her cheek. "But it's one only you can ease."

"Tell me what to do. I want to help you. Oh, Josh, please, don't block me out. Not now, when we've been through so much together."

Gently, she planted her hands on his chest, as if that would convince him of her sincerity. Unfortunately, the action assured him of a good deal more. The ache within him intensified, and every second that she stared down on him with her bright angel eyes was adding heaps of coal to a fire that was already roaring with intensity.

"Honey, it's not that kind of pain." He set her hand on his groin.

Amy's eyes jolted with surprise and flickered several times as she came to terms with what he was saying.

Josh, unfortunately, was in for a surprise of his own. If he'd thought his action would cure what ailed him, then he was sadly mistaken. Instead, a shaft of desire stabbed through him with such magnitude that for a wild moment it was all he could do to breathe.

Amy's hand trembled, or perhaps he was the one shivering, he couldn't tell for sure. He released her wrist, but she kept her fingers exactly where they were, tormenting him in ways she couldn't even begin to understand.

"Josh," she whispered, her voice filled with wonder and excitement. "I want you, too...there's so much for you to teach me."

Her eyes reflected the painful longing Josh was experiencing. Knowing she was feeling the same urgency only increased his desire for her. He knew he could handle his own needs, but how was he going to be able to refuse hers?

"No," he cried desperately, his control already stretched beyond endurance. The need in him felt savage. The woman couldn't be *that* innocent not to realize she was driving him insane.

"Amy," he cried harshly, gripping her wrist once more. "Stop."

"It's...so hot," she whispered, her low words filled with wonder. "It makes me feel so... I don't know...so empty inside."

Josh had reached the point where reason no longer controlled him. All the arguments he'd built up against there ever being anything sexual between them vanished like mist under a noonday sun. He grasped her around the waist, half dragging her onto the bed beside him. Josh barely gave her time to adjust herself to the mattress before he kissed her, thrusting his fingers into her hair and sweeping his mouth over hers.

The kiss was hot and wild. Amy seemed to sense that he was giving her an example of what was soon to follow, and she slid her hand over his shoulder, digging her nails into the muscles there. Her untamed response was enough to send the blood shooting through him until he thought his head would explode with it.

He found her hipbone and scooted her as close as he could, then he gloried in the way she intuitively churned the lower half of her body against him.

"Amy" he groaned. "You don't know what you're doing to me." She smiled, and her whole face glowed with joy as her soft, kittenlike sound was nearly his undoing. "You're wrong. I do know and I'm enjoying every second." Her hands were in his hair, encouraging him with soft, trembling sounds that came deep from the back of her throat.

The bliss was so sharp, so keen that for Josh it reached

the point of pain. The ache in his loins was unbearable. It was either take her now or stop completely.

Josh didn't have long to consider his options. His shoulders were heaving when he buried his face in the gentle slope of her neck. It took him several seconds to compose himself, and even then he felt as shaky as a tree limb caught in a hurricane.

"Josh?" Amy's voice was filled with question. "What's wrong?"

Slowly, he lifted his head, struggling to maintain the last fragment of his control before it snapped completely. Gently, he kissed her lips, while he gently pushed her away, breaking their intimate hold on one another.

"Did I hurt you?" she asked, her voice low and warm, throbbing with concern.

Her question tugged at his heart, affecting Josh more than any in his life. He'd come within a hair's space of making love with her, driven to the edge of insanity by need and desire. His burning passion had dominated his every move. He might have frightened her, or worse, hurt her. The hot ache in him had been too strong to have taken the proper amount of care to be sure this first time was right. And Amy was concerned that she'd hurt *him*.

"Josh?" She repeated her question with his name, grazing his face with gentle, caressing fingers.

"I'm fine. Did I hurt you?"

"No...never. It was wonderful, but why did you stop?"

"Remember Robo-nurse?"

It was obvious that Amy had completely forgotten Bertha White by the startled look that flashed into her soft blue eyes. "Did she...is she back?"

"No, but she will be soon enough." Bertha was an excuse, Josh realized, a valid one, but she wasn't the reason he'd pulled away. He'd been about to lose all control, and heaven help him, he couldn't allow that to happen.

For two frustrating days, Amy's visits to Josh were limited to short ten-minute stays. Her father had her running errands for him. The charity bazaar she had worked on earlier that summer needed her for another project, and then Manuela had taken sick.

Everything seemed to be working against her being with Josh. It seemed every time she came, wanting to be alone with Josh, his nurse found an excuse to linger there. Amy wondered if he had put the older woman up to it. That was a silly thought, she realized, because he didn't seem to be any more fond of Bertha than Amy was.

Her thoughts were abuzz with questions. Every time her mind focused on the things Josh had done to her, the way he had held and kissed her, she grew warm and achy inside. The pleasure had been like nothing she had ever known, and once sampled, it created a need for more. She felt as though she had stood at the precipice, seeking something she couldn't name. Now that she had gazed upon such uncharted territory she was lost, filled with questions with no one to answer them.

It was late and dark and her father had retired for the evening. Amy lay in bed, restlessly trying to concentrate on a novel. The effort was useless, and she knew it. Every thought that entered her head had to do with Josh.

Throwing aside the sheets, she reached for her satin robe and searched out her slippers, which were hiding beneath her bed. Never in all her life had she done anything so bold as what she was about to do now.

She paused outside her bedroom door in the softly lit hallway and waited for reason to lead her back where she belonged. Nothing drove her backward. Instead she felt compelled to move forward.

Thankfully, at this time of night Bertha White would be sound asleep. As silently as possible Amy closed the door, then proceeded down the wide hallway to Josh's room.

The first thing she noticed was that his reading light was on. The sight relaxed her. She hadn't looked forward to waking him.

"Hello, Josh," she said as she silently stepped into the room. She closed the door, and when she turned around, she noticed that he was sitting up, gazing at her with dark, intense eyes.

"It's late," he announced starkly.

"Yes, I know. I couldn't sleep."

He eyed her wearily. "I was just about to turn out my light."

"I won't be a minute. It's just that I have a few questions for you, and I realize this is probably pretty embarrassing, but there isn't anyone else I can ask."

He closed his book, but she noticed that he didn't set it aside. In fact, he was holding it as if the hardbound novel would be enough of a barrier to keep her away.

"Questions about what?"

"The other day when we—"

"That was a mistake."

She swallowed tightly before continuing. "I don't know why you say that. Every time you so much as touch me, you claim it was a mistake. It's unbelievably frustrating."

A hint of a smile bounced against his eyes and mouth. "What do you want to know?" he asked, not unkindly. "And I'll do my level best to answer you."

"Without making a comment about the rightness or wrongness of what's happening between us?"

"All right," he agreed.

"Thank you." She pulled up a chair and sat, her gaze level with his own. Now that she had his full attention, she wasn't sure exactly where to start. Twice she opened her mouth, only to abruptly close it again, her muddled thoughts stumbling over themselves.

"I'm waiting," he said with a dash of impatience.

"Yes, well, this isn't exactly easy." She could feel a blush work its way up her face, and was confident she was about to make a complete idiot of herself. Briefly Amy had thought that if her mother had been alive, she could have asked her, but on second thought, she realized this was something one didn't discuss with one's mother.

"Amy," he questioned softly, "what is it?"

Her gaze was lowered, and the heat creeping up from her neck had blossomed into full color in her cheeks. She absently toyed with the satin ties at the neck of her robe.

"I...when we—you know—were on the bed together, you said something that has been on my mind ever since."

"What did I say?"

Josh sounded so calm, so...ordinary, as if he had this type of discussion with women every day of the week, as if he were a doctor discussing a medical procedure with his patient. Amy's heart was thundering in her ears so loudly she could barely form a coherent thought.

He prompted her again, and she wound the satin tie around her index finger so tightly she cut off the circulation. "You were trying to undo my blouse," she whispered, nearly choking on the words.

"And?"

"And you kissed me and held me in ways no other man ever has."

"I suspected as much."

"You see I attended a private girls school and there just wasn't much opportunity for this sort of...foreplay. I realize you must think me terribly naive and...gauche."

"I don't think anything of the sort. You're innocent, or at least you were until I got my hands on you." He frowned as he said it.

"Would you do it again...touch me the way you did before."

"Amy, no..."

"Please, I need to know these things and I want you to be the one to teach me."

"You don't know what you're asking."

"I do, Josh. I'm not completely innocent and I promise you I'm a quick learner."

He closed his eyes and groaned. "I'm all too aware of that fact already."

"It felt so good to have you touch me."

"It did for me, too." Josh's voice was low and hesitant.

"Will you do it again?" she asked, her voice so quiet she could barely hear herself. Boldly she raised her eyes to his, her heart beating wildly.

She stood and walked the few short steps to his bedside and laid open her robe. Josh sat there mesmerized, his face unreadable, but he didn't say or do anything to stop her. Her fingers were trembling as she slipped the robe from her shoulders. It fell silently at her feet. She made herself vulnerable to him in ways she was only beginning to comprehend. She was so pale, she realized, wishing now that she was tan and golden for him, instead of alabaster white.

"Amy."

Her name was little more than a rasp between his lips. "Like I explained earlier you don't know what you're asking." Of their own volition, it seemed, his fingers lightly brushed the smooth skin of her throat. Instantly, her tender skin there started to throb.

His touch, although featherlight, produced an immediate melting ache in her. She pulsed in places she'd never known existed until Josh had kissed and touched her.

"Please, Josh," she whispered. "I have to know." There was more she longed to ask, more she yearned to discover, but the words withered on the end of her tongue at the look of intense longing Josh gave her.

He reached for her waist and gently urged her forward until she was close enough for him to bury his face between her breasts. Abruptly, Josh stopped and jerked his head away. For several seconds he did nothing but draw in deep, lung-rasping breaths. "Enough," he said finally. Amy clung to him, not knowing how to tell him that he hadn't answered a single inquiry. Instead he'd created even more.

"I don't want you to stop," she moaned in bewilderment. She paused, hoping to clear her thoughts, then continued raggedly. "Josh, I want to make love with you. I want you to teach me to be a woman, your woman."

"No."

Her knees would no longer support her, and she sank onto the bed, sitting on the edge of the mattress. It was then that she realized that Josh was trembling, and the knowledge that she could make him want her so desperately filled her with a heady sense of power.

Reaching out to him, Amy wasn't about to let him push her away. Not again.

"No," he cried a second time, but with much less conviction. Even as he spoke he filled his palms with her breasts and made a low, rough sound of protest. "Amy…please." His voice vibrated between them, filled with urgency and helplessness. "Not like this…not in your father's house."

She sagged, drooping her head in frustration. Josh was right. They were both panting with the effort to resist each other as it was, and in a few seconds neither one of them would be able to stop. It took everything within her to quit now.

Amy blindly reached for her robe. She would have turned and vaulted from the room if Josh hadn't reached for her wrist, stalling her. Not for anything could she look him in the eye.

"Are you going to be all right?" he asked.

She nodded wildly, knowing it was a lie. She would never be the same again.

He swore quietly, and with a muffled deep gasp of pain sat upright in the bed and reached for her, hugging her close and burying his face in the gentle slope of her neck.

"Amy, listen to me; we've got to stop this horsing around before it kills the both of us."

"Josh," she whispered, her tone hesitant. "That's the problem. I don't want to stop. It feels so wonderful when you touch me, and I get all achy inside and out." Consternation and apprehension crept into her voice. "My behavior is embarrassing you, isn't it?"

"Me?"

"I mean, the last thing you need is me making all kinds of sexual demands on you. You're lucky to be alive. Here I am, like a kid who's recently discovered a wonderful toy and doesn't quite know how to make everything work."

"Believe me, honey, it's working."

"I'm sorry, Josh, I really am—"

He silenced her with a chaste kiss. "Go back to bed. We can talk more about it in the morning, when both our heads are clear."

"Good night," she whispered, heaving a sigh.

"Good night." He kissed her once more and, with a reluctance that tore at her heart, he released her.

"Morning, Dad," Amy said as she seated herself at the table for breakfast the following morning.

Her father grumbled an inaudible reply, which wasn't anything like him. Harold Johnson had always been a morning person and boomed enthusiasm for each new day.

Amy hesitated, her thoughts in a whirl. Was it possible that her father had heard her sneak into Josh's room the night before? That thought was enough to produce a heated blush, and in an effort to disguise her discomfort, she hurriedly dished up her scrambled eggs and bacon.

Her father didn't say anything more for several minutes. Deciding it would be better to confront him with the truth than suffer this intolerable silence, Amy straightened her shoulders and clasped her hands in her lap.

"How's Josh doing?" Harold asked, reaching for the sugar bowl after pouring himself a cup of coffee.

"Better." She eyed him warily, trying to decide the best way to handle this awkward situation. Perhaps she should let him bring up the subject first.

"I talked to Mrs. White yesterday afternoon," she said with feigned cheerfulness, "and she said Josh is doing better than anyone expected."

"Good. Good."

Enthusiasm echoed in each word. Amy was absolutely positive that her father knew the reasons behind Josh's increasing strength. The crimson heat that had invaded her face earlier circled her ears like a lariat. She swallowed a bite of her toast, and it settled in her stomach like a lead ball.

"I had a chance to talk to Mrs. White this morning myself."

"You did?" she blurted out.

"Yes," he continued, eyeing her closely.

Amy did her level best to disguise her distress. She'd always been close to her father, and other than the business about him making her a part of Johnson Industries, she'd prided herself on being able to talk to him about anything.

"Amy, are you feeling all right?"

"Sure, Dad," she said energetically, knowing she wasn't going to be able to fool him.

He arched his brows and reached for his coffee, sipping at it while he continued studying her.

There was nothing left to do but blurt out the truth and clear the air before she suffocated in the tension. "You heard me last night, didn't you?"

"I beg your pardon?"

"Well, you needn't concern yourself, because nothing happened. Well, almost nothing, but not from lack of trying on my part. Josh was the perfect gentleman."

Her father stared at her with huge blue eyes. He certainly wasn't making this any easier on her. He continued to glare at her for several uneasy seconds until Amy felt compelled to explain further.

"It was late…and I couldn't sleep. I know that probably isn't a very good excuse, but I had a question that I wanted to ask Josh."

"You couldn't have asked me?"

Her startled eyes flew to him. "No!"

"Go on."

"How much more do you want to know? I already told you nothing happened."

"I believe the phrase you used a moment ago was 'almost nothing.'"

"I'm crazy about him, Dad, and I've never been in love

before, and, well, it's difficult when you…feel that way about someone…if you know what I mean?"

"I believe I do."

"Good." She relaxed somewhat. Although her appetite had vanished the instant she realized her father was waiting to confront her about what had happened in Josh's room, she did an admirable job of finishing her breakfast.

"Mrs. White said Josh would be able to join us for dinner tonight."

Amy's happy gaze flew to her father. "That's wonderful."

"I thought you'd be pleased to hear it."

"I'll have Manuela prepare a special dinner."

Her father nodded. "Good idea." He downed the last of his coffee, glanced at his watch, then stood abruptly. "I've got to go to the office. Have a good day, sweetheart."

Amy raised her coffee cup to her lips and sipped. "Thanks. You, too."

"I will." He was halfway out of the dining room when he turned around. "Amy."

"Yes, Dad."

"I'm not exactly certain I should admit this. But I didn't hear a thing last night. I slept like a log."

Eight

"It's your move," Amy reminded Josh for the second time, growing restless. Just how long did it take to move a silly chess piece, anyway?

Josh nodded, frowning slightly as he studied the board that rested on the table between them.

Amy's gaze caught her father's and she rolled her eyes. Josh was the one who'd insisted they play chess following dinner. Harold Johnson shared a secret smile with her. He pretended to be reading when in fact he was closely watching their game.

Amy had never been much of a chess player; she didn't have the patience for it. As far as she was concerned, chess was a more difficult version of checkers, and she chose to play it that way. It never took her more than a few seconds to move her pieces. Josh, on the other hand, drove her crazy, analyzing each move she made, trying to figure out her strategy. Heaven knew she didn't have one, and no one was more shocked than she was when Josh announced that she'd placed him in checkmate. Good grief, she hadn't even noticed.

"You're an excellent player," he said, leaning back and

rubbing the side of his jaw. He continued to study the board as though he couldn't quite figure out how she'd done it. Amy hoped he would let her in on the secret once he figured it out; she was curious to find out herself.

Her father rose from his wingback leather chair and crossed the room to get a book from the mahogany cases that lined two walls. As soon as he was out of earshot, Amy glanced over to Josh.

"You haven't kissed me all week," she whispered heatedly.

Josh's anxious gaze flew to her father, then to her. "I don't plan to."

"Ever again?"

Josh frowned. "Not here."

"Why not?"

"Because!" He hesitated and glanced toward her father. "Can we discuss this another time?"

"No," she answered with equal fervor. "You're driving me crazy."

"Mr. Johnson," Josh said anxiously and cleared his throat when her father started toward his chair. "Could I interest you in a game of chess?"

"No thanks, son. Amy's the champion of our family, you're going to have to demand a rematch with her." He stopped and placed his hand over his mouth, then did a poor job of feigning a yawn. "The fact is, I was thinking of heading up to bed. I seem to be tired this evening."

"It's barely eight," Amy protested. She immediately regretted her outburst. With her father safely tucked away in his bedroom, she might be able to spend a few minutes alone with Josh, which was something she hadn't been able to do in days.

"Can't help it if I'm tired," Harold grumbled and, after bidding them both good night, he walked out of the room.

Amy waited a few moments until she was sure her father was completely up the stairs. "All right, Joshua Powell, kindly explain yourself."

"The subject's closed, Amy."

She bolted to her feet, her fists digging into her hipbones as she struggled to quell her irritation. "Subject? What subject?"

"You and me...kissing."

If his face hadn't been so twisted with determination and pride, she would have laughed outright. Unfortunately, Josh was dead serious.

"You don't want to kiss me anymore? At all?"

He tossed her a look that told her she should know otherwise by now. Reaching for his crutches, he struggled to his feet. The cast had been removed from his leg, but he still had trouble walking without support.

"Where are you going?" she demanded, growing more agitated by the minute.

"To bed."

"Oh, honestly," she cried. "There's no reason to wrestle your way up those stairs so early. If you're so desperate to escape me, then I'll leave."

"Amy..."

"No." She stopped him by holding up both hands. "There's no need to worry your stubborn little head about me taking a drive alone in the cold, dark city. There are plenty of places I can go, so sit down and enjoy yourself. You must be sick of that room upstairs." With a proud thrust of her chin she marched out of the room and retrieved her purse. Glancing over her shoulder, she sighed and added, "There's no need to fret. Seattle has one of the lowest murder rates on the west coast." She had no idea if this was true or not, but it sounded good.

"Amy," he shouted, and followed her. His legs swung wide as he maneuvered his crutches around the corner of the hallway, nearly colliding with her.

She offered him a brave smile and pretended she wasn't the least bit disturbed by his attitude, when exactly the opposite was true. If he didn't want to kiss or hold her again then…then she would just have to accept it.

"Yes?" she asked, tightly clenching the car keys in her hand as though keeping them safely tucked between her fingers was the most important thing in her life.

For a long moment Josh did nothing but stare at her. A battle raged in his expression as if he was fighting himself. Whichever side won apparently didn't please him, because his shoulders sagged and he slowly shook his head. "Do you want company?"

"Are you suggesting you come along with me?"

His smile was off center. "What do you think?"

"I don't know anymore, Josh. You haven't been yourself all week. Do you think I'm so blind I haven't noticed how you've arranged it so we're never alone together anymore?"

"It's too much temptation," he argued heatedly. "We're in trouble here, Amy. We're so hot for each other it's a minor miracle that we don't burst into spontaneous combustion every time we touch."

"So you're making sure that doesn't happen again?"

"You've got that right," he returned forcefully. He was leaning heavily upon his crutches. He wiped a hand over his face as if to erase her image from his mind. "I don't like it any better than you do, Angel Eyes."

Somehow Amy doubted that. Her tight look must have said as much because Josh emitted a harsh groan.

"Do you have any idea how much I want to make love with you?" he asked her in a harsh whisper. "Every time you walk into the room, it's pure torment. Tonight at dinner, I swear I didn't take my eyes off your breasts the entire meal."

She smiled, not knowing how to answer him.

"Then you got up and walked away, and it was all I could do to keep from watching your sweet little tush swaying back and forth. I kept thinking how good it would be to place my hands there and hold you against me. Did you honestly believe I wanted seconds of dessert? The fact was, I didn't dare stand up."

"Oh, Josh." Her smile was watery with relief.

He held open his arms for her, and she walked into them the way a frightened child ducks into a family home, sensing security and safety. Using the wall to brace his shoulders, he set one crutch aside and reached for her, wrapping his arm around her waist. Slowly, he lowered his hand, lifting her toward him so he could press himself more intimately against her. "Josh…"

"Do you understand now?" he ground out, close to her ear.

"Yes," she whispered with a barely audible release of breath. She slipped her arms around his neck.

He stroked his thumb along the side of her neck and inhaled a wobbly breath before he spoke again. "Now, what was it you were saying about going for a ride?"

"Ride?" she repeated in a daze.

"Yes, Amy, a ride, as in a motorized vehicle, preferably with all the windows down and the air conditioner on full blast so my blood will cool."

She pressed her forehead to his chin and smiled before reluctantly breaking away from him. Josh reached for his crutches and followed her through the kitchen and to the garage just beyond.

A few minutes later, with Amy driving and Josh sitting in the passenger seat, they headed down the long, curved driveway and onto the street, turning east toward Lake Washington.

"I love Seattle at night," Amy said, smiling at him. "There're so many bright lights, and the view of the water is fantastic."

"Where are you taking me?"

"Lover's Leap?" she teased.

"Try again."

"All right, it isn't exactly Lover's Leap, but it is a viewpoint that looks out onto the lake. It's been a while since I've been there, but from what I remember, it's worth the drive."

"And what exactly do you know about lookout points, Amy Johnson? I'd bet my entire life's savings that you've never been there with a man."

"Then you'd lose." She tossed him a saucy grin, then pulled her gaze to the roadway, her love for him so potent she felt giddy with it.

He eyed her skeptically. "Who?"

"Does it matter? All you need to know is that I was there with a man. A handsome one, too, by anyone's standards."

"When?" he challenged.

"Well," she hesitated, not wanting to give her secret away quite so easily. "I don't exactly remember *when*. Let me suffice to say, it was several years back, when I was young and foolish."

"You're young and foolish now."

"Nevertheless, I was with a man. I believe you said you'd hand over your life savings to me." She laughed, her happiness bubbling over. "I'll take a check, but only with the proper identification."

"All right, if you're going to make this difficult, I'll guess. You were ten and your daddy was escorting you around town and stopped at this lookout point so you could view the city lights."

"How'd you guess that?" she asked, then clamped her mouth shut, realizing she'd given herself away. "I should make you pay for that, Joshua Powell."

He brushed his fingers against her nape, and when he spoke his voice was low and seductive. "I'm counting on it, Angel Eyes."

"You think once I park this car that I'm going to let you kiss me, don't you?"

Josh's laugh was full. "Baby, you're going to ask for it. Real nice, too."

Laughing, she eased the Mercedes to a stop at the end of the long, deserted street and turned off the headlights, then the ignition. The view was as magnificent as she remembered. More so, because she was sharing it with Josh. The city stretched out before them like a bolt of black satin, littered with shimmering lights that sparkled and gleamed like diamonds. Lake Washington was barely visible, but the electricity from the homes that bordered its shores traced the curling banks. The sky was cloudless and the moon full.

Amy expelled her breath and leaned her head back to gaze into the heavens. It was so peaceful, so quiet, the moment serene. It was a small wonder that this area hadn't been developed over the intervening years since she'd last been here. She was pleased that it remained unspoiled, because it would have ruined everything to have this lovely panorama defaced with long rows of expensive homes.

Josh was silent, apparently savoring the sight himself.

"All right," she whispered, her voice trembling a little with anticipation.

He turned to her, his mending leg stretched out in front of him in as comfortable a position the cramped quarters of the car could afford him. The crutches were balanced against the passenger door. "All right what?"

"You said I was going to have to ask for a kiss. I'm asking, Josh." She felt breathless, as if she'd just finished playing a set of tennis. "Please."

Josh went stock-still, and she could sense the tension in him as strongly as she could smell the fragrant grass that grew along the roadside.

"Heaven help me, Amy, I want to please you."

"You do, every time we touch."

He turned her in his arms, his kiss slow and sultry. So hot and sweet that her toes curled and she twisted, wanting to get as near to him as possible in the close confines. The console was a barrier between them, and the steering wheel prevented her from twisting more than just a little.

In their weeks together, Josh had taught her the fine art of kissing, his lessons exhaustive and detailed. Tonight, Amy was determined to prove to him what an avid student she had been. His shoulders heaved, and he drew in a sharp breath.

"Amy," he warned in a severe whisper, "you should never have gotten us started. Angel, don't you understand yet what this is eventually going to lead to—"

She pressed the tips of her fingers over his lips. "Why do you insist on arguing with me, Joshua Powell?" She didn't give him an opportunity to answer, but slid her hands up his shoulders and joined them at the base of his neck, lifting her mouth to his once more, unwilling to spend these precious moments alone debating a moot point.

Josh's kiss wasn't slow or sweet this time, but hot and urgent, so hungry that he drove the crown of her head against the headrest. He grasped the material of her skirt, bunching it up around her upper thighs as he slid his callused palm over her silk panties.

Her eyes snapped open with surprise at this new invasion. He wanted to shock her, prove to her that she was in over her head. What Josh didn't realize was that with all the other lessons he'd been giving her, she'd learned to swim. So well she wanted to try out for the Olympic team. Lifting her hips just a little to aid him, her knee came in sharp contact with the steering wheel, and she cried out softly.

"Damn."

"If you think that's bad, I've got a gear shift sticking in my ribs," he informed her between nibbling kisses. "I'm too old for this, Angel Eyes."

"I am, too," she whispered and teased him with her tongue.

"Maybe I'm not as old as I think," he amended at the end of a ragged sigh.

Amy smoothed the hair away from his face, spreading eager kisses wherever she could. "You know what I want?"

"Probably the same thing I do, but we aren't going to get it in this car."

"Honestly, Josh, you've got a one-track mind."

"Me!" he bellowed, then groaned and broke away from her to rub the ache from his right leg.

"Are you all right?" Amy asked, unable to bear the thought of Josh in pain.

"Let me put it this way," he said, a frown pleating his brow. "I don't want you to kiss it and make it better."

"Why not?" She tried to sound as offended as she felt.

"Because the ache in my leg is less than the one that

console is giving my ribs. If this is to go any farther, then it won't be in this car."

"Agreed." Without another word, she snapped her seat belt into place, turned on the ignition and shifted the gears into Reverse. Her tires kicked up loose gravel and dirt as she backed into the street.

"*Now* where are you taking me?" Josh asked, chuckling.

"Don't ask."

"I was afraid of that," he muttered.

A half hour later, they turned off the road onto the driveway that led to her family home. She drove past the garage and the tennis courts and parked directly in front of the pool.

"What are we doing here?" he demanded, looking none too pleased.

"I tried to say something earlier," she reminded him, "but you kept interrupting me. I think we should go swimming."

He groaned and shut his eyes, obviously less than enthusiastic with her suggestion. "Swimming? In case you hadn't noticed it's October, and there's a definite nip in the air."

"The pool's heated. Eighty-two degrees, to be exact."

"I don't have a suit."

"There are several your size in the cabana."

Josh closed his fingers around the door handle. Slowly shaking his head, he opened the door and, using both hands, carefully swung out his right leg. "I have the distinct notion you have an argument for every one of my objections."

"I do." She climbed out of the car, and with her arm around his waist, she guided him toward the changing room and brought out several suits for him to choose from. She kissed him, then smiled at him. "The last one in the water is a rotten egg."

By the time Amy came out of the cabana, Josh was sitting at the edge of the deep end, his long legs dangling in the pool. He was right about there being a chill in the night air. She kept the thick towel securely wrapped around her shoulders as she walked over to join him, but she did this more for effect than to ward off the cold.

"Hello, rotten egg."

"Hi, there," she said, giving him a slow, sweet smile before letting the towel drop to her feet.

The minute she did, Josh gasped and his eyes seemed to pop out of their sockets. "Oh, no," he muttered, expelling his breath in a slow exercise.

"Do you like it?" she asked, whirling around in a wide circle for him to admire her itsy-bitsy string bikini.

"You mean, do I like what there is of it?"

She smiled, pleased to the soles of her feet by his response. "I picked it up in France last summer. Trust me, this one is modest compared to what some of the other women were wearing."

"Or not wearing," he commented dryly. "You'd be arrested if you showed up in that...thing on any beaches around here."

Holding her head high to appear as statuesque as possible, she smiled softly, turned and dipped her big toe into the pool to test the temperature. "I most certainly would *not* be arrested. Admired, perhaps, but not imprisoned."

His Adam's apple moved up and down his throat, but he didn't take his eyes off her. "Have you...worn this particular suit often?"

"No. There was never anyone I wanted to see me in it until now." With that, she stood at the edge of the pool, raised her arms high above her head and dove headlong into the turquoise blue waters, slicing the surface with her slender frame.

She surfaced, sputtering and angry. "Oh, dear."

"What's wrong?"

"You don't want to know." Before he could question her further, she dove under the clear blue water and held her breath for as long as she could.

When she broke the surface, gasping for breath, Josh was in the pool beside her, treading water. He took one look at her and started to laugh.

"You lost your fancy bikini top," he cried, as if she hadn't noticed.

"I suppose you find this all very amusing," she said, blushing to the roots of her hair. To her horror, she discovered that women's breasts have the uncanny habit of floating. Trying to maintain as much dignity as possible, she pressed her splayed fingers over her breasts, flattening them to her torso. But she soon discovered that without her hands, she couldn't stay afloat. Her lips went below the waterline, and she drank in several mouthfuls before choking. Mortified, she abandoned the effort, deciding it was better to be immodest than to drown.

Josh was laughing, and it was all she could do not to dunk him. "The least you can do is try to help me find it."

"Not on your life. Fact is, this unfortunate incident is going to save me a good deal of time and trouble."

"Josh." She held out her hand. "I insist that you…keep your distance." She eyed him warily while clumsily working her way toward the shallow end of the pool.

"Look at that," he said, his gaze centering on her breasts, which were bobbing up and down at the surface as she tried to get away from him.

Her toes scraped the bottom of the pool, and once her

feet were secure, she scrunched down, keeping just her head visible. She covered her face with both hands. "This is downright embarrassing, and all you can do is laugh."

"I'm sorry."

But he didn't sound the least bit petulant.

"I wanted you to see me in that bikini and swoon with desire. You were supposed to take one look at me and be so overcome with passion that you could hardly speak."

"I was."

"No, you weren't," she challenged. "In fact you looked angry, telling me I should be arrested."

"I didn't say that exactly."

"Close enough," she cried, her discontent gaining momentum. "I spent an extra ten minutes in the cabana spreading baby oil all over my body so I'd glisten for you, and did you notice? Oh, no, you—"

Before another word passed her lips, Josh had gripped her by the waist and carried her to the corner of the pool, securing her there and blocking any means of escape with his body. His outstretched arms gripped the edge of the pool.

Wide-eyed, she stared at him, the only light coming from the full moon and the dim blue lights below the water. "It isn't any big disaster," Josh told her.

"Oh, sure, you're not the one floating around with your private parts exposed. Trust me, it has a humbling effect."

She knew he was trying not to laugh, but it didn't help matters when the corners of his mouth started quivering. "Joshua Powell," she cried, bracing her hands against his shoulders and pushing for all she was worth. "I could just—"

"Kiss me." The teasing light had vanished and he lowered his gaze to the waterline. His eyes were dark and narrowed, and her breasts felt heavy and swollen just from the way he was looking at her.

Timidly, she slanted her mouth over his, barely brushing his lips with her own.

"Not like that," he protested, threading his fingers through her wet, blond hair. "Kiss me the way you did earlier in the car." His voice was low and velvety. "Oh, baby," he moaned, slipping his moist mouth back and forth over her own. "The things you do to me." Seemingly impatient, he took advantage of her parted lips, and kissed her thoroughly and leisurely. He kissed her as he never had before, tasting, relishing, savoring her in a hungry exchange that left them both breathless.

"Wrap your legs around my waist," he instructed, his words raspy with desire.

Without question she did as he asked. Slipping her hands over the smooth-powered muscles.

"Josh?"

"Yes, love."

She didn't know what she wanted to ask.

She slipped her arms around his neck and pressed her torso against the water-slickened planes of his chest.

"Are you...hungry?" she asked, her voice little more than a husky murmur.

His response was guttural. "You know that I am."

Her head spun with all the things he was doing to her, kissing her until she was senseless.

"Angel," he whimpered, "be still for just a moment."

"I can't," she cried breathlessly.

Her nails curled into his chest, but if the action caused him any pain, he gave no indication. The need to taste him dominated every thought as she ran the tip of her tongue around the circumference of his mouth. Her breasts were heaving when she collapsed on him. "Oh, Josh, I never knew… I never knew." She was just regaining her breath when she heard the sound of voices and laughter advancing from the other side of the cabana.

Josh heard it as well and stiffened, tension filling his body. "Who's there?" he shouted, his body shielding Amy from view.

"Peter Stokes."

Josh's questioning gaze met Amy's. "He's our gardener's son," she explained in a whisper. "Dad told him he could come swimming anytime…but not now."

"The pool's occupied," Josh called out. "Come back tomorrow." A low grumble followed his words, but soon the sound of the voices faded.

The moment was ruined. They both accepted it with reluctance and regret. Josh kissed her forehead, and she snuggled against him. The water lapped against them, and they hugged each other, their bodies entwined.

"Next time, angel," he said, tucking his finger under her chin and raising her eyes to his. "We don't stop."

Nine

"About last night," Josh started, looking disgruntled and eager to talk.

"That's exactly what I want to talk to you about," Amy whispered fiercely as she joined him in the dining room the following morning. "It isn't there."

Manuela had just finished serving him a plate heaped high with hot pancakes. He waited until the housekeeper was out of the room before he spoke. "What isn't there?" Josh asked, pouring thick maple syrup over his breakfast.

"My bikini top," she returned, growing frustrated. "I went down to the pool early this morning...before anyone else could find it, and it *wasn't there*." She was certain her cheeks were the same color as the cranberry juice he was drinking. It had been too dark to search for it the night before, and so cold when they climbed out of the water that Josh had insisted they wait until morning.

"I'm sure it'll show up," he said nonchalantly.

"But it's not there now. What could have possibly happened to it?" Naturally, he was unconcerned. It wasn't *his* swimsuit that was missing. The fact that he was having so much trouble suppressing a smile wasn't helping matters, either.

"It's probably stuck in the pump."

"Don't be ridiculous," she countered, not appreciating his miserable attempt at humor. "The pump would never suck up anything that big."

"Trust me, honey. There wasn't enough material in that bikini to cover a baby's bottom. Personally, I don't want to be the one to explain to your father how it got there when he has to call in a plumber."

"Funny. Very funny."

She'd just pulled out a chair to sit across the table from him when the phone rang. She turned, prepared to answer, when the second ring was abruptly cut off.

"Manuela must have gotten it," she said, noting that Josh had set his fork aside as if he expected the call to be for him. Sure enough, a couple of moments later, the plump Mexican cook came rushing into the dining room. "The phone is for you, Mr. Josh," she said with a heavy accent.

Josh nodded, and he cast a glance in Amy's direction. She could have sworn his eyes held an apologetic look, which was ridiculous, since there was nothing to feel contrite about. He scooted away from the table and stood with the aid of his cane. Her gaze followed him, and she was surprised when he walked into the library and deliberately closed the door.

"Well," Amy muttered aloud, pouring herself a cup of coffee. So the man had secrets. To the best of her knowledge, Josh had never received or made a phone call the entire time he had spent with them. But then, she wasn't with him twenty-four hours a day, either.

An eternity passed before Josh returned—Amy was on

her second cup of coffee—but she was determined to drink the entire pot if it took that long.

He was leaning heavily upon the cane, his progress slow as he made his way into the dining room. This time his eyes avoided hers.

"Your breakfast is cold," she said, standing behind her chair. "Would you like me to ask Manuela to make you another plate?"

"No, thanks," he said, and his frown deepened.

Amy strongly suspected his scowl had little or nothing to do with his cold breakfast.

"Is anything the matter?" She would have swallowed her tongue before she'd directly inquire about the phone call, but something was apparently troubling Josh, and she wanted to help if she could.

"No," he said.

He gave her a brief smile that was meant to hearten her, but didn't. His unwillingness to share, plus his determined scowl, heightened her curiosity. Then, in a heartbeat, Amy knew.

"That was Jasmine, wasn't it?" Until that moment she'd put the other woman completely out of her mind, refusing to acknowledge the possibility of Josh loving someone else. It shocked her now that she had been so blind.

"Jasmine?"

"In the hospital you murmured her name several times… apparently you had the two of us confused."

"Amy, I don't know anyone named Jasmine." His eyes held hers with reassuring steadiness.

"Then why would you repeat her name when you were only half-conscious?"

"Good grief, I don't know," he returned resolutely.

He looked like he was about to say something more, but

Amy hurried on. "Then I don't need to worry about you leaving me for another woman?" She gave a small laugh, not understanding his mood. It was as if he had erected a concrete wall between them, and she had to shout to gain his attention.

"I'm not going to leave you for another woman." His eyes softened as they rested on her, then pooled with regret. "But I *am* leaving you."

He stated it so casually, as if he was discussing breakfast, as if it was something of little consequence in their lives. Amy felt a fist closing around her heart, the winds of his discontent whipping up unspoken fears.

"I'm sorry, Angel Eyes."

She didn't doubt his contrition was sincere. She closed her hands deliberately over the back of the dining room chair in front of her. "I... I don't think I understand."

"That was SunTech on the phone."

Amy swallowed tightly, debating whether she should say anything. The decision was made simultaneously with the thought. She had to! She couldn't silently stand by and do nothing.

"You couldn't possibly mean to suggest you're going back to work? Josh, you can't—you're not physically capable of it. Good grief, this is only the first day you haven't used your crutches."

"I'll be gone as soon as I've finished packing."

She blinked, noting that he hadn't bothered to respond to her objections. He never intended to discuss his plans with her. He told her, and she was to accept them.

"Where?" she asked, feeling sick to her stomach, her head and her heart numb.

"Texas."

315

She sighed with relief; Texas wasn't so far. "How long?" she asked next.

"What does it matter?"

"I… I'd like to know how long it will be before you can come back."

He tensed, his back as straight as a flagpole. "I won't be coming back."

"I see." He was closing himself off from her, blocking her out of his life as if she was nothing more than a passing fancy. The pain wrapped itself around her like ivy climbing up the base of a tree, choking out its life by degrees.

Without another word of explanation, Josh turned and started to walk away from her.

"You intend to forget you ever knew me, don't you?"

He paused in the doorway, his back to her, his shoulders stiff and proud. "No."

Amy didn't understand any of this. Only a few hours before he'd held her in his arms, loved her, laughed with her. And now…now, he was casually turning and strolling out of her life with little or no excuse. It didn't make any sense.

Several minutes passed before Amy had the strength to move. When she did, she vaulted past Josh as he slowly made his way up the stairs one at a time. Poised at the top, she forced a smile to her lips, although they trembled with barely suppressed emotion.

"You can't leave yet," she said with a saucy grin, placing a hand on her hip and doing her best to look sophisticated and provocative. "We have some unfinished business. Remember?"

"No, we don't."

"Josh, you're the one who claimed that the next time we don't stop."

"There isn't going to be a next time."

He was so cold, so callous, so determined. Removing her hand from her hip, Amy planted it on her forehead, her thoughts rumbling in her mind, deep and dark. Lost. "I think I'm missing out on something here. Last night—"

Josh stopped her with a glare, telling her with his eyes what he said every time he touched her. *Last night was a mistake.*

"All right," she continued, undaunted. "Last night probably shouldn't have happened. But it did. It has in the past, and I was hoping—well, never mind, you know what I was hoping."

"Amy…"

"I want to know what's so different now? Why this morning instead of yesterday or the day before? It's as though you can't get away from me fast enough. Why? Did I do something to offend you? If so, I think we should talk about it and clear the air…instead of this."

He reached the top of the stairs, his gaze level with her own. He tried to disguise it, but Amy saw the pain in his eyes, the regret.

"The last thing I want to do is hurt you, Amy."

"Good, then don't."

He cupped her face in his hand and gazed deeply into her eyes as if to tell her that if there had been any way to avoid this, he would have chosen it. He dropped his hand and backed up two small steps. Once more, Amy noted how sluggish his movements were, but this time she guessed it wasn't his leg that was bothering him, but his heart. She looked into his eyes and saw so many things she was certain he meant to hide from her. Confusion. Guilt. Rationalization.

Without another word, he walked past her and to his room. Not knowing what else to do, she followed him.

"You can't tell me you don't love me," she said, stepping inside after him. Immediately, her eyes fell on the open suitcase sitting atop the bed and a sick, dizzying feeling assaulted her. Josh had intended to leave even before the phone call, otherwise his suitcase wouldn't be where it was. "You *do* love me," she repeated, more forcefully this time. "I know you do."

He didn't answer, apparently unwilling to admit his feelings either way.

"It's the money, isn't it? That ridiculous pride of yours is causing all this, and it's just plain stupid. I could care less if you have a dime to your name. I love you, and I'm not going to stop loving you for the next fifty years. If you're so eager to go to Texas, then fine, I'll go with you. I don't need a fancy house and a big car to be happy…not when I have you."

"You're not following me to Texas or anyplace else," he said harshly, his words coated with steel. "I want that understood right now." While he was speaking, he furiously stuffed clothes into the open piece of luggage, his movements abrupt and hurried.

Amy walked over to the window and gripped her hands behind her back, her long nails cutting into her palms. "If you are worried about Dad's—"

"It isn't the money," he said curtly.

"Then what is it?" she cried, losing patience.

He pressed his lips together, and a muscle leaped in his lean jaw.

"Josh," she cried. "I want to know. I have the right, at least. If you want to walk out of my life, then that's your business, but tell me why. I've got a right to know."

He closed his eyes and when he opened them again, they were filled with a new determination, a new strength. "It's you. We're completely different kinds of people. I told you when we met I had no roots, and that's exactly the way I like my life. I like jobs that take me around the world and offer fresh challenges. You need a man who's going to be a father to those babies you talked about once. And it's not going to be me, sweetheart."

She flinched at the harsh way he used the term of affection. Sucking in her breath, she tried again. "When two people love each other, they can learn to compromise. I don't want to chain you to Seattle. If you want to travel, then I'll go with you wherever you want."

"You?" He snickered once. "You're used to living the lifestyles of the rich and famous. Jetting off in your daddy's plane, shopping in Paris, skiing in Switzerland. Forget it, Amy. Within a month, you'd be bored out of your mind."

"Josh, how can you say that? Okay, I can understand why you'd think I'm a spoiled rich kid, and…and you're right, our lifestyles *are* different, but we're compatible in other ways," she rushed on, growing desperate. "You only have to think about what…what nearly happened in the pool to realize that."

He paused, and his short laugh revealed no amusement. "That's another thing," he said coldly. "You with your hot little body, looking for experience. I'm telling you right now, I'm not going to be the one to give it to you."

"You seemed willing enough last night," she countered, indignation overcoming the hurt his words caused.

He granted her that much with a cocky grin. "I thank the good Lord that your gardener's son showed up when he did, otherwise there could be more than one unpleasant complication to our venture into that pool."

"I'm not looking for experience, Josh, I'm looking for love."

"A twenty-four-year-old virgin always coats her first time with thoughts of love—it makes it easier to justify later. It isn't love we share, Amy, it's a healthy dose of good old-fashioned lust." He stuffed a shirt inside his suitcase so forcefully it was a miracle the luggage remained intact. "When it comes to making love, you're suffering from a little retarded growth. The problem is, you don't fully realize what you're asking for, and when you find out, it's going to shock you."

"You haven't shocked me."

"Trust me, I could."

He said this with a harshly indrawn breath that was sharp enough to make Amy recoil.

"Sex isn't romance, Angel Eyes, it's hot mouths and grinding hips and savage kisses. At least it is with me, and I'm not looking to initiate a novice."

"It seems we've done our share of...that."

"You wouldn't leave me alone, would you? I tried to stay out of your way. I went to great pains to be sure we wouldn't be alone together—to remove ourselves from the temptation. But you would have none of that—you threw yourself at me at every opportunity."

That was true enough, and Josh knew it.

"I'm a man, what was I supposed to do, ignore you? So I slipped a couple of times. I tried to ward you off, but you were so eager to lose your virginity, you refused to listen. Now the painful part comes, I was as much of a gentleman as I could be under the circumstances. It wasn't as if I didn't try." He slammed the lid of his suitcase closed, shaking the bed in the process.

A polite knock sounded at the door, and Josh turned slowly toward it. "Yes, what is it, Manuela?"

"Mr. Josh, there is taxi here for you."

"Thank you. Tell him I'll be down in a couple of minutes."

Amy blinked as fast as she could to keep the burning tears from spilling down her cheeks. "You're really leaving me, aren't you?" She was frozen with shock.

"I couldn't make it any more clear," Josh shouted. "You knew the score when I met you. I haven't lied to you, Amy, not once. Did you think I was joking when I told you I was walking out that door and I didn't plan on coming back? Accept it. Don't make this any more difficult than it already is."

"Go then," she whispered, pride coming to her rescue. "If you can live with the thought of another man holding and kissing me and making love with me then…go." *Go,* she cried silently, *before I beg you to stay.*

For a moment, Josh stood stock-still. Then he reached for his suitcase, closing his fingers viciously around the handle, and dragged it across the bed. He held it in one hand and his cane in the other. Without looking at her, he headed toward the stairs.

Amy stood where she was, tears raining down her face in a storm of fierce emotion. By the time the shock had started to dissipate and she ran to the head of the stairs, Josh was at the front door.

"Josh," she cried, bracing her hands against the railing.

He paused, but he didn't turn and look at her.

"Go ahead and walk out that door… I'm not going to do anything to stop you."

"That's encouraging."

She closed her eyes to the stabbing pain. "I… I just wanted you to know that you can have all the adventures you want and travel to every corner of the world and even… and even make love to a thousand women."

"I intend on doing exactly that."

He was facing her now, but the tears had blinded her and all she could make out was a watery image. "Live your life and I'll... I'll live mine, and we'll probably never see each other again, but... I swear to you...one day you're going to regret this." Her shoulders shook with sobs. "One day you're going to look back and think of all that you threw away and realize..." She paused, unable to go on, and wiped the moisture from her eyes.

"Can I go now?"

"Stop being so cruel."

"It's the only thing you'll accept," he shouted, his anger vibrating all the way up the stairs. He turned from her once more.

"Josh," she cried, her hands knotting into tight fists at her sides.

"Now what?"

The air between them crackled with electricity and the longest moment of her life passed before she could speak. "Don't come back," she told him. "Don't ever come back."

Josh rubbed his eyes with his thumb and index finger and sagged in the seat of the yellow cab.

"Where to, mister?"

"Sea-Tac Airport," Josh instructed. His insides felt like a bowl of overcooked oatmeal tossed in a campfire. Surviving the explosion had been nothing compared to saying goodbye to Amy. He would gladly have run into another burning building rather than walk away from her again. He had to leave, he had known that the minute he climbed out of the pool the night before. It was either get out of her life before their lovemaking went too far or marry her.

For both their sakes, he was leaving.

But it hadn't been easy. The memory of the way her eyes had clouded with pain would haunt him until the day he died. He shut his mind to the image of her standing at the top of the stairs. Her anguish had called to him in an age-old litany that would echo in his mind far beyond the grave.

What she said about him regretting leaving her had hit him like a blow to the solar plexus. He hadn't even been away five minutes, and the remorse struck him the way fire attacks dry timber.

She was right about him loving her, too. Josh hadn't tried to lie about his feelings. He couldn't have, because she knew. Unfortunately, loving her wouldn't make things right for them. It might have worked, they may have been able to build a life together, if she wasn't who she was—Harold Johnson's daughter. Even then Josh had his doubts. There was only one absolute in all this—he wasn't ever going to stop loving her. At least not in this lifetime.

"Hey, buddy, are you all right back there?" the cab driver asked over his shoulder. He was balding and friendly.

"I'm fine."

"You don't look so fine. You look like a man who's been done wrong by his woman. What's the matter, did she kick you out?"

Josh met the driver's question with angry silence.

"Listen, friend, if I were you, I wouldn't put up with it." His laugh was as coarse as his words.

Josh closed his eyes against fresh pain. Amy's words about another man making love to her had hit their mark. Bull's-eye. If he had anything to be pleased about, it was the fact that he had left her with her innocence intact. It had come so close in the pool. He had managed to leave her pure and sweet for some other man to initiate into lovemaking.

A blinding light flashed through his head, and the pain

was so intense that he blinked several times against its un-expected onslaught.

"Hey, friend, I know a good lawyer if you need one. From the looks of it, you two got plenty of cold cash. That makes it tough. I know a lot of people who've got money, and from what I see, it sure as hell didn't buy happiness."

"I don't need a lawyer."

The taxi driver shook his head. "That's a mistake too many men make, these days. They want to keep everything friendly for the kids' sake. You got kids?"

Josh's eyes drifted closed. Children. For a time there, soon after they had returned from Kadiri, Josh had dreamed of having children with her. He dreamed a good deal about making those babies, too. He smiled wryly. If he had learned anything in the months he had spent lov-ing Amy, it was the ability to imagine the impossible. He would wrap those fantasies around him now the way his Aunt Hazel tucked an afghan around her shoulders in the heart of winter.

"I got two boys myself," the driver continued, apparently unconcerned with the lack of response from his passenger. "They're mostly grown now, and I don't mind telling you they turned out all right. Whatever you do, buddy, don't let the wife take those kids away from you. Fight for 'em if you got to, but fight."

Josh was battling, all right, but the war he was waging was going on inside his head. It didn't take much imagina-tion to picture Amy's stomach swollen with his child and the joy that would radiate from her eyes when she looked at him. Only there wouldn't be any children. Because there wouldn't be any Amy. At least not for him.

"Buddy, you sure you don't want the name of that law-yer? He's good. Real good."

"I'm sure."

The cab eased to a stop outside the airport terminal, and the chatty driver looped his arm around the back of the seat and twisted around to Josh. "Buddy, I don't mean to sound like a know-it-all, but running away isn't going to solve anything."

Josh dug out his wallet and pulled out a couple of bills. "This enough?"

"Plenty." The cabbie reached for his wallet. "No, sir, the airport is the last place in the world you should be," he muttered as he drew out a five-dollar bill.

Josh already had his hand on the door. He needed to escape before he realized how much sense this taxi driver was making. "Keep the change."

"Amy." Her father tapped gently against her bedroom door. "Sweetheart, are you all right?"

She sat with her back against the headboard, her knees drawn up. The room was dark. Maybe if she ignored him, her father would go away.

"Amy?"

She sniffled and reached for another tissue. "I'm fine," she called, hoping he would accept that and leave her alone. "Really, Dad, I'm okay." She wasn't in the mood for conversation or father-daughter talks or anything else. All she wanted was to curl up in a tight ball and bandage her wounds. The pain was still too raw to share with her father, although she loved him dearly.

Contrary to her wishes, he let himself into her room and automatically reached for the light switch. Amy squinted and covered her face. "Dad, please, I just want to be by myself for a while." It was then that she noticed the illuminated dial on her clock radio. "What are you doing home this time of day, anyway?"

"Josh phoned me from the airport on his way out of town."

"Why? So he could gloat?" she asked bitterly.

Harold Johnson sat on the edge of his daughter's bed and gently patted her shoulder. "No. He wanted to thank me for my hospitality and to say you probably needed someone about now. From the look of things, he was right."

"I'm doing quite nicely without him, so you don't need to worry." And she would—in a few months or a few years, she added mentally.

"I know you are, sweetheart."

She blew her nose and rubbed the back of her hand across her eyes. "He loves me…in my heart I know he does, and still he walked away."

"I don't doubt that, either."

"Then why?"

"I wish I knew."

"I… I don't think we'll ever know," she sobbed. "I hurt so much I want to hate him and then all I can think is that the…the least he could have done was marry me for my money."

Her father chuckled softly and gathered her in his arms. "Listen, baby, a wise man once stated that happiness broadens our hearts, but sorrow opens our souls."

"Then you can drive a truck through mine."

He held her close. "Try to accept the fact Josh chose to leave, for whatever reason. He's gone. He told me when he first came that was his intention."

"He didn't tell me," she moaned. "Dad, I love him so much. How am I ever going to let him go?"

"The pain will get better in time, I promise you."

"Maybe," she conceded, "but it doesn't seem possible right now." Knowing Josh didn't want to marry her was difficult enough, but refusing to make love with her made his rejection all the more difficult to bear.

"Come downstairs," her father coaxed. "Sitting in your room with the drapes closed isn't helping anything."

She shook her head. "Maybe later."

"How about a trip? Take off with a friend for a while and travel."

She shook her head and wiped a tear from her cheek. "No, thanks. It isn't that I don't appreciate the offer, but I wouldn't enjoy myself. At least not now."

"Okay, baby, I understand." Gently he kissed her crown and stood.

"Dad," she called to him when he started to walk out of her room. "Did Josh say...anything else?"

"Yes." His eyes settled on her and grew sad. "He said goodbye."

The knot in her stomach twisted so tight that she sucked in her breath to the surge of unexpected pain. "Goodbye," she repeated, and closed her eyes.

The next morning, Amy's alarm clock rang at six, rousing her from bed. She showered and dressed in her best suit, primly tucking in her hair at her nape in a loose chignon.

Her father was at the breakfast table when she joined him. His eyes rounded with surprise when she walked into the room.

"Good morning, Dad," she said, reaching for the coffee. She didn't have Josh, but she had her father. Harold Johnson had the courage of a giant and the sensitive heart of a child. Just being with him would help her find the way out of this bitter unhappiness.

"Amy." It looked as if he wasn't quite sure what to say. "It's early for you, isn't it?"

"Not anymore. Now, before we head for the office, is there anything you want to fill me in on?"

For the first time Amy could remember, her father was completely speechless.

Ten

"There was a call for you earlier," Rusty Everett told Josh when he returned from lunch.

Josh's heart thudded heavily. "Did you catch the name?"

"Yeah, I wrote it down here someplace." Rusty, fifty and as Texan as they come, rummaged around his cluttered desk for several moments. "I don't know what I did with it. Whoever it was said they'd call back later."

"It didn't happen to be a woman, did it?" One that had the voice of an angel, Josh added silently. He'd gone out of his way to be sure Amy never wanted to see or talk to him again, and yet his heart couldn't stop longing for her.

"No, this was definitely a man."

"If you find the name, let me know."

"Right."

Leaning upon his cane, Josh made his way into the small office. Since he was still recovering from the explosion, Josh was pushing a pencil for SunTech. He didn't like being cooped up inside an office, but he didn't know if he should attribute this unyielding restlessness to the circumstances surrounding his employment or the gaping hole left in his life without Amy. He had the feeling he could be tanning on the lush white sands of a tropical paradise and still find plenty of cause for complaint.

As painful as it was to admit, there was only one place he wanted to be, and that was in Seattle with a certain angel. Instead, he was doing everything within his power to arrange a transfer to the farthest reaches of planet earth so he could escape her. The problem was, it probably wouldn't matter where he ran, his memories would always catch up with him.

He was wrong to have abruptly left her the way he did, to deliberately hurt her, but, unfortunately, he knew it was the right thing for them both, even if she didn't.

He'd been noble, but he'd behaved like a jerk.

He had to forget her, but his heart and his mind and his soul wouldn't let him.

Wiping a hand across his face, Josh leaned back in his chair and rubbed the ache from his right thigh. The pain in his leg was minute compared to the throbbing anguish that surrounded his heart.

With determination, Josh reached for the geological report he wanted to read, but his mind wasn't on oil exploration. It was on an angel who had turned his life upside down.

"Hey, Josh," Rusty called from the other room. "You've got a visitor."

Josh stood and nearly fell back into his chair in shock when Harold Johnson casually strolled into his office.

"Hello, Josh."

Amy's father greeted him as if they were sitting down to a pleasant meal together. "Mr. Johnson," Josh replied stiffly, ill at ease.

The two shook hands, eyeing each other. One confident, the other dubious, Josh noted. Without waiting for an invitation, Harold claimed the chair on the other side of the desk and crossed his legs as though he planned to sit and chat for a while. All he needed to complete the picture was a snifter of brandy and a Cuban cigar.

"What can I do for you?" Josh asked, doing his level best to keep his voice crisp and professional.

"Well, son," Harold said, and reached inside his suit jacket for the missing cigar. "I've come to talk to you about my daughter."

Vicious fingers clawed at Josh's stomach. "Don't. I made it clear to her, and to you, that whatever was between us is over."

"Just like that?"

"Just like that," Josh returned flatly, lying through clenched teeth.

A flame flickered at the end of the cigar, and Harold took several deep puffs, his full attention centered on the Havana Special. "She's doing an admirable job of suggesting the same thing."

Perhaps something was wrong. Maybe she had been hurt or was ill. Josh struggled to hide his growing concern. Amy's father wouldn't show up without a good reason.

"Is she all right?" Josh asked, unable to bear not knowing any longer.

Harold chuckled. "You'd be amazed at how well she's doing at pretending she never set eyes on you. She hasn't so much as mentioned your name since the day you left. She's cheerful, happy, enthusiastic. If I didn't know her so well, I could almost be fooled."

Relief brought down his guard. "She'll recover."

"Yes, I suspect so. She's keeping busy. The fact is, the girl surprised the dickens out of me the morning after you left. Bright and early she marched down the stairs, dressed in her best business suit, and claimed it was time she started earning her keep. Accounting never knew what hit them." The older man chuckled, sounding both delighted and proud.

If Amy's father had meant to shock him, he was doing an admirable job of it.

"The girl's got grit," Harold continued.

"Then why are you here?" Josh demanded.

"I came to see how you were doing, son."

"A phone call would have served as well."

"Tried that, but your friend there said you were out to lunch, and since I was in town, I thought I'd stop by so we could chat a bit before I flew home."

"How'd you know where to find me?"

Harold inhaled deeply on the cigar. "Were you in hiding?"

"Not exactly." But Josh hadn't let it be known where in Texas he was headed.

"I must say you're looking well."

"Thanks," Josh murmured. Most days he felt as though he wanted to hide under a rock. At least it would be dark and cold, and perhaps he could sleep without dreaming of Amy. The last thing he needed was a confrontation with her father, or to own up to the fact he was dying for news of her.

"Fact is, you look about as well as my daughter does."

Josh heaved a sigh and lowered his eyes to his paperwork, hoping Harold Johnson would take the hint.

"By the way," the older man said, a smile teasing the corners of his mouth, "you wouldn't happen to know anything about a swimsuit I found at the bottom of my pool the day you left, would you?"

It took a good deal to unsettle Josh, but in the course of

five minutes Harold Johnson had done it twice. "I… Amy and I went swimming."

"Looks like one of you decided to skinny-dip," Harold added with an abrupt laugh.

His amusement bewildered Josh even more. "We…ah… I know it looks bad."

"That skimpy white thing must have belonged to my daughter, although I'll admit that I'd no idea she had such a garment."

"Sir, I want you to know I… I didn't…"

"You don't have to explain yourself, son. My daughter's a grown woman, and if nothing happened, it's not from any lack of trying on her part, I'll wager."

Josh hadn't blushed since he was a boy, but he found himself doing so now.

"She must have been a tempting morsel for you to walk away from like that."

Josh swallowed with difficulty and nodded. "She was."

Harold Johnson puffed long and hard on his cigar once more, then held it away from his face and examined the end of it as if he suspected it wasn't lit. When he spoke again, his voice was nonchalant. "I knew a Powell once."

Josh stiffened. "It's a common enough name."

"This Powell was a successful stockbroker with his own firm situated on Wall Street. Ever hear of a fellow by the name of Chance Powell?"

A cold chill settled over Josh. "I've heard of him," he admitted cautiously.

"I thought you might have." Harold nodded, as if confirming the information he already knew. "He's one of the most successful brokers in the country. From what I understand he has offices in all fifty states now. There's been a real turnaround in his business in recent years. I understand he almost lost everything not too long ago, but he survived, and so did the business."

Josh didn't add anything to that. From the time he'd walked away from his father, he'd gone out of his way *not* to keep track of what was happening in his life, professional or otherwise.

"From what I know of him, he has only one child, a son."

If Harold was looking for someone to fill in the blanks, he was going to be disappointed. Josh sat with his back rigid, his mouth set in a thin line of impatience.

Harold chewed on the end of the cigar the way a child savors a candy sucker. "There was a write-up in the *Journal* several years back about Chance's son. I don't suppose you've heard of *him?*"

"I might have." Boldly Josh met the older man's stare, unwilling to give an inch.

"The article said the boy showed promise enough to be one of the brightest business minds this country has ever known. He graduated at the top of his class at MIT, took the business world by storm and revealed extraordinary insight. Then, without anyone ever learning exactly why, he packed up his bags and walked away from it all."

"He must have had his reasons."

Harold Johnson nodded. "I'm sure he did. They must have been good ones for him to walk away from a brilliant future."

"Perhaps he was never interested in money," Josh suggested.

"That's apparently so, because I learned that he served for several years as a volunteer for the Peace Corps." Harold Johnson held the cigar between his fingers and lowered his gaze as if deep in thought. "It's unfortunate that such a keen business mind is being wasted. Fact is, I wouldn't mind having him become part of my own firm. Don't know if he'd consider it, though. What do you think?"

"I'm sure he wouldn't," Josh returned calmly.

"That's too bad." Harold Johnson heaved a small sigh. "His life could be a good deal different if he wished. Instead—" he paused and scowled at Josh "—he's wasted his talents."

"Wasted? Do you believe helping the less fortunate was squandering my—his life?"

"Not at all. I'm sure he contributed a good deal during the years he served with the Peace Corps. But the boy apparently has an abundance of talent in other areas. It's a shame he isn't serving where he's best suited." He stared directly at Josh for a lengthy, uncomfortable moment. "It would seem to me that this young man has made a habit of walking away from challenges and opportunities."

"I think you may be judging him unfairly."

"Perhaps," Amy's father conceded.

Josh remained silent. He knew what the older man was saying, but he wanted none of it.

Harold continued to chew on his cigar, apparently appreciating the taste of the fine Cuban tobacco more than he enjoyed smoking it. "I met Chance Powell several years back, and frankly, I liked the man," Harold continued, seeming to approach this conversation from fresh grounds.

"Frankly," Josh echoed forcefully, "I don't."

The older man's eyes took on an obstinate look. "I'm sorry to hear that."

Josh made a show of looking at his watch, hoping his guest would take the hint and leave before the conversation escalated into an argument. Harold didn't, but that wasn't any real surprise for Josh.

"Do you often meddle in another man's life, or is this a

recent hobby?" Josh asked, swallowing what he could of the sarcasm.

The sound of the older man's laughter filled the small office. "I have to admit, it's a recent preoccupation of mine."

"Why now?"

Harold leaned forward and extinguished his cigar, rubbing it with unnecessary force in the glass ashtray that rested on the corner of Josh's crowded desk. "What's between Chance Powell and his son is their business."

"I couldn't agree with you more. Then why are you bringing it up?"

Any humor that lingered in the older man's gaze vanished like sweet desserts in a room filled with children. "Because both you and Amy are about to make the biggest mistakes of your lives, and I'm finding it downright difficult to sit back and watch."

"What goes on between the two of us is our business."

"I'll grant you that much." Releasing his breath, Harold stood, his look apologetic. "You're right, of course, I had no right coming here. If Amy knew, she'd probably never forgive me."

Josh's tight features relaxed. "You needn't worry that I'll tell her."

"Good."

"She's a strong woman," Josh said, standing and shaking hands with a man he admired greatly. "From everything you said, she's already started to rebound. She'll be dating again soon."

The smile on his lips lent credence to his words, but the thought of Amy with another man did things to his heart Josh didn't even want to consider. It was far better that he never know.

"Before you realize it, Amy will have found herself a

decent husband who will make her a good deal happier than I ever could," Josh said, managing to sound as though he meant it.

Harold Johnson rubbed the side of his jaw in measured strokes. "That's the problem. I fear she already has."

Amy sat in the office of the accounting supervisor for Johnson Industries. Lloyd Dickins would be joining her directly, and she took a few moments to glance around his neat and orderly office. Lloyd's furniture was in keeping with the man, she noted. His room was dominated by thick, bulky pieces that were so unlike her own ultramodern furnishings. A picture of Lloyd's wife with their family was displayed on the credenza, and judging by its frame, the picture was several years old. The one photograph was all there was to fill in the blanks of Dickins's life outside the company. Perhaps his need for privacy, his effort to keep the two worlds separate, was the reason Amy had taken such a liking to Lloyd. It was apparent her father shared her opinion.

Lloyd had welcomed Amy into the accounting department, although she was convinced he had his reservations. Frankly, she couldn't blame him. She was the boss's daughter and if she was going to eventually assume her father's position, albeit years in the future, she would need to know every aspect of managing the conglomerate.

"Sorry to keep you waiting," Lloyd mumbled as he sailed into the office.

Amy swore the man never walked. But he didn't exactly run, either. His movements were abrupt, hurried, and Amy supposed it was that which gave the impression he was continually rushing from one place to the other. He was tall and thin, his face dominated by a smile that was quick and unwavering.

"I've only been waiting a minute," she answered, dismissing his apology.

"Did you have the chance to read over the Emerson report?" he asked as he claimed the seat at his desk. He reached for the file, thumbing through the pages of the summary. The margins were filled with notes and comments.

"I read it last night and then again this morning."

Lloyd Dickins nodded, looking pleased. "You've been putting in a good deal of time on this project. Quite honestly, Amy, I wasn't sure what to expect when your father told me you'd be joining my team. But after the last three weeks, I don't mind telling you, you've earned my respect."

"Thank you." She'd worked hard for this moment, and when the praise came, it felt good.

"Now," Lloyd said, leaning back in his chair, "tell me what you think?"

Amy spent the next twenty minutes doing exactly that. When she'd finished, Lloyd added his own comments and insights and then called for a meeting of their department for that afternoon.

When Amy returned to her office, there were several telephone messages waiting for her. She left Chad's note for last. Chad Morton worked in marketing and had been wonderful. He was charming and suave and endearing, and best of all, nothing like Josh. In fact, no two men could have been more dissimilar, which suited her just fine. If she was going to forget Josh, she would have to do it with someone who was his complete opposite.

Chad was the type of man who would be content to smoke a pipe in front of a fireplace for the remainder of his life. He was filet mignon, designer glasses and BMW personality.

"Chad, it's Amy." She spoke into the receiver. "I got your message."

"Hi, Angel Face."

Amy closed her eyes to the sudden and unexpected flash of pain. She was forced to bite her tongue to keep from asking him not to call her anything that had to do with angels. That had been Josh's line, and she was doing everything within her power to push every thought of him from her life.

"Are you free for dinner tonight?" Chad continued. "Brenn and James phoned and want to know if we can meet them at the country club at six. We can go to a club afterward."

"Sure," Amy responded quickly, "why not? It sounds like fun." Keeping busy, she'd discovered, was the key. If she wasn't learning everything she could about her father's business, she was throwing herself into social events with the energy of a debutante with a closet full of prom dresses.

Rarely did she spend time at home anymore. Every room was indelibly stamped with memories of Josh and the long weeks he had spent recovering there. She would have given anything to completely wipe out the time spent at his side, but simultaneously she held the memories tightly to her chest, treasuring each minute he'd been in her life.

She was mixed up, confused, hurting and pretending otherwise.

It seemed Josh had left his mark in each and every room of her home. She couldn't walk into the library and not feel an emptiness that stabbed deep into her soul.

Only when she ventured near the pool did she feel his presence stronger than his absence, and she left almost immediately, rather than have to deal with her rumbling emotions.

* * *

When Amy arrived home that evening, she was surprised to discover her father sitting in the library in front of the fireplace, his feet up and a blanket draped over his lap. It was so unusual to find him resting that the sight stopped her abruptly in the hallway.

"Dad," she said, stepping into the room. "When did you get back?" Still perplexed, but pleased to see him, she leaned over to affectionately kiss his cheek. He'd been away several days on a business trip and wasn't expected home until the following afternoon.

"I landed an hour ago," Harold answered, smiling softly at her.

Amy removed her coat and curled up in a chair beside him. "I didn't think you'd be home until tomorrow night. Chad phoned, and we're going out to dinner. You don't mind, do you?"

He didn't answer her for several elongated moments, as if he was searching for the right words. This, too, was unlike him, and Amy wondered at his mood.

"You're seeing a good deal of Chad Morton, aren't you? The two of you are gallivanting around town every night of the week, it seems. Things seem to be getting serious."

Amy sidestepped the question. As a matter of fact, she'd been thinking those same thoughts herself. She *had* been seeing a good deal of Chad. He'd asked her out the first day she started working at Johnson Industries, and they'd been together nearly every night since.

"Do you object?" she asked pointedly. "Chad would make an excellent husband. He comes from a good family, and seems nice enough."

"True, but you don't love him."

"Who said anything about love?" Amy asked, forcing

a light laugh. As far as she was concerned, falling in love had been greatly overrated.

If she was going to become involved with a man she would much rather it was with someone like Chad. He was about as exciting as one-coat paint, but irrefutably stable. If there was anything she needed in her life, it was someone she could depend on who would love her for the next fifty years without demands, without questions.

As an extra bonus, there would never be any threat of her falling head over heels for Chad Morton and making a fool of herself the way she had for Josh Powell. No, it wasn't love, but it was comfortable.

Her father reached for his brandy, and Amy poured herself a glass of white wine, savoring these few minutes alone with him. They seldom sat and talked anymore, but the fault was mainly her own. In fact, she had avoided moments such as this. Her biggest fear was that he would say something about Josh, and she wouldn't be able to deal with it.

"I may not love Chad, but he's nice," she answered simply, hoping that would appease the question burning in her father's deep blue eyes.

"Nice," Harold repeated, his smile sad and off-center. He made the word sound trivial and weak, as if he was describing the man himself.

"Chad works for you," she said as a means of admonishment.

"True enough."

"So how was the trip?" she asked, turning the course of the conversation. She hadn't said she would accept Chad's proposal when he offered it, only that she fully expected him to tender one soon. She hadn't made up her mind one way or the other on how she would answer such a question. A good deal would depend on what her father thought.

Since the two men would be working closely together in the future, it would be best if they liked and respected each other...the way Josh and her father seemed to have felt.

Josh again. She closed her eyes to the thought of him, forgetting for the moment that he was out of her life and wouldn't be back.

Once more her father hesitated before answering her question. "The trip was interesting."

"Oh?" Rarely did her father hedge, but he seemed to be doing his fair share of it this evening.

His gaze pulled hers the same way a magnet attracts steel. "From Atlanta I flew down to Texas."

Amy rotated the crystal stem between her open palms, her heart perking like a brewing pot of coffee. Josh had claimed he was heading for Texas, but it was a big state and...

She blinked a couple of times, hoping desperately that she had misread her father, but one look from him confirmed her worst suspicion. Instantly, her throat went dry and her tongue felt as if it was glued to the roof of her mouth.

"You...talked to Josh, didn't you?"

Without the least bit of hesitation, Harold Johnson nodded, but his eyes were weary, as if he anticipated a confrontation.

Her lashes fluttered closed at the intense feelings of hurt and betrayal. "How could you?" she cried, bolting to her feet. Unable to stand still, she set the wineglass aside and started pacing the room, her movements crisp enough to impress the military.

"He put on a brave front—the same way you've been doing for the last three weeks."

Amy wasn't listening. "In all my life, I've never ques-

tioned or doubted anything you've ever done. I love you...
I trusted you." Her voice was trembling so badly that it was
amazing he could even understand her. "How could you?"

"Amy, sit down, please."

"No!" she shouted. The sense of betrayal was so strong,
she didn't think she could remain in the same room with
him any longer. Through the years, Amy had always considered her father to be her most loyal friend. He was the
safe port she steered toward in times of trouble. Since she
was a child he'd been the one who pointed out the rainbow
at the end of a cloudburst. He was the compass who directed the paths of her life.

Until this moment, she had never doubted anything he'd
done for her.

"What possible reason could you have to contact Josh?"
she demanded. "Were you looking to humiliate me more?
Is that it? It's a wonder he didn't laugh in your face... Perhaps he did, in which case it would serve you right."

"Amy, sweetheart, that isn't the reason I saw Josh. You
should know that."

Furious, she brushed away the tears that sprang so readily to her eyes and seared a wet trail down her cheeks. "I
suppose you told him I was wasting away for want of him?
No doubt you boosted his arrogance by claiming I'm still
crazy about him...and that I'll probably never stop loving him."

"Amy, please—"

"Wasn't his leaving humiliation enough?" she shouted.
"Who...gave you the right to rub salt in my wounds? Didn't
you think I was hurting enough?" Without waiting for his
reply, Amy stormed out of the library, so filled with righteous anger that she didn't stop until she was in her bedroom.

No more than a minute had passed before her father pounded on her door.

"Amy, please, just listen, would you?"

"No...just go away."

"But I need to explain. You're right, I probably shouldn't have gone to see Josh without talking with you about it first, but there was something I needed to discuss with him."

Although she remained furious, she opened her bedroom door and folded her arms across her chest. "What possible reason could you have to talk to Joshua Powell...if it didn't directly involve me?"

Her father stood just outside her door, a sheen of perspiration moistening his pale forehead and upper lip. He probably shouldn't have come racing up the stairs after her. He looked ashen, and his breathing was labored, but Amy chose to ignore that, too angry to care.

"Dad?" she repeated, bracing her hands against her hips. "Why did you talk to Josh?"

Her father's responding smile was weak at best. "I have a feeling you aren't going to like this, either." He hesitated and wiped a hand across his brow. "I went to offer him a job."

"You did what?" It demanded everything within Amy not to explode on the spot. She stood frozen for a moment, then buried her face in her hands.

"It isn't as bad as it seems, sweetheart. Joshua Powell is fully qualified. I was just looking to—"

"I know what you were trying to do," Amy cried. "You were looking to *buy* him for me!" Before it had been her voice that trembled. Now her entire body shook with outrage. Her knees didn't feel as if they were going to support her any longer.

But that didn't stop her from charging across the room

to her closet and throwing open the doors with every ounce of strength she possessed. She dragged out her suitcases and slammed them across the bed.

"Amy, what are you doing?"

"Leaving. This house. Johnson Industries. And you."

Her calm, rational father looked completely undone. If he was colorless before, he went deathly pale now. "Sweetheart, there's no reason for you to move out." The look in his eyes was desperate. "There's no need to overreact... Josh turned down the offer."

The added humiliation was more than Amy could handle.

"Of course he did. He didn't want me before. What made you think he would now?" Without stopping, she emptied her drawers, tossing her clothes in the open suitcase, unable to escape fast enough.

"Amy, please, don't do anything rash."

"Rash?" she repeated, hiccuping on a sob. "I should have moved out years ago, but I was under the impression that we...shared something special...like trust, mutual respect...love. Until tonight, I believed you—"

"Amy."

Something in the strangled way he uttered her name alerted her to the fact something was wrong. Something was very, very wrong. She whirled around in time to see her father grip his chest, roll back his eyes and slump unconscious to the floor.

Eleven

Josh lowered the week-old *Wall Street Journal* and let the newspaper rest on his lap while his mind whirled with troubled concern. Mingling with his worries was an abundance of ideas, most of them maverick—but then he had been considered one in his time.

"What part of the world are you headed for now, dear?" his Aunt Hazel inquired, her soft voice curious. She sat across the living room from him, her fingers pushing the knitting needles the way a secretary worked a keyboard. Her white hair was demurely pinned at the back of her head, and tiny wisps framed her oval face. Her features, although marked with age, were soft and gentle. Her outer beauty had faded years before, but the inner loveliness shone brighter each time he stopped to visit. Without much difficulty, Josh could picture Amy resembling his aunt in fifty or so years.

"I'm hoping to go back to Kadiri," he answered her, elbowing thoughts of Amy from his mind.

"Isn't that the place that's been in the news recently?" she asked, sounding worried. "There's so much unrest in this world. I have such a difficult time understanding why people can't get along with one another." She pointedly glanced in his direction, her hands resting in her lap as her tender brown eyes challenged him.

Over the years, Josh had become accustomed to his aunt inserting barbed remarks, thinly veiled, about his relationship with his father. Josh generally ignored them, pretending he didn't understand what she meant. He preferred to avoid a confrontation. As far as he was concerned, his Aunt Hazel was his only relative, and he loved her dearly.

"What's that you're reading so intently?"

Josh's gaze fell to the newspaper. *"The Wall Street Journal."* Knowing his aunt would put the wrong connotation into the subject matter, since he normally avoided anything that had to do with the financial world, he hurried to explain. "I have a...friend, Harold Johnson, who owns and operates a large conglomerate. With all the traveling I do, it's difficult to keep in contact with him, so I keep tabs on him by occasionally checking to see how his stock is doing."

"And what does that tell you?"

"Several things."

"Like what, dear?" she asked conversationally.

Josh wasn't certain his aunt would understand all the ins and outs of the corporate world, so he explained it as best he could in simple terms. "Stock prices tell me how he's doing financially."

"I see. But you've been frowning for the last fifteen minutes. Is something wrong with your friend?"

Josh picked up the newspaper and made a ceremony of folding it precisely in fourths. "His bond rating has just been lowered."

"That's not good?"

"No. There's an article here that states that Johnson Industries' stock price is currently depressed, which means the value has fallen below its assets. With several long-term bonds maturing, the cost of rolling them over may become prohibitive."

His Aunt Hazel returned to her knitting. "Yes, but what does all that mean?"

Josh struggled to put it into terminology his aunt would understand. "Trouble, mostly. Basically it means that Johnson Industries is a prime candidate for a hostile takeover. He may be forced into selling the controlling interest of the business he's struggled to build over a lifetime to someone else."

"That doesn't seem fair. If a man works hard all his years to build up a business, it's not right that someone else can waltz right in and take over."

"Little in life is fair anymore," Josh said, unable to disguise his bitterness.

"Oh, Josh, honestly." His aunt rested her hands in her lap and slowly shook her head, pressing her lips together tightly. "You have become such a pessimist over the years. If I wasn't so glad to see you when you came to visit me, I'd take delight in shaking some sense into you."

Although his aunt was serious, Josh couldn't help laughing outright. "Harold's going to be just fine. He's a strong man with a lot of connections. The sharks are circling, but they'll soon start looking for weaker prey."

"Good. I hate the thought of your friend losing his business."

"So do I." Setting the newspaper aside, Josh closed his eyes, battling down the surge of long-forgotten excitement. The adrenaline had started to pound through his blood the minute he had picked up the *Wall Street Journal*. It had been years since he had allowed himself the luxury of remembering the life he'd left behind. Since the final showdown with his father, he had done everything he could to forget how much he loved plowing into problems with both hands, such as the one Johnson Industries was currently experiencing. Before he realized what he was doing, his mind was churning out ways to deal with this difficulty.

Releasing his breath, Josh closed his mind to the thought of offering any advice to Amy's father. The cord had been cut, and he couldn't turn back now.

"Your father is looking well," his aunt took obvious delight in informing him.

Josh ignored her. He didn't want to discuss Chance, and Aunt Hazel knew it, but she did her best to introduce the subject of his father as naturally as possible.

"He asked about you."

Josh scoffed before he thought better of it.

"He loves you, Josh," Hazel insisted sharply. "If the pair of you weren't so unbelievably proud, you could settle this unpleasantness in five minutes. But I swear, you're no better than he is."

The anger that shot through Josh was hot enough to boil his blood and, unable to stop his tongue, he blurted out, "I may not be a multimillionaire, but at least I'm not a crook. My father should be in prison right now, and you well know it. You both seem to think I was supposed to ignore the fact that Chance Powell is a liar and a cheat."

"Josh, please, I didn't mean to reopen painful wounds. It's just that I've seen you fly from one end of the world to the other in an effort to escape this difficulty with your father. I hardly know you anymore... I can't understand how you can turn away from everything that ever had any value to you."

The older woman looked pale, and Josh immediately regretted his outburst. "I'm sorry, Aunt Hazel, I shouldn't have raised my voice to you. Now, what was it you said you were cooking for dinner?"

"Crow," she told him, her eyes twinkling.

"I beg your pardon?"

She laughed softly and shook her head. "I seem to put my foot in my mouth every time I try to talk some sense into you. No matter what you do with the rest of your life, Joshua, I want you to know I'll always love you. You're the closest thing to a son I've ever had. Forgive an old woman for sticking her nose where it doesn't belong."

Josh set aside the paper and walked over to sit on the arm of her overstuffed chair. Then he leaned over and kissed her cheek. "If you can forgive me for my sharp tongue, we'll call it square."

That night, Josh wasn't able to sleep. He lay on the mattress with his hands supporting the back of his head and stared into empty space. Every time he closed his eyes, he saw Harold Johnson sitting across the desk from him, discussing his current financial difficulties. Amy's father was probably in the most delicate position of his business career. The sheer force of the older man's personality was enough to ward off all but the most bloodthirsty sharks. But Josh didn't know how long Harold could keep them at bay. For Amy's sake, he hoped nothing else would go wrong.

His first inclination had been to contact her father with a few suggestions. But Harold Johnson didn't need him, and for that matter, neither did Amy. According to her father, she was seriously dating someone else. In fact, he had claimed she would probably be wearing an engagment ring before long.

Josh hadn't asked any questions, although he would have given his right hand to have learned the name of the man who had swept her off her feet so soon after he had left. More than likely, Josh wouldn't have known the other man, and it wouldn't have mattered if he had.

When he had flown out of Seattle, Josh had hoped Amy would hurry and fall in love with someone else, so there was no reason for him to be unsettled now. This was exactly what he had wanted to happen. So it made no sense that he was being eaten alive with regrets and doubts.

The answer as to why was obvious. He was never going to stop loving Amy. For the first time since his conversation with her father, he was willing to admit what a fool he had been to have honestly believed he had meant it. Just the thought of her even *kissing* another man filled him with such anger that he clenched his fists with impotent rage.

If that wasn't bad enough, envisioning Amy making love with her newfound friend was akin to having his skin ripped off his body one strip at a time. The irony of this was that Amy had told him as much. She'd stood at the top of her stairs and shouted it to him, he recalled darkly. *If you can live with the thought of another man holding and kissing me and making love to me then...go.*

Josh *had* walked away from her, but she had been right. The image of her in the arms of another man caused him more agony than his injuries from the explosion ever had.

Harold Johnson's words came back to haunt him, as well. They had been talking, and Amy's father had stared directly at him and claimed: *This young man has made a habit of walking away from challenges and opportunities.*

At the time it had been all Josh could do not to defend himself. He had let the comment slide rather than force an argument. Now the truth of the older man's words hit him hard, leaving him defenseless.

Josh couldn't deny that he had walked away from his

father, turned his back on the life he had once enjoyed, and had been running ever since. Even his love for Amy hadn't been strong enough to force him to deal with that pain. Instead, he had left her and then been forced to deal with another more intense agony. His life felt like an empty shell, as if he were going through the motions, but rejecting all the benefits.

In his own cavalier way, he'd carelessly thrown away the very best thing that had ever happened to him.

Love. Amy's love.

Closing his eyes to the swell of regret, Josh lay in bed trying to decide what he was going to do about it. If anything.

He didn't know if he could casually walk into Amy's life after the way he had so brutally abandoned her. The answer was as difficult to face as the question had been.

Perhaps it would be best to leave her to what happiness she had found for herself.

Doubts pounded at him from every corner until he realized sleep would be impossible. Throwing back the blankets, he climbed out of bed, dressed and wandered into the living room. His aunt's bedroom door had been left slightly ajar, and he could hear her snoring softly in the background. Instead of being irritated, he was comforted by the knowledge that she was his family. He didn't visit her as often as he should, and he was determined to do so from now on.

Josh sat in the dark for several minutes, reviewing his options with Amy and her father. He needed time to carefully think matters through.

In the wee hours of the morning, he turned on the television, hoping to find a movie that would help him fall asleep. Instead, he fiddled until he found a station that broadcast twenty-four-hour financial news. The article in the *Wall Street Journal* was a week old. A great many things could have happened to Johnson Industries in seven days. It wasn't likely that he would learn anything, but he was curious nonetheless.

"Josh, what are you doing up at this time of night?" his aunt demanded, sounding very much like a mother scolding her twelve-year-old son. She stood and held the back of her hand over her mouth as she yawned. She was dressed in a lavender terry-cloth robe that was tightly cinched at the waist, and her soft hair was secured with a thin black net.

"I couldn't sleep."

"How about some warm milk? It always works for me."

"Only if you add some chocolate and join me."

His aunt chuckled and headed toward the kitchen. "Do you want a bedtime story while I'm at it?"

Josh grinned. "It wouldn't hurt."

She stuck her head around the corner. "That's what I thought you'd say."

Josh stood, prepared to follow her. He walked toward the television, intent on turning it off, when he heard the news. For one wild moment, he stood frozen in shock and disbelief.

"Aunt Hazel," he called once he found his voice. "You'd better cancel the hot chocolate."

"Whatever for?" she asked, but stopped abruptly when she turned and saw him. "Josh, what's happened? My dear boy, you're as pale as a ghost."

"It's my friend. The one I was telling you about earlier—he's had a heart attack and isn't expected to live."

For most of the evening, Josh had been debating what he should do. He had struggled with indecision and uncertainty, trying to decide if it would be best to leave well enough alone and let both Amy and her father go on with their lives. At the same time, he had begun to wonder if he could face life without his Angel Eyes at his side.

Now the matter had been taken out of his hands. There was only one option left to him, and that was to return. If Johnson Industries had been a prime candidate for a hostile takeover *before* Harold's heart attack, it was even more vulnerable now. Sharks always went after the weakest prey, and Johnson Industries lay before them with its throat exposed. Josh's skills might be rusty, but they were intact, and he knew he could help.

Amy would need him now, too. Father and daughter had always been especially close, and losing Harold now would devastate her.

"Josh." His aunt interrupted his musings, her hand on his forearm. "What are you going to do?"

Josh's eyes brightened and he leaned forward to place a noisy kiss on his aunt's cheek. "What I should have done weeks ago—get married."

"Married? But to whom?" A pair of dark brown eyes rounded with surprise. Flustered, she patted her hair. "Actually, I don't care who it is as long as I get an invitation to the wedding."

Like a limp rag doll, Amy sat and stared at the wall outside her father's hospital room. He was in intensive care, and she was only allowed to see him for a few minutes every hour. She lived for those brief moments when she could hold his hand and gently reassure him of her love, hoping to lend him some strength. For three days he'd lain in a coma, unable to respond.

Not once in those long, tedious days had she left the hospital. Not to sleep, not to eat, not to change clothes. She feared the minute she left him, he would slip into death and she wouldn't be there to prevent it.

Hurried footsteps sounded on the polished floor of the hospital corridor, but she didn't turn to see who was coming. So many had sat by her side, staff requesting information, asking questions she didn't want to answer, friends and business associates. But Amy had sent them all away. Now she felt alone and terribly weary.

The footsteps slowed.

"Amy."

Her heart thudded to a stop. "Josh?" Before she was entirely certain how it happened, she was securely tucked in his embrace, her arms wrapped around his neck and her face buried in his chest, breathing in his strength the way desert-dry soil drinks in the rain.

For the first time since her father's heart attack, she gave in to the luxury of tears. They poured from her eyes like water rushing over a dam. Her shoulders jerked with sobs, and she held on to Josh with every ounce of strength she possessed.

Josh's hands were in her hair, and his lips moved over her temple, whispering words she couldn't hear over the sound of her own weeping. It didn't matter; he was there, and she needed him. God had known and had sent him to her side.

"It's my fault," she wailed with a grief that came from the bottom of her soul, trying to explain what had happened. "Everything is my fault."

"No, angel, it isn't, I'm sure it couldn't be."

No one seemed to understand that. No one, and she was too weak to explain. Stepping back, she wiped the tears from her eyes, although it did little good because more poured down her face. "I caused this... I did...we were ar-

guing and…and I was so angry, so hurt that I wanted to…
move out and…that was when it happened."

Josh gripped her shoulders, and applying a light pressure, he lowered her into the chair. He squatted in front of
her and took both her hands between his, rubbing them. It
was then that Amy realized how cold she felt. Shivering
and sniffling, she leaned forward enough to rest her forehead against the solid strength of his shoulder.

His arms were around her immediately.

"He's going to be all right," Josh assured her softly.

"No…he's going to die. I know he is, and I'll never be
able to tell him how sorry I am."

"Amy," Josh said, gripping the sides of her head and
raising her face. "Your father loves you so much, don't you
think he already knows you're sorry?"

"I… I'm not sure anymore."

She swayed slightly and would have fallen if Josh hadn't
caught her.

He murmured something she couldn't understand and
firmly gripped her waist. "When was the last time you had
anything to eat?"

She blinked, not remembering.

"Angel," he said gently, "you've got to take care of yourself, now more than ever. Your father needs to wake up and
discover you standing over him with a bright smile on your
face and your eyes full of love."

She nodded. That was exactly how she pictured the scene
in her own mind, when she allowed herself to believe that
he would come out of this alive.

"I'm taking you home."

"No." A protest rose automatically to her lips, and she
shook her head with fierce determination.

"I'm going to have Manuela cook you something to eat

and then I'm going to tuck you in bed and let you sleep. When you wake up, we'll talk. We have a good deal to discuss."

Something in the back of her head told Amy that she shouldn't be listening to Josh, that she shouldn't trust him. But she was so very tired, and much too exhausted to listen to the cool voice of reason.

She must have fallen asleep in the car on the way home from the hospital because the next thing she knew, they were parked outside her home and Josh was coming around to the passenger side to help her out.

He didn't allow her to walk, but gently lifted her into his arms as if she weighed less than a child and carried her in the front door.

"Manuela," he shouted.

The plump housekeeper came rushing into the entryway at the sound of Josh's voice. She took one look at him and mumbled something low and fervent in Spanish.

"Could you make something light for Amy and bring it to her room? She's on the verge of collapse."

"Right away," Manuela said, wiping her hands dry on her blue apron.

"I'm not hungry," Amy felt obliged to inform them. She would admit to feeling a little fragile and a whole lot sleepy, but she wasn't sick. The one they should be taking care of was her father. The thought of him lying so pale and so gravely ill in the hospital bed was enough to make her suck in her breath and start to sob softly.

"Mr. Josh," Manuela shouted, when Josh had carried Amy halfway up the stairs.

"What is it, Manuela?"

"I say many prayers you come back."

Amy wasn't sure she understood their conversation. The

words floated around her like dense fog, few making sense. She lifted her head and turned to look at the housekeeper, but discovered that Manuela was already rushing toward the kitchen.

Josh entered her bedroom, set her on the edge of her bed and removed her shoes.

"I want a bath," she told him.

He left her sitting on the bed and started running the bathwater, then returned and looked through her chest of drawers until he found a nightgown. He gently led her toward the tub, as if she needed his assistance. Perhaps she did, because the thought of protesting didn't so much as enter her mind.

To her consternation, Amy had to have his help unbuttoning her blouse. She stood lifeless and listless as Josh helped remove her outer clothing.

A few minutes later, Manuela scurried into the bedroom, carrying a tray with her. Frowning and muttering something in her mother tongue, she pushed Josh out of the room and helped Amy finish undressing.

Josh was pacing when Amy reappeared. She had washed and blow-dried her hair, brushed her teeth and changed into the soft flannel pajamas covered with red kisses.

Instantly Josh was at her side, his strong arms encircling her waist.

"Do you feel better?" he inquired gently.

She nodded and noted the way his eyes slid to her lips and lingered there. He wanted to kiss her, she knew from the way his gaze narrowed. Her heart began to hammer when she realized how badly she wanted him to do exactly that. Unhurried, his action filled with purpose, Josh lowered his head.

His mouth was opened over hers. Amy sighed at the

pleasure and wrapped her arms around his neck, glorying in the feel of him until he broke off the kiss. "Manuela brought you a bowl of soup," Josh insisted, leading her to the bed.

Like a lost sheep, Amy obediently followed him to where the dinner tray awaited her. Josh sat her down on the edge of the mattress and then placed the table and tray in front of her.

After three bites she was full. Josh coaxed her into taking that many more, but then she protested by closing her eyes and shaking her head.

Josh removed the tray and then pulled back the covers, prepared to tuck her into bed.

"Sleep," he said, leaning over and kissing her once more.

"Are you going away again?"

"No," he whispered, and brushed the hair from her temple.

She caught his hand and brought it to her lips. "Promise me you'll be here when I wake up... I need that, Josh."

"I promise."

Her eyes drifted shut. She heard him move toward the door and she knew that already he was breaking his word. The knowledge was like an unexpected slap in the face and she started to whimper without realizing the sounds were coming from her own throat.

Josh seemed to understand her pain. "I'm taking the tray down to the kitchen. I'll be back in a few minutes, angel, I promise."

Amy didn't believe him, but when she stirred a little while later, she discovered Josh sitting in a chair, leaning forward and intently studying her. His forearms were resting on his knees.

He reached out and ran his finger down the side of her

face. "Close your eyes, baby," he urged gently. "You've only been asleep a little while."

Amy scooted as far as she could to the other side of the mattress and patted the empty space at her side, inviting him to join her.

"Amy, no," he said, sucking in his breath. "I can't."

"I need you."

Josh sagged forward, indecision etched in bold lines across his tight features. "Oh, angel, the things you ask of me." He stood and sat next to her. "If I do sleep with you, I'll stay on top of the covers. Understand?"

She thought to protest, but hadn't the strength.

Slowly, Josh lowered his head to the pillow, his eyes gentle on her face, so filled with love and tenderness that her own filled with unexpected tears. One inglorious tear-drop rolled from the corner of her eye and over the bridge of her nose, dropping onto the pillow.

Josh caught the second droplet with his index finger, his eyes holding hers.

"Oh, my sweet Amy," he whispered. "My life hasn't been the same from the moment I met you."

She tried to smile, but the result was little more than a pathetic movement of her lips. Closing her eyes, she raised her head just a little, anticipating his kiss.

"So this is how you're going to make me pay for my sins?" he whispered throatily.

Amy's eyes flickered open to discover him studying her with sobering intensity.

"Don't you realize how much I want to make love with you?" he breathed, and his tongue parted her lips for a deep, sensual kiss that left her shaken. She raised her hand and tucked it at the base of his neck, then kissed him back. Although she was starved for his touch, having him in bed with her didn't stir awake sexual sensations, only a deep sense of love and security.

He closed his hand possessively over her hip, dragging her as close as humanly possible against him on the mattress. He kissed her again.

Beneath the covers he slid his hand along her midriff. There was much she wanted to tell him, much she wanted to share. Questions she longed to ask but to her dismay, she was forced to stop in order to yawn.

He seemed to understand what she wanted. "We'll talk later," he promised. "But first close your eyes and rest."

She nodded, barely moving her head. Her lashes drifted downward, and before she knew what was happening, she was stumbling headlong on the path to slumber.

Sometime later Amy stirred. She blinked a couple of times, feeling disoriented and bemused, but when she realized that she was in her own bedroom, she sighed contentedly. The warm, cozy feeling lulled her, and her eyes drifted closed once more. It was then that she felt the large male hand slip wrapped around her middle.

With a small cry of dismay, her eyes flew open, and she lifted her head from the thick feather pillow. Josh was asleep at her side, and she pressed her hand over her mouth as the memories rolled into place, forming the missing parts of one gigantic puzzle.

"No," she cried, pushing at his shoulder in a flurry of anger and pain. "How dare you climb into my bed as though you have every right to be here."

Josh's dark eyes flashed open and he instantly frowned, obviously perplexed by her actions. He levered himself up on one elbow, studying her.

"Kindly leave," she muttered between clenched teeth, doing her best to control her anger.

"Angel Eyes, you invited me to join you, don't you remember?"

"No." She threw back the covers with enough force to pull the sheets free from between the mattress and box springs. To add to her dismay, she discovered that her nightgown had worked its way up her body and was hugging at her waist, exposing a lengthy expanse of leg, thigh and hip. In her rush to escape, she nearly stumbled over her own two feet.

"Will you please get out of my bedroom…or I'll… I'll be forced to phone the police."

"Amy?" Josh sat up and rubbed the sleep from his eyes as though he expected this to be a part of a bad dream. "Be reasonable."

"Leave," she said tersely, throwing open the door to be certain there could be no misunderstanding her request.

"Don't you remember?" he coaxed. "We kissed and held each other and you asked me to—"

"That was obviously a mistake, now get out," she blared, unconsciously using his own phrase. She wasn't in the mood to argue or discuss this—or anything else—rationally. All she knew was that the man she'd been desperately trying to forget was in her bed and looking very much as though he intended to stay right where he was.

Twelve

"Amy," Josh said, his voice calm and low, as though he was trying to reason with a deranged woman.

"Out," she cried, squeezing her eyes shut as if that would make him go away.

"All right," he returned, eyeing her dubiously. "If that's what you really want."

The audacity of the man was phenomenal. "It's what I *really* want," she repeated, doing her level best to maintain her dignity.

Josh didn't seem to be in any big rush. He sat on the end of the bed and rubbed his hand down his face before he reached for his shoes. It demanded everything within Amy not to openly admire his brazen good looks. It astonished her that she could have forgotten how easy on the eyes Josh was. Even now, when his expression was impassive, she was struck by the angled lines of his features, as sharp as a blade, more so now as he struggled not to reveal his thoughts.

He stood, but the movement was marked with reluctance. "Can we talk about this first?"

"No," she said, thrusting out her chin defiantly.

"Amy—"

"There's nothing to discuss. I said everything the day you left."

"I was wrong," he admitted softly. "I'd give everything I own if I could turn back time and change what happened that morning. From the bottom of my heart, I'm sorry."

"Of course you were wrong," she cried, fighting the urge to forgive and forget. She couldn't trust Josh anymore. "I knew you'd figure it out sooner or later, but I told you then and I meant it—I don't want you back."

Manuela appeared, breathless from running up the stairs. "Miss Amy… Mr. Josh, the hospital is on phone."

In her eagerness to expel Josh from her room, Amy hadn't even heard it ring. "Oh no…" she murmured and raced across the room, nearly toppling the telephone from her nightstand in her eagerness.

"Yes?" she cried. "This is Amy Johnson." Nothing but silence greeted her. Frantically, she tried pushing on the phone lever, hoping to get a dial tone.

"I unplugged it," Josh explained and hurriedly replaced the jack in the wall. At her fierce look, he added, "I wanted you to rest undisturbed."

"This is Amy Johnson," she said thickly, her pulse doubling with anxiety and fear.

Immediately the crisp, clear voice of a hospital staff member came on the line. The instant Amy heard that her father was awake and resting comfortably, she slumped onto the mattress and covered her mouth with her hand as tears of relief swamped her eyes.

"Thank you, thank you," she repeated over and over before hanging up the phone.

"Dad's awake…he's apparently doing much better," she

told Manuela, wiping the moisture from her face with the side of her hand. "He's asking for me."

"Thank the good Lord," Josh whispered.

Amy had forgotten he was there. "Please leave." She cast a pleading glance in Manuela's direction, hoping to gain the housekeeper's support in removing Josh from her bedroom.

"Mr. Chad come to see you," Manuela whispered, as though doing so would prevent Josh from hearing her. "I tell him you sleep."

"Thank you, I'll phone Mr. Morton when I get back from the hospital."

"I also tell him Mr. Josh is back to stay," Manuela said with a triumphant grin.

"If you'll both excuse me," Amy said pointedly, "I'd like to get dressed."

"Of course," Josh answered, as if there had never been a problem. He winked at her on his way out the door, and it was all Amy could do not to throw something after him.

She was trembling when she sat on the edge of her mattress. The emotions battling within her were so potent, she didn't know which one to respond to first. Relief mingled with unbridled joy that her father had taken a decided turn for the better.

The others weren't so easy to identify. Josh was here, making a dramatic entrance into her life when she was too wrapped up in grief and shock to react properly.

Instead, she'd fallen into his arms as though he was Captain America leaping to the rescue, and the memory infuriated her. He could just as easily turn and walk away from her again. She'd suffered through a good deal of heartrending pain to come to that conclusion. And once burned, she knew enough to stay away from the fire.

By the time she had dressed and walked down the stairs,

Josh was nowhere to be seen. She searched the living room, then berated herself for looking for him. After all, she had been firm about wanting him to leave. His having left avoided an unpleasant confrontation.

No sooner had the thought passed through her mind when the front door opened and he walked into the house as brazen as could be.

Amy pretended not to see him and stepped into the dining room for a badly needed cup of coffee. She ignored the breakfast Manuela had brought in for her and casually sought her purse and car keys.

"You should eat something," Josh coaxed.

Amy turned and glared at him, but refused to become involved in a dispute over something as nonsensical as scrambled eggs and toast.

"I've got a rental car, if you're ready to go to the hospital now."

"I'll take my own," she informed him briskly.

Josh leaned across the table and reached for the toast on her plate. "Fine, but I assume it's still at the hospital."

Amy closed her eyes in frustration. "I'll take another vehicle then."

"Seems like a waste of gasoline since I'm going that way myself. Besides, how are you going to bring two cars home?"

"All right," she said from between clenched teeth. "Can we leave now?"

"Sure."

Any told Manuela where she could be reached and walked out to Josh's car, which was parked in front of the house. She climbed inside without waiting for him to open the door for her and stiffly snapped her seat belt into place.

They were in the heavy morning traffic before either

spoke again. And it was Josh who ventured into conversation first. "I can help you, Amy, if you'll let me."

"Help me," she repeated with a short, humorless laugh. "How? By slipping into my bed and forcing unwanted attentions on me?" She couldn't believe she had said that. It was so unfair, but she would swallow her tongue before she apologized.

Josh stiffened, but said nothing in his own defense, which made Amy feel even worse. She refused to allow herself to be vulnerable to this man again, least of all now, when she was so terribly alone.

"I'd like to make it up to you for the cruel way I acted," he murmured after a moment.

Her anger stretched like a tightrope between them, and he seemed to be the only one brave enough to bridge the gap.

Amy certainly wasn't. It angered her that Josh thought he could come back as easily as if he'd never been away, apparently expecting to pick up where they'd left off.

"I'd like to talk to your father," he said next.

"No," she said forcefully.

"Amy, there's a good deal you don't know. I could help in ways you don't understand, if you'll let me."

"No, thank you," she returned, her voice hard and inflexible, discounting any appreciation for his offer.

"Oh, Amy, have I hurt you so badly?"

She turned her head and glared out the side window, refusing to answer him. The fifteen-minute ride to the hospital seemed to take an hour. Josh turned into the parking lot, and she hoped he would drop her off at the entrance and drive away. When he pulled into a parking space and turned off the engine, she realized she wasn't going to get her wish.

Biting back a caustic comment, she opened the door and climbed out. Whether he followed her inside or not was his own business, she decided.

She groaned inwardly when the sound of his footsteps echoed behind her on the polished hospital floor. The ride in the elevator was tolerable only because there were several other people with them. Once they arrived on the eighth floor, Amy stopped at the nurses' station and gave her name.

"Ms. Johnson, I was the one who called you this morning," a tall redheaded nurse with a freckled face said. "Your father is looking much better."

"Could I see him, please?"

"Yes, of course, but only for a few minutes."

Amy nodded, understanding all too well how short those moments would be, and followed the nurse into the intensive-care unit.

Harold Johnson smiled feebly when she approached his bedside. Her gaze filled with fresh tears that she struggled to hide behind a brilliant smile. His color was better, and although he remained gravely ill, he was awake and able to communicate with her.

"This is an expensive way to vacation," she said, smiling through the emotion.

"Hi, sweetheart. I'm sorry if I frightened you."

Her fingers gripped his and squeezed tightly. "I'm the one who's sorry...more than you'll ever know. Every time I think about what happened, I blame myself."

A weak shake of his head dismissed her apology. He moistened his mouth and briefly closed his eyes. "I need you to do something."

"Anything."

His fingers tightened around hers, and the pressure was

incredibly slight. "It won't be easy, baby...your pride will make it difficult."

"Dad, there isn't anything in this world I wouldn't do for you. Don't waste your strength apologizing. What do you need?"

"Find Joshua Powell for me."

Amy felt as if the floor had started to buckle beneath her feet. She gripped the railing at the side of his bed and dragged in a deep breath. "Josh? Why?"

"He can help."

"Oh, Daddy, I'm sure you mean well, but we don't need Josh." She forced a lightness into her voice, hoping that would reassure him.

"We need him," her father repeated, his voice barely audible.

"Of course, I'm willing to do whatever you want, but we've gotten along fine without him this far," she countered, doing her best to maintain her cheerful facade. Then it dawned on her. "You think *I* need him, don't you? Oh, Dad, I'm stronger than I look. You should know by now that I'm completely over him. Chad and I have a good thing going, and I'd hate to throw a wrench into that relationship by dragging Josh back."

"Amy," Harold said, his strength depleting quickly. "I'm the one who has to talk to him. Please, do as I ask."

"All right," she agreed, her voice sagging with hesitation.

"Thank you." He closed his eyes then and was almost immediately asleep.

Reluctantly, Amy left his side, perplexed and worried. Josh was pacing the small area designated as a waiting room when she returned.

"How is he?"

"Better."

"Good," Josh said, looking encouraged. His gaze seemed to eat its way through her. "Did you tell him I was here?"

"No."

"You've got to, Amy. I can understand why you'd hesitate, but there are things you don't know or understand. I just might be able to do him some good."

She didn't know what to make of what was happening, but it was clear she was missing something important.

"We've got to talk. Let me buy you breakfast—we can sit down and have a rational discussion."

Amy accepted his invitation with ill grace. "All right, if you insist."

His mouth quirked up at the edges. "I do."

The hospital cafeteria was bustling with people. By the time they had ordered and carried their orange trays through the line, there was a vacant table by the window.

While Amy buttered her English muffin, Josh returned the trays. When he joined her, he seemed unusually quiet for someone who claimed he wanted to talk.

"Well?" she asked with marked impatience. "Say whatever it is that's so important, and be done with it."

"This isn't easy."

"What isn't, telling the truth?" she asked flippantly.

"I never lied to you, Amy. Never," he reinforced. "I'm afraid, however," he said sadly, "that what I'm going to tell you is probably going to hurt you even more."

"Oh? Do you have a wife and family securely tucked away somewhere?"

"You know that isn't true," he answered, his voice slightly elevated with anger. "I'm not a liar or a cheat."

"That's refreshing. What are you?"

"A former business executive. I was CEO for the largest conglomerate in the country for three years."

She raised her eyebrows, unimpressed. That he should mislead her about something like this didn't shock her. He had misrepresented himself before, and another violation of trust wasn't going to prejudice her one way or the other. "And I thought you were into oil. Fancy that."

"I was, or have been for the past several years. I left my former employer."

"Why?" She really didn't care, but if he was willing to tell her, then she would admit to being semi-curious as to the reason he found this admission to be such a traumatic one.

"That's not important," he said forcefully. "What is vital now is that I might be able to help your father save his company. These are dangerous times for him."

"He's not going to lose it," she returned confidently.

"Amy, I don't know how much you're aware of what's going on, but Johnson Industries is a prime candidate for a hostile takeover by any number of corporate raiders."

"I know that. But we've got the best minds in the country dealing with his finances. We don't need you."

"I've been there, I know how best to handle this type of situation."

She sighed expressively, giving the impression that she was bored with this whole conversation, which wasn't entirely false. "Personally, I think it's supremely arrogant of you to think you could waltz your way into my father's business and claim to be the cure of all our ills."

"Amy, please," he said, clearly growing frustrated with her.

Actually she didn't blame him. She wasn't making this easy for a reason. There were too many negative emotions tied to Josh for her to blithely accept his offer of assistance.

"The next time you see Harold, ask him about me," he suggested.

The mention of her father tightened Amy's stomach. It was apparent that Harold already knew, otherwise he wouldn't have pleaded with her to find Josh. Nor would he have offered Josh a position with the firm. But they both had kept Josh's past a secret from her. The pain of their deception cut deep and sharp. Her father she could forgive. But Josh had already hurt her so intensely that another wound inflicted upon one still open and raw only increased her emotional anguish.

Valiantly, she struggled to disguise it. What little appetite she possessed vanished. She pushed her muffin aside and checked her watch, pretending to be surprised by the time. With a flippant air, she excused herself and hurried from the cafeteria.

Blindly, she stumbled into the ladies' room and braced her trembling hands against the sink as she sucked in deep breaths in an effort to control the pain. The last thing she wanted was for Josh to know he still had the power to hurt her. The sense of betrayal by the two men she'd loved the most in her life grew sharper with every breath.

Running the water, Amy splashed her face and dried it with the rough paper towel. When she'd composed herself, she squared her shoulders and walked out of the room, intent on returning to the intensive care unit.

She stopped abruptly in the hallway when she noticed that Josh was leaning against the wall waiting for her. Her facade was paper-thin, and he was the last person she was ready to deal with at the moment.

"I suppose I should mention that my father asked me to find you when I spoke to him this morning," she said when she could talk.

Josh's dark eyes flickered with surprise and then relief. "Good."

"You might as well go to him now."

"No," he said firmly, and shook his head. "We need to clear the air between us first."

"That's not necessary," she returned flatly. "There isn't anything I want to say to you. Or hear from you. Or have to do with you."

He nodded and tucked his hands in his pants pockets as if he had to do something in order not to reach out to her. "I can understand that, but I can't accept it." He paused as two orderlies walked past them on their way into the cafeteria. "Perhaps now isn't the best time, but at least believe me when I say I love you."

Amy pretended to yawn.

Josh's eyes narrowed and his mouth thinned. "You're not fooling me, Amy, I know you feel the same thing for me."

"It wouldn't matter if I did," she answered calmly. "What I feel—or don't feel for you—doesn't change a thing. If you and my father believe you can help the company, then more power to you. If you're looking for my blessing, then you've got it. I'd bargain with the devil himself if it would help my father. Do what you need to do, then kindly get out of my life."

Josh flinched as if she had struck him.

Amy didn't understand why he should be so shocked. "How many times do I have to tell you to leave me alone before you believe me?"

"Amy." He gripped her shoulders, the pressure hard and painful as he stared into her eyes. "Did I do this to you?"

"If anyone is at fault, I am. I fell in love with the wrong man, but I've learned my lesson," she told him bitterly. Boldly, she met his stare, but the hurt and doubt in his dark eyes were nearly her undoing. Without another word, she freed herself from his grasp and headed toward the elevator.

Josh followed her, and they rode up to the eighth floor in an uncomfortable silence. She approached the nurses' station and explained that her father had requested to talk to Josh.

She had turned away, prepared to leave the hospital, when the elevator doors opened and Chad Morton stepped out.

"Amy," he cried, as if he expected her to vanish into thin air before he reached her. "I've been trying to see you for two days."

"I'm sorry," she said, accepting his warm embrace.

"I stopped off at the hospital yesterday, but I was told you'd gone home. When I drove to the house, Manuela explained that you were asleep."

"Yes, I... I was exhausted. In fact, I wasn't myself," she said pointedly for Josh's benefit.

"With little wonder. You'd been here every minute since your father's heart attack. If you hadn't gone home, I would have taken you there myself."

Amy could feel Josh's stare penetrate her shoulder blades, but she ignored him. "I was just leaving," she explained. "I thought I'd check in at the office this morning."

Chad's frown darkened his face. "I... I don't think that would be a good idea."

"Why not?"

It was clear that Chad was uncomfortable. His gaze shifted to the floor, and he buried his hands in his pockets. "The office is a madhouse with the news and...and, well, frankly, there's a good deal of speculation going around—"

"Speculation?" she asked. "About what?"

"The takeover."

"What are you talking about?" She'd known that their situation was a prime one for a hostile takeover—in theory at least—but the reality of it caused her face to pale.

Chad looked as though he would give his right arm not be the one to tell her this. He hesitated and drew in a breath. "Johnson shares had gone up three dollars by the time Wall Street closed yesterday. Benson's moved in."

George Benson was a well-known corporate raider, the worst of the lot, from what little Amy knew. His reputation was that of a greedy, harsh man who bought out companies and then proceeded to bleed them dry with little or no compassion.

Amy closed her eyes for a moment, trying to maintain a modicum of control. "Whatever you do, you mustn't tell my father any of this."

"He already knows," Josh said starkly from behind her. "Otherwise, he wouldn't have asked for me."

Chad's troubled gaze narrowed as it swung to Josh. "Who is this?" he asked Amy.

Purposely, she turned and stared at Josh. "A friend of my father's." With that she turned and walked away.

Josh lost track of time. He and Lloyd Dickins had pored over the company's financial records until they were both seeing double. They needed a good deal of money, and they needed it fast. George Benson had seen to it that they were unable to borrow the necessary funds, and he had also managed to close off the means of selling some collateral, even if it meant at a loss. Every corner he turned, Josh was confronted by the financial giant who loomed over Johnson Industries like black death. Harold Johnson's company was a fat plum, and Benson wasn't about to let this one fall through his greedy little fingers.

"Are we going to be able to do it?" Lloyd Dickins asked, eyeing Josh speculatively.

Josh leaned back in his chair, pinched the bridge of his nose and sadly shook his head. "I don't see how."

"There's got to be some way."

"Everything we've tried hasn't done a bit of good."

"Who does George Benson think he is, anyway?" Lloyd flared. "God?"

"At the moment, he's got us down with our hands tied behind our backs," Josh admitted reluctantly. The pencil he was holding snapped in half. He hadn't realized his hold had been so tight.

"The meeting of the board of directors is Friday. We're going to have to come up with some answers by then."

"We will." But the confidence in Josh's voice sounded shaky at best. He had run out of suggestions. Years before, his ideas had been considered revolutionary. He never *had* been one to move with the crowd, nor did he base his decisions on what everyone else was doing around him. He had discovered early on that if he started looking to his colleagues before making a move he would surrender his leading edge to his business peers. That realization had carried him far. But he had been out of the scene for too many years. His instincts had been blunted, his mind baffled by the changes. Yet he had loved every minute of this. It was as if he was playing a good game of chess—only this time the stakes were higher than anything he had ever wagered. He couldn't lose.

"I think I'll go home and sleep on it," Lloyd murmured, yawning loudly. "I'm so rummy now I can't think straight."

"Go ahead. I'll look over these figures one more time and see what I can come up with."

Lloyd nodded. "I'll see you in the morning." He hesitated, then chuckled, the sound rusty and discordant. "Looks like it *is* morning. Before much longer this place is going to be hopping, but as long as it isn't with Benson's people, I'll be content."

Josh grinned, but the ability to laugh had left him several hours ago. A feeling of impending doom was pounding at him like a prizefighter's fist, each blow driving him farther and farther until his back was pressed against the wall.

There had to be a way…for Amy and her father's sake, he needed to find one. With a determination born of desperation, he went over the numbers one last time.

"What are you doing here?"

Amy's voice cracked against his ears like a horsewhip. His eyes flew open, and he blinked several times against the bright light. He must have dozed off, he realized. With his elbows braced against the table, he rubbed the sleep from his face. "What time is it?"

"Almost seven."

"Isn't it a little early for you?" he asked, checking his watch, blinking until his eyes focused on the dial.

"I… I had something I needed to check on. You look absolutely terrible," she said, sounding very much like a prim schoolteacher taking a student to task. "You'd better go to your hotel and get some sleep before you pass out."

"I will in a minute," Josh answered, hiding a smile. Her concern was the first indication she still loved him that she'd shown since the morning she awoke with him in her bed. That had been…what? Two weeks ago? The days had merged in his mind, and he wasn't entirely certain of the date even now.

"Josh, you're going to make yourself sick."

"Would you care?"

"No…but it would make my father feel guilty when I tell him, and he's got enough to worry about."

"Speaking of Harold, how's he doing?"

"Much better."

"Good."

Amy remained on the other side of the room. Josh gestured toward the empty chair beside him. "Sit down and talk to me a minute while I gather my wits."

"Your wits are gathered enough."

"Come on, Amy, I'm not the enemy."

Her returning look said she disagreed.

"All right," he said, standing, "walk me to the elevator then."

"I'm not sure I should…you know the way. What do you need me for?" She held herself stiffly, as far on the other side of the office as she could get and still be in the same room with him.

"Moral support. I'm exhausted and hungry and too tired to argue. Besides, I have a meeting at nine. It's hardly worth going to the hotel."

"My dad has a sofa in his office…you could rest there for an hour or so," she said, watching him closely.

Josh hesitated, thinking he'd much rather spend the time holding and kissing her. "I could," he agreed. "But I wouldn't rest well alone." Boldly his eyes held hers. "The fact is, I need you."

"You can forget it, Joshua Powell," she said heatedly. She was blushing, very prettily, too, as she turned and walked out of Lloyd Dickins's office.

Josh followed her. When she stepped into her father's office, he dutifully closed the door.

"I…think there's a blanket around here somewhere." She walked into a huge closet that contained supplies. Josh went in after her, resisting the temptation to slip his arms around her and drag her against him.

"Here's one," she said and when she turned around he was directly behind her, blocking any way of escape. Her startled eyes clashed with his. Josh loved her all the more as she drew herself up to her full height and set her chin at a proud, haughty angle. "Kindly let me go."

"I can't."

"Why not?" she demanded.

"Because there's something else I need far more than sleep."

She braced one hand against her hip, prepared to do battle. Only Josh didn't want to fight. Arguing was the last thing on his mind.

"What do you want, Joshua?" she asked.

"I already told you. We should start with a kiss, though, don't you think?"

Astonished, she glared at him. "You've got to be out of your mind if you think I'm going to let you treat me as though I was some brainless—"

Josh had no intention of listening to her tirade. Without waiting for her to pause to breathe, he clasped his hands around her waist and dragged her against his chest. She opened her mouth in outrage, and Josh took instant advantage.

Amy tried to resist him. Josh felt her fingernails curl into the material of his shirt as if she intended to push him away, but whatever her intent had been, she abruptly changed her mind. She may have objected to his touching her, but before she could stop herself, she was kissing him back and small moaning sounds were coming from her throat. Or was he the one making the noise?

"Oh…oh…"

At the startled gasp, Josh broke off the kiss and shielded Amy from probing eyes.

Ms. Wetherell, Harold Johnson's secretary, was standing in the office, looking so pale it was a wonder that she didn't keel over in a dead faint.

Thirteen

Matters weren't looking good for Johnson Industries. Amy didn't need to attend the long series of meetings with Josh and the department executives to know that. The gloomy looks of those around her told her everything she needed to know. Lloyd Dickins, usually so professional, had been short-tempered all week, snapping at everyone close to him. His movements were sluggish, as if he dreaded each day, so unlike the vivacious man whose company she'd come to enjoy.

Twice in the past two weeks, Amy had found Ms. Wetherell dabbing at her eyes with a spotless lace hankie. The grandmotherly woman who'd served her father for years seemed older and less like a dragon than ever.

Amy sincerely doubted that Josh had slept more than a handful of hours all week. For that matter, she hadn't either. In the evenings when she left the office, she headed directly for the hospital. Josh had made several visits there himself once her father was moved out of the intensive-care unit, but the older man always seemed cheered after Josh had stopped by. Amy knew Josh wasn't telling Harold the whole truth, but, despite their differences, she approved and didn't intervene.

For her part, Amy had avoided being alone with Josh since that one incident when Ms. Wetherell had discovered them. She had learned early on that she couldn't trust Josh, but he taught her a second more painful lesson—*she couldn't trust herself around him.* Two seconds in his arms and all her resolve disappeared. Even now, days later, her face heated at the memory of the way she had opened to his impudent kisses.

"How's he doing?"

Amy straightened in her chair beside her father's hospital bed. Josh, the very object of her musings, entered the darkened room. "Fine. I think."

"He's sleeping?"

"Yes."

Josh claimed the chair next to her and rubbed a hand down his face as if to disguise the lines of worry, but he wasn't fooling her. Just seeing him caused her heart to throb with concern. He looked terrible. Sighing inwardly, Amy guessed that she probably wasn't in much better shape herself.

"When was the last time you had a decent night's sleep?" she couldn't help asking.

He tried to reassure her with a smile, but failed. "About the same time you did. Amy, I'm sorry to tell you this but it doesn't look good. You know as well as I do how poorly that meeting went with the board of directors this afternoon. We're fighting even more of an uphill battle than we first realized. Half are in favor of selling out now, thinking we might get a better price, and no one's willing to speculate what Benson will be offering next week."

"We...we can't let my father know."

Josh shrugged. "I don't know how we can keep it from him. He's too smart not to have figured it out. We've done everything we can to hide it, but I'm sure he knows."

Amy nodded, accepting the truth of Josh's statement. She was all too aware of the consequences of the takeover. It would kill her father as surely if George Benson was to shoot him through the heart. Johnson Industries was the blood that flowed through her father's veins. Without the business, his life would lack purpose and direction.

Josh must have read her thoughts. His hand reached for hers, and he squeezed her fingers reassuringly. "It's going to work out," he told her. "Don't worry."

"It looks like you're doing enough of that for the both of us."

He tried smiling again, this time succeeding. "There's too much at stake to give up. If I lose this company," he said, his eyes holding hers, "I lose you."

Amy's gaze fell to her lap as his words circled her mind like a lariat around the head of a steer. "You lost me a long time ago."

The air between them seemed to crackle with electricity. Amy could almost taste his defeat. So much was already riding on Josh's shoulders without her adding her head as a prize. Whatever happened happened. What was between them had nothing to do with that.

"I can't accept that."

"Maybe you should."

"You can't fool me, Amy. You love me."

"I did once," she admitted reluctantly, "but, as you so often had told me in the past, that was a mistake. Chad and I—"

"Chad!" He spat out the name as if it were a piece of

spoiled meat. "You can't honestly expect me to believe you're in love with that spineless pansy?"

A tense moment passed before she spoke again. "I think we'd best end this conversation before we both lose our tempers."

"No," he jeered. "We're going to have this out right now. I'm through playing games."

"Talk this out? Here and now?" she flared. "I refuse to discuss anything of importance with you in my father's hospital room."

"Fine. We'll leave."

"Fine," she countered, nearly leaping to her feet in her eagerness. She felt a little like a boxer jumping out from his corner at the beginning of a new round. Every minute she was with Joshua, he infuriated her more.

At a crisp pace, she followed him out of the hospital to the parking lot. "Where are we going?" she demanded, when he calmly unlocked the passenger side of his car door.

"Where do you suggest?" he asked, as casually as if he was seeking her preference for a restaurant.

"I couldn't care less." His collected manner only served to irritate her all the more. The least he could do was reveal a little emotion. For her part, she was brimming with it. It was all she could do not to throw her purse to the ground and go at him with both fists. The amount of emotion churning inside her was a shock.

"All right then, *I'll* decide." He motioned toward the open car door. "Get in."

"Not until I know where we're headed."

"I don't plan on kidnapping you."

"Where are we going?" she demanded a second time, certain her eyes must be sparking with outrage and fury.

"My hotel room."

Amy slapped her hands against her thighs. "Oh, brother," she cried. "Honestly, Josh, do I look that stupid? I simply can't believe you! There is no way in this green earth that I'd go to a hotel room with you."

He stood on the driver's side, the open door between them. "Why not?" he asked.

"You...you're planning to seduce me."

"Would I succeed?"

"Not likely."

Unconcerned, Josh shrugged. "Then what's the problem?"

"I..." She couldn't very well admit that he was too damn tempting for her own good.

"We're closer to my hotel than your house, and at least there we'll be afforded some privacy. I can't speak for you, but personally, I'd prefer to discuss this in a rational manner without half of Seattle listening in."

He had her there. Talk about taking the wind out of her sails! "All right, then, but I'd rather drive there in my own car."

"Fine." He climbed inside his vehicle, leaned across the plush interior and closed the passenger door, which he had opened seconds earlier for her.

The ride to the hotel took only a few minutes. There was a minor problem with parking, which was probably the reason Josh had suggested she ride with him. Since there wasn't any space on the street, she found a lot, paid the attendant and then met Josh in the lobby.

"Are you hungry?"

She was, but unwilling to admit it. The hotel was the same one where he had been staying when she had first met him. The realization did little to settle her taut nerves. "No."

"If you don't object, I'll order something from room service."

"Fine."

The air between them during the elevator ride was still and ominous, like the quiet before a tornado touches down.

Josh had his key ready by the time they reached his room. He unlocked the door and opened it for her to precede him. She stopped abruptly when she realized that even the *room* was identical to the one he'd had months earlier. How differently she'd felt about him then. Even then she'd been in love with him.

And now…well, now, she'd learned so many things. But most of those lessons had been painful. She'd come a long way from the naive college graduate she'd been then. Most of her maturing had come as a result of her relationship with Josh.

"This is the same room you had before," she said, without realizing she'd verbalized her thought.

"It looks the same, but I'm on a different floor," Josh agreed absentmindedly. He reached for the room-service menu and scanned its listings before heading toward the phone. "Are you sure I can't change your mind?"

"I'm sure." Her stomach growled in angry protest to the lie. Amy gave a brilliant performance of pretending the noise had come from someone other than herself.

Josh ordered what seemed like an exorbitant amount of food and then turned toward her. "All right, let's get this over with."

"Right," she said, squaring her shoulders for the coming confrontation.

"Sit down." He motioned toward a chair that was angled in front of the window.

"If you don't mind, I'd like to stand."

"Fine." He claimed the chair for himself.

Amy had thought standing would give her an advantage. Not so. She felt even more intimidated by Josh than at any time in recent memory. Garnering what she could of her emotional fortitude, she squared her shoulders and met his look head on, asking no quarter and giving none herself.

"You wanted to say something to me," she prompted, when he didn't immediately pick up the conversation.

"Yes," Josh reiterated, looking composed and not the least bit irritated. "I don't want you seeing that mamma's boy again."

Amy snickered at the colossal nerve of the man. "You and what army are going to stop me?"

"I won't need an army. You're making a fool of him and an even bigger one of yourself. I love you, and you love me, and frankly, I'm tired of having you use Chad as an excuse every time we meet."

"I was hoping you'd get the message," she said, crossing her arms over her waist. "As for this business of my still loving you," she said, forcing a soft laugh, "any feeling I have for you died months ago."

"Don't lie, Amy, you do a piss poor job of it. You always have."

"Not this time," she told him flatly. "In fact, I can remember the precise moment I stopped loving you, Joshua Powell. It happened when you stepped inside a taxi that was parked outside my home. I... I stood there and watched as you drove away, and I swore to myself that I'd never allow a man to hurt me like that again."

Josh briefly closed his eyes and lowered his head. "Leaving you that day was the most difficult thing I'd ever done in my life, Amy. I said before that I'd give anything for it never to have happened. Unfortunately, it did."

"Do you honestly believe that a little contrition is going to change everything?"

Josh leaned back in the chair, and his shoulders sagged with fatigue. "I was hoping it would be a start."

"A few regrets aren't enough," she cried, and to her horror, she felt the tears stinging in the back of her eyes. Before they brimmed and Josh had a chance to see them, she turned and walked away from him.

"What do you want?" he demanded. "Blood?"

"Yes," she cried. "Much more than that... I want you out of my life. You...you seem to think that...that if you're able to help my father, that's going to wipe out everything that's happened before and that... I'll be willing to let bygones be bygones and we can marry and have two point five children and live happily ever after."

"Amy..."

"No, Josh," she cried, and turned around, stretching her arm out in front of her in an effort to ward him off. "I refuse to be some prize you're going to collect once this craziness with George Benson passes and my father recovers."

"It's not that."

"Then what is it?"

"I love you."

"That's not enough," she cried. "And as for my not seeing Chad Morton again...there's something you should know. I...plan on marrying Chad. He hasn't asked me yet, but he will, and when he does, I'll gladly accept his proposal."

"You don't love Chad," Josh cried, leaping from his chair. "I can't believe you'd do anything so stupid!"

"I may not love Chad the way I love—used to love you, but at least if he ever walks out on me it won't hurt nearly as badly. But then, Chad never would leave me—not the way you did at any rate."

"Amy, don't do anything crazy. Please, Angel Eyes, you'd be ruining our lives."

"Chad's wonderful to me."

Momentarily, Josh closed his eyes. "Give me a chance to make everything up to you."

"No." She shook her head wildly, backing away from him, taking tiny steps as he advanced toward her. "Chad's kindhearted and good."

"He'd bore you out of your mind in two weeks."

"He's honorable and gentle," she continued, holding his gaze.

"But what kind of lover would he be?"

Amy's shoulders sagged with defeat. Chad's kisses left her cold. Josh must have known it. A spark of triumph flashed from his eyes when she didn't immediately respond to his taunt.

"Answer me," he demanded, his eyes brightening.

Amy had backed away from him as far as she could. Her back was pressed to the wall.

"When Chad touches you, what do you feel?"

The lie died on the end of her tongue. She could shout that she came alive in Chad Morton's arms, insist that he was an enviable lover, but it would do little good. Josh would recognize the lie and make her suffer for it.

Slowly, almost without her being aware of it, Josh lifted his hand and ran his fingertips down the side of her face. Her nerves sprang to life at his featherlight stroke, and she sharply inhaled her breath, unprepared for the onslaught of sensation his touch aroused.

"Does your Mr. BMW make you feel anything close to this?" he asked, his voice hushed and ultra-seductive.

It was a strain to keep from closing her eyes and giving in to the sensual awareness Josh brought to life within her. She raised her hands, prepared to push him away, but the instant they came into contact with the hard, muscular planes of his chest, they lost their purpose.

"I don't feel anything. Kindly take your hands off me."

Josh chuckled softly. "I'm not touching you, angel, you're the one with your hands on me. Oh, baby," he groaned, his amusement weaving its way through his words. "You put up such a fierce battle."

Mortified, Amy dropped her hands, but not before Josh flattened his against the wall and trapped her there, using his body to hold her in check.

Amy's immediate reaction was to struggle, pound his chest and demand that he release her. But the wild, almost primitive look in his eyes dragged all the denial out of her. His pulse throbbed at the base of his throat like a drum, hammering out her fate. He held himself almost completely rigid, but Amy could feel the entire length of him pulsating with tension.

It came to her then that if she didn't do something to stop him, he was going to make love with her. The taste of bitter defeat filled her throat. Once he became her lover, she would never be able to send him away.

Her breath clogged her throat and she bucked against him. Her eyes flew to his face, and he smiled.

"That's right, angel," he urged in a deep whisper. "You want me as much as I want you."

"No I don't," she murmured, but her protest was feeble at best.

He kissed her then. Slow and deep, as if they had all the time in the world. Against every dictate of her will, blistering excitement rushed through her and she moaned. Her small cry seemed to please him, and he kissed her again, and she welcomed his touch, wanting to weep with abject frustration at the treachery of her body.

His hands were at the front of her blouse.

Knowing his intention, Amy made one final plea. "Josh...no...please."

His shoulders and chest lifted with a sharp intake of breath.

The polite knock against the door startled them both. Josh tensed and sweat beaded his fervent face.

"Josh," she moaned, "the door...someone's at the door."

"This time we finish," he growled.

The knock came a second time. "Room service," the male voice boomed from the other side. "I have your order."

"Please," she begged, tears filling her eyes. "Let me go."

Reluctantly, he released her, and needing to escape him, Amy fled into the bathroom. From inside she could hear Josh dealing with the man who delivered the meal. She ran her splayed fingers through her mussed hair, disgusted with herself that she'd allowed Josh to kiss and hold her. It shocked her how quickly she'd given in to him, how easily he could manipulate her.

"Amy. He's gone."

Leaning against the sink, she splashed cold water on her face and tried to interject sound reason into her badly shaken composure.

When she left the bathroom, it demanded every ounce of inner strength she possessed. As she knew he would be, Josh was waiting for her, prepared to continue as if nothing had happened.

She raised her shoulders and focused her gaze just past him, on the picture that hung over the king-size bed. "You proved your point," she said, shocked by how incredibly shaky her voice sounded.

"I hope to high heaven that's true. You're going to marry me, Amy."

"No," she said flatly. "Just because I respond to you physically...doesn't mean I love you, or that I'm willing to trust you with my heart. Not again, Josh, never again."

Before he could say or do anything that would change her mind, she grabbed her purse and left the room.

Amy spent the next four days with her father, purposefully avoiding Josh. In light of what had happened in his hotel room, she didn't know if she would ever be able to look him in the eye again. If the hotel staff hadn't decided to deliver his meal when they had, there was no telling how far their lovemaking would have progressed.

No, she reluctantly amended, she *did* know where it would have ended. With her in his bed, her eyes filled with adoration, her body sated with his lovemaking. Without question, she would have handed him her heart and her life and anything else he demanded.

"You haven't been yourself in days," Chad complained over lunch. "Is there anything I can do?"

No matter what Josh believed about the other man, Chad had been wonderful. He'd anticipated her every need. Amy didn't so much as have to ask. More often than not, he arrived at the hospital, insisting that he was taking her to lunch, or to dinner, or simply out for a breath of fresh air.

Rarely did he stay and talk to her father, and for his part, Harold Johnson didn't have much to say to the other man, either.

"How's everything at the office?" she asked, recognizing that she was really inquiring about Josh and angry with herself for needing to know.

"Not good," Chad admitted, dipping his fork into his

avocado and alfalfa-sprout salad. "Several of the staff have turned in their resignations, wanting to find other positions while they can."

"Already?" Amy was alarmed, fearing her father's reaction to the news. She hoped Josh would shield him from most of the unpleasantness.

"When Powell left, most everyone realized it was a lost cause. I want you to know that I'll be here for however long you and your father need me."

"Josh left?" Amy cried, before she could school her reaction. A numb pain worked its way out from her heart, rippling over her abdomen. The paralyzing agony edged its way down her arms and legs until it was nearly impossible to breathe or move to function normally.

"He moved out yesterday," Chad added conversationally. "I'm surprised your father didn't say anything."

"Yes," she murmured, lowering her gaze. For several moments it was all she could do to keep from breaking down into bitter tears.

"Amy, are you all right?"

"No... I've got a terrible headache." She pressed her fingertips to her temple and offered him a smile.

"Let me take you home."

"No," she said, lightly shaking her head. "If you could just take me back to the hospital. I...my car is there."

"Of course."

An entire lifetime passed before Amy could leave the restaurant. On the ride to the hospital, she realized how subdued her father had been for the past twenty-four hours. Although his recovery was progressing at a fast pace, he seemed lethargic and listless that morning, but Amy had been too wrapped up in her own problems to probe. Now it all made sense.

Debbie Macomber

When the going got tough, Josh packed his bags and walked out of their lives. He hadn't even bothered to say goodbye—at least not to her. Apparently, he hadn't been able to face her, and with little wonder. Harold had needed him, even if she didn't. But none of that had mattered to Josh. He had turned his back on them and their problems and simply walked away.

"Why didn't you tell me?" Amy demanded of her father the moment they were alone. Tears threatened but she held them in check. "Josh left."

"I thought you knew."

"No." She wiped away the moisture that smeared her cheeks and took in a calming breath before forcing a brave front for her father's sake. "He didn't say a word to me."

"He'll be back," her father assured her, gently patting her hand. "Don't be angry with him, sweetheart, he did everything he could."

"I don't care if he ever comes back," she cried, unable to hold in the bitterness. "I never want to see him again. Ever."

"Amy..."

"I'll be married to Chad before Josh returns, I swear I will. I detest the man, I swear I hate him with everything that's in me." She had yet to recover from the first time he had deserted her, and then in their greatest hour of need, he had done it a second time. If her father lost Johnson Industries, and in all likelihood he would, then Amy would know exactly who to blame.

"There's nothing left that he could do," her father reasoned. "I don't blame him. He tried everything within his power to turn the tide, but it was too late. I should have realized it long before now—I was asking the impossible. Josh knew it, and still he tried to find a way out."

"But what about the company?"

"All is lost now, and there's nothing we can do but accept it."

Amy buried her face in her hands.

"We'll recover," her father said, and his voice cracked. He struggled for a moment to compose himself before he spoke again. "I may be down, but I'm not out."

"Oh, Daddy." She hugged him close, offering what comfort she could, but it was little when her own heart was crippled with the pain of Josh's desertion.

Fourteen

By the weekend, Amy came to believe in miracles. Knowing that her father was about to lose the conglomerate he had invested his entire life building, she had been prepared for the worst. What happened was something that only happened to those who believe in fairy tales and Santa Claus. At the eleventh hour, her father sold a small subsidiary company that he had purchased several years earlier. The company, specializing in plastics, had been an albatross and a money loser, but an unexpected bid had come in, offering an inflated price. Her father and the corporate attorneys leaped at the opportunity, signing quickly. Immediately afterward, Johnson Industries was able to pay off its bondholders, all within hours of its deadline. By the narrowest of margins, the company had been able to fend off George Benson and his takeover schemes.

The following week, her father was like a young man again. His spirits were so high that his doctors decided he could be released from the hospital the coming Friday.

"Good morning, beautiful," Harold greeted his daughter when she stopped in to see him on her way to work Monday morning. "It's a beautiful day, isn't it, sweetheart?"

Not as far as Amy was concerned. Naturally, she was pleased with the way matters had turned out for her father, but everything else in her life had taken a sharp downward twist.

Carefully, she had placed a shield around her heart, thinking that would protect her from Josh and anything he might say or do. But she had been wrong. Having him desert her and her father when they needed him most hurt more the second time than it had the first.

Amy found it a constant struggle not to break down. She could weep at the most nonsensical matters. A romantic television commercial produced tears, as did a sad newspaper article or having to wait extra long in traffic. She could be standing in a grocery aisle and find a sudden, unexplainable urge to cry.

"It's rainy, cold and the weatherman said it might snow," she responded to her father's comment about it being a beautiful day, doing her best to maintain a cheerful facade and failing miserably.

"Amy?" Her father's soft blue eyes questioned her. "Do you want to talk about it?"

"No," she responded forcefully. It wouldn't do the least bit of good. Josh was out of their lives, and she couldn't be happier or more sad.

"Is it about Josh?"

Her jaw tightened so hard her back teeth ached. "What possible reason would I have to feel upset about Joshua Powell?" she asked, making his question sound almost comical.

"You love him, sweetheart."

"I may have at one time, but it's over. Lately... I think I could hate him." Those nonsensical tears she had been experiencing during the past two weeks rushed to the corners of her eyes like water spilling over a top-full barrel. Once more, she struggled to disguise them.

Narrowing his gaze, Harold Johnson motioned toward the chair. "Sit down, sweetheart, there's a story I want to tell you."

Instead, Amy walked to the window, her arms cradling her waist. "I've got to get to work. Perhaps another time."

"Nothing is more important than this tale. Now, sit down and don't argue with me. Don't you realize, I've got a bad heart?"

"Oh, Dad." She found herself chuckling.

"Sit." Once more he pointed toward the chair.

Amy did as he asked, bemused by his attitude.

"This story starts out several years back…"

"Is this a once-upon-a-time tale?"

"Hush," her father reprimanded. "Just listen. You can ask all the questions you want later."

"All right, all right," she said with ill grace.

"Okay, now where was I?" he mumbled, and stroked his chin while he apparently gathered his thoughts. "Ah, yes, I'd only gotten started.

"This is the story of a young man who graduated with top honors at a major university. He revealed an extraordinary talent for business, and word of him spread even before he'd received his MBA. I suspect he came by this naturally, since his own father was a well-known stockbroker. At any rate, this young man's ideas were revolutionary, but by heaven, he had a golden touch. Several corporations wanted him for their CEO. Before long he could name his own terms, and he did."

"Dad?" Amy had no idea where this story was leading, but she really didn't want to sit and listen to him ramble on about someone she wasn't even sure she knew. And if this was about Josh, she would rather not hear it. It couldn't change anything.

"Hush and listen," her father admonished. "This young man and his father were apparently very close and had been for years. To be frank, the father had something of a reputation for doing things just a tad shady. Nothing illegal, don't misunderstand me, but he took unnecessary risks. I sincerely doubt that the son was fully aware of this, although he must have guessed some of it was true. The son, however, defended his father at every turn."

Amy glanced at her watch, hoping her father got her message. If he did, it apparently didn't faze him.

"It seems that the son often sought his father's advice. I suppose this was only natural, being that they were close. By this time, the son was head of a major conglomerate, and if I said the name you'd recognize it immediately."

Amy yawned, wanting her father to arrive at the point of this long, rambling fable.

"No one is exactly certain what happened, but the conglomerate decided to sell off several of its smaller companies. The father, who you remember was a stockbroker, apparently got wind of the sale from the son and with such valuable inside information, made a killing in the market."

"But that's—"

"Unethical and illegal. What happened between the father and son afterward is anyone's guess. I suspect they parted ways over this issue. Whatever happened isn't my business, but I'm willing to speculate that there was no love lost between the two men in the aftermath of this scandal. The son resigned his position and disappeared for years."

"Can you blame him?"

"No," her father replied, his look thoughtful. "Although it was a terrible waste of talent. Few people even knew what had happened, but apparently he felt his credibility had been weakened. His faith in his father had been destroyed, no doubt, and that blow was the most crushing. My feeling is that he'd lived with the negative effects of having money for so many years that all he wanted was to wash his hands of it and build a new life for himself. He succeeded, too."

"Was he happy?"

"I can't say for certain, but I imagine he found plenty of fulfillment. He served in the Peace Corps for a couple of years and did other volunteer work. It didn't matter where he went, he was liked by all. It's been said that he never met a man who didn't like him."

"Does this story have a punch line?" Amy asked, amused.

"Yes, I'm getting to that. Let me ask you a couple of questions first."

"All right." She'd come this far, and although she hadn't been a willing listener, her father had managed to whet her appetite.

"I want you to put yourself into this young man's place. Can you imagine how difficult it would be for him to approach his father eight years after this estrangement?"

"I'm confident he wouldn't unless there was a good reason."

"He had one. He'd fallen in love."

"Love?" Amy echoed.

"He did it for the woman, and for her father, too, I suspect. He knew a way to help them, and although it cost him everything, he went to his father and asked for help."

"I see," Any said, and swallowed tightly.

"Amy." He paused and held his hand out to her. "The company that made the offer, the company that *saved* us, is owned by Chance Powell, Josh's father."

Amy felt as if she had received a blow to the head. A

ringing sensation echoed in her ears, and the walls started to circle the room in a crazy merry-go-round effect. "Josh went to his father for us?"

"Yes, sweetheart. He sold his soul for you."

Although Amy had been to New York several times, she had never appreciated the Big Apple as much as she did on this trip. The city was alive with the sights and sounds of Christmas. Huge boughs of evergreens were strung across the entryways to several major stores. The city was ablaze with lights, had never shone brighter. A stroll through Central Park made Amy feel like a child again.

Gone was the ever-present need to cry, replaced instead with a giddy happiness that gifted her with a deep, abiding joy for the season she hadn't experienced since the time she was a child and the center of her parents' world.

With the address clenched tightly in her hand, Amy walked into the huge thirty-story building that housed Chance Powell's brokerage. After making a few pertinent inquiries, she rode the elevator to the floor where his office was situated.

Her gaze scanned the neat row of desks, but she didn't see Josh, which caused her spirits to sag just a little. She'd come to find him, and she wasn't about to leave until she'd done exactly that.

"I'm here to see Mr. Powell," Amy told the receptionist. "I don't have an appointment."

"Mr. Powell is a very busy man. If you want to talk to him, I'm afraid you'll have to schedule a time."

"Just tell him Amy Johnson is here...you might add that I'm Harold Johnson's daughter," she added for good measure, uncertain that Josh had even mentioned her name.

Reluctantly, the young woman did as Amy said. No

sooner had she said Amy's name than the office door opened and Chance Powell himself appeared. The resemblance between father and son was striking. Naturally, Chance's looks were mature, his dark hair streaked with gray, but his eyes were so like Josh's that for a moment it felt as if she was staring at Josh himself.

"Hello, Amy," he said, clasping her hands in both of his. His gaze slid over her appreciatively. "Cancel my ten o'clock appointment," he said to the receptionist.

He led the way into his office and closed the door. "I wondered about you, you know."

"I suppose that's only natural." Amy sat in the chair across from his rich mahogany desk, prepared to say or do whatever she must to find Josh. "I don't know what Josh said to you, if he explained—"

"Oh, he said plenty," the older man murmured and chuckled, seemingly delighted about something.

"I need to find him," she said fervently, getting directly to the point.

"Need to?"

Any ignored the question. "Do you know where he is?"

"Not at the moment."

"I see." Her hands tightened into a fist around the strap of her purse. "Can you tell me where I might start looking for him?" Her greatest fear was that he'd headed back to Kadiri or someplace else in the Middle East. It didn't matter, she would follow him to the ends of the earth if need be.

Chance Powell didn't seem inclined to give her any direct answers, although he had appeared eager enough to meet her. He scrutinized her closely, and he wore a silly half grin when he spoke. "My son always did have excellent taste. Do you intend to marry him?"

"Yes." She met his gaze head-on. "If he'll have me."

He laughed at that, boisterously. "Josh may be a good many things, but he isn't a fool."

"But I can't marry him until I can find him."

"Are you pregnant?"

Chance Powell was a man who came directly to the point, as well.

The color screamed in Amy's cheeks, and for a moment she couldn't find her tongue. "That's none of your business."

He laughed again, looking pleased, then slapped his hand against the top of his desk, scattering papers in several directions. "Hot damn!"

"Mr. Powell, please, can you tell me where I can find Josh? This is a matter of life and death." His death, if he didn't quit playing these games with her. Perhaps she'd been a fool to believe that all she had to do was fly to New York, find Josh and tell him how much she loved him so they could live happily ever after. It had never entered her mind that his father wouldn't know where he was. Then again, he may well be aware of precisely where Josh was at that very moment and not plan to tell her.

"Do you have any water?" she said, feigning being ill. "My...stomach's been so upset lately."

"Morning sickness?"

She blushed demurely and resisted the temptation to place the back of her hand to her brow and sigh with a good deal of drama.

"Please excuse me for a moment," Chance said, standing.

"Of course."

A moment turned out to be five long minutes, and when the office door opened, it slammed against the opposite wall and then was abruptly hurled closed. The sound was forceful enough to startle Amy out of her chair.

Josh loomed over her like a ten-foot giant, looking more furious than she could ever remember seeing him. His eyes were almost savage. "What did you say to my father?"

"Hello, Josh," she said, offering him a smile he didn't return. Bracing her hands against the leather back of the chair, she used it as a shield between the two of them. The little speech she had so carefully prepared was completely lost. "I… I changed my mind about your offer. The answer is yes."

"Don't try to avoid the question," he shouted, advancing two steps toward her. "You told my father you're pregnant. We both know that's impossible."

He looked so good in a three-piece suit. So unlike the man who had asked to share a picnic table with her along the Seattle waterfront all those months ago. He had been wearing a fringed leather jacket then, and his hair had been in great need of a trim. Now…now he resembled a Wall Street executive, which was exactly what he was.

"What do you mean, you changed your mind?"

"I'm sorry I misled your father. I never came out directly and told him I was pregnant. But he didn't seem to want me to know where you were, and I had to find you."

"Why?"

He certainly wasn't making this easy on her. "Well, because…" She paused, drew in her breath and straightened her back, prepared for whatever followed. "Because I love you, Joshua Powell. I've reconsidered your marriage proposal, and I think it's a wonderful idea."

"The last I heard you were going to marry Chad Morton."

"Are you kidding? Don't you know a bluff when you hear one?"

He frowned. "Apparently not."

"I want to marry *you*. I have from the day you first kissed me on the Seattle waterfront and then claimed it had been a mistake. We've both made several of those over the past months, but it's time to set everything straight between us. I'm crazy about you, Joshua Powell. Your father may be disappointed, but the way I figure it, we could make him and my father grandparents in about nine months. Ten at the tops."

"Are you doing this out of gratitude?"

"Of course not," she said, as though the idea didn't even merit a response. "Out of love. Now please, stop looking at me as if you'd like to tear me limb from limb and come and hold me. I've been so miserable without you."

He closed his eyes, and his shoulders and chest sagged. "Oh, Amy…"

Unable to wait a moment longer, she walked into his arms the way a bird returns to its nest, without needing directions, recognizing home. A sense of supreme rightness filled her as she looped her arms around his neck and stood on her tiptoes. "I love you too, Angel Eyes," she said for him.

"I do, you know," he whispered, and his rigid control melted as he buried his face in her hair, rubbing his jaw back and forth against her temple as if drinking in her softness.

"There're going to be several children."

Fire hardened his dark eyes as he directed his mouth to hers in a kiss that should have toppled the entire thirty-story structure in which they stood. "How soon can we arrange a wedding?"

"Soon," she mumbled, her lips teasing his in a lengthy series of delicate, nibbling kisses. She caught his lower lip between her teeth and sucked at it gently.

Josh fit his hand over the back of her head as he took control of the kiss, slanting his mouth over hers with a hungry demand that depleted her of all strength. "You're playing with fire, angel," he warned softly, his dark eyes bright with passion.

She smiled up at him, her heart bursting with all the love she was experiencing. "I love it when you make dire predictions."

"Amy, I'm not kidding. Any more of that and you'll march to the altar a fallen angel."

She laughed softly. "Promises, promises."

Epilogue

"Amy?" Josh strolled in the back door of their home, expecting to find his pregnant wife either taking a nap or working in the nursery.

"I'm in the baby's room," he heard her shout from the top of the stairs.

Josh deposited his briefcase in the den, wondering why he even bothered to bring his laptop home. He had more entertaining ways of filling his evenings. Smiling, he mounted the stairs two at a time, while working loose the constricting silk tie at his neck. Even after five years, he still wasn't accustomed to wearing a suit.

Just as he suspected, he discovered Amy with a tiny paintbrush in her hand, sketching a field of wildflowers around several large forest creatures on the nursery wall.

"What do you think?" she asked proudly.

Josh's gaze softened as it rested on her. "And to think I married you without ever knowing your many talents." He stepped back and observed the scene she was so busy creating. "What makes you so certain this baby is a boy?"

Her smile was filled with unquestionable confidence. "A woman knows these things."

Josh chuckled. "As I recall, you were equally confident Cain would be a girl. It was darn embarrassing, bringing him home from the hospital dressed entirely in pink."

"He's since forgiven me."

"Perhaps so, but I haven't." He stepped behind her and flattened his hands over her nicely rounded abdomen. Her stomach was tight and hard, and his heart fluttered with excitement at the thought of his child growing within her. "I can think of a way for you to make it up to me, though," he whispered suggestively in her ear, then nibbled on her lobe. He felt her sag against him.

"Joshua Powell, it's broad daylight."

"So?"

"So..."

He could tell she was battling more with herself than arguing with him. Josh hadn't known what to expect once they were married. He had heard rumors about women who shied away from their husbands after they had spoken their vows. But in all the years he had been married to Amy, she had greeted his lovemaking with an eagerness that made him feel humble and truly loved.

"Where's Cain? Napping?"

"No...he went exploring with my father," she whispered.

"Then we're alone?" He stroked her breasts, and his loins tightened at how quickly her body reacted to his needs. No matter how many times they made love, it was never enough, and it never would be. When he was ninety, he would be looking for a few private moments to steal away with her.

"Yes, we're the only ones here," she told him, her voice trembling just a little.

"Good." He kissed the curve of her neck, and she relaxed against him. "Josh," she pleaded, breathless. "Let me clean the brush first."

He continued to nibble at her neck all the while, working on the elastic of her jeans.

"Josh," she begged. "Please," she moaned.

"I want to please you, angel, but you need to take care of that brush, remember."

"Oh, no, you don't," she cried softly. "You've got to take care of *me* first. You're the one who started this." Already she was removing her top, her fingers trembling, her hurried movements awkward. "I can't believe you," she cried, "in the middle of the day with Cain and my father due back any moment. We're acting like a couple of teenagers."

"You make me feel seventeen again," Josh murmured. He released her and started undressing himself.

Amy locked the door, then turned and leaned against it, her hands behind her back. "I thought men were supposed to lose their sexual appetite when their wives were pregnant."

Josh kicked off his shoes and removed his slacks. "Not me."

"I noticed."

He pinned her against the door, his forearms holding her head prisoner. "Do you have any complaints?"

"None," she whispered, framing his face lovingly with her hands. She kissed him, giving him her mouth She looped her arms around his neck as she moved her body against him.

"I want you," he managed.

"Right here?" Her eyes widened as they met his. "Now?" Amy closed her eyes, sagged against the door and sighed.

"You okay?"

"Oh, yes," she whispered.

* * *

By the time Josh had drifted back to earth, Amy was spreading kisses all over his face. He marveled at her, this woman who was his wife. She was more woman than any man deserved, an adventurous lover, a partner, a friend, the mother of his children, a keel that brought balance to his existence and filled his life with purpose.

Gently he helped her dress, taking time to kiss and carress her and tell her how much he loved her. Some things he had a difficult time saying, even now. Her love had taken all the bitterness from his life and replaced it with blessings too numerous to count.

As he bent over to retrieve his slacks, Josh placed a hand in the small of his back. "Remind me that I'm not seventeen the next time I suggest something like this."

"Not me," Amy murmured, tucking her arms around his neck and spreading kisses over his face. "That was too much fun. When can we do it again?"

"It may be sooner than you think."

Amy kissed him, and as he wrapped his arms around the slight thickening at her waist, he closed his eyes to the surge of love that engulfed him.

"Come on," she said with a sigh, reaching for her paintbrush. "All this horsing around has made me hungry. How about some cream cheese and jalapeños spread over a bagel?"

"No, thanks." His stomach quivered at the thought.

"It's good, Josh. Honest."

He continued to hold her to his side as they headed down the stairs. "By the way, my father phoned this afternoon," he mentioned casually. "He said he'd like to come out and visit before the baby's born."

Amy smiled at him. "You don't object?"

"No. It'll be good to see him. I think he'd like to be here for the baby's arrival."

"I think I'd like that, too," Amy said.

Josh nodded. He had settled his differences with his father shortly before he had married Amy. Loving her had taught him the necessity of bridging the gap. His father had made a mistake based on greed and pride, and that error had cost them both dearly. But Chance deeply regretted his actions, and had for years.

In his own way, Josh's father had tried reaching out to Josh through his sister-in-law, but he had never been able to openly confront Josh. However, when Josh had come to him, needing his help, Chance had been given the golden opportunity to make up to his son for the wrong he had done years earlier.

Amy set a roast in the oven and reached for an orange, choosing that over the weird food combination she'd mentioned earlier.

"Mommy, Mommy." Three-year-old Cain crashed through the back door and raced across the kitchen, his stubby legs pumping for all he was worth. "Grandpa and I saw a robin and a rabbit and a…a worm."

Josh waylaid his son, catching him under the arms and swinging him high above his head. "Where's Grandpa?"

"He said Mommy wouldn't want the worm inside the house so he put it back in the garden. Did you know worms live in the dirt and have babies and everything?"

"No kidding?" Amy asked, pretending to be surprised.

Harold Johnson came into the kitchen next, his face bright with a smile. "It looks like Cain gave you a run for your money, Dad," Amy said, kissing her father on the cheek. "I've got a roast in the oven, do you want to stay for dinner?"

"Can't," he said, dismissing the invitation. "I'm meeting the guys tonight for a game of pinochle." He stopped and looked at Josh. "Anything important happening at the office I should know about?"

"I can't think of anything offhand. Are you coming in on Tuesday for the board of directors' meeting?"

"Not if it conflicts with my golfing date."

"Honestly, Dad," Amy grumbled, washing her son's hands with a paper towel. "There was a time when nothing could keep you away from the business. Now you barely go into the office at all."

"Can't see any reason why I should. I've got the best CEO in the country. My business is thriving. Besides, I want to live long enough to enjoy my grandchildren. Isn't that right, Cain?"

"Right, Gramps." The toddler slapped his open palm against his grandfather's, then promptly yawned.

"Looks like you wore the boy out," Josh said, lifting Cain into his arms. The little boy laid his cheek on his father's shoulder.

"He'll go right down after dinner," Harold said, smiling broadly. "You two will have the evening alone." He winked at Josh and kissed Amy on the cheek. "You can thank me later," he whispered in her ear.

* * * * *